a marriage that behind closed doors is cruel and brutal.

Annabel has no choice but to flee, and will do everything to save herself, and her unborn baby, from destitution. But the very rich and very powerful expect to get what they want – and Richard wants only one thing – Annabel…

One

Would *he* be there that evening? Annabel Tarleton wondered as she discarded yet another of her dresses and selected one she had earlier rejected as having been worn too often in the past. Yet what did it matter if the evening gown was last season's? She did not suppose *he* would be there for one moment. And she wasn't likely to meet anyone else in the least interesting; it would be the same crowd as usual and she would be bored long before the evening was out. In fact, if she thought about it, she didn't particularly want to go.

She gave herself a long, critical look in the cheval mirror, turning all ways to see her reflection. She supposed the dress she was wearing would do for the Munsters' dance at a pinch. The cut and style were good for it had come from the House of Worth and been expensive when new, but she had worn it more than a dozen times already. However, there was absolutely no chance of her having anything new for the foreseeable future, nor would she dream of asking her brother for money at such a time. Just as she had almost decided to change again, the bedroom door opened and her younger sister came in.

'Mother sent me to see if you were ready,' Hetty Tarleton said. 'Tom and Selina have arrived. They're having a sherry in the library but he wants to get off because they encountered some patchy fog on the way here.'

'Jonah told me it was going to be a bad night,' Annabel said and pulled a face at her reflection. The dress was last season's and nothing was going to change that, though she'd added some silk flowers to the bodice and her evening shawl was new, a birthday present from Selina Manners, Tom Brocklehurst's sister. Oh, what did it matter? 'Is it bad out, Hetty?'

'Look for yourself. It seems to be coming thicker now.'

Annabel turned to glance out of the window and sure enough the mist had begun to swirl about the flat countryside surrounding Tarleton Towers. 'How does Jonah know these things and why does he forecast gloom and doom all the time?'

'That's our Jonah for you.' Hetty laughed; her face lighting with mischief. As children they had all enjoyed tormenting their long-suffering gardener and she was secretly rather fond of him. She thought Annabel was too, though she wouldn't have admitted it. 'I think he tries to live up to his name.'

'That's quite possible.' Annabel cast her eyes upwards and then sighed. 'I look awful in this wretched dress but I suppose it will have to do. Mary

Hadleigh knocked wine over my best one at the last bash and it's still being cleaned. I doubt if the stain will come out.'

'Now you sound just like Jonah,' Hetty said and pulled a face. Annabel's evening bag lay on the bed, its contents spilled out on the cover. She picked up a pretty silver compact, which their brother had bought at Liberty of London as a birthday present for Annabel, and replaced it in the silk evening purse together with a lace handkerchief. 'You look gorgeous as usual, Belle, and no one will care if you've worn the dress before. You're so lucky to be going to yet another dance. I just wish I could go to one.'

Annabel glanced at her sister and smiled. Hetty's hair was darker and thicker than her own; a honey blonde similar to Lady Tarleton's rather than the fine, spun gold Annabel had been blessed with. Her brother Benedict's colouring was a match for hers, but then they were twins, alike in many ways and not just in looks. Hetty took after her mother and was generally thought not to be as pretty as her sister, though she had a wide, generous mouth and a lovely smile. Annabel thought her sister was like a young colt, all long legs and tossing hair.

'Your turn will come, poppet,' Annabel said. 'Another couple of years that's all. I shall be married off by then and hopefully you will be able to have more clothes than I have. If my husband is rich, I'll spend some of it on you, and that's a promise.'

'I'm not sure I care much about clothes.'

'You will,' Annabel said. She dropped a kiss on her sister's head in passing. 'When I marry a rich man I'll take you shopping and buy you lots of lovely things.'

'Just as long as you marry someone you care about,' Hetty said, looking at her with anxious eyes. 'Ben was telling me he intends to marry for money. He says he doesn't care if she looks like a horse as long as she comes with a fat settlement.'

'Ben has a large house in danger of falling down around him,' Annabel said. 'The poor darling has to marry a fortune or sell the estate. He should have sold all Father's investments after he died, but he was too young to understand what was going on, and Father's lawyers told him it would be best to leave the money where it was until he was ready to deal with it himself.'

It had been bad advice as it turned out, though well intentioned. Their father had invested most of his money in America and when the Wall Street Crash came in October 1929, it had taken most of what they had. Benedict Tarleton was still reeling from the shock of being told he had virtually nothing, other than the estate itself and was desperately trying to save himself from bankruptcy.

'That would be a bit of a shame,' Hetty admitted. She loved the big, shabby, rather ugly old house for all its faults and inconveniences and knew that she would hate to see it sold. And yet she wanted her brother to be happy. 'But Ben should find some other way to make his fortune.'

'Father lost most of our money trying to make his fortune. Everything seemed to be booming when he bought all those shares. It would have been much safer in land, but he wanted a better return for us all,' Annabel said, a sad expression in her deep blue eyes. It was the constant worry about money that had brought on the illness, which had led, a year or so earlier, to her father's sudden death at the age of fifty-three. 'Ben will make up his own mind what he's going to do – but Mother wants him to marry Helen Winters, because of the money her grandfather left her and he probably will when it comes to it.'

'I still think he should wait until he falls in love. He might fall for a rich girl as easily as a poor one.'

'Perhaps he will.' Annabel picked up her shawl. 'I haven't got time for this, Hetty. Tom will be getting impatient.'

Hetty watched as she left the room, and then went over to the dressing table to borrow a spray of perfume from the pretty cut glass bottle. The perfume was French and expensive and had been a present from Major Brocklehurst on Annabel's twentieth birthday in June. He had given Hetty something similar for her own birthday in the spring.

She liked Tom and Selina. They were distant cousins and had been good to the family since Sir William's death; it was to Tom that Ben had turned for advice after the shock of the crash, though he had refused to accept a loan, mainly because he knew that Tom would never allow him to repay it. And Selina was the reason Annabel had been invited to so many parties and dances. She was a widow, quite well off, and had a large circle of friends she entertained both in London and at her brother's country house.

'I've no one else but you,' she'd told Hetty's mother once when Hetty was in the room. 'Your children and my brother *are* my family. If I can be of help to the girls it will be a pleasure.'

'You are so kind, Selina.' Lady Tarleton had taken full advantage of the offer. 'If you could just introduce Annabel to some of your friends? I'm sure something can be arranged for her, even though she is a difficult girl to please.'

Hetty knew their mother wanted Annabel to make a good marriage. In her own opinion, she thought Belle was beautiful, intelligent, and good natured so it ought to be easy to find her a rich husband. She suspected that Tom Brocklehurst was a little in love with her himself, though at past forty he was perhaps too old and set in his ways to be considered a good catch. Yet Hetty thought if it were her, she would rather marry him than most of the young men who came courting her sister.

Having helped herself to Annabel's perfume, she began to tidy away the clothes her sister had discarded, holding the ones she liked up against her figure. She didn't know why Belle was in such a fuss over the dance. It was surely no different from any of the others.

*

Annabel's heart missed a beat as she caught sight of *him* across the room, her stomach clenching with nerves. She had been so sure he wouldn't be here this evening. He seldom attended little dances like this, because he was more often in London or at Newmarket for the racing. They had met on only one other occasion and she'd felt an instant attraction, though she wasn't certain he was interested. He'd smiled, asked her to dance, talked about his passion for racehorses, briefly mentioned the business passed on to him by his late father, and then left her to rejoin his friends.

Tall and lean, with dark hair, and an attractive face, Richard Hansen was very wealthy. Everyone knew that he was the heir to a vast manufacturing empire. His grandfather had started with some mills in the North Country but his father had expanded the business and become both wealthy and influential. Richard had been sent to the best schools and then to Oxford, where he had somehow managed to survive without being sent down despite his reputation for being wild. Perhaps because of his charm, which seemed to embrace everyone he met and sent more than one young woman's heart on a dizzy whirl. It was a little way he had of making you feel that you were special that drew women to him, as moths to the naked flame.

Even as Annabel watched, she saw him charming an older woman who was known for her sour disposition but who now simpered and blushed as he twisted her around his little finger. Annabel watched the woman laughing like a young girl and then flushed herself as his eyes told her he'd become aware of her gaze.

'You're wasting your time,' a mischievous voice said at her ear and Annabel turned to smile at her friend Georgina Barrington. Georgie was dark haired, pretty and full of fun, a year or so younger than Annabel. Wearing a short dress with fringes that sparkled as she moved, she was a true reflection of the age. Much more than a flapper, she was intelligent and full of the joy of life. 'Ma told me to give him a wide berth, Belle. Mr Hansen is a charmer but spoiled – and some say he's bad, though they won't say why.'

'What do you mean – bad?' Annabel asked, unwilling to accept that Richard could be less than the perfect young god he appeared and yet knowing that her friend was far from malicious. 'He seemed pleasant enough to me when we met.'

Georgie had been her best friend since they'd met two years earlier, when the Barringtons were staying with friends in Cambridge. The family visited every few months and Georgina had written to say she would be at the Munsters' dance that evening.

'It's just whispers,' Georgie said. 'I think he probably gets drunk and does reckless things – but Ma never tells me the whole story. You know what mothers are like.'

'Yes, I do,' agreed Annabel with a rueful look. 'Your mother is better than most though, Georgie. She gives you a lot of freedom. This is 1929 but I sometimes think my mother is still living in Victorian times. She hardly lets me out without a chaperone.'

'Lady Tarleton is a little anxious for you sometimes,' Georgie said diplomatically and glanced across the room to her own mother. 'She wants you to make a good marriage. Priscilla says she doesn't care who I marry as long as I am happy. That's partly because of Jessie, I believe. She's wonderful, Belle.'

'Jessie? Is she your uncle's wife?' Annabel vaguely recalled hearing something about her. 'Isn't she the…?' A faint blush coloured her cheeks but she recovered. 'She married him after his accident and helped him set up his business, didn't she?'

'You don't have to be tactful,' Georgina said and laughed. 'Jessie was born in the East End of London. She trained as a nurse during the war and went to work for the Kendle family as a nursery maid.'

'Yes, I had heard something,' Annabel admitted. Her mother had considered it something to be swept under the carpet and spoken of only in whispers. *A gentleman marrying his nursery maid! Shocking!* 'Jessie sounds rather special?'

'Jessie is a marvel,' Georgie enthused. 'The family couldn't have survived without her after the accident. She does so much for everyone and she's always cheerful. I adore her. I think you would too. I'm going down to Kendlebury for a few weeks soon – why don't you come with me?'

'I couldn't possibly impose – and just before Christmas. They don't know me…' Annabel ended, pink with embarrassment.

'I'm going down to help out. They are busy at this time of the year. You wouldn't be imposing – not if you are willing to do your share.'

'Of what?'

Annabel was curious but before her friend could explain they were approached by two young men who asked them to dance. Since dancing was the business of the evening they accepted and it was not until much later that they had another chance to talk.

Annabel was a popular girl, liked for her smile and her easy going nature, and never without a partner for long. She made friends without really trying, passing from one group to another as she tangoed, fox-trotted and performed the Charleston creditably with the Hon. Charles Fortescue.

'I say, Belle,' he enthused after their dance. 'You're a topping girl. You dance better than anyone I know. I don't suppose you would marry me, would you?'

'Oh, Charlie,' Annabel laughed. He was enthusiastic about most things, and likeable, though not exactly good looking because of his long aristocratic nose. 'That's the fourth time you've asked me this month.'

'I suppose the answer is still no?' He looked mournfully at her, his eyes reminding her of a King Charles spaniel her father had once owned. She knew he was one of the Bentley Boys, part of a wild crowd of young men who drove fast cars, gambled, spent time on the Riviera at the appropriate time of year, and lived life as if there was no tomorrow. His frequent proposals meant nothing and he would have been shocked if she had accepted.

'I don't think your mother would approve, Charlie. I don't have any money.'

'Nor do I,' he said regretfully. 'If only I was as rich as that blighter over there you might take me seriously.'

Annabel glanced in the direction he indicated and her heart skipped a beat. Richard Hansen was staring at her in rather an intimate way. He arched one eyebrow and then smiled at her in a way that was meant to tell her she was the only person in the room for him. She'd dreamt of meeting him again like this, but she feared he would have forgotten her. After all, he could have any woman he chose, so why would he choose Annabel? People said she was beautiful but she could never see anything remarkable in her dressing mirror and thought it just flattery. Richard had everything: looks, charm, money and that power of authority that made both women and men defer to him.

Why did he keep staring at her? Was he coming over – or did he just think she looked like a provincial nothing in her old dress? Her heart began to thump madly and she felt breathless as he began to cross the room, knowing from his deliberate stride that he was heading for her.

'Be careful, Belle,' Charlie hissed before leaving her. 'Rich as Croesus but dangerous with it. Believe me, he's not your type.'

Annabel ignored the warning. Charlie was probably a little jealous of the older man, because although he had an impeccable family, he had little else to attract the heiress he needed so badly. She was tingling all over, her chest tight as she felt the excitement mount deep down inside her. Richard might be dangerous if someone upset him, perhaps, but no one else had ever made her feel like this. She wanted to be near him, to have him touch her, yet she made herself wait. Nothing would be worse than seeming too eager and she broke eye contact, breathing deeply to steady herself.

'You dance the Charleston well, Miss Tarleton.'

'Thank you,' she said, her voice husky. 'Charlie is a good dancer. I just follow him.'

'To be honest I didn't notice. I was looking at you and I liked what I saw. I liked it very much.'

'You're very kind, sir.'

'No, I'm not kind, Miss Tarleton. I may be many things but kind isn't one of them. I always say what I mean.'

Surely he was flirting with her? Annabel lifted her eyes to his, saw the amusement there and her heart leapt. Life could be so very dull at home these days and Richard was mysterious, exciting, the kind of man that all young girls dreamt of. People hinted at something dark but for Annabel that night it only enhanced his aura and made her long to know him better – to be a part of the charmed circle he moved in.

'My name is Annabel. You don't need to be so formal. We're all friends here, aren't we?'

What on earth had made her say that? It was too bold for a girl of her upbringing but she wanted him to notice her, to remember her. She was almost begging him to flirt with her and she could see by his eyes, which suddenly had the gleam of wet slate, that he intended to take up the invitation.

'I sincerely hope we shall be good friends, Annabel,' he murmured and something in his tone sent delicious shivers down her spine. 'Can I persuade you to dance this next waltz with me – since we are friends?'

His voice was like cream and whisky, the magic of his personality warming her, making her reckless. He was the picture book image of the man about town, sophisticated, rich, sought after – heady stuff for a girl used to the Charlie Fortescues of this world, who were sweet but dull.

She was walking on thin ice. Something warned Annabel that she ought to draw back now while she still had the chance, but her heart was dictating something very different. Richard Hansen might not be perfect husband material, but he was exciting, and she was so tired of the boring routine of her own small world. She needed something to change… something new and interesting, and Richard might be the gateway to a whole new world.

She smiled at him, slipping her hand into his, feeling a thrill of excitement shoot through her as his fingers closed possessively about hers, as though he already believed she was his for the taking.

Annabel should have been warned by his predatory manner, but she was floating on clouds, her body responding to the challenge from his, feeling as light as air as he whisked her expertly around the dance floor. It was such heaven to be dancing with him! Nothing else had ever come close. She wanted it to go on and on forever, and when a little later he took her outside for a sneaky cigarette, she was waiting for his kiss, longing for it to happen and yet afraid too. Annabel had never been properly kissed, though some of the men she met at parties had made a swift pass at her and ended up slobbering over her neck if they'd had too much to drink. Richard, she knew instinctively, would kiss her in the way she wanted to be kissed.

When he reached for her she melted into his arms, her body pressed close to his in a passionate embrace that left her breathless, in the delight of that moment forgetting all her mother's warnings about allowing men to think her forward. As his mouth and tongue explored hers with a sweet tenderness that had her heart melting, she pressed closer, wanting and expecting so much. A mood of recklessness had taken over her. Just for a little while she was going to do what she wanted, to enjoy this feeling of excitement that had come over her the moment Richard smiled at her. The kiss seemed to go on and on, melding them together in a sensuous bliss that made her ache for even more. This was all a part of the world that lay tantalisingly just outside her reach, the place of sophistication and danger that lured her, making her feel so adult all of a sudden, tearing her from her safe childish world. Just for this short time she was free of all the restrictions and rules her mother had laid down all her life.

'Well,' he murmured against her ear. 'You are something special, Annabel. I suspected as much when I watched you dance the Charleston; you really let yourself go, not like some of the prim and proper young ladies here tonight.'

'I'm a very proper young lady really,' Annabel told him, giving him a shy look now as the warning bells jangled louder. She had behaved badly in allowing him to kiss her – and responding so eagerly – and her mother would be shocked if she knew. 'It's just – just that you go to my head.' Her cheeks went red hot as he laughed. 'Oh, I shouldn't have said that, should I?' She must have had too much champagne!

'Possibly not,' he said in an amused drawl. He drew on his cigarette and then tossed it carelessly into the shrubbery. 'We had better go back in before the gossips start shredding your good name, my dear. You do realise that I'm not fit company for young ladies, don't you?'

'I enjoy being in your company. I don't care what they think – the old cats are only happy when they're destroying someone's reputation.' Annabel tossed caution aside because she had to take this chance to make him notice her now or it would pass by and he would drift out of her life.

'Yes, aren't they,' Richard agreed, and tipped her face up with one finger, looking down at her, a faint smile on his lips. She was far more amusing than he had thought the first time they met, and what he badly needed was someone to amuse him. 'You intrigue me, Annabel. You *are* a properly brought up young lady, I have that on good authority – and yet there is fire beneath that demure exterior. Will you come out with me for a drive one afternoon if I call for you?'

'Yes,' she said a trifle defiantly. 'Why shouldn't I?'

'I think you know why,' Richard said and smiled, then kissed her nose. 'You've been warned about men like me – but you're willing to take a risk, aren't you? Well, it might be amusing for both of us, though don't expect it to lead anywhere, Belle – because I'm not the marrying kind. At least, not yet.'

'It's just as friends, understood,' Annabel said, flicking down her lashes to hide her thoughts. She wasn't sure she wanted anything more than a stolen kiss or two, but she did want to be a part of his world, to experience the thrill of living life in the fast lane. Annabel knew that many of her friends felt as she did; they were so lucky to have escaped the horrors of the Great War that had decimated a generation. It was the reason men like Charlie drank too much champagne and did wild things; she thought it might be guilt, because someone else had been shot at and killed for them, or fear that it could happen again.

Richard's intense gaze thrilled and yet terrified her. He was too attractive for her peace of mind, the lean chiselled features of his face as handsome as any film star's. The excitement of being here alone with him was making her heart race and she was prepared to ignore his warning. Men like Richard always played the field, but in time they settled down to marriage. Besides, she wasn't going to let him do more than kiss her. She wasn't a fool whatever he might think! 'Yes, I should love to come for a drive with you, Richard. When will you pick me up?'

'Sunday afternoon?' He raised his fine brows. 'Or have you something else in mind?'

'No, nothing that matters.' Annabel recklessly jettisoned tea with her mother's friends. 'I'll look forward to seeing you then.'

'Yes,' he murmured. 'I dare say you will. Be good, Belle. I'll be seeing you. Don't have bad dreams, will you?'

'I never do.'

'The sleep of the blameless,' he mocked and took out his gold cigarette case. It bore an Art Deco motif in diamonds on the front and had probably come from Garrard's or some other exclusive jeweller, as expensive as everything else he owned no doubt. His clothes were from Savile Row, his shoes hand made of the finest leather, shrieking wealth and money, a gold ring with a large diamond on the little finger of his right hand. 'Run along in, little one. I'm going to have another cigarette in the garden.'

Annabel hesitated as he left the veranda and walked into the darkness, wanting to follow yet knowing herself dismissed. She sighed as she went back to the light and heat of the ballroom. She still wasn't sure that he really liked her and suspected he was just amusing himself at her expense. She was beginning to feel foolish and wish she hadn't responded to that kiss so readily, or that she hadn't let him see what a naïve child she was underneath.

Georgie Barrington came up to her as she re-entered the ballroom.

'Your friends were looking for you just now,' she said. 'I think Major Brocklehurst wants to leave soon because of the fog.'

'It didn't seem too bad when I was on the veranda,' Annabel replied. 'Not that I mind leaving early for once.' She didn't really want to dance with anyone else after Richard; it would be an anti-climax. Her bedroom and dreams of Richard, so that she could relive that kiss, appealed far more than dancing with Charlie or his friends again.

'You will think about coming down to Kendlebury with me?'

'Yes, perhaps,' Annabel said. 'Why don't you come for tea one day and tell me about it? Only not on Sunday, because I'm going out.'

'Sunday is out for me too,' Georgie replied, looking thoughtful. 'What about Monday afternoon? I'm free then.'

'Yes, I should like that. Come on Monday, Georgie – and now I had better go or Tom will be annoyed. I don't want to upset either him or Selina, they've been such bricks to me this past year.'

'Tom is rather a dear,' Georgie said. 'I danced with him several times this evening, and Selina is fun, isn't she?'

'Yes, rather.'

Annabel left her friend as she saw Selina coming towards them.

'I'm sorry if I've kept you waiting,' she said. 'I went out on the veranda to get some air.'

'It doesn't matter in the least, my dear. I wouldn't have thought of leaving for another hour but Tom is worried about getting us all home safely in this wretched weather. He's an old woman sometimes, but he does take his duties seriously and that's a good quality overall I think – don't you?'

'Tom is a dear,' Annabel said. 'I wouldn't dream of keeping him waiting if he wants to leave. Besides, I'm quite ready to go home.'

Selina smiled. She was a very attractive woman in her late thirties with dark blonde hair which had been cut in an asymmetrical style that suited her elfin face. Her lips were heavily rouged with a dark plum shade and her nails varnished to match. She was wearing an ankle length, figure hugging dress that evening, with rhinestone straps and a long string of huge pearls; they had been an engagement present from her late husband and were a prized possession. Very much a woman of the twenties, Selina enjoyed life and she liked Annabel, who seemed a modest girl and was always good mannered.

'Yes, it has been a little slow this evening,' she agreed. 'Not many new faces. I shall have to take you to London with me in the spring, Belle. Perhaps we'll find someone exciting for you there.'

Annabel blushed and shook her head. 'I didn't mean that I hadn't enjoyed myself, just that I don't mind leaving. But I would love to come and stay with you, Selina. You give the very best parties. Everyone says so.'

'Yes, I do, don't I?' Selina said and laughed huskily. 'That's because I invite all the reprobates, artists, writers and black sheep. Far more interesting than the cream of society, which is all you will meet at an affair like this. Though I did see you dancing with Richard Hansen. He's one of the blackest sheep, darling Belle. Have fun with him by all means, but don't expect him to offer marriage – and run as fast as you can if he should. You wouldn't enjoy being married to Richard.'

'Why do you say that?' Annabel asked but her question went unanswered as they saw Tom beckoning to them. 'Oh, we'd better go, Selina. Tom has our wraps. He's ready to leave.'

'I'm sorry to rush you, Annabel,' Tom Brocklehurst said as he helped her on with her velvet evening cloak. 'The fog doesn't seem too bad here because of all the lights, but it looks like freezing and will be worse when we get on to those narrow roads around your house; that's the trouble with living in this part of the country, my dear. I always think fen mists are the worst; they seem to hug the land and linger forever.'

'Yes, it is cold,' Selina agreed as they went out into the night air. 'I can feel it nipping at my nose. 'You were right to insist on leaving, Tom. Besides, Belle and I have both had enough of that dreary dance.'

'I didn't say that,' Annabel denied with a giggle.

'No, but I did,' Selina said and gurgled with laughter. 'I have a houseful of guests coming for Christmas, Belle. If you can spare the time you must stay for a few days.'

'I may be going away for a while before Christmas,' Annabel said. 'But you know I would love to come when I can. Mother has her own guests over Christmas, naturally, and I must be at home then, but perhaps in the New Year.'

'Oh dear,' Selina said. 'Tom and I are going to France for a holiday after Christmas. But failing all else I'll take you to London for a few weeks in the spring.'

'Lovely,' Annabel said. She peered out of the window. 'It is getting dreadfully thick now, isn't it?'

'Don't you worry, Annabel,' Tom said without turning his head to look at her. 'I'll have you home safely soon enough.'

'Jonah was right,' Annabel said. 'He told me it was going to be a terrible night.'

Actually, the old man had told her it was a bad night for her personally and that she would be better not to venture out at all. She shuddered as the car slid a little on the icy road, suppressing her cry of fear as Tom fought the wheel and his car brushed against the verge, barely avoiding tipping into a deep dyke at the edge of the narrow road. However, they hadn't been going fast enough to do any damage, and a short time later she was home and Tom and Selina were kissing her goodnight.

'Thank you for taking me this evening,' Annabel said as Tom kissed her cheek. She smiled and pressed his hand. 'You are sure you won't stay tonight? I know Mother would be glad to offer you a bed.'

'We're only a couple of miles down the road,' Tom replied, giving her an affectionate glance. His feelings for Annabel were those of a fond friend, though if he'd been a dreamer they might have been more. He wasn't and he knew she would have been horrified if he'd tried to court her so he kept his feelings on a tight rein. 'We'll be fine. Go to sleep and don't worry your pretty head over us.'

'Goodnight then,' Annabel said. 'And thank you again.'

She waved to him as he returned to the car, and then went inside the house. As she ran upstairs, Lady Tarleton came out of her bedroom wearing a pink silk dressing gown, her face slick with the vanishing cream she applied every night. Her complexion was still good but her mouth had a sour downturn.

'You're back safely then,' she said and looked inquiringly at her daughter. 'It is a dreadful night – but did you have a lovely time? Was there anyone special there this evening?'

'I had a very nice time, thank you, Mother,' Annabel said casually, keeping her tone even. 'No, I don't think I met anyone special this evening. I danced with Charlie Fortescue and all the same crowd as usual – Oh, there was someone. His name is Richard Hansen and we've met before. He asked me to dance once and said he might call on Sunday afternoon.'

'I don't think I've met Mr Hansen,' Lady Tarleton said and frowned. 'Is he suitable for you to know, Annabel? I allow you to go to these parties without my supervision because I think you are sensible. I hope you won't let me down.'

'Well, I think you might say Richard was in trade, because his grandfather started with some mills in the north, but his father became very rich and he went to Oxford…'

'That Richard Hansen!' Lady Tarleton's eyes lit with sudden excitement as she realised her daughter was talking about one of the richest men in the country. 'Why didn't you say it was him for a start? I suppose there is a connection to trade, but it is perfectly acceptable in his case. Besides, money is money these days, Annabel. After your father lost all our money, we must do what we can. We can't be that choosy – as I am continually telling your brother.'

Poor Ben, Annabel thought, but kept her thoughts to herself.

'It doesn't mean Richard is interested in me, Mother. He only said he might call to take me for a drive. He probably won't so don't make too much of it.'

'I am hardly likely to, am I?' her mother said in a disapproving tone. 'You have disappointed me these past months, Annabel. After all the parties, dinners and dances you've attended, and you've received not one proposal – I cannot understand it. Unless you are deliberately keeping yourself aloof?'

'Charlie asked me to marry him again this evening.'

'I meant a serious proposal as you very well know.'

'Yes, Mother.' Annabel sighed inwardly. She felt guilty, knowing how desperate the situation was for her family and that it was her duty to marry well. Yet she could not bring herself to marry someone she did not at the very least like and respect, and she wanted some fun and freedom first. 'I am terribly sorry to disappoint you – but I can't make someone propose to me, can I?'

'You could encourage it,' Lady Tarleton replied, a sour twist to her mouth. 'In my day the girls knew what they were about. You young things of today don't seem to realise the importance of making a good marriage. If you don't find someone soon you may have to think about taking work of some kind. Your brother can't be expected to keep funding us all forever, Annabel.'

'I should be very happy to work, Mother. You've always said it was out of the question.'

'That was when I thought you would soon find a husband,' her mother replied waspishly. 'You have all the advantages of beauty, intelligence, and an adequate education, Annabel.'

'Then I should be able to find suitable work, shouldn't I?'

'Oh, really!' Lady Tarleton's exasperation had reached its limit. 'That is a last resort as you well know. You have no real talents. Unless you want to end up as some kind of a drudge you had better try a little harder to find yourself a husband. Think of what you might be able to do for your sister and brother. You are such a selfish girl!'

'I'll do my very best, Mother,' Annabel promised and went into her bedroom, closing the door. She leant against it, taking a moment to recover her composure.

Her mother's scolding occasionally brought her to the verge of tears, but that evening she was able to ignore the unkind taunts. Lady Tarleton would be furious if she knew that her daughter had already turned down proposals from two very suitable gentlemen, both of whom were wealthy, considerate and reasonably attractive. Annabel had not told her mother about either proposal and discouraged the gentlemen in question from approaching either Lady Tarleton or Ben.

Gazing at her reflection in the mirror she wondered if she had been right to refuse so finally. It was true that if she married well she might be able to help both her brother and sister. Perhaps her mother was right and she ought to have accepted the most suitable, because she wasn't exactly cut out for making a success of anything else. She had refused because she was hoping that the right man would come along... and perhaps he had, she mused, a smile beginning to curve her mouth as she remembered *that* kiss.

Richard Hansen had warned her not to think of him as a husband, and she had received other warnings concerning him, but she preferred not to take any notice. He was exciting, far more exciting than any of the other men she knew, and just this once she was willing to take a risk.

Two

'Terrible night last night,' Jonah said to Annabel as she saw him in the garden the following morning. 'Told you it would be, didn't I?'

'Yes, you did,' she replied with a smile as he chewed on the stem of his pipe, regarding her from eyes that were surprisingly bright for a man of nearly eighty. His face was wrinkled and brown from exposure to all weathers, his hands gnarled with the rheumatics that caused him such pain at times, the result of living in the damp atmosphere of the fens all his life. However, his spirit was still youthful. 'But as you see, I returned home safe and sound. Major Brocklehurst is a good driver.'

'Aye, he be that, Miss Belle,' the old man replied. 'A good man the major. And his sister is a looker for all her wild ways in Lun'un.'

'Mrs Manners isn't wild,' Annabel said and laughed. He was the only person she knew that ever talked to her like this and she loved him for it. 'You're a wicked tease, Jonah. I think you're in love with her but she won't have you.'

Jonah chuckled and sucked at his empty pipe. 'And you're a naughty puss, Miss Annabel. Her wouldn't ever look at the likes of I even if I be thirty years younger.'

'But you like looking at her,' Annabel said, and laughed as she saw the expression in his eyes. 'I think you were a terrible flirt when you were young, Jonah. You must have had all the young ladies after you.'

'Ah, mebbe,' he said, a wicked gleam in his eyes. 'You take them chrysanthemums in to her ladyship now and mind your step. It's frosty this morning. We don't want you slipping over and laid up in bed now do we?'

'I shall be very careful, thank you,' Annabel said and turned away.

As she went into the house, she found her sister replacing the telephone on its stand in the hall.

'It was just Tom ringing to tell you that they arrived home safely last night,' Hetty said. 'He didn't ask for you so I took the message.'

'Oh, it was good of him to ring,' Annabel said. 'But then he is always so thoughtful.'

'I like Tom,' Hetty said, giving her sister a searching look. 'Why don't you marry him, Belle? He's rich enough to give you plenty of clothes and holidays in France. He told me they are going away in the New Year. I should love to go to France in January, wouldn't you?'

'Yes, it might be nice, get away from the worst of the winter,' Annabel said. 'But in answer to your question, Tom hasn't asked me to marry him, and I don't think I would if he did. I'm very fond of him, but I'm not in love with him.'

'It would be better than having Mother go on at you about marriage,' Hetty said and pulled a wry face. 'I heard her last night, Belle. It isn't fair. You didn't make Father lose all his money.'

'No, I didn't,' Annabel agreed. 'And Ben hasn't said anything about wanting me out of the way. It might be different when he gets married. I don't suppose his wife will want us all here then.'

'He'll have the Dower House done up for us, I expect,' Hetty said. 'I heard Mother telling one of her friends that Ben was getting an estimate of the work needed. I shan't mind as long as I can still walk in the gardens and ride. Besides, I'm going to do something with my life as soon as I'm seventeen. I want to travel, Belle – and I think I should like to be an artist.'

Annabel looked at her in surprise. 'You do paint well, Hetty,' she agreed. 'But you can't think you could do it well enough to make a living?'

'Why not?' Hetty gave her a rebellious stare, her pretty mouth set in a stubborn line. 'Just because everyone else in the family is obsessed with marriage doesn't mean I have to be. Women do work these days. I might not become a great artist overnight, but I could probably find work in commercial art. I want to go to college and study. I'm not going to marry a man for his money, whatever Mother says – and if I were you I wouldn't either.'

'Mother will never allow you to go to Art College, will she?' Annabel said looking at her anxiously. 'You know what she's like.'

'She isn't as bad with me as she is with you,' Hetty said. 'She doesn't think I'm pretty enough to make a good marriage so she said she would consider letting me go to college in Bournemouth – providing I live with a friend of hers who will keep an eye on me.'

'Well, if it's what you want – and if Mother agrees,' Annabel laughed, feeling pleased that her sister would be spared the pressure she was under at the moment. 'I think that's rather wonderful. I can't believe Mother actually said yes.'

'Selina persuaded her,' Hetty said ruefully. 'Last night, I think, while they were waiting for you. She told her that I wasn't likely to settle for marriage for some years, and that it was perfectly respectable for young women to work these days. Selina knows people – she has offered to introduce me to friends of hers who might help me.'

'I'm so thrilled for you, dearest,' Annabel said. 'But you're not seventeen yet.'

'I shall be in the spring,' Hetty said, that rebellious light in her eyes once more. 'Selina is going to take me on a visit with her before that. She will help me to enrol in the college and make sure everything is as Mother would like it.'

'Then I wish you good luck,' Annabel said. 'I'm going to arrange these flowers now. Jonah picked them for Mother. Aren't they gorgeous? Do you want to help me?'

'I've promised Mother I'll take a note to the Vicarage for her,' Hetty said, not wanting to be stuck indoors all morning. 'Besides, you don't need me to help, you always do the flowers so well.'

'I shall see you later then,' Annabel said, taking her flowers through to the back scullery to arrange them. She was humming a tune to herself as she sorted through the vases, selecting a cut glass vase and a smaller, rather special Rene Lalique bowl with an Art Nouveau design in the glass, which she rather liked, for her own room.

It had surprised her that Lady Tarleton had given even a tentative agreement to Hetty's request, but perhaps Annabel's failure to find a rich husband had made her realise that her younger daughter might have similar difficulty. Perhaps she could find a job herself, Annabel thought, though she wasn't artistic like her sister, and she really didn't know what she might do.

Sighing, Annabel carried her vase of beautifully arranged flowers through to her mother's favourite sitting room, relieved that Lady Tarleton wasn't yet seated in her usual place by the window. Her own talents were perfectly suited to filling the role her mother had planned for her, because she would make a good society hostess – but marriage to a man she couldn't love did not appeal to her.

She could only carry on as she was and hope that one day she would meet the man she could love, and that in the meantime Ben wasn't forced to sell the estate out from under them.

*

Annabel's heart raced as she saw the expensive car draw up in the drive. He had come and she hadn't been sure that he would, because there were plenty of other girls who would love to go driving with Richard. She ran down the stairs, arriving a little breathlessly just as he was being shown into the hall.

'Ready?' he asked. 'Or do I have to be approved by Mama?'

'No, certainly not,' Annabel said stung by the mocking expression in his eyes. 'Mother would love to meet you, naturally, but I don't have to have her permission to go out for a drive with you; this is 1929 not the Victorian age.' She raised her head with a little defiance as she said it, although as far as Lady Tarleton was concerned, time had not moved on.

'I am relieved to hear it,' he murmured. 'Come on then. I've an appointment to see a horse and I thought you might enjoy that. You do like horses, don't you?'

'Absolutely,' she said. 'I've been riding since I was three.'

'That's all right then,' he replied and opened the passenger side door of his car for her to get in. She did so, inhaling the scents of leather, tobacco and lastly cedar wood, which she thought came from his cologne.

'This is a beautiful car. It's a Rolls Royce, isn't it?'

'Yes.' He smiled at her. 'I like the best in everything, as you will discover if our friendship continues, Belle.'

'Is it going to continue?' she asked, giving him a rather shy glance.

'That rather depends on you,' he replied as he started the car. 'I thought you might have been warned not to come with me this afternoon. Didn't your mother tell you I wasn't suitable for you to know?'

Afterwards, Annabel never understood why she replied in the way she did, but it just seemed to come out without her intending it to.

'My mother wants me to marry a rich man,' she said, a hint of bitterness in her voice. 'It wouldn't matter what kind of reputation he had or what he had done, just as long as he had money and was willing to marry me.'

Her reply startled Richard for a moment and then he laughed.

'Well, that's the most honest reply I've ever heard,' he said. 'I take it that you haven't told her I'm not the marrying kind.'

'You don't tell my mother that kind of thing,' Annabel replied, relieved that he had thought it funny, because it was really rather dreadful of her. 'After a few months she may tell me I'm wasting my time, but for now you are at the top of her list.' There, she'd said it and he could think what he liked!

'It must be trying for you at times,' he said, clearly amused by her frankness. She saw the laughter but was there more? Annabel thought that perhaps she'd intrigued him and that pleased her. 'But perhaps you feel the same way about marriage as your mother?'

'No, I don't,' Annabel replied with such feeling that he laughed. 'I want someone I can love and care for. I've already turned down two proposals of marriage, though my mother doesn't know. She would be furious if she found out who they were.'

'You're quite a girl,' Richard said and put his foot down. 'Hang on, Belle, I'm in a bit of a hurry. I want this horse and I happen to know that someone else wants it too...'

Annabel took a deep breath as the car rounded a corner at high speed, its back wheels sliding out slightly. He certainly wasn't as careful a driver as Major Brocklehurst, and she wasn't sure whether she was more scared or excited, but she laughed because she thought Richard would expect it of her and it was rather thrilling.

He continued to drive at breath-taking speed until they arrived at their destination, then slowed down as his car entered a long drive leading to a large, well known stud situated at the edge of the small town of Newmarket.

'I know Tom came here some weeks ago to buy a horse for himself,' Annabel remarked as the car stopped. 'He needed something up to his weight and found just what he wanted here.'

'Your brother?' Richard arched his brows at her.

'No – Major Brocklehurst. He is a distant cousin of my father's and he and his sister are family friends.'

Richard nodded, losing interest as he saw a man coming to greet him. He got out of the car without commenting or asking Annabel to go with him. She watched him walk off in the direction of the stables, feeling as if she'd been deserted. Not that it would have been a good idea for her to go far since her shoes were not at all suitable for walking, but she didn't much enjoy being left to sit on her own, especially as Richard was gone for more than half an hour. He might at least have asked if she wanted to see the horse.

She hunted for something to look at, finding a copy of The Times on the back seat, but she had already seen the paper and it didn't hold her interest for long, because the main article was about the Nazi party having won a big election. Annabel had never heard of them and wondered why the paper was so disapproving. She found a copy of T.E. Lawrence's *Revolt in the Desert*, which was very popular at the moment, but couldn't get past the first page. Feeling bored, she got out of the car and leant against it. She saw another, slightly shabby, car draw up and a man got out. He was carrying a large flat case that looked as if it might contain drawings or plans of some kind. He glanced her way and smiled, hesitating and then approaching her.

'You wouldn't be Miss Harding I suppose?'

'No, I'm sorry,' Annabel said. His clothes were rather smarter than his car, but he obviously came from what her mother would call the "working class", though he had probably got on in the world and wasn't short of a few pounds. 'I'm just waiting for a friend. He's looking at a horse. Have you come about a horse?'

'No. I don't much care for them,' the man said. 'I'm here about some printing work – advertising for the stables. I was told to see Miss Jane Harding. I'd better go on up to the office I expect. I believe it is around here somewhere.'

'I expect so,' Annabel said. 'I'm sorry I can't be of help. I haven't been here before.' She gave him a warm smile, because there was something about him that she liked, despite the gap between their two worlds. A gap her mother would consider unbridgeable. 'I'm Annabel Tarleton. It was nice to have met you, Mr…?'

'Paul Keifer,' he said and offered her his hand. She took it and liked his firm clasp. 'It was nice talking to you but I mustn't be late. I think I am a few minutes behind as it is. Goodbye, Miss Tarleton.'

Annabel watched as he walked off. He had seemed pleasant, she thought, not wildly attractive like Richard, but nice in his own way, his hair a dark brown and his eyes the greenish brown that some people called hazel. She thought there might just have been a trace of a North Country accent in his voice.

'Sorry to have been so long,' a voice said from behind her and she turned to discover that Richard had returned without her noticing. 'Who were you talking to just now?'

'Just someone looking for Jane Harding,' she said. 'He thought I might be her.'

'I've met her and she looks nothing like you,' Richard said, his frown deepening.

'I don't suppose he knows what she looks like.'

'No…' His frown cleared. 'Anyway, it doesn't matter now. I got my horse. She's a damn good mare and I shall put her to stud in my own yard. I'll take you there one day if you like, when you're wearing suitable footwear.'

'Perhaps,' Annabel replied but didn't smile. He was taking her just a little too much for granted, though that might be her own fault. By being outspoken she may have given him the impression that she was easy and that annoyed her.

'Miffed, are you?' Richard said, guessing that she hadn't liked to be kept waiting for so long. 'Never mind, I'll take you out for tea somewhere nice on the way back.'

'Yes, all right,' she said but she still didn't smile. It might do him good to be kept guessing instead of getting his own way all the time.

*

'Did you enjoy your drive?' Hetty asked, when she came in to say goodnight that evening. 'I saw you going off in that expensive car. Who is he? Anyone interesting?'

'I thought he might be,' Annabel said and sighed as she took off her shoes, which were high heeled black suede courts and expensive. Maybe if she hadn't worn these Richard would have taken her with him to look at the horse, but if he'd told her where they were going in the first place, she would have been better prepared. 'But now I'm not sure that I like him very much after all.'

'You always say that,' Hetty observed and sat on the bed, picking up a magazine with an article about Ivor Novello and staring at the photograph. 'He is so moody, but terribly handsome, don't you think?'

'Yes, he is rather,' Annabel said with an amused look. Her sister was a romantic, and perhaps a bit of a dreamer. She hoped that wouldn't lead to Hetty getting hurt one day. 'You can take that if you like, Hetty. Someone gave it to me but I don't really want it.'

'Thank you, I shall,' Hetty said. 'I suppose you want some peace so I'll leave you to it. I still think you should marry Tom. He really likes you, Belle, and I'm sure he would marry you if you hinted you were willing.'

'I shall do no such thing,' Annabel replied and threw a pillow at her. 'And if you dare to say anything to him I'll skin you alive.'

Hetty raised her brows and Annabel smiled as the door closed behind her. Her sister was a scamp, but there were times when Hetty's presence in the house was the only thing that made her life bearable. Sometimes, she felt she'd been a fool to turn down the offers of marriage she'd had, because there were times when she would do anything to escape from her mother's constant disapproval.

She had already endured a grilling from her mother on the subject of Richard Hansen and had begun to wish that she had never gone out with him in the first place! Annabel knew that Lady Tarleton wouldn't let her forget that he'd been interested enough to take her for a drive, and she would silently disapprove if she had missed the opportunity to snaffle a rich husband. It just wasn't worth thinking about and she would put the whole thing out of her mind – think about something else.

She remembered that Georgie Barrington was coming the next day and smiled. It might be a good idea to go away for a few days, let her mother forget all about Richard Hansen.

*

'Your uncle's wife sounds like an enterprising lady,' Annabel said when Georgie had finished explaining about the situation at Kendlebury Hall the following afternoon. 'And you're going to help out with the pre-Christmas rush?'

'I rather enjoy joining in and doing all sorts of work,' Georgie said and grinned at her. 'It's all very informal. One day I might be working in the shop, another I might be making beds for the guests.'

'Is it a hotel then?' Annabel asked, still not quite clear what went on. 'They seem to do all kinds of things, what with the workshops, their tea rooms and lodgers.'

'No, it's not quite like that,' Georgie said. 'The guests are just a few regulars that come and stay for a week or so once or twice a year. You see, when people discovered how good the food was at Kendlebury they started saying they would like to visit more often, and after Sir Joshua and then Lady Kendle died, Harry thought it might be a good idea to take selected guests for short periods. A lot of people like to come for a visit before Christmas. And during the last three weeks of December they do evening meals as well as teas in the annexe.'

'Gosh, that must make them really busy,' Annabel said. 'But it does sound rather intriguing. I'm not much use at anything. I make my own bed, of course, and I can do flowers and write letters neatly, that sort of thing.'

'Jessie will find you a job,' Georgie replied with a grin. 'There are so many small tasks that need doing. We all get roped in for something.'

'Are you sure I shan't be in the way?'

'Jessie never lets anyone feel useless,' Georgie said. 'I wasn't much use the first time I offered to help out, but I soon learned. You're not stupid, Belle. It's just that your mother has never let you do much except arrange flowers.'

'She says housework is what the servants are for.' Annabel wrinkled her nose. 'Poor Mrs Bumble isn't as good on her legs as she used to be so Hetty and I do what we can to help out. Hetty is more practical than me. She goes into the kitchen sometimes and lends a hand with the cooking. She has been doing it since she was about ten and I think they've got used to her, though Mother grumbles if she knows what she's been up to. Mostly she doesn't, because no one tells her. I usually tidy the rooms we use, just picking up stuff and putting it away. I'm up ages before Mother most mornings so she doesn't know. But there's only Mr and Mrs Bumble and Ruth these days, and Ruth doesn't always come in if she doesn't feel like it.'

'I know what that's like,' Georgie said and laughed. 'We had a maid like that once. Mother soon sorted her out!'

'My mother tried but she says it's too difficult to find new staff willing to work in such an isolated area, and Ruth does do all the rough work when she's here.' Annabel pulled a wry face. 'We used to have three gardeners when I was little, but there's only one now and he's eighty. Jonah does what he can in the garden and his grandson helps out when he has time. Eric usually works on the farm. His father is Ben's tenant and I imagine the family has been here as long as ours. My great grandfather bought the property when he retired from a career in the army. He was a younger son but unexpectedly inherited the title when his elder brother died. The family had money then but my father managed to lose most of it, as I expect you've been told.'

Georgie nodded but made no comment as Annabel continued. 'It wasn't all Daddy's fault. His own father gambled excessively and that started the rot. Daddy just made unwise investments trying to make more money for us. And then the crash more or less wiped us out.'

'That can happen to anyone,' Georgie agreed. 'My father did well with his investments after the war but a lot of people didn't.'

'Ben is doing his best to turn things round but it isn't easy for him.'

'It must be difficult to manage a house like this.' Georgie glanced round the pretty sitting room, which was decorated in shades of cream and green and was clearly Annabel's domain because of the touches of modernity which were missing from the rest of the house. Annabel was an admirer of Art Deco and a lot of her possessions had that influence. Situated at the back of the house, the room looked out onto the kitchen gardens and beyond that, the fens themselves. The fog had lingered for days but was at last clearing and because the house was set on a small rise, it was possible to see for miles across the flat countryside behind them; fields, deep dykes and hedges, but very few trees. 'It's one of those rambling houses, isn't it? All passages, small dark rooms and freezing in winter. Mother says they are an abomination and should all be pulled down.' She blushed as she realised what she'd said. 'Oh, sorry, I didn't mean it the way it sounded.'

'You're so right,' Annabel said and laughed. 'My mother is always complaining about the cold and damp – that's why she sits at the front of the house. The sun comes in more that way and there are some fine windows; the rooms are bigger too. I prefer to be here, because I rather like the view. I know most people think the fens are dull and boring, but they have a fascination all their own. You should see the sunset sometimes, it's really beautiful out there.' At other times there was a haunting stillness in the surrounding countryside, but no one who hadn't been born to the fens could understand the way it touched the heart.

Georgie saw the pensive look in her eyes and wondered if she chose this room to escape from her mother, but didn't voice her thoughts aloud.

'Old houses can be so difficult to keep in order, especially when you can't find enough servants to look after them. Mother says Jessie has a problem at Kendlebury, though most of her people don't live in now. They come and go and it's not as bad as when she first went there, because there is a good bus service now. I think at one time they found it almost impossible to keep girls; they prefer the factories or shops.'

'Yes, I've heard that's pretty common these days,' Annabel agreed. 'I often wonder what it must have been like before the war – when there was plenty of money about and people rode in carriages with splendid horses to pull them. It must have been nice to have lots of big house parties, people staying at weekends and everything run like clockwork. Mother says people knew their place in those days and it made life much easier.'

'I suppose there are still some people lucky enough to live like that,' Georgie said, keeping her opinions on such old-fashioned thinking to herself. 'Mother manages with a housekeeper and a secretary who looks after all her correspondence and clothes, but we don't have a big old house. Ours is small compared to this and modern. My mother insisted on it when Father retired from his post in the Government. He's on the board of several companies now, and they spend a lot of their time at the London house. I was at boarding school until last year as you know, now I visit friends and flit about as I like most of the time. I enjoy travelling.'

'Hetty says she wants to travel,' Annabel said and wrinkled her brow. 'I've never thought about it much. I don't really know what I want to do with my life – except that I want it to be different from this…'

Georgie reflected privately that her friend had never been allowed to think for herself. Lady Tarleton had decided she should make a good marriage and Annabel had simply allowed her mother to dictate to her.

'Well, come to Kendlebury with me,' she urged. 'It might help you to decide what you want, Belle.' And it would do her good to get right away from her mother for a few weeks!

'Yes. Yes, I will,' Annabel said and smiled at her. 'To tell you the truth I've been feeling a bit low and this will make a nice change.'

'I'll pick you up in my car,' Georgie said. 'Daddy bought it for my last birthday, the darling, and he taught me to drive himself so I'm quite safe. You ought to learn, Belle, it's awfully good fun – and it makes one independent.'

'Yes, it sounds fun,' Annabel said. She didn't add that she had asked her brother to teach her but her mother had made such a fuss that they had given up the idea. 'Perhaps I shall one day.'

'I'll give you a go when we're at Kendlebury,' Georgie promised and picked up her bag. 'I had better go. Mother has arranged something for this evening and I don't want to be late.'

'No, of course not—' Annabel broke off as someone came into the room and then gave a little cry of pleasure. 'Ben! I didn't know you were coming home today.'

'I didn't expect to,' he said. 'But I had some news so I thought I might as well get it over with.' He stopped, his cheeks colouring as he saw Georgie preparing to leave. 'Hello. I'm sorry if I've interrupted. I didn't realise Belle had a friend with her.'

'It's perfectly all right,' she said and smiled at him. They had met on a couple of occasions but she hadn't really got to know him and she suspected that he didn't recognise her. 'I'm Georgie Barrington.'

'Yes, I thought so,' he said and looked rueful. 'We danced once. I'm most awfully sorry. My mind was elsewhere and I didn't recognise you immediately.'

'Why should you?' Georgie asked. 'We've only met a couple of times and I've had my hair cut since you last saw me.'

'Yes, you have, and very nice it looks too,' he replied. 'I like the way young women are cutting their hair these days. Belle's is still long and a real nuisance to her at times.'

'I've thought about cutting it, especially when it's hot,' Annabel said. 'But Mother says I shouldn't because it wouldn't suit me.'

'You should ignore her,' Ben said and rolled his eyes skywards. 'I say, Georgie, is that little roadster I saw parked in the drive yours?'

'Yes, it is,' she replied and laughed as she saw his expression. 'It's an Alfa Romeo Spider and the latest thing. I'm very lucky. My father tends to spoil me when it comes to presents.'

'You wouldn't give me a spin down the road, would you?'

Georgie laughed at his enthusiasm. Most young men of her acquaintance felt very much the same when they saw the car.

'It will have to be a quick one, because I mustn't be late back.' She glanced at Annabel. 'I'm afraid there are only two seats.'

'Oh, take Ben,' Annabel said. 'I shall have my ride when you call for me on Friday.'

'Yes, certainly,' Georgie said. 'Goodbye for now, then.'

Annabel smiled to herself as they went out together. Georgie was a lively girl, fun to be with, and much more Ben's kind of girl than Helen Winters who, in her opinion, was rather a shrew. She wondered about her twin's news and hoped it wasn't what she suspected. If he had made up his mind to marry she would have to start thinking seriously about the future.

She had been trying not to think of Sunday afternoon, which was still inclined to rankle in her mind, even though Richard had tried to compensate for his mistake. He had taken her to tea at a very nice hotel after they left the stables and made polite conversation until he'd brought her home again. He had thanked her for her company but hadn't tried to kiss her. She wasn't sure if she was sorry or glad about that, because although a part of her had wanted him to, the other part was still smarting from the way he had simply abandoned her at the stables.

Perhaps it was because she'd been cool towards him afterwards that he hadn't tried to kiss her, Annabel thought, and after he'd driven away, saying merely that he would see her sometime, she'd begun to wish she'd behaved differently. After all, her shoes hadn't been suitable for the stable yard – but she would still have liked to have been asked. It was his careless attitude that had upset her rather than the fact that she'd had to sit and wait. Her friends had warned her about him, and perhaps they were right, she decided. Richard could be fun, and oozed charm when he wished, but he wasn't the sort of comfortable man a sensible girl would choose for a husband.

Annabel sighed as she prepared to go upstairs and change for the evening. Marriage remained a distant prospect and what was she going to do if Ben brought a wife home?

*

It was just as she was about to go downstairs for dinner that her brother knocked at the door of her bedroom, asking if she was decent.

'Yes, of course,' she said, opening it to him. 'I was about to go down, Ben.' She saw that he had changed his clothes for the evening and smiled. He was extremely good looking as well as being good natured, and she was very fond of him. 'We'll go together if you like.'

'I wanted a word in private first.'

'Come in,' she invited. 'You look bothered – what's the matter?'

'Nothing. I've made up my mind but I wanted to tell you first – that's why I came to you when I got home. By the way Georgie's car is fantastic! I wouldn't mind something like that myself.' He frowned. 'Not that I've money to spare for new cars. My own will have to do for the moment, but things may get better once I'm married.'

'Are you going to be married?' she asked.

'I'm engaged to Helen,' he replied. 'The wedding won't be until next June, when she's nineteen and I'll be twenty-one. Her father insisted on the engagement period, but it doesn't bother me that much. I told him I needed time to make some changes here anyway and he's agreed to help me out financially. He thinks I should put some modern plumbing in and I agree with him. He's giving us a small house in London as a wedding present and Helen will have five thousand a year from her trust fund once we're married. She says it will enable us to take holidays in France and live decently, and it will certainly make things easier for me if she has her own money.'

'Is that what you want?' Annabel asked, looking at him anxiously. 'In your heart, Ben? Don't do this just because Mother thinks it's a good idea. You could sell the house and the farm and be free – live your own life.'

'And what happens to you, Hetty and Mother?' he said with a lift of his brows. 'I know you will probably marry sooner or later but it will be a while before Hetty settles down. Besides, I happen to be quite fond of the house, even if it is a dinosaur and a millstone around my neck.'

'But marriage is forever,' Annabel pressed on. 'I know people do divorce these days, but it isn't for you, Ben. You're not ruthless enough. I know you. If you marry Helen you'll stick by her.'

'Yes, I probably shall,' he replied with a lop-sided grin. 'Don't think I haven't given all this a lot of thought, Belle, because I have. Mother made it clear after we lost the money that I either had to make some quickly or marry a rich wife. Well, I've tried everything I can think of and I've managed to clear Father's debts at last. I've bought a couple of good fields recently with the money Grandmother left me, which will help with the income from the farm, but I'm down to my last few hundred now. And although I can make a reasonable living from the land and my freelance writing for the magazine, I know I'll never be a rich man.

'Besides, Helen is all right. I think she really loves me and I'm fond of her. I know you don't like her much, but that's because she isn't at her best with you. She's jealous because you're my twin and she thinks she'll never be as close to me as you are.'

'Oh, Ben,' Annabel said and sighed. Her brother had considerable talent as a writer, but articles on the countryside for a glossy magazine brought in just a few pounds a month and were never going to solve his problems. It was a pity he couldn't write a play like Noël Coward and become famous, but somehow it didn't seem likely. Ben just didn't have what it took to make a raging success of his life. He was loveable, kind and generous, but never dynamic. 'People don't understand about twins, do they? It's true that there's a bond between us that can never be broken, but it doesn't stop us loving other people.'

'I've tried to explain, but Helen is possessive,' he said. 'I don't mind it too much really. Her father is going to settle ten thousand on us when we marry and that will make things much easier all round. It's the best way for me, Belle. Please try to understand. I don't want my marriage to cause a rift between us.'

'As if it could or would,' she said and kissed him on the cheek. 'I love you more than anyone else in the world, Ben. I want you to be happy, and if this is what you really want I'm pleased.'

'Are you?' he asked and lifted his brows. 'Well, try to be because it's done now and I'm going to tell Mother this evening.'

'She will be delighted. Hetty will think you're mad, but take no notice of her. Do you know she wants to go to Art College?'

'No – does she?' He grinned. 'That will ruffle some feathers.'

'Actually, Mother has agreed. Selina persuaded her.'

'Ah, that explains it,' he said. 'Mother is quite impressed by Selina, you know. So what about you – have you met *the* man yet? The one who will sweep you off your feet and dance you into a sunlit future?'

'How romantic. If only...' She laughed huskily as she hugged his arm. 'I've come to the conclusion there is no such thing as the perfect man. Perhaps I shall take the next man who makes an offer for me.'

'Don't be an idiot,' her twin said sharply. 'You don't have to marry just yet. I'm not pushing you. Take your time, Belle. I want you to be happy.'

'Thank you.' She glanced up at him, knowing that he meant it. 'I'm going to stay with Georgie's family for a while. It's a working holiday and may help me to make up my mind what I want to do with my life.'

'Good,' he said and nodded approvingly. 'It's time you made a bid for independence.'

'Just don't tell Mother,' she warned. 'She knows I'm staying with Georgie but she doesn't know we'll be helping out, and I would rather she didn't for the moment.'

'When did I ever tell Mother more than I need?' her brother asked. 'But I'm glad you're doing this, Belle. If Mother has her way you'll be married before you've had time to see any life at all.'

'It's a breathing space,' Annabel said. 'Mother doesn't know but I've already turned down two offers of marriage. I thought I'd met someone but I'm not sure – besides, he's not the marrying kind.'

'Why don't you just forget about all that for a while and enjoy yourself?' Ben suggested. 'You've had so much pressure on you since you came out of the schoolroom, just put it all out of your mind and have a good time – that's my advice.'

'And very good advice,' she told him, hugging his arm. 'That's exactly what I intend to do for the next three weeks…'

Three

'Oh, what a lovely house,' Annabel exclaimed as she saw Kendlebury Hall for the first time. 'No wonder your family is willing to work so hard to hang on to it. We're quite fond of our house, but it's nothing like this.'

'It is rather lovely, isn't it?' Georgie said. 'I took it for granted when Mother used to bring us here to stay as children, but it was a bit run down then. Jessie has really brought the house and the gardens back to life. And the workshops are a little community all on their own. Everyone is so friendly that it's like coming home each time I visit.'

'I can understand why you want to come now,' Annabel said. The house was ancient but had a mellow charm that appealed to her instantly, and the surrounding park had wonderful old trees that looked as if they had stood forever. 'I'll bet those roses in front of the veranda are a picture in the summer. All this must take some looking after.'

'Jessie does some of the gardening herself,' Georgie said. 'But you'll meet her in a minute and then you'll see what I mean.'

A woman who looked to be in her late fifties had come out of the house to greet them and Annabel wondered if she was the lady of the house, then decided that she couldn't be: Jessie was younger.

'Hello, Mrs Pottersby,' Georgina said and went to kiss the woman on the cheek. 'Annabel, this lady is Jessie's Aunt Elizabeth – my friend, Annabel Tarleton.'

Elizabeth Pottersby smiled and came forward to take one of Annabel's suitcases. She was clearly a very strong, robust woman and had a cheerful, welcoming manner.

'I'm very pleased to meet you, Miss Tarleton. It's good of you to come down to help us out.'

'I'm not sure I can be of much help,' Annabel said, her cheeks pink. 'Though I am very willing to try.'

'Don't worry, Jessie will find you a job,' Elizabeth said and chuckled. 'She gets us all in the end. I was running my own bakery and teashop in London until three years ago, then, after years of trying, she finally persuaded me to sell and come here to live – and it was the best thing I ever did. I have no responsibilities and a very comfortable home, and I like being a part of the family.'

'It is certainly a beautiful house,' Annabel agreed. 'I can understand why people want to come and stay here.'

'We could have visitors all year round if we wanted,' Elizabeth said. 'But Harry thinks we all work hard enough as it is and we're managing well as we are, so for the moment it is just the favoured few.'

Elizabeth led the way into the house. A man of about sixty or so came forward to take the case she was carrying and also one of Georgie's.

'It's good to see you here again, Miss Georgie – and your friend.'

'Thank you, Carter,' she said. 'This is Annabel Tarleton. She is going to help out for a while.'

'We're very busy,' he told her. 'A party of six arrived this morning for a week so there's plenty to do.'

'Is Jessie here?'

'Not at the moment,' Elizabeth answered as Carter went on ahead of them with the cases. 'She drove herself into Torquay to order some things she needs for Christmas, but she will be back by tea time.'

Carter had taken the cases into a large bedroom, which the girls were to share; he then departed without saying anything more, leaving Elizabeth to settle them in.

'I hope you won't mind sharing,' she said. 'But with so many guests we're rather short of good rooms. There are a couple empty on the floor above but I thought you would prefer this.'

'We don't mind sharing, do we, Belle?'

'No, of course not. It's rather fun – and we'll keep it tidy so we shan't make more work for you, Mrs Pottersby.'

'That's the spirit,' Elizabeth replied. 'Shall you come down for tea in the kitchen, Georgie? Or would you rather show your friend around first? You can have it in the annexe if you wait until three thirty.'

'Oh no, we'll have it with you,' Georgie said. 'It's much nicer in the kitchen. Besides, we're here to work, not to be waited on. I'll take Annabel round later, and we can unpack afterwards.'

Annabel had already opened her small case. She took out her dressing case and put it on a table by the window, opening it to remove her hairbrushes and combs. Georgie borrowed one to save unpacking her own and they both powdered their noses, applying the merest touch of lipstick.

'We'll do,' Georgie said. 'I'm dying for a cup of tea and a bun. Cook and Mrs Pottersby are both marvels in the kitchen. The wonder is that they agree, but Mrs Pottersby only helps out with the cooking when we're busy. Most of the time she looks after the house. The housekeeper left just after Jessie married into the family and they managed without one for ages – but now Mrs Pottersby runs it all like clockwork, giving Jessie time for other things.'

'I'm looking forward to meeting her.'

'I am sure you will like her.'

Georgie led the way to the kitchen, using the back stairs this time. As they approached the area Lady Tarleton always referred to as *downstairs* Annabel could hear the echo of laughter and several excited voices all talking at once. When they went into the kitchen she saw a rather attractive woman, probably in her thirties, with soft brown eyes and lovely dark hair worn in a twist at the nape of her neck, laughing with the others. She was dressed in a pair of grey wide-legged trousers with a soft silk blouse that tied at the neck, and a pair of pearl earrings set off the casual but very elegant ensemble. She looked up as the girls walked in and smiled, coming forward at once.

'Hello, Georgie darling,' she said. 'And you must be Annabel. I'm sorry I wasn't here to greet you when you arrived, but I know my aunt looked after you. You must be dying for a cup of tea, as am I. I've been indulging myself in the shops and Harry will have a fit when he discovers how much I've spent – but it had to be done.'

Jessie kissed her niece on the cheek, then smiled at Annabel, decided she liked what she saw and kissed her too. Taking her by the hand she led her forward and introduced her to the other women in the kitchen.

'This is Cook, who looks after us all so well and without whom we should all come to a standstill,' she said, her eyes bright with mischief. Jessie was actually older than Annabel had thought, getting towards the end of her thirties now, but one of those women who seem eternally young. 'This is Maggie. She is a married lady and has two lovely children, so she can only come for a few hours while they're at school. This is Pam Bates, who helps me in so many ways – and this is my friend Alice Rawlings. She is a singer and an actress, but she's between engagements at the moment and so she has come down to help us for a while. Just a few months ago she was in a successful show with the Tiller Girls at the London Plaza!'

Annabel looked suitably impressed and Alice laughed.

'What Jessie really means is that I'm not a very successful singer,' Alice said and held out her hand to shake Annabel's. 'Every now and then I get some work from a friend of mine who owns a nightclub, and I was in that show for a while, but most of the time I work in Jessie's gift shop. If they need help at table in the evenings I do that too. I used to be a housemaid here.'

'At least you know what you want to do with your life,' Annabel said, deciding that she liked the other girl. Georgie had already told her that Alice had had a child although she wasn't married. Annabel's mother would have found that very shocking, but she thought it was very brave of Alice to keep the child despite all the difficulties it must have made for her over the years. 'I'm afraid I'm not much use at anything. I don't have any talents at all.'

'Now that I don't believe,' Jessie said. 'I imagine you haven't had any need to develop them but I'm sure you have plenty.'

'Well, I can arrange flowers and write neatly.'

'That's brilliant,' Jessie said. 'You can help with the plants and do the flowers for the house for starters, and if your handwriting is very good, you can do some menus for us. I like to see them hand-written sometimes.'

'I told you Jessie would find you a job,' Georgie said. 'Have you made seed cake, Cook? Scrummy! It's my favourite. A large slice for me please.'

'You're as bad as your mother. Miss Priscilla was always one for my seed cake,' Cook said, her three chins wobbling. She was a very large lady but her girth appeared not to bother her and she seemed very pleased with life, Annabel thought. 'What about you, Miss Annabel?'

'I wouldn't mind the seed cake,' Annabel said. 'But are those tarts coconut? I'm rather partial to coconut tarts.'

'Help yourself, my dear,' Cook invited, looking pleased. 'We don't stand on ceremony here as you can see – and I like to see a girl enjoy her food.'

'I'm going to leave you now,' Jessie said. 'I think Harry is back and he wanted me to check some orders for him this evening. I shall see you girls at dinner. There's nothing for you to do today, just relax and enjoy yourselves. I'll find you plenty to do tomorrow.'

They took her at their word, tucking into the splendid feast Cook had provided before Georgie decided it was time she showed Annabel around outside.

'If we don't go now it will be dark,' she said. 'But the shop is still open and so are some of the workshops. Harry's main workshop is in Torquay but he has another here in the old barn. I'll take you to one or two of the others but you can find your own way about after that. There aren't many rules here, Belle. As I said before, everyone is friendly and pleased to see you if you're interested in what they're doing.'

'Well, I'm certainly interested,' Annabel said as they left the house and set off in the direction of what had clearly once been a stable block. 'As long as we're not being a nuisance.'

'Stop worrying,' Georgie told her. 'You're at Kendlebury now, not Tarleton Towers.'

Annabel nodded, smiling at her. 'It just seems a little strange at first. Your aunt seems to treat her staff as friends.'

'Well, they are her friends,' Georgie said. 'I know it isn't what you've been used to but you'll soon take it for granted.'

Some of the craft units were in darkness, others had their lights burning. After popping into the gift shop, which was just about to close for the day, they visited two of the workshops. One of the units was occupied by several men and women making baskets and wicker work hampers, another was very small and Annabel was fascinated to see rather stylish leather handbags being sewn by a man working alone.

'What are the other workshops producing?' she asked as they walked on. 'There are no lights.'

'Harry's people make wonderful furniture, but that's in the barn not the old stable block. One of them is a small pottery making souvenirs for the gift trade. They sell a lot of that very modern stuff, bright colours and odd shapes. But the owner only works here part time, he does more in the summer; the visitors like to see the wheel working. I think he has a little shop in Torquay – and the other workshop is a small printing firm. The owner of that isn't here very often either. He has a larger printing works somewhere now but he still keeps the workshop on. I'm not sure why.'

'Oh…' Annabel looked at her curiously. 'That's a bit odd, isn't it?'

'I believe Paul has always been a little in love with Jessie, though I suppose she is a few years older than him,' Georgie said. 'There's nothing going on; she adores Harry and the children. You haven't met them yet. They have two sons, Jonathan and Walter, and a daughter, Catherine. Catherine is probably in the annexe helping to lay tables for the evening. They will serve dinner in there as there are paying guests at the moment. Catherine likes to do that, though she can't cope with serving the customers.' Georgie bit her lip. 'I haven't told you about Harry's daughter. He had her with Mary, his first wife, and she isn't quite the same as you and me. She isn't stupid, don't think that, she knows what's going on all right, but she's a little slow at times. However, Jessie thinks the world of her and she makes sure Catherine is never left out of anything we're doing. She'll help with all the Christmas decorations and she makes beds beautifully. I suppose that proves everyone has some talents. She helps Cook in the kitchen too sometimes, though she can't do too much because she isn't strong.'

'What is the matter with her?'

'I'm not sure,' Georgie said, wrinkling her brow. 'I think she has a weakness in her heart. At one time they thought she might not live very long, but she isn't often ill; it's just that she gets tired suddenly and needs to sleep. But both the boys are fine. Jonathan is at boarding school and Walter goes to a day school in Torquay.'

'I shall be interested to meet Catherine,' Annabel said. 'Everything you tell me about your aunt makes me admire her, Georgie. They didn't know if your uncle would ever walk again when she married him, did they?'

'Jessie had made up her mind he wasn't going to be allowed to sit around in that chair forever,' Georgie said and smiled. 'But he isn't really well. He can get about on his own if he takes things slowly, and his mind is as sharp as a razor, but he tires easily and needs to rest more than he used to before the accident. Jessie is the driving force behind the estate. Without her it would all have been sold long ago.'

'Well, she seems to have plenty of energy. I wish I could be more like her. It must be wonderful to know exactly what you want to do when you get up in the mornings.'

'Well, you'll know what to do tomorrow morning,' Georgie said and laughed. 'Jessie will expect us both to be ready bright and early.'

*

Annabel was thoughtful as she left the kitchen and began to walk towards what had once been the old stable block but was now a hive of activity. It was a dull morning but the lights were shining at the windows of all the workshops, and she could see that the gift shop had customers. She had spent her morning addressing Christmas card envelopes for Jessie, almost a hundred of them, and helping Pam Bates to clean silver. Now she was going to the shop to ask if they needed their stock of homemade jams and preserves replenishing.

Alice was serving a customer when she went in, and another girl was checking the shelves. Alice smiled but didn't speak; the other girl turned as she noticed Annabel and beckoned to her.

'Hello,' she said. 'I know what you've come for. We've had a run on the brandy peaches and Cook's special strawberry preserve, but we're all right for everything else.'

'Have you been very busy?'

'Yes, all week,' the girl replied. 'We haven't met before but I think you must be Annabel. I'm Sarah. I usually come in in the mornings three times a week, but Jessie asked me if I could come every day up until Christmas. My sister Jane was here when you came in the other evening. She's having a day off but she told me about you. Are you settling in now?'

'Yes, thank you. It's incredible that I've been here almost a week now. The time has gone so quickly that I hardly know where I am.'

'It does when you're busy, doesn't it?

'I'd better go back and see if Cook has what you need,' Annabel said. 'Some new guests are arriving this afternoon and I've promised to do the flowers for their rooms.'

As she began to walk back the way she had come, Annabel saw a man leave the unit Georgie had told her was a small printing works. He was probably thirtyish, wearing old corduroy slacks and a tweed jacket with patched elbows. He began to walk towards the house, then stopped suddenly and swung round, bumping into her as he did so.

'I'm so sorry,' he apologised instantly. 'My mind was elsewhere I'm afraid.'

'You didn't realise I was so close behind you,' she said, and then wrinkled her brow as she stared at him. 'Haven't we met somewhere recently?'

'I don't think... yes, now I think about it. I have seen you – in Newmarket, wasn't it? I thought you were someone else.'

'Yes, of course,' Annabel said. 'I couldn't recall for a moment. I was waiting for someone and you had a portfolio with you. You'd come about some printing work.'

'Yes, that's right,' he agreed and smiled as the memory slotted into place. 'Your name – let me think, it will come to me.'

'Why should it?' she asked, and smiled. 'I'll forgive you, Mr Keifer – it's Annabel.'

'Tarleton, that's it,' he said and laughed. 'I've had a lot on my mind recently, Miss Tarleton. I don't normally forget pretty girls.'

A faint blush touched her cheeks and she shook her head. 'Please, call me Annabel. Have you come to stay with the family?'

'I'm staying in Torquay at an apartment I rent sometimes,' he replied. 'It's handy for when I work down here and I like to spend some time there in the summer.'

'It must be beautiful then,' Annabel said. 'Jessie took Georgie and I in one day to do a little shopping and I thought how nice it would be when the weather was warm.'

'Yes, this area is rather attractive. I particularly like it here on the estate. We're peaceful at Kendlebury, except for a few weeks in summer when the visitors descend in huge numbers.'

'They seem busy in the shop this week.'

'The people visiting now are local or regulars,' Paul told her. 'In the summer we get hordes of folk, of all types. I sometimes wonder how Jessie can bear to have her precious home and gardens invaded – but I know that's what keeps them going.'

'Yes. I think it is wonderful. I only wish my brother could do something similar at home. Unfortunately, our house is isolated. We're at the edge of the fens, close to a small village, but too far off the beaten track to make a business like this work.'

'The fens can be rather beautiful in their own way,' he said. 'I've printed a series of postcards from photographs I took myself and they sell quite well. People do love to send postcards home – although the humorous ones are often the most popular.'

'Really? I should like to see your photos of the fens,' Annabel responded eagerly. 'Most people don't see the beauty. I think it is an acquired taste. You aren't from the fens, Mr Keifer?'

'If I'm going to call you Annabel you must call me Paul.' His eyes dwelt on her face for a moment and she felt a tremor inside. 'No, I've stayed in the fens a few times but my home was in Newcastle originally. My father went down the mines when he was nine and died at the age of twenty-nine. I vowed then that I would never follow in his footsteps. When I was eight, my mother died of a fever exacerbated by malnutrition and I left the north after they buried her in a pauper's grave.'

'At eight years of age?' Annabel stared at him, fascinated. 'That's terrible. What did you do? I can't imagine what that must have been like. I was thoroughly spoilt at that age – until my father died I suppose.' A shadow hovered as she remembered the devastation she'd felt when he died.

'Look after your mother for me, Belle,' he'd told her when she'd gone up to wish him goodnight as he lay ill in his bed. 'I fear I've failed you all – but it is your mother who will feel it the most...'

'How did you manage alone at that age?'

'Do you really want to know?' Paul asked.

'Yes, I do,' she said. 'I seem to know so little of life. I've learned an awful lot since I came here. Please tell me, Paul. If you don't think it rude of me to ask.'

'I lived rough on the streets of London, stealing food from the barrows in the market until one of the men caught me. He gave me a good hiding, then took me home and fed me. His name was Bob Smith and he put me to work for him on his stall. When I was fifteen I was apprenticed at a printing works and Bob took me to political meetings with him. I was an active member of the labour movement until the war came and I joined up. Afterwards, I couldn't find work and I travelled the country persuading men to join the unions because I believed the working man needed to stand up for himself. I'm still a supporter of the Labour Party but I've given up my political work.'

'What an extraordinary life you've have had,' Annabel said, awed by his story. 'And now you have your own business. You must work very hard.'

'I've been lucky with my friends,' Paul said. 'Jessie asked me to print and distribute some leaflets for her and I took the workshop here on the strength of it, though I wasn't often here myself in the early days. And then someone I knew died and left me his bookshop in London. I'd helped Archie out in the shop for years and looked after him when he was ill; he had no one else and he liked me. I thought he might leave everything to Jessie, because he was fond of her, but he said he wanted me to have it. I sold the property for more than I would ever have dreamed of earning in a lifetime and with that I was able to invest in a larger printing works in Manchester. Fortunately, that is thriving and I've never looked back.'

'How exciting,' Annabel said. 'I do admire you for your enterprise, Paul. If you had stayed in Newcastle you might have been working in the mines.'

'As I saw it, I had no choice.'

'I think it was very brave of you to leave your home.'

'We didn't really have a home after my father died. We were kicked out of our cottage and slept wherever we could find a roof over our heads, in deserted sheds or old warehouses.' He smiled crookedly as she looked horrified. 'I don't know why I told you all that, Annabel. It took me years before I opened up to Jessie.'

They had reached the kitchen door now. His last remark had brought a flush to her cheeks, and she hesitated.

'I'd better get back to work now. It was nice talking to you, Paul.'

'I don't suppose you would like to go somewhere this evening – to a dance or the cinema? *The Jazz Singer* is showing this week, starring Al Jolson.'

Annabel was startled. Her mother would have a fit if she knew that a man of Paul's background had asked her out, and on such slight acquaintance. She ought to say no at once, but somehow she found herself agreeing.

'Could we go to the cinema?' she asked. 'You'll think this very odd, but I've never been. My mother doesn't quite approve.'

'She wouldn't approve of me either, would she?' Paul's eyes narrowed, seeming to darken. 'Perhaps I shouldn't have asked?'

'I'm very glad you did,' Annabel said quickly. 'It doesn't matter what my mother would think, Paul. I'm not going to tell her – and I want to come out with you this evening. If you haven't changed your mind about taking me?'

'I'm years older than you…'

'That hardly matters,' Annabel said and laughed, her eyes sparking with mischief. 'You're not asking me to marry you, only to visit the cinema. Besides,

I've said yes and you wouldn't stand me up – would you?'

'I wouldn't dream of it,' he said and chuckled. I'll call for you at about six. We can have something to eat afterwards, if you like?'

Annabel smiled. She thought she might enjoy that very much. She was feeling reckless, and she liked her new friend. Just for a little while she was going to forget who she was and what was expected of her.

*

The family gathered in the large drawing room for tea four days before Christmas. Carter had brought in a tall pine tree that smelled delicious and was in the process of being decorated with candles, silver tinsel and glass balls.

Catherine was in charge, accepting the various ornaments and putting each one in its allotted place, except for those at the very top, which Jessie did for her, crowning the tree with a pink and spangled fairy doll.

Annabel was conscious of the warmth of feeling between them all. Home for the holidays, Catherine's brothers looked after their elder sister whenever necessary and it was obvious that everyone loved her. She held a special place in all their hearts, and

Annabel knew that Catherine was fortunate to be so loved.

It was very different at Tarleton Towers, where Annabel's mother cast a shadow over the festivities as she did at any other time, her arrangements formal and nowhere near as much fun as here, where everyone joined in.

Sipping tea and nibbling at a dainty cake, Annabel wished she might stay here forever, but the time was slipping by all too quickly, perhaps because she was enjoying every minute of her stay.

She had spent nearly all her free time with Paul. He had taken her to the pictures, to a concert and to dinner and dancing. They had gone for a walk on the front at Torquay on one fine Sunday afternoon, getting to know each other and finding pleasure in each other's company.

Annabel knew she would miss seeing him when she went home. She ought to tell Paul she would be going soon, but she kept putting it off, not wanting to spoil the fun they were having. She would tell him soon though, because she was not sure what would happen when she left Kendlebury.

*

'I thought you might be staying over Christmas,' Paul said as he pulled his car to a halt in the courtyard at the back of the house later that evening. They had been to a dance in Torquay and it was on the return journey that Annabel had told him she was leaving Kendlebury shortly. 'Jessie invited me for Christmas Day. I was hoping we might spend it together.'

'I have to go home,' Annabel said, smothering a sigh. 'We were supposed to go last weekend but we delayed the journey for another few days.'

'You didn't tell me.' Paul frowned, his eyes narrowing as he looked at her face. 'Were you planning to leave without a word?'

Annabel bit her lip. She had been enjoying herself so much these past weeks that she hadn't wanted to think about leaving. She might not have spoken just yet if Paul hadn't mentioned that he had to go up to Manchester on business and would be back at the weekend.

'I didn't want to spoil things,' she admitted. 'I've had such a wonderful time, being here, working with everyone and… going out with you, Paul.'

'Have you?' Paul leaned towards her and she caught her breath as he brushed his lips softly over hers. His eyes held hers, making her pulse race and she trembled as he took her face between his hands, kissing her again, more deeply this time, but still sweetly, tenderly, asking but not demanding. 'I think

I've fallen in love with you, Annabel. I didn't intend that to happen, but it has.'

'Oh, Paul…' Annabel felt the prickle of tears behind her eyes. She stared at him unhappily, lost for an answer. It was all so hopeless, because her mother would never countenance such a match, and Annabel knew it was her duty to marry the kind of man her family would approve of. 'I've had such a lovely time with you and I do like you very much but…'

'You're not in love with me?' He tipped her chin up with one finger so that she was obliged to meet his inquiring look. 'Tell me the truth please, because I'm in danger of getting serious. I'm considering marriage, Annabel.'

What was the truth? Annabel wasn't sure. She'd had fun with Paul and she liked him more than anyone else who had shown an interest in her, but two weeks wasn't long enough to be certain. Especially when it was hopeless anyway.

'I never meant to hurt you,' she faltered. 'I am fond of you, Paul, and if it was possible to go on seeing you…'

'I could come to Cambridgeshire,' he offered. 'I told you I'd visited before. I have friends in Cambridge. We could meet and see how you feel – in a few weeks' time perhaps?'

'Perhaps.' Annabel felt close to weeping. She didn't want to go home to that damp, cheerless house where her mother's silent disapproval seemed to dog her every step. The time she'd spent here had been wonderful. She'd tasted freedom and the thought of going back to a home that now seemed much like a prison appalled her. She wished she could find a new life for herself somewhere, but her family ties were strong and if she quarrelled with her mother it would mean a breach with all of her family. 'It wouldn't be as easy for us to meet at my home, Paul.'

'Because your mother wouldn't approve?'

Suddenly she felt the withdrawal in him, sensed that she had touched a raw nerve.

'Yes.' She blushed, feeling stupid because it mattered. 'Mother expects me to marry money.'

'I'm not a poor man, though I'm not rich either. I've always expected to work for my living; that's why I kept the workshop on here. I like to work with my hands sometimes. In Manchester I'm the boss, but here I'm just another craftsman earning a living.'

'It isn't just the money…' She bit her bottom lip. How could she explain without offending him? 'My mother is a snob, Paul. She wouldn't consider a marriage between us or even friendship. She would be furious if she knew…' her voice tailed off as he moved away from her.

'That you had been out with me at all?' He was angry now, she could feel it, read it in the way he held himself, in his eyes. 'But you knew that from the beginning. What was it for you? Did you find it amusing to stray over the tracks for a while, have a fling with one of the common horde? Isn't that what girls like you call men like me? Are you one of the Flappers, Annabel – the kind of girl who wants to party all the time and is never serious about anything?'

Annabel was hurt that he could suggest such a thing. It was true that there were both men and women in her set who did fit that criteria. The twenties had a frenetic feeling, and she knew some of her friends – Charlie Fortescue for one – felt they had to run to stand still. It was as if they were running from the shadow of the war years, trying to snatch as much pleasure as they could before it was too late, but Annabel had never wanted to be a part of that set. Indeed, she had found the constant round of parties became boring in the end. She wasn't sure what she wanted to do with her life, but it wasn't to go on in the same old way.

'That's not fair, Paul,' she cried, stung by his accusation. 'It wasn't like that. I've loved being with you and I do like you very much, but I'm not sure it's enough. You don't understand what it would mean if – if I let myself love you.'

'I think I have a fair idea. If I didn't at the start then I have now.' His face had gone hard and there was ice crackling in his voice, coldness rather than the hot anger that might have driven him to do something he would regret, his feelings under an iron control. 'So that's it then – it's been nice knowing you and goodbye.'

'Please don't be angry,' Annabel begged. 'I want us to be friends.'

'Friends?' He gave a harsh laugh. 'Why isn't that enough for me?' His hand reached out to touch her cheek. 'I don't think so, Annabel. I was a fool to think you might be for me. I knew you came from a different class, but you seemed so genuine, so real, not like others I've met. I really fell for it – but that's my bad luck. Serves me right for looking above my station, doesn't it? Jessie stepped up out of her class but Harry needs her. Maybe it wouldn't have worked if he hadn't been a semi-invalid. I should've known you were just playing at being a working girl. Run back home, little butterfly. Your wings might fall off if you stay in the real world for too long.'

'You sound so bitter…' Annabel's throat felt tight. 'Don't hate me, Paul. I do care for you and I didn't mean to hurt you. I just didn't think.' The truth was she hadn't wanted to think of the future, only the moment.

'Your kind never does,' he said, a nerve flicking in his throat. 'You care but not enough to take a chance. For what it's worth, I don't hate you, Annabel. I can't be your friend, but I shan't forget you. Goodbye, pretty butterfly. I doubt we shall meet again.'

Annabel hesitated for a moment. A part of her was hurting, the regret already making her wish she could take it all back, take back the bitter words, the hurt she had unthinkingly inflicted. Then, as tears began to trickle down her cheeks, she got out of the car and ran towards the house. As she went in the back door she heard the sound of laughter from the direction of the kitchen. Usually, she would have popped in to say hello, but she didn't feel like talking to anyone at this moment. Avoiding the lights and the sound of laughter, she rushed upstairs to her bedroom, hoping it would be empty, but Georgie was there, sitting on the bed surrounded by bits of tissue and ribbon.

'I was just wrapping the last of my Christmas presents,' Georgie said and then frowned as she saw Annabel's face. 'What's wrong? Have you had a quarrel with Paul?'

'He told me he was in love with me,' Annabel said. 'He was thinking about us getting married one day.'

'Was?' Georgie stared at her and then nodded her understanding. 'He wouldn't be suitable. Your family would never agree.'

'Ben wouldn't care who I married if I was happy. Mother would disown me and she'd forbid me to see

Hetty. I might have been brave enough to accept that if – if I'd been sure. It's too soon, Georgie. I don't know if I care enough. I do like him a lot though.'

'You seemed very taken with him. You've spent all your spare time in the evenings with him, Belle. Everyone thought it might be serious for you two. Alice thinks you're in love with him.'

'Yes, I know I've spent a lot of time with Paul. It wasn't very sensible of me – but I was having fun.'

'I didn't want to say anything because you seemed happy. Perhaps I should?'

Annabel shook her head. 'I was happy. I didn't think about afterwards until Paul said he was in love with me. I had no idea he felt like that about me.'

'You were the only one who didn't guess then.'

'Was it that obvious?' Annabel blushed. 'You must think me an awful fool.'

'Because you were having fun?' Georgie frowned. 'I was pleased for you. What did Paul say when you turned him down?'

'I didn't… in so many words. I told him it would be difficult to meet because of Mother and he got angry. I wasn't very tactful. He surprised me. We've known each other such a short time.'

'Love happens that way,' Georgie said, her cheeks faintly pink. 'You're talking and then it hits you. It isn't your fault if you don't feel that way about Paul, Belle.'

'I think he's the nicest man I know,' Annabel said thoughtfully. 'Nice is such an awful word, so bland – but I really do like him. We got on so well, talked so easily, and enjoyed being together. It was as if we'd been together all our lives. I hated quarrelling with him. It really hurts, Georgie. I'm going to miss him and everyone here. I don't think I've ever been so happy.'

'Are you sure you're not in love with Paul?'

'No, I'm not sure,' Annabel admitted. 'I feel very mixed up about it. There was someone else I rather liked, but then I discovered that he wasn't a bit nice, not really. I'm such a fool. I wish I hadn't let Paul think I cared about what my mother thinks. I don't want to be like her, Georgie. I just feel obliged to do what she wants. Daddy asked me to look after her, and there's Hetty. I can't imagine what her life would be like if I defied my mother and married Paul. I'm not sure I'm brave enough to stand up to her… even if I did love Paul.' She laughed ruefully. 'What a mess! I sound hopeless, don't I?'

'You've been brought up to listen to you mother and she is a determined lady. Be careful, Belle. Don't let her push you into a marriage you hate,' Georgie said. 'It's nearly 1930. Girls don't have to do what their mother tells them these days, Belle. There's a whole new world out there waiting for you – you just have to be brave enough to go looking for it.'

Annabel shook her head because no one, not even Georgie, could understand how she felt. She'd been forced to listen to her mother dictating what her life must be for years and it wasn't easy to throw off the habits of a lifetime. The consequence would be banishment from the family, and that would hurt others besides herself.

'I wish I were more like you, Georgie. I hate hurting Paul.'

'Can't you tell Paul how you really feel? Ask him to give you some time to think.'

'He was hurt and angry. He probably won't want to see me ever again.'

'He'll want to see you. He's in love with you. You may not be sure of your feelings for him, Belle, but he knows what he wants, and that's you.'

'He's leaving early in the morning. I shan't get a chance to talk to him again.'

'Write to him,' Georgie advised. 'Leave a letter for him. When he has got over his disappointment he will realise it was partly his fault that you quarrelled. He spoke too soon. He should have waited, found a way of seeing you again. Paul will know that when he thinks things over. He'll be pleased to get your letter and I'm sure he'll be patient once he understands how things are for you.'

'You're a good friend,' Annabel said and kissed her cheek. 'You've made me feel much better.'

'Jessie is giving us a little party tomorrow evening,' Georgie said. 'We're going to exchange gifts as we shan't be here at Christmas. I bought Catherine a pair of slippers with cats on them. You know how she loves them. I also got some sweets for her. Have you got a present for her? You can give her the sweets if not. We all try to make a bit of a fuss of her at Christmas.'

'Yes, I imagine so. Catherine is a lovely girl, such a sweet nature. I bought a fluffy pink scarf and mittens for her,' Annabel said. 'I got the boys chocolate animals and Jessie a set of pens, because she's always losing hers. Everyone else has a bottle of sherry or chocolates, except you – and I'm not telling you what yours is.'

'I don't want to know until tomorrow,' Georgie said and laughed. 'I almost wish we could stay for Christmas, but my family would be disappointed if I didn't go home. It's always a big thing for us.'

Annabel wished she didn't have to leave all her new friends. Christmas at Tarleton Towers would be formal and dull after the time she'd spent here, but she had to be there, if only for Hetty's sake.

*

'Did you have a wonderful time?' Hetty asked and hugged her sister. 'I missed you. It was awful here without you. Ben wasn't around much. He went to stay with Helen for a week and he's bringing her to the party on Christmas Eve.' She made a wry face, because Ben's fiancée wasn't her favourite person.

'Mother's parties are always so formal,' Annabel said feeling the depression settle over her. She thought of the fun she'd had working at Kendlebury, the way everyone helped each other and joined in, the laughter and friendship she'd found there. 'But I suppose it's a good time to announce their engagement to all our friends.'

'We've been invited to a New Year party at the Munsters' house,' Hetty told her. 'Mother has arranged for Ben to take us. Helen will go with her parents. It's the first time I've been allowed to stay up for a party like that.'

'It's a good thing I bought you a new dress then.'

'Oh, Belle, you didn't!' Hetty cried. 'I was thinking I might borrow the one you wore last year.'

'It's your Christmas present – or one of them. I've got some surprises for you so I don't mind you knowing about the dress.' She pointed to a large cardboard box. 'You can open it now if you like. Try it on and see if it needs any alteration.'

Hetty untied the strings, lifting the lid to look inside. She gave a cry of pleasure as she saw the evening dress. It was fashioned of yellow silk taffeta and had puffed sleeves and a demurely scooped neckline, with a deep frill at the hem, which floated just above her ankles, and was entirely suitable for a young girl's first party.

'It must have cost you all your allowance for the month. You shouldn't have spent so much on me, Belle.'

'Do you like it?'

'Yes, very much. It's lovely – but how could you afford it?'

'Jessie paid us wages. I didn't expect anything but she insisted and I spent the money on Christmas presents for everyone.'

'But you only went to help out with flowers and things.'

'I did a lot more than that, but don't tell Mother,' Annabel said with a smile. 'I waited on tables in the teashop the last few days we were there and I helped to clean the guestrooms, and to polish the silver. Oh, all kinds of things, running errands, writing menus. It was great fun and I enjoyed every minute.'

'Mother would have a fit if she knew.'

'She won't know,' Annabel said. 'It was so different, Hetty. I felt really alive, needed, as if I were doing something worthwhile. I wouldn't mind working there all the time, but they don't always need extra staff. Jessie said I could go back in the summer when they're busy, but I'm not sure whether it will be possible.'

'Mother thinks you will be married by then,' Hetty said. 'Mr Hansen telephoned three times while you were away.'

'Richard Hansen?' Annabel stared at her in surprise. 'You didn't mention it in your letters.'

'I didn't know at first, besides, Mother said she would tell you. She gave him your address but perhaps he didn't want to write. Some people don't like writing letters.'

'No, perhaps he didn't like the idea of writing,' Annabel said. 'I am surprised he rang at all. He didn't say anything about seeing me again – just that he would see me around, you know.'

'Well, you will be seeing him soon,' Hetty assured her. 'I heard Mother telling him that we would be at the Munsters' on New Year's Eve. I think he is staying with them for a couple of days then.'

'Oh…' Annabel was thoughtful. She wasn't sure how she felt about the news that he had telephoned while she was away. She had forgotten him while she was at Kendlebury, forgotten that kiss and the annoyance she'd felt at being left to wait while he bought a horse. Besides, it had happened before she met Paul and that had changed things. Richard seemed unimportant now, because the girl who had rather liked him didn't truly exist anymore. That Annabel had been wild for change, her need for excitement making her reckless. Something had happened at Kendlebury, something that had changed her inside. She felt different now, happier, perhaps because she'd tasted freedom for the first time in her life. 'I didn't expect Richard to ring.'

'Well, he did, three times,' Hetty said and grinned. 'Mrs Bumble took the first two calls. She just told him you weren't in and then Mother answered the third. It was after that that she told me you would probably be married by the summer.'

'Oh no! How could she?' Annabel exclaimed. 'Richard isn't interested in marriage. He told me so at the start. I can't imagine what made Mother think he was serious. I'm not sure he really likes me at all.'

'He must like you,' Hetty said. 'He wouldn't telephone three times if he didn't – would he?'

'No, perhaps not,' Annabel said and wrinkled her nose. 'I thought...'

She didn't finish what she was going to say, because she wasn't sure any more. She hadn't expected Paul to declare his love for her and she still didn't know how she really felt about that, though she had left a letter for him with Jessie. Richard Hansen was exciting to be with at times but he wasn't nice – not the way Paul was, deep down inside. Annabel had believed she wanted the kind of high society life he could give her, money, trips to Paris to buy clothes, skiing holidays and wild parties, but staying with Jessie at Kendlebury, she'd discovered a new way of life and one she rather enjoyed…

Four

Annabel had given Paul her address and telephone number in the letter she left for him. She wasn't sure what she expected him to do, perhaps send a Christmas card or ring her, but he did neither and she was aware of a sense of deep disappointment. Yet she couldn't blame him for ignoring her. She had tried to explain her feelings on paper, though she suspected she hadn't made a very good job of it. Perhaps because she was all muddled up inside. He would probably think she was an idiot and decide that he'd had a lucky escape after all.

Ben came home on Christmas Eve, bringing his fiancée. His presence made the party bearable for Annabel and she did her best to be friendly towards Helen. The girl was her brother's choice and although Annabel was afraid he had made a terrible mistake it wasn't up to her to judge.

'I'm so pleased Ben is going to marry you,' she told Helen and kissed her on the cheek. 'I do hope we shall be friends.'

'I hope we shall,' Helen replied, sounding doubtful. She wrinkled her nose as if she thought Annabel was something the cat had dragged in. 'I wouldn't want things to be awkward between us when we live here.'

'I'm sure they won't be.'

'Well, I dare say you'll marry as soon as you can and then we shan't be forced to live in each other's pockets.'

Annabel gave her a polite smile but made no comment. It was clear that Helen didn't want her husband's twin living near her. The difference in her behaviour towards Lady Tarleton was so marked that it made her feelings all the more obvious. The pair of them got on so well that it seemed they were bosom friends already.

Annabel sometimes wondered why her mother disliked her. It hadn't been the same with her father; he'd always made a fuss of her and she'd been sure of his affection. Her mother seemed to tolerate her at best and at worst to actively dislike her. Now that she was back at home, Lady Tarleton's constant nagging was pressing on Annabel once more and she felt a return of the desperation that had made her feel she would do almost anything to escape her mother's disapproval. At times she was tempted to just leave – to run away – but then she remembered. Hetty would suffer. All privileges would be withdrawn and she would lose her dream of Art College. And there was Ben: he'd made a sacrifice for the sake of the family and a rift between Annabel and her mother could only make life harder for him.

Over the Christmas period Annabel found herself remembering her brief stay at Kendlebury with increasing fondness and regret. She had enjoyed working there and it made her wonder if she could find herself work of a permanent kind. She knew it was unlikely she would find anything as congenial as that she had discovered at Kendlebury, but perhaps she might try working as a receptionist at a small hotel – if she could get her mother's consent.

Annabel thought it would be difficult to persuade her mother to agree and yet Selina might help her. Even Lady Tarleton must see that it would be better for her eldest daughter to do something with her life once it dawned on her that Annabel wasn't going to make the right sort of marriage.

Annabel had been vaguely dissatisfied with her life before she went to Kendlebury, but now she had begun to realise how empty her days were. She took on a little more of the housework, easing the burden for Mrs Bumble and the part time maid, but she was still restless. In the end even her mother noticed.

'What on earth is wrong with you?' she asked irritably when Annabel got up and went to the window for the third time in an hour. They were sitting alone in the drawing room, Hetty having stayed in bed with a cold that day. Ben was spending the evening with his fiancée and they had no guests for dinner themselves. 'Why don't you read your book?'

'I'm not very interested in it, Mother.'

'Then find yourself another or do something useful. Find some needlework, Annabel. If you were more industrious you might be less bored. And sit down! Your restlessness is giving me a headache.'

'I'm sorry. I'll go to my room.'

'And leave me alone? It's only half past eight. You might think of my feelings for once. I really do not know what has come over you. You haven't been the same since you came home from that place.'

'I supposing I'm missing Georgie.'

'For goodness sake! I begin to think she is a bad influence on you.'

Annabel sat down and picked up her book, pretending to read it. She felt as if she could scream and her nerves were on edge as her mother lapsed into silence.

How different it would be at Kendlebury. There she would have friends to talk to – perhaps she might be out with Paul. She had never once felt bored there, she never had time to be. She laid down her book, determined to speak out.

'What is it, Annabel?' Lady Tarleton looked at her in annoyance.

'I was thinking I might look for a job in the New Year, Mother. Helen doesn't want me living here when Ben marries her. I could perhaps find something away from here.'

'Please do not be ridiculous,' her mother snapped. 'I shall be living in the cottage. You will live with me – unless you are married before then.'

'That's hardly likely,' Annabel said. 'I think I might like to work – perhaps in a hotel as a receptionist. A small, respectable establishment with decent guests, of course.'

'I shall not listen to such nonsense. You have no need to work. With a little more effort on your part you could marry. It is merely your stubbornness that has prevented it thus far.'

'Perhaps I would rather work, Mother. I'm not sure I want to marry.'

'You are being deliberately difficult, Annabel. If you cannot be sensible you might as well go to your room. My head is so painful that I shall go up soon myself.'

'Thank you. Goodnight, Mother. I am sorry your head aches.'

Annabel got to her feet and left quickly before her mother could recall her. She popped into see Hetty, who was sitting up reading a book, her cheeks still a little flushed from the cold.

'You must be better by New Year's Eve,' Annabel said. 'You don't want to miss the party.'

'That's why I stayed in bed today. Besides, Mother told me to.' Hetty smiled at her. 'It's nice being told to do something you want to do for a change.'

'Oh, Hetty,' Annabel said. 'I wish I knew what that felt like.'

'Poor Belle,' her sister sympathised. 'Why don't you get married? It would be better than living the way you do – whatever he was like.'

'Yes, perhaps you're right,' Annabel said, but a picture of Paul's face when she'd hurt him came into her mind and the tears were close. 'Sleep tight, love.'

She went into her own room but didn't undress. Instead she paced the floor like a caged tiger, feeling no more at ease than she had down in the drawing room.

It seemed there was no escape for her. Perhaps she ought to have run away with Paul when he'd told her he was in love with her. She had hesitated and thrown her chance away. Now she was so miserable that she didn't know what to do with herself. Sometimes she felt that if she didn't escape from this house, she would go mad! At least she had the party on New Year's Eve to look forward to…

*

Annabel picked up her third glass of champagne of the evening and sipped it. Her mother was busy gossiping with her friends; Hetty was talking to one of the young girls she knew, leaving Annabel to amuse herself. So far she hadn't seen anyone she felt remotely interested in spending time with and she was beginning to wish she'd claimed to feel unwell and cried off. It was all so dull and she couldn't help contrasting it with the fun she'd had that last evening at Kendlebury.

'Hello,' a voice said in her ear, almost making her spill her champagne. She glanced at Richard Hansen, unsure of how she felt at finding him suddenly so close. He was as handsome as ever, but now she looked at him with new eyes there was something about him that made her uneasy. 'I'm late but I was determined to come because Lady Tarleton told me you would be here.'

'I thought you were staying here?'

'I am, tonight and for a couple of days more.'

'My sister told me you telephoned while I was away.'

'Why didn't you tell me you were going away?'

She gazed up at him, wondering what had changed. Was it Richard or had she changed? His eyes were very dark that evening, almost black and intense. His hair was slicked back with oil so that it looked darker than she remembered. There was no denying that he was very attractive and her heart missed a beat; he still attracted her even though he also scared her.

'You didn't say you might telephone.'

'I wasn't sure I would. I fully intended to forget you, Annabel.'

'Why didn't you?' She tipped her head to one side, challenging him with her eyes, her mood becoming more reckless. What did it matter if he thought she was flirting with him? What did anything matter? Her life couldn't be any worse than it already was!

'Because it was harder than I imagined. You are very beautiful, Belle.'

'You must meet any amount of pretty girls.' She pouted at him, deliberately provocative.

'I said beautiful.' Richard stroked a finger down her bare arm, making her tingle with anticipation. 'I think you're one of, if not the, most beautiful girl I've ever met. You're special, Annabel. You get under a man's skin and disturb his dreams...'

Annabel giggled. She'd been drinking all evening, feeling lonely and miserable, wishing that she could be transported to another world, another life, and now the best looking man in the room was telling her she haunted his dreams. It was heady stuff for a girl who had lived quietly at home for most of her life.

'I'll bet you say that to all the girls…' she said and looked up at him. What she saw there was raw hunger and it sent a sudden shock of desire and need through her, because she thought it meant love. 'Richard… you shouldn't tease. I might take you seriously…' She arched her brows at him and he made a little growling sound and took hold of her arm.

'You're playing with fire…' he warned her and she felt the heat spread through her as she saw the raging blaze in his eyes.

Annabel finished her drink and took another one. She was already slightly inebriated but somehow she didn't care. Her depression had given way to something else. She was being swept along by the irresistible tide that was Richard and felt unable to stop herself falling under his power.

'Shall we find somewhere we can be alone?'

'Why not?' She gulped the rest of her drink in one go, attempting to snatch another as they passed a butler circulating with his tray. Richard jerked her away, guiding her firmly past him and out of the crowded reception room into the hall. 'I wanted another drink,' she said, a trifle petulantly.

'I think you've already had enough.'

'That's none of your business,' Annabel muttered, annoyed now. She was sick of being told what she may or may not do. 'I'm not a child. I can have as many drinks as I like.'

'I would rather you didn't,' Richard said, 'because I want to make love to you and I want you to be sober enough to understand that you belong to me and that I've no intention of letting anyone else have you…'

Annabel opened her mouth to protest but the next moment she discovered she was being dragged into a small dark room used to store things. Even as she tried to protest, Richard thrust her against the wall and started to kiss her. She pushed at his shoulders but his mouth was warm and demanding and she felt a surge of excitement deep down inside her. This kiss demanded so much – her response, her body, even her soul. He was taking her over, robbing her of the will to resist or even to think properly. Somewhere in the back of her mind, alarm bells were ringing, but she was lost in a fog of alcohol, need, loneliness and longing for love. She took Richard's words to mean that he loved her with a deep passion and her damaged heart responded to his demands. Paul had loved her…

Oh Paul… Paul… I need you…

In her befuddled state, she thought of the moment when Paul kissed her in the car and emotion swamped her, making her body cry out with loneliness. Without thinking about what she was doing, she put her arms up around Richard's neck, her fingers exploring the soft skin there as she melted into him, her body pliant and yielding as she responded to his kiss. Her head was spinning, the champagne robbing her of her natural caution, and she moaned as his hands roamed over her body, pressing her hips hard against him so that she became aware of his burning heat through her thin gown.

'This is why I couldn't forget you,' he muttered thickly against her throat. 'I've been on fire for you since that kiss. I want you, Belle. I want you more than I've ever wanted a woman in my life.'

The warning bells were clamouring in her head but she ignored them. Paul was here with her. He'd come back to claim her and to tell her he loved her and wanted her. Part of her knew that it was Richard who was making love to her and yet her responses were for Paul. At that moment all she could think of was the desire coursing through her body. The Annabel that whimpered and arched against him, aware of his arousal and responding to it, was somehow different, a woman on fire with physical need, the girl she had been lost somewhere along the way.

'My little love,' he murmured. 'You're hot for me, aren't you? I knew you would be like this. You pretend to be so cool and reserved, but under the ice there's fire.'

Annabel could feel the fire burning her up. She couldn't seem to think of anything but the man holding her, of him kissing her, stroking her where it felt good, arousing her needs, needs she hadn't known she had until this moment. He pushed down the neckline of her gown so that he could suck at her breasts, licking the nipples with his tongue, the slight rasp setting more ripples of need coursing through her. She was so hot! Burning up! Then he was inching up the skirt of her gown. She was vaguely aware that this was wrong, that she ought not to let him do this, but somehow she couldn't find the strength to stop him… didn't want him to stop. She'd missed him so much since she left Kendlebury and now he was here, holding her close.

'Paul…' she whispered hoarsely, not realising she'd spoken, as she felt his hand part her legs, and then he was lifting her, thrusting at her with something hard and warm. 'Oh yes…' She gave a cry as he suddenly thrust into her but he covered her mouth with his own, cutting off the scream of pain. Annabel realised too late what she was allowing to happen, and that it was Richard not Paul who was forcing himself inside her, the pain of his entry shocking her out of the stupor she had fallen into, terrifying her. What was she doing! This was the forbidden thing she had been warned of so many times. She pushed against his shoulders as he thrust into her against the wall, silencing her belated protests with a ruthless arrogance that shocked her to the core.

'Please...' she whispered as she felt the deep shudder go through him. 'Please don't...'

But it was too late and she felt the hopelessness wash over her as she understood what had happened, her mind clear now, facing the truth of what her foolish behaviour had brought her to.

'You were a virgin,' he said in an emotionless tone that made her want to die. As if he cared! 'I wasn't sure. Never mind, Belle. They say it only hurts once. You'll have more fun next time. We'll go somewhere more comfortable and I'll make it nice for you, I promise.'

His words made her head come up. She thrust him away from her angrily, pulling her dress straight as a shudder of disgust went through her. Love didn't take so ruthlessly. What a fool she'd been to mistake desire and selfishness for love. Richard might desire her, but he didn't love her. Her head had cleared quite suddenly of the alcohol induced fog and she realised just what a stupid fool she'd been. In her head two men had become one and her unconscious longing for Paul had made her vulnerable to Richard's assault on her senses.

'There isn't going to be a next time. Not with you.'

'Oh, come off it,' Richard drawled, reaching into his jacket to find his cigarette case. 'You'll be accusing me of rape soon. You were ready for it, Belle. Don't pretend otherwise. You wanted it as much as I did.'

Annabel felt a rush of revulsion and anger, as much for her own foolish behaviour as his ruthless seduction of her. 'I hate you. You're a ruthless devil. I must have been mad to let you bring me here.'

'You were panting for it. Now you're frightened.' He lit his cigarette, his eyes moving over her mockingly. 'Don't worry. If anything goes wrong I'll marry you. In fact I rather think I might like to marry you anyway. I've been told I need a wife to make me respectable if I want to stand as a Member of Parliament. You would suit me better than most. So don't turn on that outraged look. You told me you wanted a rich husband, now you've found one. Your mother will be delighted.'

'My mother doesn't know what you've just done.'

'Shall we tell her?'

Annabel struck out at him, but he caught her wrist, his fingers cutting into the flesh, twisting, hurting her deliberately. She saw the gleam in his eyes and knew he was enjoying this, loving the power he had over her, his ability to torment her.

'You wouldn't dare tell her. Not even you could hope to get away with rape – not if you want to be admitted to decent society. And you do, don't you, Richard? Why are you thinking of getting married? What have you done that might compromise you?'

'Don't be a fool, Belle. Push me too far and you'll regret it. As for Lady Tarleton – she would forgive me anything as long as I marry you. Your delightful mother worships money, Belle: money and breeding. I have enough of one to make up for a slight lack of the other. She told me you were a rebel and needed a firm hand. She would applaud me for teaching you who the master is.'

'I don't believe you!'

'It's quite true. She told me that she wanted you married by the summer, that she knew you'd turned down several offers from suitable men. She hinted that if I wanted you I should seduce you – providing I wanted to marry you.'

'You liar!'

'Ask her then? Tell her I've had you this evening and proposed. See what reaction you get.'

'I would rather die than marry you.' Annabel felt stone cold sober now and her pride reasserted itself. She looked at him with disdain.

'That's not the impression I received just now. You loved it until you got scared.' He reached out, cupping the back of her neck, forcing her towards him. 'I want you, Belle, and I always get what I want. Don't you know that by now? Besides, you've ruined your chance of marriage to anyone else, haven't you?'

Unfortunately, he was right. The truth of it stuck like a thorn in her flesh, making her smart with self-disgust. How could she have let herself be carried away like that? Yes, she'd had too much champagne, but even so... in her subconscious mind she'd allowed herself to think it was Paul and that's why she'd let herself respond to his kiss. Only when it was too late had she realised what she was doing.

'You really are a devil. I don't want you. I won't marry you.' She was suddenly revolted by what she had done, hating herself. How could she have let it happen? She didn't even like him.

'Oh, I think you will,' he said, a smile of satisfaction playing over his mouth. 'Your mother will see to that. What do you think would happen if this got out, my love?'

'Don't call me that! You don't know how to love.'

'No, perhaps I don't,' he agreed. 'But it suits me to marry you and that's what I'm going to do – whether you like it or not.'

'You can't mean that. You can't force me to marry you.'

'Do I really need to force you?' His brows rose. 'What else can you do with your life? Marriage to someone like me is all you're fit for. I shan't ask much of you, except more of what happened this evening and a pleasant manner when you entertain my guests. You'll have a decent house, clothes, and money to spend. You would like that, wouldn't you? Don't tell me you're happy with your life the way it is. I won't believe you. Imagine what your dear Mama would say if I told her that I'd had you and then you refused to marry me... and she might not be the only one I tell what a little wanton you are...'

Annabel stared at him dully. Her life was in ruins. She had tossed it away in a reckless moment and now she hated herself for what she had done. Her mother would never give her a moment's peace. She would never be allowed to forget the disgrace she'd brought on herself or the family. In fact, she would either have to take her own life to escape the shame or run away and hide herself from the world.

At this moment all she wanted to do was to get as far away as she could from Richard Hansen. She hated him for mocking her and wanted to wipe the smile from his face, but he had the upper hand and he was a ruthless devil who would not let go when he wanted something. If she defied him he would tell her mother what had happened; he would drop hints to other men so that her reputation would be gone – but he would twist it and make it seem as if she'd been the one who had instigated the whole thing – and Lady Tarleton would believe him, because she wanted to. She would scold Annabel night and day, making her life unbearable.

And there was always the chance that she might already be carrying Richard's child. If that happened she would be ruined – and Hetty with her, for a sister's reputation could damage her sibling without intention. It was the way of her world; the way things were whether she liked it or hated it. Yet rebellion still flared in her heart.

If only she could walk away, go somewhere she was liked and needed and could be free, but the ties of family and duty held her fast.

If Annabel ran away now Richard would lose nothing but she had already lost everything. She tried to think calmly, but she was angry and mixed up. What could she do now? Paul was lost to her now and the happiness she'd briefly glimpsed must be forgotten. Richard had put his brand on her and for a girl of her upbringing and background there was nothing she could do but accept his offer of marriage. His money would at least buy her freedom from her mother's nagging; it would give her a chance to get away and she would no longer be a burden on her brother. She could buy things for Hetty, and make sure that she wasn't made to suffer the way Annabel had been by their mother.

She really had no choice but to marry him and take what little she could from the marriage.

Her head went up as she knew what she was going to do. She would take all that he was offering, because it was the only thing she could do… and perhaps one day she would find a way to pay him back for what he'd done to her!

*

'Are you happy?' Hetty asked. She looked at Annabel in her expensive ivory silk wedding dress. It floated just above her ankles with a scalloped lace edge, which was matched by the same lace on the dropped waist, and the dress had a squared neckline heavily encrusted with diamante and pearls. Her head-dress was a shoulder length veil attached to a diamond and pearl tiara, one of the many gifts Richard had presented to his beautiful fiancée. 'I mean – do you love him?'

'I'm not sure I know what love is,' Annabel said, hating it that she was lying to her sister but not wanting her to guess the truth. 'Richard is very attractive. He is also rich and generous – and Mother is deliriously happy.'

'You're not marrying him just to get away from her, are you? I know I said you should, Belle, but I didn't really mean it. I thought you might have Tom. I know he cares for you. He would have been kind.'

'Tom didn't ask me,' Annabel reminded her with a smile. 'Don't worry, dearest. My marriage has nothing to do with anything you said. Richard decided he wanted a wife and he has a lot to offer so I accepted.'

She hadn't told anyone about the methods Richard had used to persuade her. Her memory was a little hazy about the events leading up to that moment, though she remembered the feeling of panic that had spread over her too late, and the anger when the mist cleared. Sometimes she thought she must have been mad to give into Richard's bullying, but she had and he hadn't given her a chance to change her mind. Before she knew what was happening their engagement was being announced and the gleam in her mother's eyes told her there was no going back.

The wedding had been arranged with indecent haste. It was now only the second week in February and she was about to become Mrs Richard Hansen. Her mother had taken complete charge, becoming suddenly full of energy as she carried Annabel off to London in triumph to buy clothes and be fitted for her wedding dress at an exclusive establishment. Annabel had allowed herself to be taken over, drifting through the preparations in a haze of disbelief. This wasn't really happening to her; she would wake up and discover it was all a bad dream.

She couldn't really be marrying a man she didn't even like very much – but she was trapped and felt as if there was no way out that would not hurt others.

Of Richard she had seen very little, though gifts, letters and flowers arrived daily. He had a lot of work to get through so that he could take time off for their honeymoon in Paris.

'We can buy you some decent clothes then,' he'd told her on one of his flying visits. 'Once we're married you can dump the stuff your mother chose. I don't want my wife to look like a country frump.'

'Thank you very much,' Annabel replied. 'I'm glad to know what you think of my taste.'

'You've been the dutiful daughter too long. When you're my wife you'll have to start to think for yourself.'

Her brows rose. 'I imagined you would take over the role. You seem to think you have the right to dictate to me as you please.'

'Don't be so damned stupid! And don't act the martyr with me, Belle. You're getting plenty out of the arrangement. 'I've told you what I want from you, the rest is up to you. I'm too busy to run your life, even if I wanted to – which I don't.'

What did he really want? Annabel asked herself the question a hundred times. What had made him suddenly decide he needed a wife? Was it that he thought she was a pretty doll who would do as she was told? She was under no illusions about Richard. He wasn't in love with her. He desired her when he was in the mood but Annabel sensed that she meant very little to him. She'd just happened to be around when it suited him to get married.

Well, it was her own fault for being careless. She'd thrown away her chance of real happiness and the resulting regret had led her into her reckless behaviour. She was trapped and there was no getting out of it. Besides, all her life she'd been told she must do her duty to her mother and her family, and her mother's smile told her that she believed that was exactly what Annabel was doing.

'Let's go, Hetty,' she said and picked up her bouquet. 'We don't want them thinking the bride has cold feet.' She looked at her sister, who was wearing a dress of pale green in a style that was fashionable with a dropped waist and a hemline halfway up her calf. 'You look lovely, Hetty – and I do love you, dearest.'

'Oh Belle, I love you, and I'll miss you,' Hetty said and gave her hug.

Annabel went through the ceremony feeling as if she were in a kind of stupor. It was if it was all happening to someone else, but then she wasn't Annabel any more. She was Richard's fiancée, one of his possessions, bought and paid for like his car or a horse. Except that the horse was probably more important to him than she was, she thought, and smiled to herself.

'That's better,' Richard said to her as they were driven to the reception at an expensive hotel. 'You looked as if you were on your way to the stake all through the ceremony. Do you want everyone to think it was a forced marriage?'

'They think that already,' she replied and laughed, coming out of the daze. The ceremony was over. They were married and she might as well make the most of it. 'It was terribly rushed, wasn't it? Everyone will be counting the months, but they will be wasting their time.'

'So you're not pregnant.' He looked thoughtful. 'I wasn't sure. You didn't say.'

'Are you disappointed?'

'There's plenty of time. I want to enjoy my beautiful wife as she is for a while.'

The gleam in his eyes sent a shiver down her spine. Richard clearly intended to get full value from their bargain. Not that she would find it so difficult to do what he wanted. She hated him but the excitement was still there when he touched her. She knew that her body would accept him even as her mind denied him. He had a kind of destructive charm that drew her even as she denied it. Men liked Richard were dangerous. Someone had warned her but she'd ignored it, caught by the honey of his smile.

'You do know I don't love you, Richard?'

'Hate was the word you used,' he reminded her with a cruel smile that made her feel cold all over. 'I find that arouses me, Belle. Most women fall over themselves to crawl into my bed. It will be interesting to see how long you hold out before you beg me to love you.'

'I shall never do that!'

'That's just as well, because you would be wasting your time.'

Annabel refused to rise to his goading. She smiled coolly, knowing he would prefer her to be angry. He actually liked it when she tried to hit him, and she had learned not to try. But whatever he said he couldn't hurt her. She had learned to ignore the spiteful taunts of her mother and she could learn to ignore Richard. At least, most of the time she could ignore him.

'I know exactly what to expect, Richard. Please believe me when I say there are no surprises where you are concerned.'

'Don't be too sure, Belle. You don't know me yet.'

Something about him then sent an icy shiver down her spine. She didn't know him but she would learn very soon. The fear gnawed at her stomach and she suddenly realised that she had made a terrible mistake. She had a feeling that anything would have been better than marriage to Richard.

*

'Oh, I almost forgot,' Jessie said and looked up from the artwork spread out on the table in front of her. 'Annabel left a letter for you. 'It's in my desk. When you didn't come for Christmas I forgot about it.'

'Things didn't work out as I'd planned,' Paul said, taking the letter and slipping it into his jacket pocket. 'We had several large orders come in all at once and I had to stay up there for a few days, then I popped over to France. As I explained when I rang, it was important. This could take me from being a small concern to a much larger one.'

'Yes, I know it is important to you.' She gave him an amused smile. 'I'm sorry, Paul, but when I think of what you were doing when we first met it doesn't seem possible that you've turned into a high-powered business man.'

Paul laughed ruefully. 'I was young and full of ideals then, Jessie. I suppose it sounds as if I've sold out to the enemy but I do try to keep my feet on the ground and to treat my workers as human beings. I've had a wonderful example to follow from you and Harry.'

'Well, we're different from most,' Jessie said, 'and it hasn't been easy to keep the furniture business going. Sometimes we've plenty of orders and sometimes we have to cut back, but Harry won't lay men off. We manage somehow.'

Paul nodded, his expression thoughtful. The first flush of euphoria after the war years had died away and after the disastrous crash on Wall Street, he was pretty sure that a slump was coming, which was why he'd chased the orders that came his way rather than take up the invitation to stay with his friends over Christmas. Lean times were ahead and he needed to build up a little fat to see him through.

'You always manage very well. I admire you, Jessie. It hasn't been easy for you these past years, has it?'

'Is life ever easy?' she said lightly. 'I'm happy. Harry keeps going somehow and the children are doing well. I count my blessings, Paul.'

'Yes, I know. Well, I must love you and leave you. I've a dinner engagement this evening.'

'Before you go, Paul, there's something I feel I ought to tell you.' She hesitated to speak, not wanting to hurt him unnecessarily and not sure what her news would mean to him.

'Is it about Annabel?'

'Yes.' She saw the tiny nerve flicking in his throat. 'Did you see it in The Times?'

'I saw the announcement of her engagement and forthcoming wedding.'

'We none of us knew it was going to happen. Georgie doesn't like him. She says he isn't a nice person.'

'It explains a good many things,' Paul said. 'Don't worry, Jessie. I shan't do anything foolish. Annabel made her feelings clear before Christmas. I knew there was no chance of developing our… friendship.'

'She didn't tell you she was practically engaged?'

'Perhaps it is in her letter.' Paul offered a twisted smile and then changed the subject. 'So you approve of what I've suggested for you this season? I'll set the work in hand, shall I?'

'Yes, please. Are you going to stay down here for a while?'

'No. I've been offered some work for an American company. It's a film studio actually. I'm leaving for the States in a couple of days. I may be away for some months.'

'Oh, Paul, how exciting,' Jessie said. 'I had no idea you were becoming so famous.'

'Apparently the studio saw some posters I did for a theatrical company here and want to talk. It may come to nothing.'

'I'm sure they will love your ideas.'

'Well, if they do it's all due to you, Jessie. You started me in the right direction. I would still have been printing penny leaflets if you hadn't told me I owed you a favour.'

'I don't believe that but if I helped I'm glad.' She smiled at him. 'And I wish you lots of luck over there. You won't decide to stay for good, will you?'

'No, not forever, but perhaps for a while.'

Until he got over the sense of loss and regret knowing Annabel had given him, Paul thought as he took his leave of Jessie. Work was the only remedy he knew for an aching heart. He read Annabel's letter in the car, smiling at first and then frowning over the muddled plea for understanding. If he hadn't known she was already married he might have been encouraged by her words. A little spiral of pain set up inside him. She had a special way of smiling, hesitant, uncertain, almost begging for reassurance and then, when it was given, the sun burst through. And like a fool he'd fallen for it, believed she was as innocent and genuine as she was lovely. All the time she must have known she was going to marry Richard Hansen.

How could she? Paul's stomach churned with disgust. He knew Hansen only slightly but the whispers he'd heard concerning the man were enough to make Paul despise him. He pitied any woman fool enough to marry someone like that and wished it hadn't been Annabel. The thought of her with Hansen made him want to vomit and he felt the grinding anger gnawing at his guts. But she'd made her choice, had probably been laughing inside while she was going out with Paul, thinking it amusing when he'd made his clumsy bid for her affections.

Regret became a bitter taste in his mouth and he ripped the letter in two, starting the car as he fought the emotions inside him. She wasn't worth thinking about, but he didn't hate her. He hoped she wouldn't regret her marriage but he was very much afraid that she would. It was bound to be a shock to a girl like Annabel when she realised just what kind of a man she'd married – and where a lot of his money came from.

*

Annabel stared at herself in the mirror. Whatever she did the bruise on her cheek was going to show. Powder wouldn't cover it so she would just have to brazen it out and tell everyone it had been an accident. In a way it was, of course. Richard hadn't meant to hit her that hard. He'd inflicted several bruises in the two weeks of their honeymoon, but they were usually where they didn't show. This time she'd made him so angry that he'd struck out thoughtlessly in retaliation, and it was all because she'd accidentally damaged a bronze and ivory figurine of a dancing girl. It was an expensive piece, beautifully crafted by one of the top artists of the Art Nouveau period, but surely a small thing to lose your temper over? Richard had been furious and she'd realised that the expensive pieces of art he collected were more important to him than his wife.

'It's going to show. Whatever I do it will show.'

'I'm sorry,' Richard said as she turned to him, her head lifted proudly, a challenge in her eyes. 'I didn't mean to do that. It won't happen again, Belle.'

'You were angry.' She shrugged her shoulders, her face registering the cool, superior look that she knew had begun to irritate him beyond the point of restraint. 'But it's going to be noticeable this evening. Perhaps it would be better if I didn't join your guests?'

'Can't you cover it?' he asked, looking slightly ashamed. She was undoubtedly a lady, refined, good mannered – everything he knew he was not despite his Oxford education. On the surface he could pass for a gentleman but underneath he was pure primitive, selfish, greedy and coarse. 'Oh damn it! Just tell them you walked into a wardrobe door. It was an accident.'

'Yes, with pleasure, if that is your wish, Richard. Are there any more lies you would like me to tell for you while I'm about it?'

How could she manage to insult him while appearing to be submissive? It was her damned breeding, and it caused him to feel pinpricks of inferiority. He flashed a look of rage at her but kept his hands balled at his sides. One bruise was enough. It was important that Annabel attended the dinner they had been invited to that evening or he would have left her behind in the apartment. They had been back from France for two days and he was going to need his wife at his side in the next few weeks.

His marriage had been necessary after that incident just before Christmas. The girl had been a cheap whore, damn it, but he hadn't meant to kill her. He'd beaten whores senseless before but none of them had died and money or threats had bought their silence. Maurice had arranged for the body to be disposed of in the river, just another one of London's unsolved crimes, to be filed, put away on dusty shelves and forgotten, but he'd laid down an ultimatum for Richard and you didn't take Maurice's threats lightly.

'Get a wife and make yourself look respectable, Richard,' he'd told him after he'd taken care of things. 'A decent girl with background and style. If word gets out about this we're finished. I can't afford to let you carry on this way. We agreed you would stand as an MP, use your influence to help us open more clubs. No one knows you're a partner in the gambling clubs I front, but if you let me down I can ruin you. If it came out that you like to beat up whores and that one of them died…' He'd left the sentence unfinished but the threat was implicit.

'It was the silly bitch's fault,' Richard muttered sullenly. 'She defied me – took the money and then refused to do what I wanted. She got what she deserved.'

'I don't care what you do with your women, Richard, but when it causes trouble for me that's it. I shan't warn you twice.'

Richard knew he wouldn't be threatened again. Another slip and he would be joining that stupid whore in the river. He was sorry that he'd been too violent with Janie. She'd been compliant and easy to control until he'd pushed her too far. The trouble was he had developed a temper of late. Most of the time he could control it but sometimes he just went wild. He was going to have to be more careful with Annabel. He couldn't afford for the bruises to show and he didn't want her to walk out on him.

'I'll buy you something,' he offered as Annabel turned away from him. He went over to her, kissing the back of her neck as she looked at herself in the mirror again. 'Just don't let anyone guess I did that.'

'All right,' she said, meeting his eyes in the mirror. 'I'll lie for you and I'll be the perfect wife. I'll say it was my fault and let them all think you are an adoring husband – but I want something in return.'

'Anything. This is important to me, Belle.'

'Separate rooms,' she said and her face had gone hard, her eyes like chips of ice. 'I'm not refusing the use of my body to you, Richard, but it will be when I say, not when you decide you're in the mood. I want a key so that I can lock you out if I don't feel like company.'

Richard swore but looking at her he knew there was no way he could do anything but agree. Annabel wasn't the impressionable fool he had seduced or the sweet innocent he'd kissed in the garden. Something had happened to her – she'd grown up very quickly.

'You're reneging on your bargain, Belle. I don't like that.'

She touched the bruise on her cheek. 'I didn't agree to be used as your punch bag, Richard, and I have no intention of carrying on this way. If you refuse my request or threaten violence to make me change my mind I shall walk out on you – and you wouldn't like that, would you? It wouldn't fit in with your plans. You married me to give you some credibility with your political friends. I don't know what you've done, but there's a nasty little secret hiding somewhere and I'm the smoke screen to deflect suspicion, aren't I?'

'Walk out on me and I might do something you would find very disturbing, my pretty little wife, but for the moment I'll play it your way. To tell the truth you're not much fun in bed anyway. But remember that I bought and paid for you, Belle. When I want you no damned lock is going to keep me out.' He glared at her. 'Get dressed! I don't want to be late.'

Annabel remained absolutely still until the door had closed behind him, then she crossed her arms over herself, trying to control the shudders coursing through her. He was cruel, evil! Someone had told her that but she hadn't listened. What a fool she had been, imagining that she could keep him at a distance simply by being cold towards him. Any excitement his touch had aroused in her had vanished during their honeymoon. The very thought of him kissing her now brought a surge of revulsion. God, how she hated him!

She had been so innocent, just a child before her marriage. She hadn't known what kind of a man Richard was, hadn't dreamt men like him existed, hadn't even imagined some of the things he did to her when he forced her to submit to him. If she had thought he would let her go she would have left him within days of their wedding, but she knew he would follow and fetch her back. She couldn't go home. Her mother would simply tell Richard to come and fetch her; she wouldn't have any comfort or sympathy for her daughter.

She could go to Ben, of course; he would sympathise but he wasn't in a position to help her. Sometimes, after Richard had finished humiliating her, hurting her, she wanted to die, but there was another part of her that refused to give in. Why should she take her own life and leave Richard free to torment some other woman? Besides, he owed her something for what he'd done to her. He'd ruined her life. She'd been foolish and inexperienced and a little drunk, but Richard had known exactly what he was doing. For some reason he needed a wife with the right background.

She knew he had political ambitions but she suspected there was more to it. Richard was hiding something. If it was something shameful, something that threatened him, she might find a way of turning the tables, making him pay for his treatment of her.

Annabel finished applying her face powder. The bruise still showed but it didn't look as bad now. If she laughed when anyone noticed and passed it off as her fault there was a good chance she might get away with it.

She fastened the pearls Richard had given her as a wedding gift around her neck. Her dress for the evening was ankle length, cut with the flair that only the French knew how to do, fitting her slender body like a second skin. The deep blue of the soft material suited her and she had brushed her hair forward so that it fell across her face. Despite the bruise she looked attractive, and she knew Richard would be pleased with her efforts.

This evening was important to him. He hadn't told her why, but she had a feeling she was going to find out very soon.

*

'It's a pleasure to meet you, Annabel. I was delighted when Richard told me he was to be married. He's a very lucky man to have found such a beautiful bride.'

'Oh no,' Annabel replied, a faint blush in her cheeks as she met the warm approval in the man's eyes. 'I am sure the benefits are mutual. Richard has been more than generous. I dare say most people would think I was the lucky one.'

'Not only beautiful, a gracious lady,' Maurice Green said and smiled at her. Then his eyes narrowed slightly as they noticed the dark mark on her cheek, which had just begun to take on a purplish tinge. 'Did you have an accident to your face?'

'Does it look awful?' Annabel asked, giving him an innocent look, her eyes wide. 'It was so foolish of me. I was laughing, turning round to look at Richard and I bumped into the wardrobe door. Richard made such a fuss. He wanted to have the doctor but I begged him not to. It was just a silly accident.' It was strange how easily the lies came, tripping off her tongue so naturally that she was almost convinced herself.

'It's only natural that a loving husband would worry,' Richard said. 'I told Belle to stay in bed this evening but she insisted on coming.'

'Of course I did,' she said, giving him a glance that appeared to be affectionate. Years of avoiding arguments with her mother had taught her to be an actress, Annabel thought with wry satisfaction. 'I wanted to meet Richard's friends.'

'We've known each other for a while,' Maurice replied. His lowered his gaze, his sandy lashes hiding the suspicion in his greenish brown eyes. 'You must bring your friends to lunch at my restaurant, Annabel. There will be no charge for you.'

'And we want to see more of you,' Laura Bristow gushed. 'John and I are very anxious that we should all be friends. If your clever husband is elected to stand as a Conservative we shall need you to help organise the campaign. I am on several committees that you might care to join, Annabel. I enjoy my charity work. We do a lot for the poor of London's East End, besides sending aid to overseas countries, and we have a lot of fundraising events. We're having a Flag Day next week actually. You might like to help with that; shake your collection tin at people and smile, and we'll collect pounds more. If they resist, pin the flag to their lapel – that's what I do and it shames them into donating. These things are expected of politicians' wives, my dear.'

'Yes, certainly. I hadn't thought about it, but if I could be of some help I would rather like to do something useful.'

'Be careful,' Laura's husband warned and patted Annabel's arm with his podgy hand. He was wearing a gold ring with a huge diamond on his right hand and when he smiled there was a flash of gold teeth. His suit was obviously expensive, but he still managed to look a little crumpled compared with Richard's sartorial elegance. 'My wife will monopolise your time if you let her.'

'Richard is busy,' Annabel said. 'He won't mind what I do during the day.'

She liked the friendly couple. They seemed pleasant, genuine people, more open and honest than Richard's other friend. Something in Maurice Green's manner made her think he was a man to be wary of, a man with secrets, though he was polite to a fault and seemed to approve of her. She decided to reserve judgement for the moment, but she had the oddest feeling that Richard was a little afraid of him.

That was ridiculous! Why should Richard be afraid of the man he claimed was his friend? It was extremely unlikely and the reason for his unease was probably due to a fear that Annabel would let the truth slip about her bruise and embarrass him in front of these people. And yet as the evening progressed and she began to laugh naturally, enjoying herself, Richard's tension seemed only to deepen.

The Bristows were heavily involved with politics. They had proposed Richard as a candidate for a vacant seat in the coming by-election and it was obvious what his relationship was with them, but Maurice Green was another matter.

Several times she noticed Maurice staring at Richard and after the meal was over, they went off together to have a smoke in the room provided, leaving the other three to take coffee in the lounge.

'It was quite a surprise when Richard announced he was getting married,' Laura Bristow said. 'But exactly what he needed to give him the right appeal to the electorate. The right kind of wife is so important, my dear.'

Annabel smiled inwardly. 'Am I the right kind of wife? I'm afraid I've never taken much interest in politics.'

'That's the last thing you need to do,' Laura said and laughed. 'We don't want you standing yourself, Annabel. Your role is to support Richard, offer tea and sympathy to his constituents when you are at a function, and get yourself seen at various charity events.'

'Do you think Richard will be elected?'

'Oh, I think so,' Laura said. 'Especially now he has you. There are always rumours about a single man, my dear, but marriage to a decent girl will help to quash anything like that.'

'I see,' Annabel said and smiled. Suddenly, the mystery was as clear as crystal: Richard had married her because he needed respectability. 'Then you think I really can be of help to my husband in his career?'

'You have already,' she replied. 'I can't wait to introduce you to all my friends. You will help with the Flag Day, won't you?'

'Yes,' Annabel said. 'I should be delighted. I have written to ask my younger sister to come and stay. I am sure she would like to help when she is with me.'

'By all means bring her. We can do with as many willing helpers as we can get. There is so much poverty in the world, Annabel. I started all this for my husband's sake when he became involved with politics, but I do it for its own sake now.'

'Yes, I can see that you might,' Annabel agreed. 'I have often felt that my life was rather useless. I shall look forward to doing all I can for you, Laura.'

At least she had found one friendship in her new life, Annabel thought. She turned to look at Richard and Maurice as they came back into the lounge. The older man's expression was inscrutable, but Richard looked like thunder. Whatever they had been talking about had obviously not pleased him.

However, when he came to join them on the sofa he was immediately smiling, attentive, and as charming as only Richard knew how to be. Anyone watching would think he adored his young wife. However, Annabel sensed the underlying tension in him, which didn't ease until after Maurice Green took his leave of them.

'I shall expect you tomorrow, Richard,' he said and then looked at Annabel. 'It must feel strange to be living in London after the country. Please remember my standing invitation – and if ever you need a friend I shall always be around.'

'Thank you. It was nice meeting you, Mr Green.

'And you, Annabel. Take care of her, Richard.'

Annabel sensed the tension in Richard as he made a casual reply. He was as tight as a coiled spring. Had Maurice guessed that the bruise on her cheek was not an accident and taken him to task over it?

Once he had gone, Richard became the life and soul of the party, charming his friends, making them laugh by telling funny stories. Annabel could see that Laura found him totally fascinating, though her husband was a little more reserved.

It was quite late when they arrived back at Richard's large and expensively furnished apartment. Annabel experienced a flicker of fear as he paid the cab and took her arm, guiding her into the elevator.

What would happen when they were alone? Was she going to be made to pay for his displeasure?

However, when the door closed behind them, he ignored her, going over to the sideboard to pour himself a whisky which he drank neat.

'I needed that,' he said and then turned to look at her. 'Go to bed, Annabel. I'll sleep in the second bedroom and tomorrow I'll move my things in there. You won't be disturbed.'

'Thank you.'

'Don't imagine it ends there,' Richard said, reaching for the decanter again. 'For the moment it suits me to let you have your way, but I intend to get value for money, Annabel. When I want you a locked door isn't going to keep me out.'

Annabel made no reply, feeling it was safer. She believed she had Maurice Green to thank for this respite and it made her wonder just how much influence he had over Richard.

Five

'I've missed you so much, Belle,' Hetty said, and hugged her when they were alone in the flat. 'I was afraid Mother wasn't going to let me come. She said she wasn't well and made a great fuss, but Ben put his foot down. He told her that she had plenty to do for his wedding and that it was time I had a little fun – and he put my suitcases in his car and took me to the station himself.'

'I would have come and fetched you myself if she hadn't,' Annabel said. 'But you've arrived at just the right time. Richard has gone up to the North with friends of his. He's going on a kind of tour, factories and things apparently. I might have gone with him but Laura Bristow said I would be of more use here. We've got rather a lot on at the moment.'

'Is that the woman who is always organising things? You wrote to me about her. Her husband works at the Conservative Party Headquarters, doesn't he?'

'Yes, that's right,' Annabel confirmed. 'There's a by-election coming up soon and Richard has agreed to stand.'

'You told me in your letter. Did you know before you married him, Belle? It all sounds rather boring to me.'

'It might sound that way,' Annabel said and smiled. Actually, the work she was asked to do as a political wife had saved her from sinking into boredom and bitterness. 'But I really quite enjoy it. Some of the meetings can be tedious. The ladies do like to hear themselves talk. Laura has no patience with them. She always wants to get on and do things, not waste time in endless talking – but the actual work they do is often worthwhile, Hetty. We had a Flag Day last month; you know, went out on the streets and rattled tins at everyone, particularly the men. We raised a lot of money for the women of the slums in an area near the dock, and we're holding a big charity sale this weekend. There are whist drives, afternoon tea dances, and tombolas and of course the big gala ball in June.'

'Ben's wedding is going to be either in June or July,' Hetty said. 'I shall be at home for that, but I go to Art College at the beginning of September. I'll be moving in with Selina's friends at the end of August.'

'It's all arranged then?'

'Yes. Selina took me to see her friends while you were in Paris, Belle. They seem very nice, not a bit stuffy. I shall enjoy staying with them.'

'I'm glad everything is going so well for you, dearest.'

Annabel was aware of her sister's curious gaze. She turned away to glance round the guest room once more, checking that it was all perfect. The décor was very modern, as was the whole of Richard's apartment. He had a collection of Art Deco silver, and the whole theme was similar, rather minimalist and even slightly bare. He knew how to choose one beautiful thing and display it to perfection. The figurine she had slightly damaged had been cast into the depths of a cupboard as though he couldn't bear to see it. However, one thing she couldn't fault him on was his taste in furnishing and fashion. He seemed to have an instinct for it.

'When you're ready I'll ring for that cab,' Annabel told her sister. 'I'm taking you to lunch at a nice restaurant. It belongs to a friend of Richard's. Mr Green insisted that I bring you and I thought it would be pleasant; the food is very good and I've been told that all the fashionable people go there. We can have a meal, go shopping and then have tea with Laura. She is looking forward to meeting my clever sister. I've told her you're going to Art College and she's very interested.'

'I'm not clever,' Hetty said. 'I don't even know if I have any real talent, but I want to try…' She laid her hand on Annabel's arm, gazing into her face. 'You seem different. I'm not sure how. Are you feeling quite well?'

Annabel hesitated. Thankfully, the bruises didn't show, but the humiliation of that awful scene with Richard before he left on his publicity tour had stayed with her. It was her own fault for resisting, she knew that, much better to have let him have his way. He gained more pleasure from her struggles than when she lay cold and passive beneath him.

'Yes, of course I'm well,' Annabel said and laughed. 'If I seem different, Hetty, it's because I've grown up. Before I was married, I had no idea how awful life is for some people. We grumble if we can't have a new dress, but Laura was telling me how women in the slums have to pawn their belongings on a Monday to pay for the food they need. Sometimes it's their husband's Sunday suit – others might pawn their wedding rings or anything else they might happen to have just to feed their children.'

'What terrible lives they must have,' Hetty's attention was caught. 'Don't their husbands work?'

'Some do – if they can find work – but even then a lot of them drink most of the money away before they get home. The wives end up with only a few shillings and if they complain the men beat them.' A shudder ran through Annabel. 'They have to pay the rent somehow or they would be thrown out of their houses, which are disgusting hovels anyway. Laura was telling me she is ashamed that some of these places still exist. They belong to the Victorian era.'

'You've taken a real interest in all this, haven't you?'

'Yes.' Annabel's smile came more naturally now. 'Laura took me to a mission she helps to run. It's near the docks and was set up to offer comfort to battered wives and their children. They can go there for a while if things get too bad at home, and they are given a meal, sometimes clothes for themselves or the children. I gave Laura quite a few of my older dresses and she told me they disappeared as soon as they were put on the rail.'

'Now that does sound worthwhile,' Hetty agreed. 'Does Laura actually go there herself? Would she take me?'

'Laura is on the board of governors but she takes a hands on approach and visits now and then to see the way it's run for her own satisfaction.'

'Could we pay a visit? It sounds more interesting than your tombola drives and charity sales.'

'I'll ask Laura,' Annabel said. 'You can ask her yourself at tea if you wish.' She smiled at her sister, who had changed into her best dress which was short and looked very smart. It looked as if Hetty had lifted the hem to just on her knees and Annabel would guess that her mother hadn't seen the way it looked now. 'If you're ready, dearest, I'll ring for that cab.'

*

'How marvellous that you came,' Maurice Green said, as he conducted the sisters to their table himself. They had been given a pleasant, secluded spot by a window that overlooked the river and lawns, where customers were encouraged to sit at little tables and drink cocktails with fantastic names, like the Bees Knees, Sidecar or the Mary Pickford during the summer. 'It is lovely to meet you, Miss Tarleton. And I've been hoping to see you here, Annabel. You mustn't shut yourself away from us when Richard is working.'

'I've been busy with Laura,' she replied. 'Can we interest you in some tickets for our prize draw? It is for a very good cause, Maurice. We're trying to raise enough money for a new hostel for unfortunate girls.'

'For you, anything,' he said and smiled. 'You shall have a cheque before you leave. Now I shall let you relax with your sister – and remember to order whatever you want – and do try our pink champagne. This is my little gift for you and Miss Tarleton. Please excuse me. I see that Sir Harold Morton and his party have arrived. They've brought that French artist with them – Henri Claremont I believe he's called. He has an exhibition on at the

Kensington Gallery at the moment, which I am told is a great success.'

'Then we mustn't keep you,' Annabel said and looked at Hetty as he walked away. 'He's an important friend of Richard's. He's asked me to bring my friends here several times so I thought we might as well come. What did you think of him?'

'Who?' Hetty was looking across the room at the party just being shown to their table by the head waiter. 'He's awfully attractive, isn't he? He reminds me of Ivor Novello in that film – What was it called? Oh yes – *The Rat*, that's it. I saw it again quite recently, though it's years old.'

'Maurice Green?' Annabel was puzzled. Their host was an older man, not ugly but not attractive enough to draw such a comment from her impressionable sister. Then she saw the man Hetty was staring at rather too intently and understood. There was a certain wildness about the artist, his hair longer than was thought respectable in society, his eyes a brilliant blue that carried a hint of devilry, and his features had that clean cut appeal that would attract a young girl. 'Oh, I see what you mean, Hetty. Yes, Henri Claremont is very attractive. I've seen his photograph in the paper and I've been meaning to go to his exhibition. Perhaps you would like to go while you're here?'

'Yes...' Hetty had at last withdrawn her gaze from the young man. 'Yes, I should like to go very much.'

'Then we shall,' Annabel promised her. 'Now – what would you like to eat? I think I shall have the smoked salmon with salad for starters. What about you?'

'Yes, that would be nice,' Hetty said. 'And the duck afterwards I think.' She gave Annabel a shy smile. 'You asked me about Mr Green, didn't you? I thought he seemed pleasant enough – nothing special. Why did you ask?'

'Oh, no particular reason,' Annabel replied. 'It was just a matter of interest.'

Perhaps she had been wrong to imagine that Richard seemed nervous of his friend. Yet there was something about him, something that made her wonder if there wasn't more to him than the smiling face he showed to the world. She knew that he had many more business interests than this exclusive restaurant, but had no idea what they might be. A tentative question to Richard had brought no response other than a sharp reminder to remember what happened to the cat.

'Curiosity killed it,' she'd replied and he'd given her a look which had suppressed any desire to pry further into affairs that were obviously off limits to her. It hadn't stopped her wondering.

Richard had married her because he wanted the respectability a wife of good background would give him. His political friends were very respectable, genuine people – but Annabel suspected that Maurice Green might be something quite different.

However, when a waiter delivered an envelope to her table and she opened it to discover a cheque for five hundred pounds for her cause, she decided that Maurice had a social conscience and that perhaps she was letting her imagination run wild. She had wondered if he might have some criminal connections, though she wasn't sure why the thought had occurred to her. It was just something she'd heard Richard say when on the telephone to him – concerning a gambling club and a warning about an imminent police raid. But of course she could have misunderstood completely – or it might have nothing to do with either Richard or Maurice.

'I like that dress you're wearing,' Hetty said, bringing her thoughts back to the present with a start. 'Do you think we could find something similar for me?'

'Oh yes, I should think so,' Annabel said. It was a very simple design with a low waist and tailored skirt, but made of a transparent silky material worn over a satin petticoat – and very expensive. 'Richard gives me a very generous clothes allowance, Hetty – and the first thing we are going to do after lunch is to buy some pretty clothes for you.'

*

It was fun being able to give her sister really good clothes, Annabel decided after a couple of hours of sheer indulgence. She took a degree of satisfaction in spending Richard's money, using the charge accounts he'd set up for her with Swann and Edgar, Harvey Nichols, Harrods and other large stores with reckless abandon.

'Should you be spending all this on me?' Hetty asked when they had purchased a very expensive matching dress and coat, completing the outfit with a smart hat, shoes and bag and three pairs of good leather gloves. 'Will Richard mind?'

'Why should he? He expects me to spend money.' It was a part of the bargain, but of course she couldn't say that to Hetty.

Annabel had asked for everything to be delivered, leaving them free to go on to their appointment with Laura unencumbered.

Laura's home was a charming Georgian terraced house in a quiet garden square just off Primrose Hill. There was an air of faded grandeur about it that Annabel loved, the square rooms and high ceilings a perfect foil for Laura's furniture. Exquisite antiques stood side by side with worn but comfortable armchairs and sofas, giving an air of warmth and security. Richard's perfectly designed apartment seemed cold in comparison, despite being so stylish and elegant.

'I love your home, Laura,' Annabel said, realising as she spoke that that was the difference. Laura's house was a home, whereas Richard's apartment was just a place to live. She glanced around the big sunny parlour, stifling a sigh. 'You *are* lucky to live here.'

'We couldn't afford to live in Mayfair as you and Richard do,' Laura said. She looked about her with a quiet satisfaction. 'But I've always liked this house. It belonged to my grandfather and he left it to me. He believed a woman should have something of her own. He was in politics, you know, and one of the men who gave women the right to retain their property when they married. He was a wonderful old rogue and I adored him.' She smiled at Hetty. 'Are you going to help us while you're staying with your sister? She has been a marvellous help to us since she married Richard.'

'Yes, if I can,' Hetty said. 'I was wondering if we could pay a visit to that hostel Annabel was telling me about earlier.'

'It isn't a very pleasant area,' Laura said with a slight frown. 'The houses are all in a disgusting state and the streets are filthy, and you will see unemployed men hanging about on street corners. Are you sure you want to go?'

'Yes, please. I think it would be interesting to see why you're raising the money rather than just helping out with teas and things.'

'Your sister seems to know her own mind,' Laura said and laughed. 'Would you like to visit the place, Annabel? I could arrange it for tomorrow afternoon – if you're both sure?'

'I think Hetty is right. It would be interesting to see for ourselves the kind of people you are trying to help.'

'Then I'll pick you up at two o'clock sharp.' Laura smiled as a maid carried in the tea tray. 'Thank you, Barbara. How nice you've made it all look for us.' After the girl had departed she busied herself with pouring their tea. 'Barbara came to me through the mission. Her husband was killed in an accident and she had a small baby to care for. They were both ill when they came to us, but they are thriving now. Barbara puts the baby with a minder while she's at work but she has decent lodgings and seems content.'

'So you took her in,' Annabel said. 'Did she have experience of domestic work?'

'None at all,' Laura said. 'It was a disaster at first but she soon learnt. And she's very loyal to me.'

Their talk turned to general activities and they stayed on to an informal supper, leaving at nine in the cab Laura called for them.

'Yes, I do like her,' Hetty said as they were driven home. 'I can see why you've made friends with her, Belle. I thought it all sounded dreadfully boring for you but Laura is fun.' Hetty was thoughtful, then, 'Amy Johnson is attempting to fly solo to Australia soon, Belle, and other women are doing daring things – so why do we have to do what Mother thinks is right all the time?'

'I'm not sure,' Annabel said a little ruefully, 'it always seems so much easier – but now that I help Laura I lead a much fuller life. She's very respectable but she isn't dull. She is full of enthusiasm for her good causes,' Annabel said, 'and somehow you find yourself wanting to help her. I see other friends, of course. When Richard is home we dine out several times a week. I shall see Selina when she comes up to London next week. She's giving a party, and you know Selina's parties are always the best. Georgie phones me sometimes, but she's visiting friends in France at the moment.'

The telephone was ringing as Annabel walked into the apartment. She went to answer it at once, thinking it would be Richard or Lady Tarleton wanting to know why Hetty hadn't telephoned her.

'Is that Annabel Hansen?' a woman's voice asked.

'Yes, this is Mrs Hansen,' she said. The woman wasn't one of her friends; her voice sounded odd, like someone trying to speak in a manner unlike their normal one. 'Who is this please?'

'It doesn't matter who I am. I've got a message for your husband. You tell him he hasn't got away with it. I know what he's done to Janie and he'll get what's coming to him.'

'What are you talking about? What has he done?' Annabel heard the click at the other end. 'Hello – are you there?' But she knew it was useless, the caller had rung off. 'Damn!'

'Is something wrong?' Hetty asked. 'You've gone white, Belle. Who was that?'

'I've no idea.' She felt a little sick but took a deep breath to steady herself. 'She didn't say.'

'What did she say? She obviously upset you.'

'It was just a stupid hoax call. Not worth repeating.'

'Has it happened before?'

'No, that was the first time. It was a message for Richard but I shan't bother to tell him.'

Hetty stared at her and then pulled a wry face. 'I know something isn't right with you, but you don't want to tell me so I shan't pester you – but if you ever need to talk about it, I'll listen.'

'Thank you, dearest,' Annabel said. 'But really, there's nothing to worry about. I'm fine. Everything is just as I expected when I agreed to marry Richard.'

It wasn't the truth, of course, but Annabel could never voice her suspicions to her innocent sister. She had reason to know that Richard was capable of violence when thwarted. He never went too far with her; the bruises on her body were the result of forceful seduction rather than a beating. He had never struck her in anger except that once, which had been a mistake. Yet she had sensed more than once that he was holding back, that he could have been brutal if he chose.

Just what had happened to Janie? Had Richard beaten her – or was his secret even more shameful?

A dreadful suspicion entered Annabel's mind but she dismissed it immediately. She could not, must not, believe such a thing of Richard, for if she did she would find it impossible to stay with him.

*

Selina's party was every bit as much fun as Annabel had expected. She was glad it had taken place while Hetty was staying with her, because it gave her sister an opportunity to attend the kind of party she would never have been allowed to at home.

As usual, Selina had invited all kinds of talented people, artists and writers, actors and a sprinkling of debutantes. Dressed in wonderful clothes, smoking cigarettes in elegant long holders and wearing jewelled headbands, they were smart women, not always rich but always interesting. One of the guests was Edith Sitwell, a woman Annabel had long admired, both for her writing and her courage. She was initially too shy to approach the much famed lady but once they were introduced, Miss Sitwell invited her to sit with her on the sofa, and Annabel soon found herself expressing ideas about the role of women in the world that she hadn't known she had until that moment.

Because she was so entranced by her companion, listening avidly when Miss Sitwell began to expound on her own beliefs, she did not notice that Hetty seemed to be spending all her time with one person. It was only when another guest arrived and Miss Sitwell summoned him with expressions of pleasure that Annabel saw her sister was in earnest conversation with a young man she seemed to recognise, and it was only as he was leaving that she remembered him. It was the artist Henri Claremont, whom Hetty had so much admired.

'Did you see him?' Hetty asked when Annabel joined her. 'I never dreamt he would be here this evening, Belle. He told me never goes to parties like this, but came because he admires Edith Sitwell. But then he stayed to talk to me about his work.'

'Is that what you were talking about the whole time?'

'Yes… Well, almost,' Hetty said and laughed. 'He said that I would make an ideal model for a painting he wants to do – it's a sort of Greek mythology thing.'

'Which would involve you sitting for him half naked I suppose? I hope you didn't fall for that one, Hetty?'

'No, of course not,' she said and blushed. 'Can you imagine what Mother would say if I did?'

'Yes, and it makes me cringe,' Annabel told her and laughed. 'I know your artist is very attractive, dearest, but he isn't the sort of man you should be making friends with.'

'No, of course not! It was just a chance meeting at a party that's all. I dare say I shall never see him again,' Hetty said, but there was an air of studied innocence about her that made Annabel wonder. 'Oh, look, is that Miss Sitwell's brother? I do believe it is. She is beckoning to you, Belle. I think she wants to introduce you. And I want to speak to Selina for a moment. She was talking to Noel Coward just now and I want to hear about his latest play. I think it's called *Private Lives* and I should love to see it when they put it on stage…'

Annabel had the feeling that her sister was trying to change the subject, and perhaps that was best. It was unlikely that Hetty would meet the French artist again, and it would be better to just forget the incident altogether.

*

'The time has passed so quickly,' Hetty said as she hugged her sister at the railway station that afternoon. 'When I came I thought two weeks was a lovely long time, but it has flown by.'

'It does when you're enjoying yourself. I shall miss you, Hetty.'

'I wish I could stay longer, Belle, but you know what Mother is. She wants me home and if I don't go she might change her mind about me going to college.'

'Don't risk it, Hetty. I shall see you at the wedding and I'm sure we'll manage something before Christmas.'

'I'll write to you. Thank you for everything. I've had so much fun. I loved visiting the art exhibition. It was a pity Henri Claremont wasn't there though. I should have liked to see him again.'

'We missed him by a few minutes,' Annabel said and smiled at her sister's look of disappointment.

'Never mind, Hetty. You will meet plenty of nice young men when you go to college.'

'Perhaps...' There was a wistful expression in her eyes. 'I admired his work so much. I would have liked to tell him – but it doesn't matter. I'm so grateful for the clothes and all the rest of it, and the records for my gramophone. I really wanted "Brown Eyes Why Are You Blue?" And "Can't Help Lovin' Dat Man". I shall take them to college with me and we can dance to the fast Charleston ones. I can't wait to start college now.'

'You mustn't let anything stand in your way,' Annabel said, suddenly urgent. 'The sketches you did of those women and children at the mission were wonderful. Laura is going to have them framed. She thinks we can sell them for quite a bit. It was good of you to give them to her.'

'My contribution to your good work,' Hetty said. 'I wasn't much help with the tombola. Some of Laura's helpers thought I made more work than I did.'

'We can't all be good at everything.' Annabel laughed as she recalled Hetty's efforts. She had tried to provide fancy food for one of their fund raising events and although the customers had enjoyed the change, Laura told her privately that the others had grumbled at all the extra work and clearing up. 'I thought it was a superior tea, dearest. The only trouble was that you probably spent more than we earned.'

'Well, at least we paid for it – or rather Richard did,' Hetty said and looked at her anxiously. 'You are happy with him, Belle? He seems to be a perfect gentleman when I'm around but I wasn't sure you were pleased to see him home a day earlier than you had expected.'

'Richard and I don't live in each other's pockets, Hetty. It isn't that kind of a marriage.'

'You don't love him, do you?' Hetty looked sad. 'I wish you were happier, Belle. You know I love you, don't you?'

'Yes, I know. Please don't worry about me. I want you to go to college and have a wonderful time. I'm content with my life – and if I weren't, I would change it.'

'Would you leave Richard?'

'Yes, if I was desperately unhappy. At the moment I'm not – but if I became desperate I would.'

'Good!' Hetty laughed and hugged her. 'That's the spirit! The guard is blowing his whistle. I shall have to go.'

Annabel stood waving as the train pulled out of the station. She felt a deep sense of loss when she could no longer see Hetty leaning out of the window. It had been good having her in the apartment, though she'd been nervous since Richard came home, afraid of what he might do in one of his moods. She hadn't wanted Hetty to guess how unhappy her marriage really was or how wretched she felt sometimes.

It was her own fault! She ought never to have married him, never gone with him that evening. She had been drinking too much, in a daze, not really thinking until it was too late. And that was because she'd heard nothing from Paul Keifer, of course. Only when it was too late had she begun to realise what she had thrown away – a chance of real happiness.

'Oh, Paul...' she murmured as the familiar ache started up inside her. 'What a fool I was.'

She had been married for just over two months and already it seemed like a lifetime. How could she go on this way for years? Yet how could she walk out on her marriage? The thought of the scandal, of her mother's recriminations, weighed on her, crushing the spark of rebellion. Annabel's head went up. She wasn't a coward. She'd made her bed, as the saying went, and she would just have to lie on it.

'Why so pensive?'

The deep voice startled her. She was standing at the back of a very long queue for cabs and hadn't noticed Maurice Green until he spoke to her.

'I didn't see you,' she said and smiled. 'I've just been seeing my sister off. Mother wanted her home.'

'Ah yes, you will miss her,' he said. 'No wonder you looked so sad. Well, at least you need not wait for a cab. I have my car waiting. You will allow me to give you a lift?'

'Oh… Yes, of course,' Annabel agreed, feeling it would be too rude to refuse. 'You are very kind, thank you.'

'Not at all. I am sure you have better things to do with your time than stand here.'

'Yes. Laura makes sure of that,' she replied and laughed. 'Your cheque was much appreciated. I didn't imagine you wanted raffle tickets so I donated it to a worthwhile cause – the new mission for unfortunate girls and their children. Times are so hard – I read that there are nearly two million unemployed now! Laura took us to see the work that goes on there. Hetty did some wonderful sketches. They were extremely poignant, touching. Laura is going to frame them and sell them.'

'Your sister must be a talented artist. I should be interested in seeing them.' They had reached his car now and he was opening the back door for her. He hesitated for a moment and then got in beside her, leaning forward to give his driver her address. 'I am always willing to support good causes, Annabel. Especially when a friend is involved.'

'You've already been very generous.'

'There will be more in the future – but tell me, how are you getting along? Shall you enjoy being a politician's wife?'

'You think Richard will be elected?'

'I should imagine there's little doubt. It's a fairly safe seat – as long as nothing untoward happens Richard should sail through. His tour went well and your picture has appeared in the local paper up there three times. That should help. You are exactly what Richard needed, Annabel.'

'Why?' she asked and twisted her expensive gloves, which she had removed in the warmth of his car. 'Why should Richard need me? I would have thought his own charm would carry him through to say nothing of his money. And his background should appeal to people who work in factories themselves. Has Richard done something he needs to hide?'

Maurice gave her a long, hard look.

'Why do you ask? Have you heard something that bothers you?'

'Not exactly.' She saw his disbelieving expression and laughed. 'You doubt me? Well, perhaps I should tell someone. I had an odd phone call a few days ago.' She repeated as much as she could recall. 'The girl wasn't educated, though she was trying to speak properly. What do you think she meant?'

'I've no idea. I should imagine it was someone playing a trick on you, Annabel. What did you think she meant?'

'I've tried not to think about it at all.'

'Very wise. Put the whole thing out of your head.' He gave her another thoughtful look. 'You haven't told Richard. Would you tell me why?'

'He would be annoyed. Besides, he has a lot on his mind. Why should I bother him with something that trivial?'

'Quite right. You are very loyal. I hope Richard appreciates you as he should.'

'You didn't mind my telling you?'

'Of course not. I hope you will always come to me with anything that troubles you, Annabel. As for your question as to why Richard needs you – it's simply that married men appeal to the electorate. People sometimes distrust single men. Marriage is seen as a steadying influence. Richard has been a bit of a man about town. Natural enough in a young man, but he is older now. He needed a wife to give him the right image. No terrible secret. Nothing to hide.'

'Yes, that is what I thought,' she lied and gave him a wide-eyed, innocent smile. 'After all, what could Richard possibly have to hide?'

'What indeed?' he said. 'Ah, here we are, Annabel. I am so glad we've had the opportunity for this little talk. You must bring some more of your friends to my restaurant. There will always be a table for you.'

She thanked him and got out of the car, feeling chilled. His manner was as easy, as affable as ever, but somehow she was convinced that he had lied to her. He did know something about Richard – something that might damage his reputation. He obviously wasn't going to reveal it to her. Perhaps both he and Richard were involved in whatever it was?

She recalled the telephone conversation of which she had heard just a tiny snatch – something about Richard having heard there was to be a police raid at a certain nightclub. Could that be the secret they shared? Were they involved in things that might not bear the light of day? Annabel was aware that there was a world of crime swirling beneath the surface of London life, an unpleasant, sickening activity that condoned the kind of depravity she could hardly imagine: prostitution, gambling, the corruption of children. Sometimes she read articles in the newspapers but that kind of thing had always seemed so far away. She had never thought it could touch her. Now she was not so sure. Just what kind of a man had she married?

A shiver ran through her as she walked into the foyer of the exclusive apartment block, smiled at the friendly porter, stopped to ask after his wife, and then ran up the stairs. She seldom took the lift unless Richard was with her. She had thought he might be at home but there was no sign of him.

Annabel went through to her bedroom to tidy her hair, feeling restless. The apartment seemed lonely and empty without Hetty. Glancing at the clock she decided it was too late to go out again. Richard would be back shortly and they were going out for the evening.

Returning to the living room, Annabel stared at her reflection in the huge gilt mirror. The face looking back at her belonged to a stranger, a woman she didn't know any more. There was nothing for her to do here. The rooms were cleaned regularly by the in-house service, and she had only to pick up the telephone to have a delicious meal sent up. Without the charity work her life would be empty and useless.

Feeling miserable, Annabel thought about phoning a friend but there was no one she could talk to about any of this. No one she could confide in. Georgie might understand but she was visiting friends in France. Perhaps Selina...

Her hand was moving towards the phone when it rang, making her jump. 'It's Richard. I shall be late this evening. You'll have to cancel our table at the hotel. You can order a meal sent up, can't you?'

'Yes, if I'm hungry. Are you working late? There's nothing wrong?'

'Why should there be?' He sounded impatient. 'You'll have to get used to this, Annabel. Once I'm elected I'll be out until all hours. Ask someone over if you're lonely.'

'Yes, of course. I shan't wait up, Richard.'

'I didn't imagine you would.'

Annabel felt sick inside as the phone went dead. Was this what she had to look forward to – a lifetime of sitting alone?

She poured herself a glass of sherry and took it back to the sofa. She needed to talk to someone. Without really thinking she reached for the phone and dialled a number. It was answered almost immediately.

'Hello, Jessie Kendle speaking. How may I help you?'

'It's Annabel – Annabel Tarleton that was. I was just wondering how you all were. Is Catherine well and Harry?'

'Catherine had a little chill but she has recovered now, and Harry is well, thank you, Annabel. It's lovely to hear from you. How are you getting on?'

'Oh, fine. I'm very busy with my charity work. Perhaps Georgie told you?'

'She did mention something before she went dashing off to Paris last month. I saw that your husband is putting up for the Conservatives in the by-election. It must be exciting for you.'

'Yes, it is. I wondered – Paul isn't with you I suppose?'

'He's in America. He has been away since just after Christmas. I imagine he will be coming back soon. I gave him your letter, Annabel.'

'Oh yes, thank you.' Suddenly Annabel realised how foolish she was being. 'Well, I must go now. We're going out this evening. Goodbye.'

Replacing the receiver, Annabel sat staring into space for a few minutes, then she bent her head and wept. She cried for a while and then decided it was foolish to be miserable just because she felt so alone – but what was she going to do with herself? She wasn't hungry. She would have a nice hot bath and go to bed with a book. She was just getting up to go into the bathroom when the telephone rang.

'Annabel Hansen...'

'Mrs Hansen. It's Fred, the porter from downstairs. I've got a young lady here wants to see you – says her name is Alice. I thought I'd better ask before I sent her up. 'She says she's an actress and a friend of yours but I wasn't sure.'

'Alice...' Annabel wrinkled her forehead. 'Oh, of course, Alice! Please send her up, Fred. She *is* a friend of mine.'

She had just finished powdering her shiny nose when the doorbell rang and went to answer it immediately. Alice was looking very smart in a blue costume with a gored skirt and tailored jacket, worn with a blouse tied at the neck in a soft bow.

She looked a little nervous as she said, 'I hope you didn't mind my coming, Annabel? I'm working in London at the moment and I thought it might be nice to call and see you. Is it convenient? I hope I haven't come just when you want to get ready to go out? Only this is my night off and…'

'I'm on my own and feeling neglected,' Annabel said, smiling warmly as she drew her inside. 'Please don't worry, Alice. You have no idea how pleased I am that you decided to come this evening…'

Six

'It's just the same for me,' Laura said when Annabel told her Richard had been working late every night for the past week. 'Though every night for a week is rather a lot when you've only been married a short while. You should have jumped in a taxi and come over to me, my dear. You can always visit us if you're feeling lonely, if we're here, of course; that's what we political wives are good at, supporting each other.'

'Thank you. I shall remember that if I feel low,' Annabel told her. 'It was a bit lonely that first evening, but then a friend came to see me. She's an actress and she invited me to go and watch her at the theatre whenever I feel like it. I've been for two performances – it's a musical show and Alice is playing the second lead. She sings beautifully. It's her first major part in a musical and she was very excited to get it. Apparently, the girl who had been in the role left without notice a few weeks back. They tried someone else who wasn't a success and then gave Alice the chance. She is doing very well. We went out to supper together last night; it was fun.'

'An actress in a musical show? How thrilling for you, Annabel.'

Laura sounded a little dubious despite her attempt to be enthusiastic and Annabel laughed. 'Don't be a prude, Laura. Alice is perfectly respectable, a very nice girl. I met her while I was staying at Kendlebury before Christmas. As a matter of fact, I like her very much.'

'I wasn't suggesting…' Laura looked uncomfortable. 'It's just that you need to be careful, Annabel. Especially just before the election. It's next week and everything has been going so well.'

'My having a friend who sings like an angel isn't going to affect that surely? Anyone would think we were living in the age of Queen Victoria.'

'No, of course not – as long as there's no scandal. Where did you go to have your supper?'

'Nowhere flashy or smart,' Annabel said. 'Just a little Italian restaurant where Alice knows the owners. They were all very friendly and nice, and there was no one present that I was acquainted with, Laura.'

'Well, I suppose there was no harm in it – but if she asks you to go to a nightclub with her just say no. You might find your picture splashed all over the morning papers.'

'Surely not?' Annabel was annoyed. Laura was being a snob and she didn't like it. 'What difference is there in me being friendly with an actress and you employing a girl from your mission? You think Barbara is respectable, well, so is Alice.'

'I'm not suggesting...' Laura broke off and sighed. 'I'm not being a snob whatever you might think, Annabel. I am only giving you a hint as a friend. Richard might not care for your friendship with an actress or singer or whatever – and I think you should be careful for the moment.'

'I think that's pretty unfair. You haven't even met Alice – and she thinks the work you do is wonderful. She even asked me if she could do something to help. Give a little concert one evening with a few of her friends.'

'Did she?' Laura pulled a face. 'Oh dear, that makes me sound awful, doesn't it? I really didn't mean to offend you, Annabel. Please, don't let's quarrel over it any more. I'm sure your friend is very nice. It's just that Richard has so much riding on this by-election. He would be so upset if he lost – as would quite a few others. We're experiencing stronger opposition from the Labour Party candidate than we had imagined and I suppose I'm a little worried that things might go wrong.'

'Surely they won't? Maurice Green said it was a safe seat.'

'The country is going through hard times, Annabel. There's a lot of unemployment and I think it is going to get worse before long. Besides, you cannot be sure of anything these days. The electorate is nothing if not fickle.'

'I promise to be careful,' Annabel told her. 'I won't get drunk in a nightclub and be photographed brawling as I leave. Don't imagine you will see my picture splashed all over the society magazines.'

'The very idea!' Laura exclaimed and laughed. 'I never imagined you would, my dear. I'm sorry if I seemed to criticise. It wasn't intentional.'

'It's just that Alice is a friend,' Annabel said, unable to explain that being with Alice made her remember the time she'd spent at Kendlebury.

'Yes, of course. You must do as you please. I do hope you will forgive me? I should hate it if we were to fall out over this.'

'No, of course we shan't,' Annabel said. 'But what do you think of the idea of a concert? Alice says she can get several of her friends to come and perform. It would have to be on a Monday, though, because that is the night they have off from the show.'

'Let me think about it,' Laura said. 'We should need a venue, of course, just a small one. Not a theatre but perhaps a community room – the same sort of thing as we use for our tombola and whist drives. Yes, I shall give it some thought, Annabel. And now, I was going to suggest a visit to the new building we're thinking of buying. I have an appointment this afternoon, and I wondered if you might like to come with me?'

'Yes, of course I would,' Annabel agreed. 'I shall be very interested to see it.'

'I don't suppose it will be in the best of condition,' Laura said. 'For the price they are asking it's bound to need a lot of work, but we are used to that. We couldn't afford to buy if it was pristine.'

*

Richard was at the apartment when Annabel returned that afternoon. He looked at her as she entered, a frown of annoyance creasing his brow.

'Where have you been?'

'To inspect a building that Laura's charity is thinking of buying. Why do you ask?'

'You're late,' he muttered, clearly in one of his moods. 'Had you forgotten we're going out this evening?'

'No, Richard, I'm not the one who conveniently forgets or cancels these things.'

'God, you can be a bitch,' he said, eyes narrowed. 'I sometimes wonder why I ever imagined you would make a nice docile wife.'

'If I'm a bitch you taught me how to be one.'

'I haven't finished teaching you your lessons,' Richard said and the tone of his voice was so menacing that she had to fight herself to not shrink from him as he approached.

'Leave me alone, Richard. If you want me to be ready in time, just don't touch me. Remember this is an important evening for you. Some of your constituency members will be there. I'm wearing a sleeveless gown and it wouldn't look too good if I had a bruise on my arm, would it?'

'One of these days I'll shut your mouth permanently for you, Belle! If you go running behind my back to Maurice again it will be sooner rather than later.'

'He offered me a lift. I didn't run to him.'

'But you talked a lot while you had the chance.' His hands balled at his sides. She sensed that he was keeping his temper on a tight rein and that it was difficult for him. 'Don't worry, Belle. I shan't hit you, not tonight – but keep your mouth shut.'

'I only told him about a phone call…'

'You should have told me. Have there been any more?'

'No. Only that one.'

'Tell me if it happens again.'

'If that's what you want,' Annabel said. 'But it was just someone being spiteful, at least that's what Maurice thought.'

'And what did you think?'

'I didn't think anything,' Annabel replied with a shrug of her shoulders. 'It doesn't matter to me one way or the other.'

She went into her bedroom, locking the door before going to take a bath. With Richard in this mood she didn't want him walking in on her when she was at her most vulnerable. Thank goodness they were going to an important function, otherwise he would have taken his temper out on her.

*

The evening was an unqualified success. Richard was his usual public, charming self and Annabel did a lot of smiling and talking, wondering as she did so how people could be so easily deceived. It was easy for her to see now that Richard was false, his charm merely a veneer to hide his true character. If only she had waited, got to know him better – but she had been over this a thousand times in her mind and it always came back to the same thing. She was trapped and there was very little she could do about it other than leave her husband.

She didn't think she had the courage to do it. Perhaps if she was desperate she might be driven to leaving, but at the moment she was simply unhappy. There were parts of her life she enjoyed. Being able to buy fashionable gowns from Lavin and the House of

Worth was exciting, but she wasn't sure it was adequate compensation for her unhappiness. It had felt good to shower her sister with presents and Richard hadn't made a murmur about the bills.

'You must be proud of your husband,' a woman gushed to her. 'Such a charming man. He will be an asset to the Party and a shining light in the Government when we are re-elected, as I am sure we shall be soon enough.'

'Yes, I am sure he will,' Annabel replied, feeling like an awful fraud. 'We must hope he is elected next week.'

'Oh, there cannot be any doubt,' the woman said. 'Now tell me, Mrs Hansen, do you have a space free for the Tuesday following the election? I'm giving a luncheon for wives only and I wanted to add you to my list. I organise hospital visitors and I was hoping I could persuade you to join my little band of helpers.'

'Yes, possibly,' Annabel said. 'May I consult my diary and let you know? I'm not exactly sure what I have on that week.'

The woman looked slightly annoyed, as if she had expected Annabel to jump to attention. They had been introduced at some point, Annabel knew, but it was not until later, when she was talking to Laura, that she realised the woman was the wife of an important member of the opposition front benches.

'Oh dear,' Annabel said. 'I really must pay more attention when I'm introduced to someone. I told her I had to consult my diary.'

'She is a little pushy,' Laura said. 'It may do her good to be kept waiting for once, but I wouldn't make a habit of it, Annabel. You don't want to spoil Richard's chances of being invited to join the shadow cabinet – and perhaps the Government after the next election.'

'No...' Annabel was thoughtful. 'I was thinking he would be in the clear once he was elected, but I suppose there's more to it than that, isn't there?'

'Yes, of course,' Laura said. 'Richard is an ambitious man. He won't want to sit on the back benches forever.'

'No, I see that,' Annabel said and smiled.

'What are you smiling at?'

Laura was curious but Annabel kept her thoughts private. She had suddenly realised that she had a powerful weapon with which to control Richard's brutality. Spending recklessly on clothes, music, books and jewellery didn't seem to bother him, but a threat to his credibility might have the desired effect.

'Nothing in particular,' she said. 'Just that I'm beginning to realise what all this means.'

'Yes, it is rather awesome, isn't it?' Laura agreed, completely misunderstanding. 'Such a responsibility to one's husband.'

Annabel hadn't been thinking about what she could do for Richard, but what she might threaten to do if he became too violent.

*

'Where do you think you're going?' Richard asked as she walked past him towards her bedroom later that evening. 'We have unfinished business.'

'No, I don't think we do,' Annabel said and turned to look at him, her head held proudly as she saw that his mood hadn't improved during the evening. 'I was asked to lunch by the wife of a member of the shadow cabinet this evening, Richard. I shall go of course. I could volunteer to join her hospital visiting list – or I could refuse. I could even drop hints that I don't think you are suitable material for the cabinet when your party is re-elected.'

'You little bitch!' Richard moved towards her menacingly, his fists balling at his sides. 'I'll teach you to threaten me.'

'Hit me and I'll go to hospital and tell the doctors and nurses that you beat me. I don't imagine you would be thought a suitable candidate then, do you, Richard? It would be bound to be in all the morning papers.'

'I'll thrash you so hard you won't be able to get out of bed!'

'But even if you're elected I'm still your wife,' she said, smiling coldly. 'If I go to Laura and tell her what a brute you are she will believe me – and so will others. I could ruin your reputation if I chose, Richard.'

'Damn you! What do you want?' He glared at her, frustrated and angry. 'I ought to break your neck.'

'Do it,' she challenged. 'I suppose you could say I'd had an accident, but you might not be believed. I've written a letter to a friend that will be opened in the event of my death – so I should think twice about getting rid of me that way, Richard.' She hadn't of course, but it was a threat worth using and would make him think before he abused her again.

His eyes narrowed as he looked at her. 'You think you've been very clever, don't you, Annabel? Push me too far and you might get a shock.'

'Nothing you could do – or have done – could surprise me,' she said. 'I'm asking that you stay out of my bed, Richard, that's all. I've had enough of being used in that way.'

'You're not much fun anyway,' he muttered looking sour. 'And if I agree to your terms?'

'Then I shall continue to be the discreet little wife you need, Richard.'

He was so very angry! She could see that he wanted to hit out at her, to force her to do what he wanted, but he was holding back, controlling his fury as best he could.

'You'll be sorry one of these days,' he muttered and turned away. 'But you needn't worry, I shan't disturb you. I've got another damned headache!'

Annabel took a deep breath. She had won the battle this time, but there was a primitive beast inside Richard and one day it would break out. For the moment he had accepted her terms. She had a breathing space, time to decide what to do with the rest of her life.

*

'I thought you'd given me up,' Alice said when Annabel went round to her dressing room one evening a few weeks later. 'Now that your husband is an MP I thought perhaps you would think twice about knowing me.'

'Don't be a snob,' Annabel said. 'I'm not so don't treat me as one.'

'I know that, I was just teasing,' Alice replied and smiled at her. 'I suppose you've been too busy to come?'

'Richard has been to one official function after another,' Annabel said with a sigh. 'I've had to go to all of them.'

'Doesn't that get boring?'

'Sometimes. But there are the nights when he's sitting late at the House like tonight. I hadn't got any engagements myself – so here I am. Have you got time to come out this evening?'

'You're welcome to join us,' Alice said but looked doubtful. 'A group of us are going to a nightclub. It's a new one, opened only last month. I haven't been before and don't know much about it, but apparently an American blues singer is appearing there at the moment.'

'Is it legal?' Annabel asked, remembering Laura's warning. 'I should like to come with you, but I have to be a bit careful.'

'Yes, I'm sure it is,' Alice told her. 'I wouldn't go otherwise, believe me. They get a lot of showbusiness people there so I've heard. Film stars from America and even some minor royalty.'

'Oh well, that should be all right then. Yes, I would love to come, Alice – if I'm dressed for the part?' She looked down at her smart costume in comic dismay.

'I could lend you an evening gown,' Alice offered. 'I keep several here in case I'm invited somewhere special. I should think you could find one to fit you, we're not much different in size, are we?'

'No, not much,' Annabel agreed. She looked through the rail Alice indicated. 'Most of the dresses were rather more glamorous than she usually chose for herself, but she found one that was fashioned of satin and lace in dark blue, with a slim skirt and bodice and a little bolero to cover the dipping neckline. 'May I borrow this one?'

'Yes, of course,' Alice said and nodded approval of her choice. 'Jessie gave me that dress and I had it altered to fit me. It should suit you, Annabel, and those shoes will go with it nicely.'

Annabel went behind the screen to change, emerging after a few minutes to look at herself in the mirror. The dress fitted well and the colour was flattering.

'Why don't I do your hair differently?' Alice asked. 'I think it would look good brushed back close to your head in waves and curls.'

'Like Marlene Dietrich or Betty Grable?' Annabel asked. 'How are you going to manage that? My hair is too straight for the style.'

'Not if I use these curling tongs,' Alice offered. 'They are Marcel waving tongs and you just heat them up on the gas ring. It would give you a whole new look, Belle.'

'No, I don't think so,' Annabel said and laughed. 'I think I'll stay as I am for the moment – though I have thought of cutting my hair and having a permanent wave.'

'That would be fun,' Alice said. 'I've thought about it but I'm not sure I want to go through all that palaver. You have to sit for ages with your hair wired up to this weird machine – and sometimes it gets burned off. That happened to a friend of mine and she ended up with little bubble curls all over her head. It looked nice, but I need to be able to change my hair for my work.'

'I don't think I would like that,' Annabel said made a face. 'Perhaps I'll just stay as I am.'

Alice had gone behind the screen to change and emerged wearing a slinky green satin dress with a low back. She had a matching shawl, which she draped over her arm, and declared herself ready.

'Shall we go? The others are meeting us in the foyer.'

'Who are the others?' Annabel asked belatedly.

'Oh, they're all boys and girls from the show,' Alice said carelessly, 'and an American film producer. He's over here looking for talent for a big musical that he's producing in Hollywood. They want a lot of new faces for the chorus apparently. It's going to be a real spectacular.'

'It sounds exciting,' Annabel said. 'Are you hoping to be offered a part? Are you going to be another Lilian Gish or Gloria Swanson?''

'I should be so lucky,' Alice said raising her brows. 'Our show finishes next month so I would be off like a shot if I got the chance, but it isn't likely is it? We all dream of Hollywood but few of us make it.'

'Well, you never know,' Annabel said. 'What would you do with your daughter if you went?'

'She is in a boarding school,' Alice said. 'I didn't want her shoved from pillar to post and I never know how long I'm going to stay anywhere. She stays either with Jessie or my mother during the holidays and I go down to be with her when I can.'

'What is her name? I knew you had a child but no one told me her name.'

'She's called Elizabeth after Mrs Pottersby,' Alice said. 'Jessie and her aunt were both good to me when I was having her and afterwards.'

'Yes, they are good friends to have,' Annabel said thoughtfully. 'I missed them all when I left Kendlebury.'

'But surely you had so much to look forward to – with your wedding and all?'

'I didn't know I was getting married then,' Annabel said. 'It happened quickly – and it was a mistake.'

'Oh, Belle!' Alice looked shocked. 'You don't mean that?'

'Yes, I do – but I haven't admitted it to anyone else, so please don't say anything.'

'No, of course not. I wouldn't gossip about you to anyone, Belle.'

'I know. I suppose that's why I told you. I've wanted to talk and there's no one I can tell...'

'I'll come round to your place one evening,' Alice promised. 'We can't talk about it now. We shan't have much chance for the rest of the evening.'

'No, of course not,' Annabel said. 'It's nothing desperate, Alice. It will keep.' She smiled. 'I'm looking forward to having a little fun this evening, and to hearing the singer you were telling me about.'

'We're going to have a good time,' Alice said and smiled at her. 'By the sound of it it's time you had some fun.'

*

Richard had taken Annabel to a nightclub in Paris but since their return to London they had attended only private parties and functions, other than the occasional trip to the theatre or the opera. The club she attended with Alice was crowded, noisy and rather dark inside, but the music was good and the atmosphere exciting.

Alice's friends had accepted her as one of them and she was given a cocktail as soon as she sat down. Some of the girls were dancing, others were listening to the music; the rest were hanging on to the film producer's every word as he talked about the musical extravaganza he was planning.

Someone asked Annabel to dance but she refused, preferring to sit quietly taking it all in and listening to the singer, who was really very good. Richard didn't appreciate this kind of music, but Annabel loved it when she had the chance to hear it, especially live.

The singer on the stage wasn't someone she'd heard of, but reminded Annabel of Ma Rainey and Bessie Smith, whose records she collected whenever she could.

She got up from the table and moved closer to the stage, joining a group of fans who were watching and listening eagerly, and clapped as enthusiastically as anyone else when the singer retired from the stage. Instead of going back to the table immediately, she went to the ladies' cloakroom, which was done out discreetly in pale pinks and blues. She spent a few moments there, retouching her face powder and lipstick, then returned to the main salon. A band was playing dance music now and the floor was crowded with couples enjoying themselves. Annabel had to edge her way round the perimeter in the semi darkness and managed to bump into a man who had just risen from his table.

'Oh, I am so sorry,' she apologised. 'Did I tread on your toes?'

'It was my fault... Annabel?'

She knew his voice instantly, looking at him intently as her heart took a flying leap. He had been just a shadow in the gloom now he had become someone she knew – someone who was never far from her thoughts.

'Paul? Jessie told me you were in America.'

'I got back a couple of days ago,' he said. 'I've been doing some publicity posters for a film company. One of the producers I was working with is here this evening. He brought some girls and boys here from a London show – looking for new talent I believe.'

'Alice is one of them,' Annabel said. 'I'm wearing a dress I borrowed from her. I went to see her at the theatre earlier and she invited me to join her and her friends.'

'Are you about to rejoin them?'

'Yes, I was,' Annabel said. 'I suppose I should…'

She sounded reluctant even to herself and Paul smiled. 'Why don't I come with you?' he asked. 'I was invited to join the party this evening, that's why I'm here.'

'You're alone?'

'I met some friends on the way in,' he said. 'But I'm not with them.'

'I'm sure Alice would love to see you,' Annabel said, her heart beginning to beat wildly. She had never dreamt that she would see Paul this evening and her feelings were a mixture of confusion and hope – though what she had to hope for she couldn't think, but insensibly her spirits were soaring.

'I'll escort you there,' Paul said. 'It's a bit of a scrum this evening. I've never been before. I understand it's a new club and it seems to be popular.'

'Yes, doesn't it?' Annabel said. The evening had suddenly become a success for her. She only hoped he couldn't see how she was affected or feel the excitement just being with him had aroused in her.

Alice was dancing with the film producer when they reached their table. Annabel introduced Paul to the others; he shook hands all round, smiled and then asked her if she would care to dance with him.

'Yes,' she said. 'Yes, I think I should.'

Paul took her hand and led her out onto the floor, drawing her into his body as the band began a soft, smoochy number. It felt so good to be in his arms. Annabel closed her eyes, laying her head against his shoulder as they moved to the rhythm of the romantic song. She never wanted the music to end; it was sheer heaven, bliss to be close to him, to feel the warmth of his body.

Neither of them spoke. It was a moment out of time, a moment to be treasured and held somewhere safe where it couldn't be touched or exposed to the cruel light of reality. This was how it should have been between them from the beginning. She knew it now, too late, knew it deep down inside her and sensed that he felt the same.

'Annabel…' Paul said as the song ended but she touched her fingers to his mouth, preventing him from speaking.

'Not now, Paul,' she whispered. 'Let's go back to the others. We'll talk some other time.'

'I have to go up to Manchester tomorrow. In fact I ought to leave now, because I have an early start.'

'Telephone me when you get back,' she said. 'We'll meet. We need to talk, Paul – don't we?'

'Yes,' he said and reached out to run a finger down her cheek. 'I think we should talk. We owe ourselves that at least…'

Annabel smiled up at him. As he led her back to their table she was unaware that someone was staring at her from his vantage point above the room. The window was discreetly placed so that the club's owners could watch without being observed. Hardly anyone was aware that it was there.

Alice was excited when she returned Annabel's costume the next morning and collected her dress, her news bubbling out of her as soon as she was inside the door of the apartment.

'You'll never guess,' she cried. 'I still can't believe it, Annabel – I've been offered a part in Milo's new film.'

'That's wonderful,' Annabel congratulated her warmly. 'I'm so very pleased for you. You didn't think you stood a chance, did you?'

'No, not a real chance,' Alice said. 'I'm not sure that I can go, because of Beth. I might be away for some months.'

'You couldn't take her with you?'

'Not at first,' Alice said. 'She's doing well at school and I'm not sure how things will work out. I don't want to uproot her and then find I'm out on my ear. Of course if I decided to stay over there for longer I could come back and fetch her – or get someone to bring her out to me.'

'You are afraid she might miss you?'

'I try to see her as often as possible.' Alice pulled a face. 'I know she can stay with my mother sometimes and Jessie is always pleased to have her – but I don't want her to forget she has a mother or to feel resentful about it.'

'No, of course not,' Annabel agreed. 'Why don't you go and see her? Tell her that it is a good chance for you and ask her if she minds you being away for a while. If you explain it all to her she might understand.'

'She's a sensible girl and quite grown up for her age.' Alice looked at her, seeming hesitant. 'I don't suppose you could come with me, Belle? Help me talk to her...'

'Where is she at school?'

'It's not far from Torquay.'

'That would mean an overnight stay, wouldn't it?' It would be awkward for Annabel to get away but she could see that this meant a lot to her friend and she spoke without thinking as she agreed. 'Of course I'll come with you,' she said. 'We might get a chance to see Jessie and the others while we're there. When do you want to go?'

'It can't be until next month, after the show finishes,' Alice said, her face lighting up. 'I'll arrange a date with the school and then let you know. I could go on my own, of course, but I'd be happier if you would go with me. Beth is such a serious child and I'm never sure what she's thinking.'

'And what will you tell the film producer?'

'I'll tell him I'll go,' Alice said. 'I'm sure Beth will understand, especially if you tell me what to say to her.'

'I'm not sure that I know,' Annabel said, but she knew that all Alice really needed was a little moral support. 'I think the best thing is just to make sure she knows you love her and tell her you will come back for her as soon as you can.'

*

To Annabel's surprise Richard accepted the news that she was going to stay with a friend for a day or so without argument. She explained that she would be visiting a young girl at boarding school and that she would stay with her friends at Kendlebury for a night before coming back.

'Do as you please,' he said seeming indifferent. 'It hardly matters to me whether you are here or not, does it?'

'That's not fair, Richard. I do most things you ask and I try to make a good impression for you.'

'Oh yes, you're the perfect little wife,' he snarled. 'Except that you lock me out of your bedroom and refuse my rights as your husband.'

'I wouldn't refuse if you didn't hurt me,' Annabel said defensively. 'You could try being a little nicer to me, Richard.'

'You want me to beg?' His mouth curled in a sneer. 'Oh no, my dear, I like my women to beg. You won't bring me to heel that way – and if I wanted you no lock would keep me out. Just remember that.'

Annabel stilled the sharp retort that leapt to her tongue. It didn't matter. Nothing he said could hurt her because she felt nothing for him. At least he hadn't forbidden her to visit her friends.

*

'Did your husband mind you coming with me?' Alice asked when they boarded the train together. 'I wondered if he might object to your being my friend, with him being an MP these days.'

Richard isn't bothered with what I do,' Annabel said, not quite truthfully. 'Besides, why should he object?'

'You know the answer to that as well as I do,' Alice said. 'I'm an actress and I've got an illegitimate child. The newspapers could have a field day with that, couldn't they?'

'I suppose it could be made to sound as if I were mixing with unsuitable company if they tried hard enough,' Annabel said. 'But why should they? You don't get drunk, behave scandalously or act in a lewd manner, Alice, and I happen to like having you as a friend. If Richard doesn't approve that's his problem. Besides, he doesn't even know. I told him I was going to stay at Kendlebury and he can't object to that.'

'You didn't tell me why your marriage was a mistake.' Alice looked at her thoughtfully. 'You're not in love with him, Belle? Why did you marry him?'

'Because he seduced me at a party and then threatened to tell everyone if I didn't marry him.' Annabel saw the shock in her face and smiled. 'It does sound awful when you put it like that, doesn't it? I should have told him to go to hell, of course, but I didn't have the courage. I was such a child then and it was my own fault for having too much champagne, but I was feeling miserable – and that was my own fault, too. I suppose I'm a coward at heart, Alice.'

'I don't think you're a coward. I think you just got scared and did what you thought was best. When I knew Beth was on the way I wanted to have an abortion, but Jessie talked me out of it. If it hadn't been for her I wouldn't have had the courage to have my child, let alone keep her.' Alice looked at her intently. 'You made a mistake, Belle, but you don't have to pay for it for the rest of your life. Leave him if he makes you miserable. And don't say you're not brave enough, because if you really want to, you'll find the courage.'

'Perhaps,' Annabel said. 'I have thought about it – but do I have the right to just walk out on him like that? I did promise to have and to hold until death do us part. I suppose that counts for something. It's a bit selfish if I just say I've had enough and walk out on my promises, isn't it? Divorce might ruin Richard's career.'

'What is the alternative?' Alice asked. 'Must you sacrifice the rest of your life because you made one mistake? Besides, if he forced you into it he would be getting what he deserved.' Alice saw something in her eyes and frowned. 'You're not afraid of him are you – of what he might do if you crossed him?'

'No, of course not,' Annabel said. 'Anyway, I don't want to think about Richard today. I'm looking forward to meeting your Beth...'

*

Beth was a shy, serious child with dark hair, grey eyes and a quiet manner, but when she smiled her whole face lit up. It lit up when she saw her mother and ran to greet her outside the main building of the small, rather exclusive school she was attending. Alice caught her up in a hug, swinging her round and kissing her affectionately.

There was no doubt about the love between them, Annabel thought and found herself experiencing a kind of wistfulness. Her relationship with her mother had never been like that and she realised how much she had missed.

'This is my friend, Annabel,' Alice told the child. 'We've come to take you out for the day. Say hello to Annabel, darling.'

'Hello,' Beth said, giving her a shy look. 'Have you known Mummy long?'

'Not very long,' Annabel said. 'But we're good friends. I hope we shall be friends, too, Beth.'

Beth nodded but didn't answer, seeming tongue tied and awkward at first. However, as the day progressed through a shopping trip to buy her a new jumper and shoes and a really nice tea at one of the better hotels in the area, she began to come out of her shell and talk about her friends at school.

'What do you like to do best?' Annabel asked. 'Do you enjoy singing like your mother?'

'I don't sing as well as Mummy,' Beth said. 'I like to draw and paint pictures best.'

'My sister likes that too,' Annabel said. 'She wants to be an artist. She is going to Art College soon.'

'I should like to be an artist when I grow up.'

'Then perhaps you will, if you want it enough.'

Beth smiled but didn't say anything. She looked at her mother as Alice took her hand and began to talk.

'I may be going to America for a while,' she said hesitantly. 'If I do go I won't be able to visit for a while, Beth. I would write letters and send things as I do now – but I couldn't visit.'

'How long will you be away?' Beth was frowning but Annabel suspected she wasn't sure where America was or what it meant. 'Where shall I go for the holidays?'

'I might be away for a few months, Beth. You'll stay with Jessie and your grandmother for your holidays as usual.'

'But you won't be there?'

'Not this time.'

Beth stared at her solemnly for a moment, then nodded her head. She turned her serious gaze on

Annabel. 'Will you come to see me while Mummy is away?'

'Would you like that?' Annabel asked, feeling as if the child had tugged at her heartstrings. She looked so lonely in that moment, so vulnerable that she never thought of refusing. 'I could visit you now and then, take you out to tea sometimes, Beth – if you wanted?'

'Yes, please,' Beth said and smiled suddenly. 'You're nice. I'm glad Mummy brought you today. I would like it if you visited when Mummy can't.'

'Then I shall,' Annabel promised and bent down to kiss her cheek. She was surprised when Beth hugged her and felt a prick of tears behind her eyes. 'I should like that, Beth. I'll be your friend and you'll be mine.'

'And you won't mind if I'm away for a while? I don't want to leave you, darling, but it's a job – a good chance for Mummy to do something special,' Alice asked.

'I wish you didn't have to go away,' Beth told her truthfully and hugged her again. 'But I don't mind if it's what you want.'

'Thank you. We'll spend lots of time together when I get back, I promise.'

Beth nodded; her expression was almost stoic, as if she knew that separation from her mother was something that had to be endured.

'You will write to me?'

'Yes, all the time,' Alice promised. 'Sacred word of honour!'

Beth giggled as her mother gave her a salute. 'Will you write to me, Annabel?'

'Yes, of course, if you would like that,' Annabel said. 'I'll write every week and I'll visit when I can.'

Beth seemed to accept this and made no further comment. She seemed perfectly happy when they returned her to the school, though there was something a little sad in her expression as she waved them goodbye.

'It tears the heart out of me to leave her,' Alice told Annabel as they were driven to the station in a taxi. 'If I could earn a bit from film work in America I might decide to live out there and keep her with me. They aren't as stuffy about things like that out there. Besides, I might be able to afford a nice house over there, somewhere to call home, with a housekeeper to look after Beth while I'm working.'

Annabel smiled but made no comment. Alice would have to be very lucky to find work that paid her that well, she thought, but didn't want to discourage her. Perhaps this job she'd been offered would turn out to be the start of big things for her.

Seven

'I'm looking forward to seeing Jessie,' Annabel said when they got off the train at Kendlebury. It had turned chilly now, and she pulled her coat collar up around her ears. 'She was surprised when I told her I wanted to stay but seemed pleased that I was coming.'

'Jessie is always like that,' Alice said. 'She stood by me when my father refused to have anything to do with me, allowed me to see my mother at Kendlebury. He got over it before he died, I'm glad to say. Really loved Beth in his heart, but could never quite forgive me for running off and not getting married in the proper way.'

'Did you want to marry Beth's father?'

'Yes, at first, but afterwards I saw we shouldn't suit. I've never regretted what I did.'

'Have you ever wanted to marry anyone else?'

'No. I've had a few friends...' Alice went a bit pink. 'You know what I mean, Belle – but no one serious. I like being a singer and an actress, even if I'm not a very successful one.'

'I'm sure that's not true. You've been in several shows, haven't you?'

'I've had my share of work, but I've never really reached the top,' Alice said and sighed. 'Perhaps that's why I want to take this job, to give myself a chance of getting there.'

'Perhaps you will. I think you should take the opportunity, Alice. Otherwise you will always wonder.'

'I've made up my mind. I feel better now I've talked to Beth. She will be all right. She likes you, Belle. She was pleased when you said you would write to her.'

'I shall, and visit when I can manage it.'

Carter was waiting for them at Kendlebury station.

'You won't be able to use this station for much longer,' he said as he greeted them. His cheerful manner in giving bad news reminded Annabel of Jonah, their long-suffering gardener, and she smiled to herself. 'It's being closed soon. It will be the bus or the car then.'

'That's bad news,' Annabel said, realising what it could mean for local people. 'Is Jessie worried about it affecting her business?'

'Most people come by car or the bus these days. I dare say we shall survive.'

'Yes, I expect so.'

It was like coming home, Annabel thought as the car glided smoothly along the gravel drive, its wheels making a satisfying crunching noise. The light had almost gone from the sky now but there was subdued lighting on the veranda and in the gardens, highlighting the rose beds and giving the old house a subtle beauty. Once again she was aware of the welcoming atmosphere as she followed Alice into the kitchen.

Jessie was there, sharing a pot of tea with Cook, Pam Bates and another young girl who was introduced as Sally.

'Sally has just started with us,' Jessie said. 'It's her first day so we're all having a cup of tea to get to know one another. Come and join us. We've put you in the room you shared with Georgie last time, Annabel. You'll be going home I suppose, Alice?'

'Yes. I haven't come to work this time, Jessie. In fact I've got some exciting news to tell you.'

She sat down at the kitchen table, accepting a cup of tea and a rock bun as she told them of her good fortune. Everyone was pleased about Alice's exciting news and Jessie teased her about becoming a famous film star.

'It will be sixpence to know you,' Cook said. 'Next time you come we'll be charging for your autograph.'

'If only,' Alice said and laughed, knowing they were all delighted for her good fortune. 'But it's an opportunity and I have to take it. We've been to see Beth and told her the news.'

'You won't be able to come for the holidays,' Jessie said. 'Don't worry, Alice. We'll see she has a good time.'

'Thank you,' Alice said. 'I know you and Mum will look after her. Belle is going to visit her sometimes so I don't need to worry.' She finished drinking her tea, then got to her feet. 'I should be on my way now, Mum is expecting me. I shan't see you tomorrow, Belle. I'm leaving on the early train to London.'

'I shall go later,' Annabel replied. 'But we'll talk before you leave for America.'

'Yes, of course.'

'Well, I must get on,' Jessie said. 'Could we have a word, Annabel? I'll come upstairs with you if I may?'

They left the kitchen together. Annabel looked at her uncertainly.

'You didn't mind my asking if I could stay?'

'You know you are always welcome here. I was surprised when you rang and a little uncertain, because Paul had told me he was coming down today. I saw him earlier. He wants to talk to you, Annabel. He has a meeting this evening but will be here at nine in the morning. I don't know how you feel about that?'

'I should like to see him,' Annabel said. 'We need to talk.'

'Yes, I gathered that from Paul's manner. Not that he told me anything and I didn't ask – but I knew that at Christmas he felt something for you and I thought you liked him?'

'At Christmas I was a silly young girl who didn't know her own mind.'

'And you're not now?'

'I've grown up the hard way.'

'I see.' Jessie nodded. 'I shan't ask questions, Annabel, but if you want to talk at any time I'm usually here. I hope you regard me as a friend you can trust?'

'Yes, I do.' Annabel smiled at her. 'I almost told you the night I rang. My marriage was a mistake, Jessie.'

'It was very sudden – or had you planned it before you came to us?'

'No, it wasn't planned then. It happened very quickly. I can't explain but it was wrong from the beginning. I shouldn't have married him. I should have waited. As I said, I've learnt the hard way.'

'I'm sorry.' Jessie touched her arm in sympathy. 'I shan't offer advice. We all have to work out our own problems, but you are always welcome here if you need a place to stay. I'll leave you now but I shall be in the study with Harry. Come and have a drink with us after you've unpacked?'

'Thank you. I appreciate your offer of a place of refuge, Jessie. I shan't forget.'

Alone in her room, Annabel unpacked the few things she'd brought with her and sat down at the dressing table to brush her hair. She hadn't expected Paul to be here but the thought of seeing him the next morning made her heart beat strongly as nervous excitement surged inside her. She desperately wanted to see him and yet what could she say to him? Perhaps more importantly, what would he say to her?

*

'You look lovely,' Paul said as she went out to greet him in the yard the next morning. She had seen him arrive from the landing window and was feeling as uncertain as a schoolgirl on her first day at school; she looked at him shyly, her cheeks warmed by his compliment. 'But then you always do.'

'Thank you. It was a surprise when Jessie told me you were here. I came down with Alice. We visited her daughter to tell her about Alice's new job in America. I thought she took it very well.'

They turned by mutual consent and began to walk in the seclusion of the rose gardens, needing to be alone as they talked. Paul looked at her, his expression thoughtful, a little reserved.

'Beth is a sweet child. A little serious but I suppose that comes from having been left by her mother so often.'

'You don't approve?'

'Not completely. Do you?'

'I think Alice has done the best she could for her daughter in the circumstances. She could have given her up for adoption but she kept her. I think that was brave.'

'Yes. But she could have stayed here, made a life for herself at Kendlebury. Jessie would have given her her job back after the child was born,'

'She wanted more. Is that wrong, Paul?'

Annabel stopped walking for a moment to gaze into his face. In the distance she could see a heron flying, its long legs like a banner beneath it. Ravens were calling from some tall trees, but otherwise the scene was one of peace and tranquillity.

'No, of course not.' His mouth twisted into a rueful smile. 'I didn't intend to argue about Alice. I wanted to talk about us.'

'What about us?' Annabel asked. 'I threw my chance of that away, didn't I? I should have run away with you when you kissed me at Christmas. Instead, I made a mess of my life.'

'I wasn't wrong then. You are unhappy?'

'Yes,' she said and sighed. 'Is it so obvious?'

'To me, yes. You've changed, Annabel.'

'I've grown up, I suppose.'

'It's more than that. I don't know – there's something in your eyes.'

Annabel decided to be completely honest; there was no point in hiding anything. 'I don't love Richard. I never did. He doesn't love me either. He married me because I am the right kind of wife and he is ambitious.'

'Why did you marry him? Did your mother force you?'

Paul's eyes sent little shivers down her spine; he was so intense, so obviously caught in some strong emotion that made her feel her answer was important to him. Taking a deep breath, she steadied her nerve and told him, not glossing over things as she had to Alice, but giving him every sordid detail. She wanted him to know what a fool she'd been and to understand why she had let herself be pushed into a marriage she had never wanted. When she had finished he was silent, looking at her so oddly that she wished she could take it all back. She shouldn't have told him! He would despise her now.

'Say something! Even if it's only that you despise me for being a fool.'

'I'm the fool, Annabel.'

'Because you thought I was worth loving?'

'No, of course not. I let you slip through my fingers because of my stupid pride.'

'It was hardly your fault, Paul. I was a silly, useless child—' she broke off as he grabbed her by the shoulders and then kissed her. It was a long, deep passionate kiss that left her shaken but in no doubt of his feelings. Her eyes were wide with shock as he let her go. 'Paul...'

'I know I had no right to do that but I had to stop you. It seemed as good a way as any.'

'It was.'

His serious gaze softened as it dwelt on her face.

'Let me see if I understand you. You were drinking champagne at the party because you were miserable – and in the main reason for that was because I hadn't answered your letter?' She nodded wordlessly. 'I didn't get your letter until after your wedding had been announced in the paper. When I read it I thought that perhaps you had regretted our parting – but you were getting married. And your letter wasn't clear. I wasn't sure what it meant.'

Annabel smiled ruefully. 'That's hardly surprising. I didn't know myself. I believed I might be falling in love with you but I wasn't sure then. I was too uncertain and silly to know my own heart, Paul. If we could have talked again... but you were angry and I didn't know how to reach you.'

'That doesn't explain why you went with him.'

'No, I know. How can I explain when I don't understand myself? I was just miserable. I was unhappy at home, tired of being nagged at by my mother, desperate because we had quarrelled. I had been drinking that evening, more than I was used to. I'd met Richard before and I thought he was exciting and attractive. No! Please don't look like that, Paul. As far as I knew I had killed any interest you had in me and I was too naïve to know what kind of a man he was. I know I was stupid, but believe me, I have paid for my mistake.'

'Does he hurt you?' Paul asked and looked grim, as she remained silent, reading her shadowed look as an affirmative. 'There were rumours about him when he was at Oxford. Nothing was proven but I knew someone whose sister killed herself after seeing him a few times, a friend of mine from way back. She was working as a waitress and I suppose he was just amusing himself with her. Robert blamed Hansen, said he'd hurt her in some way, but he had no proof, nothing that could put the responsibility on Richard.'

'He can be violent if he doesn't get his own way. He hasn't hurt me recently. I threatened to ruin his career if he did.' She nibbled at her lower lip, and then looked into Paul's eyes. 'I've locked him out of my bedroom, Paul.'

'How does Richard feel about that?'

'He is angry but he doesn't really care. He doesn't love me. All he wants is a docile wife to charm his friends.'

'You sound bitter – as if you hate him?'

'I don't exactly hate Richard. He means nothing to me.'

'Then leave him, Annabel. Make a new life for yourself.'

'With you, Paul?'

'Perhaps – if that's what you want. I love you but I wouldn't want to push you into another mistake. If we married in the future it would be because we both wanted it.'

'Oh, Paul.' Her eyes stung as she looked at him. 'I wish I could say yes. I wish I need never go back to Richard, that we could run away together this minute.'

'I'll take you anywhere you want to go, Annabel.'

'But I can't do that, Paul. Not just like that. Perhaps I'm a fool but I feel some responsibility.'

'You will be a fool if you let him ruin your life. You've told me he doesn't love you. Where is the sense in staying with him?'

She stared at him helplessly. 'There isn't any. I know that, Paul. Deep down, I know it, but we've only been married a few months. I can't walk out on him so soon. He would look a fool and he would hate that.'

'Are you afraid of him?'

'No, of course not.'

'Tell me the truth, Annabel.'

'Sometimes. Yes, sometimes I am afraid of him. I think…' she took a shaky breath. 'I think he may have done something terrible to a girl called Janie.'

'What makes you say that?' She explained the phone call and Paul frowned. 'If you're right Richard doesn't deserve your consideration, Annabel. You could even be in danger yourself – if you continue to defy him.' He moved towards her, a note of urgency in his voice. 'You have to think about leaving him, Annabel. You owe it to yourself. I knew there were stories about him, but this could mean the worst of those stories were true.'

'If the girl was badly hurt…' she faltered and stared at him.

'Or killed,' Paul said. 'It's a pity we can't find out more about this girl, Janie. The woman who telephoned didn't give you any more clues?'

'No – but I told Richard's friend Maurice Green and he dismissed it as spite. Richard was angry when he heard that I'd spoken to his friend. He said I should have told him.'

'Why didn't you?'

'I knew he would be angry.' Annabel shivered. 'I'm not sure why I told his friend either. There's something about Mr Green that makes me uncomfortable. He seems to be respectable, a successful restauranteur – but I think there's more to him. I think he and Richard are involved in things that might not bear the light of day.'

'What kind of things?'

'Gambling clubs – vice.' Annabel laughed and shook her head. 'It sounds so fantastic, doesn't it? I'm sure I'm mistaken, but I think I heard Richard warning him about a police raid at a club. I could have got it all wrong, of course.'

'No, that makes sense,' Paul said. 'I've heard whispers that back up what you've just told me, nothing concrete, of course. Richard would be very careful to keep that kind of thing under cover.'

'But why would he risk it? Surely it would ruin his political career if it got out?'

'As would the beating of a girl he used for his own pleasures,' Paul said. 'Perhaps that was why he needed a girl from the right background to marry, Annabel.'

'Yes...' She looked at him thoughtfully. 'It has crossed my mind. When we first met he wasn't looking to marry, and then at Christmas it was as if he had set out to trap me into marriage. I couldn't think why he would do that – unless he needed the respectability suddenly.'

'I would say Maurice Green knows more than a little of Richard's affairs. It might be a good idea to have him investigated, Annabel.'

'That might be dangerous, Paul. I think he could be ruthless if someone threatened him. I think Richard is a little afraid of him.'

'He probably has something on him, something incriminating,' Paul said and frowned. 'If I could bring you proof of their activities – proof beyond doubt that Richard isn't worth your consideration – would you leave him?'

'Yes. Yes, I would,' she said. 'I would leave him now if I could – but I was brought up to have a conscience, Paul. I suppose that sounds weak to you and perhaps it is, but I'm too much my mother's daughter.'

'Please understand that I'm not pushing you to marry me after divorcing Richard. I love you but I'm prepared to wait for you, Annabel.'

'Oh, Paul,' she said, and the tears were in her eyes. 'I do love you. I realised it when it was too late. I would give anything to go back to that night—'

He bent his head to brush his lips lightly over hers, quieting her.

'We can't go back, Annabel, much as we might both wish it – but we can go forward. I'm going to get some friends of mine to do a little digging into

Maurice Green and Richard. I'm warning you that you may be shocked by what they discover.'

'No,' she said. 'I doubt very much that I shall be shocked. It might be a relief to know the truth, Paul.'

'Then let's forget Richard and his nasty friends,' Paul said and smiled at her. 'We shan't have many opportunities to be together. Will you let me take you somewhere nice for lunch and then I'll drive you back to London?'

'Yes, please,' she said. 'Just for today we'll pretend that Richard doesn't exist.'

*

Richard was sitting in an armchair smoking a cigarette, a glass of whisky on the small wine table beside him. He shot her a look of annoyance when she entered and put down her overnight bag.

'What time do you call this?'

Annabel glanced at her watch, feeling guilty as she saw it was past ten. 'I didn't realise it would be quite so late. Besides, I didn't expect you to be here.'

'Obviously. Where have you been? Your train got in ages ago.'

'I've been having a meal with a friend.'

'Is that the actress you went to a nightclub with – or the man you met there?'

'What are you talking about?' Annabel said, feeling flustered. How could he know about that night? She hadn't told anyone. Had someone seen her there? 'I danced with a man certainly, but I didn't go there to meet him.'

'Are you sure about that?' Richard had risen to his feet. She was aware of him towering over her, menacing and powerful. 'I don't like being made a fool of, Belle. If I thought you'd been with a man I should have to teach you a lesson.'

'Of course I haven't,' Annabel replied, her head up now, prepared to lie for as long as she had to, defiant and angry. 'I'm your wife. If I wanted someone else I should leave you.'

'Don't even let the thought enter your mind,' Richard said, his gaze narrowed and angry. 'I would make you wish you had never been born.'

'You couldn't make me stay with you if I wanted to leave.'

The air seemed to crackle with tension around them.

'You think not?' There was something in his look at that moment that terrified her and her fear must have shown in her face because he smiled unpleasantly. 'Yes, you're beginning to realise now. I've been easy on you thus far, my dear. You are useful to me and I don't want to spoil that pretty face of yours but if you try to leave me I'll make sure no one else wants you. And I can get to him too if you play me false.' He reached out, drawing his finger down her cheek, sending icy shivers down her spine. There was no doubting he meant his threat.

'I have no intention of playing you false, Richard. I don't know who has been telling tales but it was merely a dance, nothing more.'

'You haven't been with him since that night?'

'I stayed at Kendlebury. Telephone Jessie and ask her if you don't believe me.'

'I shall believe you for now since you tell me,' he said, his smile making her feel cold all over. 'But I don't like you seeing this actress. You won't see her again. Do you understand me?'

'Alice is a friend. You can't tell me who I can have as my friends, Richard.'

His hand shot out, closing about her wrist, gripping so hard that it hurt. 'I am telling you not to see her. Ignore my warning and you will regret it. She isn't the sort of woman I want my wife to be seen with.'

Annabel didn't answer him. She had every intention of continuing her friendship with Alice and would see her again before she left for America, but there was no point in pushing Richard too far.

'If that's what you want,' she said and shrugged. 'But don't try to stop me seeing my other friends – and remember it's my brother's wedding next week.'

'I hadn't forgotten. I shan't be able to come with you, but I don't suppose that will bother you much.'

'Not at all,' she said, as brutally frank as he had been. 'The less I see of you the better, Richard. I've noted your threats but don't forget mine. If you value your career don't come near me. I've made friends these past months and I think you might regret it if I dropped a few hints.'

She walked away from him, going into the bedroom and locking the door from inside. Her heart was beating like a frantic war drum and she felt sick. Richard's threats had really frightened her this time, not only for herself but for Paul. She believed that Richard would try to harm Paul if she left him.

Once again she found herself wishing she'd accepted Paul's offer to take her away. If they went far enough perhaps they would be safe – and yet Paul had his business to think of. Could she ask him to risk everything for her sake?

Sitting on the edge of the bed, Annabel felt the despair wash over her. For a while in Paul's company she had managed to forget Richard and her wretched marriage, the mess she had made of her life. Being with Paul had been wonderful. She'd felt loved and respected, a proper woman again, all the things she never felt with Richard.

How she longed to be free of him! But he had warned her not to think of leaving him and when she faced the truth, Annabel knew that deep down she was afraid of Richard – afraid of what he might do if she pushed him too far.

There was nothing she could do for the moment. To walk out on her husband so soon after their wedding was unthinkable and would cause a terrible scandal. She was chained to him and there was no key to set her free. Paul was set on making enquiries into Richard's affairs, and she needed time to think. Her brother's wedding was imminent and a scandal could ruin it for him. She must wait a little longer, until Ben was married and Hetty had settled at her college. If Annabel rocked the boat too soon Lady Tarleton might keep her younger daughter at home.

It was all so difficult, Annabel thought. She should never have married Richard, but she had and for now all she could do was to live with the consequences.

But one thing she was determined about, she was going to see Alice before she left for America. No matter what Richard thought or said, he wasn't going to stop her seeing her friends.

*

'I'm so nervous now,' Alice said as they sat together in the small, discreet restaurant where Annabel had asked to meet for lunch. 'Supposing I fail? I shall have to come home with my tail between my legs and ask Jessie for a job in the teashop.'

'You're not going to fail,' Annabel said and smiled at her encouragingly. 'You're going to be a huge success and go on to star in fabulous shows in America.'

'If I do I shall take Beth to live out there,' Alice said. 'I'm going to hate leaving her, Annabel, but I have to take my chance – don't I?'

'Yes, of course you do,' Annabel replied and signalled to the waitress for the bill. 'I'm sorry but I must rush off, Alice. I'm expecting Richard home early this evening. He has an important function and I have to wash my hair before I get dressed.'

'Yes, of course. I know you're busy and it's good of you to promise to go down and see Beth when you can. You won't forget will you?'

'On my honour,' Annabel said and laughed. She stood up, moved round the table and kissed Alice's cheek, realising how close they had become of late and that she would miss her while she was away. 'I'm leaving for the country in the morning; it's my brother's wedding. You'll be on your way so I shan't see you again before you go. Send me a postcard occasionally.'

'Yes, I shall. Thanks for everything,' Alice said and watched as Annabel paid the bill on her way out. She looked around the restaurant, thinking how nice it was. Perhaps if she did well in the show she would be able to come to places like this more often and bring Beth. Picking up her bag she went to leave the restaurant, but as she did so one of the waitresses came after her and handed her a handkerchief. It wasn't the girl who had served them their tea, but another she had noticed clearing a nearby table.

'I think you dropped this, Miss. It was at your table.'

'No, it isn't mine,' Alice said as she looked at it. 'It might have been Mrs Hansen's perhaps.'

'I thought it was her,' the girl said, glancing over her shoulder as if she was afraid of something. 'But I wasn't sure. Would you give it to her please?'

'I'm not sure. Yes, all right,' Alice agreed, taking the pretty lace handkerchief. 'Just a minute...' As soon as she touched the handkerchief she knew there was something inside it. The girl shot her a desperate look and went back inside the exclusive restaurant. Alice lingered for a moment, looking at the small package inside the scrap of lace. It was an envelope with Annabel's name on it and done in a poor hand as if it had been scribbled hastily.

Why had the girl been so anxious to give Annabel this letter? Alice considered what to do with it. Should she take it round to her friend's apartment or pop it in the post to her?

Perhaps she ought to see what was inside the letter before she did anything? It was addressed to Annabel but there was no home address so the young waitress obviously didn't know it. She must have scribbled the letter in a hurry when she saw Annabel in the restaurant and clearly wanted her to have it, but supposing it was unpleasant? If it was some kind of a threat, maybe Alice ought not to pass it on. Now why had that odd thought popped into her head? Yet the girl had seemed so strange in her manner.

Alice walked a few paces up the road to a small park and sat down on a bench, opening the envelope. There was just one sheet of paper, actually the back of a restaurant bill, and the words on it were so shocking that Alice felt sick. Who would want to write such a letter to Annabel? Well, she knew the answer to that one, of course – but why?

Stuffing it into her coat pocket, Alice got up and went for a walk as far as the lake. What was she going to do about the letter now she knew the contents? Should she give it to Annabel or simply destroy it?

No, Alice decided as she began to walk home. If this letter was true it was valuable to the person concerned. Alice had had to work hard all her life and unless she was very lucky she would never have enough money to look after her daughter the way she wanted. But the information in this letter could be worth a lot of money. It might be worthwhile confronting the man it named while Annabel was away at her brother's wedding.

Of course she wouldn't have done it if Annabel had been happy, if she had loved her husband, but she didn't. Richard Hansen had made her unhappy. Alice's eyes gleamed with excitement suddenly. It would be a way of making him pay for being unkind to his wife and earn her a nice little sum into the bargain!

*

'I wish you happiness, Ben, you know I do,' Annabel said and kissed her twin, clinging to him for a few minutes as he thanked her for her wedding gifts of a beautiful Art Deco silver tea and coffee service for Helen and an elegant Rene Lalique bowl for Ben. It was the first chance they'd had to be alone since she'd arrived. Helen had gone upstairs to change out of her wedding gown into a smart grey travelling costume and a matching cloche hat with a red bow. 'You must be happy! One of us has to be.'

Ben looked at her pale, intense face and frowned. 'You aren't happy, are you, Belle? Hetty told me she thought something was wrong. Why did you marry him if you didn't love him?'

'It was a combination of all sorts of things,' Annabel said. 'But I didn't mean to worry you, especially today. It's just that if... I should leave him...'

'Of course I would understand,' her brother assured her at once. 'I wouldn't want you to stay with Richard if you are miserable, love. You must do whatever you think best – and don't bother about Mother either.'

'It won't be just yet,' Annabel said. 'I haven't made up my mind and besides, I want Hetty settled at her college before I do anything that might upset Mother.'

'You should think of yourself first. I wish I had time to talk to you, Belle, but I don't. Helen is coming down now. I have to go to her.'

'Yes, of course you must,' Annabel said and smiled. 'Don't worry about me, Ben. I shall be fine. Cross my heart.'

'You would say that,' he admonished with an affectionate smile. 'We'll meet when I get back from Paris. I'll come up to town and we'll go somewhere for lunch and have a really good talk. I haven't had time to think recently, but it should be better now that the wedding is over.'

'Yes, lovely,' she agreed and then gave him a little push as the appropriate gasps and noises heralded the bride's return.

After that, Ben was too busy to do more than wave at her as he left in a flurry of rice and confetti with his bride, who really did look rather pretty, Annabel thought generously as she stood in the drive and waved them off.

'Do you think he will be miserable?' Hetty said at her side in a hushed voice. 'I do. She thinks she can tell him what to do all the time and it's only because of the money. Ben has sold himself for five thousand a year.'

'I hope you didn't let him know you thought that?'

'No, of course not. Ben is a dear. I wouldn't hurt him for the world – but Helen isn't so nice. She throws a tantrum whenever she feels like it and Ben and Mother dance around her, doing everything to please her. I'm glad I shall be at college in a few weeks.'

'Has it really been that bad?'

'Worse,' Hetty said and pulled a face. 'Thank goodness Selina and Tom are taking me to France when Ben gets back. I shall be away for three weeks and then it won't be long before I leave this place for good.'

'For good?' Annabel was startled. 'You will come back for holidays, surely?'

'Not if I can help it,' Hetty said and looked stubborn. 'It was bad enough before Ben married her. I can't imagine what it will be like in the future.'

'But where will you stay when term is over?'

'With Selina or you,' Hetty said. 'I can come to you sometimes, can't I, Belle?'

'Yes, of course,' Annabel said, trying to sound confident. She wasn't sure where she would be in a few months' time, but she couldn't tell Hetty that now. 'You know I love you, dearest. Wherever I am, there will always be a place for you.'

Hetty looked at her curiously. Something in Annabel's tone had given her away and she would have questioned her further had not their mother approached at that moment.

'You're looking very well, Annabel,' Lady Tarleton said. 'I hope you intend to stay with us for a day or so?'

'For this evening at least,' Annabel replied. 'I do have several engagements in London, Mother, so I shall have to leave sometime tomorrow.'

'Well, really,' her mother replied sharply, giving her a sour look. 'Our friends have been looking forward to seeing you… now that you're married.'

Now that she was a politician's wife, of course, and had her picture in the papers every so often. Annabel smiled inwardly. It seemed that her mother thought that made her more important, a valuable asset at her tea and dinner parties. If only she knew the truth! A shudder ran through Annabel but she controlled it and smiled at her mother.

'Perhaps another time,' she said. 'When I'm not so busy. Unfortunately, being married to a politician doesn't leave me much free time, Mother.'

She felt an unworthy pleasure at the sight of her mother's expression of chagrin. Lady Tarleton had been used to having her daughter at her beck and call and her orders obeyed, albeit reluctantly at times, but now she was forced to accept that her wishes were no longer paramount.

'Well, I suppose you are useful to Richard,' her mother said. 'Such a dear man. It was a great pity he couldn't spare the time to come today.'

'Yes, wasn't it,' Annabel agreed innocently as Lady Tarleton shot her a suspicious glance.

Lady Tarleton had invited a few friends for a supper party at home after the hotel reception, and Annabel was pleased to see that Selina was amongst the guests.

'I was sorry not to have been at your brother's wedding,' Selina told her. 'But unfortunately Tom had a nasty chill that turned to pneumonia at the weekend and I've been almost permanently at the hospital until now. He seems a little better today and he insisted that I come this evening.'

'Mother mentioned that Tom wasn't well,' Annabel said, feeling genuinely upset by this news. 'But she didn't tell me it was so serious. I am so sorry, Selina. I am fond of Tom as you know.'

'Yes, my dear, I do know – and he has always been fond of you. I don't suppose you could find time to visit him while you're here, could you?'

'I was going back to London tomorrow,' Annabel said. 'But I certainly want to see Tom. I'll go tomorrow afternoon and take him some flowers and grapes.'

'That should cheer him up no end,' Selina told her and smiled. 'I am so pleased, my dear. Now, tell me, how are you? You look a little tired. Nothing wrong I hope?'

'No, of course not. I am perfectly well, thank you.'

'And happy?' Selina's eyes were serious as they lingered on her face. 'I wondered how you were getting on, Annabel.'

'Oh, very well, busy, you know.' Annabel knew this wasn't the time to confide in Selina, she had enough worries of her own. 'Hetty tells me you are taking her to Paris for a few days. Of course that will depend on whether Tom is well enough to leave.'

'Oh, he should be better by then,' Selina said. 'At least, I do hope so.'

The conversation was turned and Selina wisely asked no more questions, though she was certain Annabel was keeping something from her. She took her leave later in the evening, saying that she would telephone her brother at the hospital in the morning and tell him to expect a visit from Annabel.

'Well, really,' Lady Tarleton said when Annabel told her she was going to catch the train to Cambridge in the morning and perhaps stay overnight in a hotel before returning to London the following day. 'When I asked you to stay for a day or so, you said you were too busy.'

'I do have engagements, Mother, but I've decided to cancel dinner with my friend Laura. She will understand. Besides, Selina and Tom have been so good to us that I couldn't simply ignore them. I didn't realise that Tom had been so ill. You didn't tell me it was pneumonia and that he was in hospital.'

'There was nothing you could do. Really, all this fuss about nothing.'

'Tom could have died,' Annabel said, her expression becoming as cold as her mother's. 'I can't believe that you can be so unfeeling. Selina and Tom are some of our very best friends.'

'And I can't believe that you can speak to your own mother that way. Marriage certainly hasn't improved your manners.'

'Perhaps not,' Annabel replied. 'I'm sorry if you think me rude, Mother, but I happen to be very fond of both Selina and her brother. Goodnight. I think I shall go to bed now.'

'Annabel!' Lady Tarleton stared after her as she walked away but Annabel didn't falter. Nor did she look back.

Eight

'Of course I don't mind,' Laura said when she telephoned her from the railway station in Cambridge. 'Naturally you want to see your friend. It must be a very worrying time for his sister.'

'Selina and Tom are the best of friends,' Annabel told her. 'She would be devastated if anything happened to him, and I think I would too. He has been like a second brother to me and to Hetty. Laura, would you mind doing me a favour?'

'You know I'm always happy to help out when I can.'

'I've tried telephoning Richard three times at home. Last night and this morning, but I can't get through to him. I don't have an office number for him but I thought your husband might. Perhaps someone could let Richard know that I won't be home until tomorrow?'

'Yes, of course, my dear. I'm sure he can be contacted and given your message. Don't you worry about anything. Let me know if I can be of further help.'

'Thank you.' Annabel replaced the receiver, hesitated and then picked it up again. She dialled the number of Paul's flat in London and held her breath.

When he answered she almost put it down again, her heart racing with a mixture of excitement and fear.'

'Annabel?' he said, when she managed to say his name. 'What's wrong?'

'I shouldn't have phoned you.'

'Of course you should. I've been hoping you would.'

'I'm in Cambridge. I'm visiting a friend in hospital this afternoon. He has been very ill. I was supposed to go home today – I've been to my brother's wedding – but I decided to stay overnight.'

'Alone?'

'Yes, I'm alone.'

'Where will you be staying?' Annabel gave him the name of the hotel she had booked from her mother's home. 'I'll be there at around seven. We can have dinner and talk. I have a few things to tell you.'

'And I have some to tell you. Richard threatened to… he forbade me to see you or Alice.'

'We'll talk this evening. Don't worry too much, Annabel. Richard doesn't frighten me. If I had my way, you would leave him right now.'

'I'll see you this evening. I have to find a cab now or I shall miss some of my visiting time at the hospital.'

Annabel replaced the telephone. She left the railway station and found a cab waiting outside. Giving the driver instructions to stop at a shop she wanted to visit in the town centre before going on to the hospital, Annabel climbed inside.

The hospital was a Victorian building fairly central to the city and pleasantly situated. Patients would be able to see cherry trees in bloom from the windows of the upper wards at the right time of year, which must cheer them up a little, she thought as she went inside. The smell of antiseptic met her as she walked down corridors with shining floors and scrubbed gloss painted walls in dark cream and green. And Matron saw to it that the place was kept scrupulously clean.

Tom was in a small side ward that held only three beds. He was the only patient and was lying propped up against a pile of pillows with his eyes shut. She had been given permission to visit him by a rather prim and proper Sister, but was a little worried that she might be disturbing him, and did not speak immediately. However, he opened his eyes almost at once.

'I knew it was you,' he said and smiled. 'Selina sent a message that you were coming and I could smell your perfume. You always wear the same one and it is delightful, so fresh and delicate – like you.'

Annabel blushed. Tom had never paid her such pretty compliments in the past.

'Thank you. What a lovely thing to say.'

'I wish I had paid you more compliments,' Tom replied as she laid her gifts on his bedside cabinet and bent to kiss his cheek. 'You might have married me then instead of Hansen. Selina is worried about you, my dear. She thinks you are unhappy.'

For some reason Annabel found herself unable to lie as she sat on the edge of the bed and took the hand he extended to her. 'Please don't worry about me, Tom dearest. I may not be as happy as I would like to be but I shall work things out.'

'That's what I told Selina. You're not a child, Annabel, and you're stronger than some would imagine.' He smiled oddly. 'It's surprising how a brush with death clears the mind. I would never have dreamt of talking to you like this before. Now I realise that I should have done.'

'Yes, perhaps you should.'

'Would you have married me if I'd asked?'

'I might have done, but it wouldn't have been right for either of us, Tom. You are a very dear friend; I love you but I'm not in love with you. In the end that might have made you unhappy.'

'I would have been content with affection from you and you've always given me that. I've always loved you dearly. I'm too old for you, of course, but I wanted you to know that I love you, Annabel. Just in case something should happen.'

Annabel felt a catch at her heart. 'You mustn't think like that, Tom. You're over the worst now.'

'So they tell me.' He smiled at her. 'It was lovely of you to come and see me. I feel much better for it, my dear. You seem to have brought a breath of fresh air with you. It's difficult to breathe in here at times.'

'It does smell of carbolic,' Annabel agreed and laughed. 'Hospitals are not the nicest places to be, are they? Never mind, when you're better you will be able to take a lovely visit to Paris – think of all the flowers and the sunshine.'

Tom pressed her hand. 'There you are, you see, you've taken me out of here already. I should have married you a year ago, Annabel. We could have had some happy months together.'

'Yes, I think we might have been happy for a while,' she said. 'But I have met someone, Tom.'

'Someone you love?'

'Yes, I think so.'

'Then you should leave Richard,' he said, and looked at her urgently. 'He wasn't right for you, Annabel. I should have said something at the time but I didn't like to – now I want to, before it is too late. We should all snatch what happiness we can, my dear, sometimes at the cost of seeming selfish to others. I left it too late, but it isn't too late for you. Promise me you won't waste your life in regret.'

Something in his eyes compelled her to make the promise. He smiled and lay back against the pillows, closing his eyes. He seemed very tired and she wondered whether her visit was too much for him but as she tried to remove her hand, his fingers tightened around it.

'Not yet,' he said. 'Just sit here with me for a bit longer.'

'Yes, of course. As long as I'm not tiring you?'

'I would never be too tired to be with you,' he said, but his eyes remained closed and she knew he was very close to sleeping.

Annabel sat there for half an hour and then the nurse came to ask her if she would leave.

'He isn't strong enough for long visits at the moment,' she said. 'He will probably sleep for some time now.'

'Yes, I'll go,' Annabel said. Tom had released her hand as he slept and she stood up, then bent to kiss his cheek. 'Goodbye, my friend.'

She walked in silence from the ward, not asking the nurse the questions that trembled on her tongue. Common sense told her that Tom was very ill. Selina believed that he was over the worst and would be home soon, she could only pray that she was right.

*

Annabel met Paul in the hotel lobby and they went into the bar, finding a table in a corner to sit and have drinks before dinner. It was a quiet, old-fashioned place and they were the only people there for a start, though one or two others came in after they were settled.

'You said Richard threatened you?' Paul's gaze was intent, serious.

'Yes. Someone saw us dancing at that nightclub, Paul.'

'I'm not surprised. It is registered in Maurice Green's name but I have reason to believe that Richard is a sleeping partner – as he is in several other clubs, some of them far less respectable.'

Annabel stared at him, her stomach feeling slightly queasy. 'You're talking about gaming clubs, aren't you?'

'Amongst other things,' Paul said. 'I haven't found anything I can offer as proof yet, Annabel, nothing on paper that ties them together – but my informant is quite certain that they are partners in several ventures that operate near to or on the other side of the law.'

'Richard wouldn't be such a fool – would he? He must know that the slightest hint of that would ruin his career, and any chance he has of continuing in polite society. He would be ostracised if this got out.'

'I imagine the political career was designed to help them gain respectability,' Paul said. 'They've made a lot of money in the past from their nefarious activities and now they are probably trying to cover their tracks, open legitimate clubs that will eventually earn them even more than their illegal vice dens.'

'You think they will close the others down?'

'Or bury the ownership so deep that they can't be traced. They will set up a system of front men so that their own names are clean. It was just by chance that I knew of someone who had dealings with Maurice Green in the past. He was a known villain at one time but he has kept himself out of trouble for years and most people have forgotten that he used to run a protection racket.'

'I've read about something like that,' Annabel said. 'It means that businesses and clubs, restaurants, pubs, all have to pay to stop their premises being attacked, isn't that right?'

'Yes, that's right. Small shops, too, and even market stall owners have been targeted – that's how I knew about Maurice Green's activities. I have friends in Petticoat Lane and they've known about him for years. You can put the past behind you and think you've covered your tracks, but people have long memories. He might be able to bribe some members of the police and certain lawyers, even a judge or two, I've been told, but you can't keep the ordinary man's mouth shut – especially men who've stood up to bullies like those he employed.'

A little shudder ran through Annabel. No wonder Richard had threatened her. If he was involved in something like that he was more dangerous than she had ever dreamed.

'Richard told me he would make me sorry if I left him – and he said something would happen to you. I thought he meant he would ruin your business, but now I wonder…' She shook her head. 'Do you think Richard is capable of murder – are his friends?'

'You mean Maurice Green and his cronies?' Paul frowned. 'I suppose it's possible. Don't worry about me, Annabel. I can take care of myself. I grew up on the streets of London. I'm not afraid of Green or Richard – or their friends.'

'I'm afraid for you, Paul.'

'You mustn't be,' he said and reached across the table to take her hand in his. 'You have to think of yourself, my dearest. You shouldn't stay with Richard. He will hurt you badly one of these days. You haven't seen the worst of him yet.'

'I know…' Annabel drew a deep breath. 'Perhaps soon. When my sister is at Art College. It will cause such a scandal when I leave him, Paul. You don't know my mother. If she can't get to me she will punish my sister. College means so much to Hetty. I don't want to ruin things for her.'

'Can't I persuade you to leave him now? We could find a way to help your sister. If you were afraid of Richard we could go abroad, to America. I have friends there and we could start a new life together.'

'Oh, Paul,' she said and caught back a sob. 'I want that so much – but I can't walk out just like that. Even though you've confirmed what I suspected, I have to wait a little longer. For Hetty's sake.'

'I shan't try to persuade you,' Paul said, 'but if you're afraid for any reason just telephone me. I'll come and fetch you, at any time of the day or night. And you don't have to marry me if you don't want to. I'm there to help and protect you whatever you decide.'

She smiled at him, loving him for his unselfish attitude. 'I know and I do wish we could be together…' A sigh escaped her. 'I was talking to my friend Tom Brocklehurst this afternoon and he made me promise I wouldn't waste my life. He told me he had always loved me but never dared to ask me to marry him because he was too old for me. I think he believes he's going to die, Paul.'

'Didn't you tell me his sister thought he was over the worst?'

'Yes, but…' She shook her head as a chill went down her spine. 'Something… I don't know. Perhaps it was just being in that place, but it seemed to me that Tom was saying goodbye to me. He was so tired and then he went to sleep...'

'Pneumonia is a horrible illness,' Paul said. 'It does kill a great many of those who go down with it, but if the doctors caught it in time he should be all right. Don't be too sad, Annabel. He may recover.'

'He is a very dear friend,' she said. 'I'm fond of him but not in love with him. He said he wished he'd asked me to marry him but if I had I would probably have made him unhappy.'

'It would have been better than marriage to Richard.'

'Yes, it would,' Annabel said. A single tear was trickling down her cheek. She brushed it away and smiled at him. 'Oh, Paul, I do love you. I wish I were free to be with you.'

'You know I love you.' His fingers tightened around hers. 'Let me take you away – now, tonight?'

She shook her head regretfully. 'You don't know how much I wish I could say yes...' She raised her head and looked at him. 'But we could stay here tonight – together. I mean really together, Paul.'

His hand clasped hers so tightly that she almost cried out.

'You don't mean that? It isn't what you really want.'

'Yes, it is,' she said. 'I do mean it, Paul. I love you. I want to be with you. It will give me something to cling to, something to think about when Richard is being nasty to me.'

'Are you certain? Perhaps you should think about this, Annabel?'

'Thinking about it won't change the way I feel,' she said and laughed. 'But perhaps it isn't what you want, Paul?'

'Don't be a damned fool!' he said. 'You know I do!'

'Then stay with me tonight?'

'If you're sure – but not here,' Paul said. 'Go up and pack your things and I'll take you to a place I know. No one will know you there and we can be all alone.'

'I'll go up and pack my bag. I don't have much,' Annabel said. 'And then I'll settle the bill.'

'I'll do that for you.' Paul smiled at her. 'I love you, darling.'

'I know. I love you, too.'

*

'This is wonderful,' Annabel said as she turned in Paul's arms and he kissed her. 'I can feel the motion of the water moving the boat. Are you sure your friends won't mind us using it?'

'It's mine whenever I want it,' he replied and kissed her lingeringly on the mouth. 'I told you that I often come this way and Charles only uses the boat for a few weeks in the year. It's moored here all the time and I have my own key. I telephoned him while you were packing and he said it was fine for me to use it. In the morning I can get milk and something for breakfast from a farm just across the way. And I'll take you home in my car.'

Annabel had been surprised when he'd brought her to the houseboat moored at the side of the river in a quiet spot. It was peaceful, almost idyllic with the willows lapping the edge of the water, and so much nicer than the hotel room she'd booked in Cambridge where the decor was shining mahogany and brass, very elegant and modern. And it was far less embarrassing than having to go through all the pretence of booking in at another hotel.

'I'm glad you brought me here,' she said, reaching up to run her fingers through his hair. It was strong and wiry to the touch, rather like him, she thought. But Paul was also gentle, his loving as tender as Richard's was cruel – but she didn't want to think about her husband now. 'It's so peaceful and romantic.'

'I didn't want to make love to you in a hotel bedroom for the first time,' Paul said and stroked her back as he smiled at her. 'That's so sleazy and it isn't for us, Annabel. I love you. I don't want a hole in the corner affair with you. I want to marry you. I want to be with you for the rest of my life.'

'I want that too,' she whispered, kissing his chest, her fingers moving in the dark hair. 'I didn't know how happy I could be until now, Paul. In three weeks' time Hetty goes to Paris with Selina. I'll leave Richard then. We could go to Paris, talk to my sister there and then…' She kissed him. 'I don't know, Paul. You will be giving up so much for me. Your business is here – your friends…'

'None of that is important compared to you,' he said. 'You are the woman I love. If being in America means you'll feel safer that's where we'll go – I can come back sometimes if I need to. I told you, I can look after myself. I have friends too: the kind of friends who could warn Richard off if he became too much of a nuisance. It isn't something I would do unless forced to, but I'm not going to let him make your life a misery, my love.'

'Oh, Paul,' she murmured, her breathing uneven as he pulled her closer, his strong body throbbing against hers, throbbing with the desire they both felt. 'I do love you so very much.'

Making love with Paul was beyond anything she had ever dreamt, the pleasure, the sensuality, and the rushing desire that consumed them both as if they were on fire. Their bodies fitted together as if they had been made for one another. The sensation of loving was so exquisite, so delightful, that she felt she would never have enough of him, her body was limp with exhaustion as they lay quiet at last, but still entwined. She felt as if she never wanted him to let her go.

*

The flat was empty when Annabel let herself in. She sighed with relief, glad that she had cut the day short even though she had been reluctant to part from Paul.

'I don't want Richard to suspect anything,' she told him. 'Especially not now – after last night.' Richard would go wild if he knew where she'd been, what she'd done, Annabel thought. But there was no reason for him to find out.

She went into the bathroom and ran herself a bath, sinking in to it with pleasure and closing her eyes as she relived the hours she had spent in Paul's arms. It was the most wonderful night of her life. She would never, never forget it, always treasure the memory, even if… but she would not let herself think that way. She was going to leave Richard. In three weeks.

She had made up her mind. Everything was settled with Paul. In three weeks Hetty would be in Paris with Selina and Annabel would be free to leave

Richard. Hetty was going straight to her college afterwards and could resist Lady Tarleton's demands to return home if she wished.

She felt slightly guilty knowing that she was breaking marriage vows that she had taken such a short time before – but in truth she had already broken them with Paul. Leaving Richard was the inevitable conclusion to what she had done the previous night. There was no going back. Nor did she want to change her mind. She wished that she could have stayed with Paul and not come back at all, but she hadn't wanted to spoil things for Hetty. Her sister would have the holiday in Paris and perhaps Lady Tarleton would have calmed down by the time she returned.

Annabel decided she wasn't going to feel guilty any more. Richard had bullied her into marrying him, and she didn't owe him anything. It was his own fault that she had come to hate him. After the way he'd treated her, he didn't deserve anything more from her – especially if what Paul believed was true.

*

'It's nice to see you, Mrs Hansen,' the porter said as she went down to collect the evening paper some days later. 'If you'd rung I'd have brought this up to you.'

'It's no trouble to come down,' Annabel told him with a smile. 'How are you, Fred – and the family?'

'I'm fine,' he replied. 'The wife has had a bit of a cold recently but she's muddling along. We'll all be better for a bit of sunshine. It hasn't been very nice this week, has it?'

'No, not all. What you want is a nice trip to France to warm you up,' Annabel said. 'My sister is going soon for a visit.'

'That's nice,' he replied. 'You should get away more yourself. Your husband works too hard.'

'Yes, he does,' Annabel agreed. 'He has been late every night this week.'

She didn't add that she was thankful for it. She'd hardly seen Richard since she came back from Cambridgeshire, and she was glad. She was counting the hours until Hetty went to France with Selina, counting the days until she was free.

She went back upstairs, going into the small kitchen to make herself a pot of tea. Carrying it back into the sitting room, she sat down and opened her paper. There was a story about some women taking the plunge in the Serpentine wearing bright coloured bathing suits that held Annabel's interest for some minutes, then she turned the page and was caught by a headline.

'Actress found dead in river. Murder suspected.'

Annabel stared at the short article for some time, too stunned to really take in what she was reading. They were talking about Alice – but they couldn't be. It must be someone else with the same name! Of course it was. Alice had gone off to America to be in a musical on Broadway. Yet that was her name… her description… and it said that she had been due to leave for America some days ago but hadn't shown up for the meeting with the friends with whom she had arranged to travel that day.

Her body had been pulled out of the river and apparently she had been beaten before being strangled and dumped in the water at a lonely spot. Her body might not have been found for ages had a fisherman not caught her on his hook. It was thought she had been in the water a matter of some days.

Annabel was stunned, completely numbed by what she was reading. How could this be? Alice should be in America. She should have been on her way to fame and fortune instead of lying dead on a mortuary slab. It was shocking, unfair – unbelievable.

Why would someone want to kill her? Alice had never harmed anyone in her life. And what was going to happen to her daughter? Beth, poor little Beth, she would be so terribly hurt. Someone would have to tell her that her mother was dead.

But surely it must be a mistake. It couldn't be true. Yet she knew that it was. Annabel read the article twice more, then picked the phone up and telephoned Paul. He wasn't at home and she remembered him saying he would be going up north on business for a week or two.

'I'll be back by the time you need me,' he'd told her. 'And if you need help in the meantime you can telephone a friend of mine.'

He'd given her a number she could ring but Annabel didn't think she wanted to talk to anyone else about this. She laid the paper down and picked up her cup, sipping at her tea, which had started to go cold. She was shivering, feeling sick and uneasy as she remembered Richard warning her that she would be sorry if she disobeyed him by meeting Alice again. And of course she had, at that restaurant – but he couldn't know that. Unless he was having her followed?

Surely Richard couldn't have had anything to do with Alice's murder? Annabel was letting her imagination carry her away. Her husband was a bully and she hated him – but was he a murderer?

No, no, she couldn't let herself believe that, for then she would have been the cause of her friend's death.

*

Annabel was still sitting on the sofa when Richard walked in. She looked up, startled, and then realised that they were supposed to be dining with friends that evening.

'I thought you would be ready,' Richard said irritably. 'Have you forgotten we're going out? I need the bathroom now. We can't both get ready together.'

'Alice is dead,' she replied, heedless of his quick frown. 'You remember the actress you forbade me to see again? She has been murdered.'

'What has that got to do with anything?' Richard asked, going to pour himself a glass of whisky. 'If you want a bath you'd better be quick about it.'

'I don't. I'm not going with you this evening. You can tell them I'm ill – whatever you like. I'm not going anywhere with you ever again. She got to her feet. I'm finished with you, Richard. I'm leaving you.'

'To go with your lover I suppose?'

'No, of course not,' she lied automatically, aware now that she had aroused his anger. 'I haven't got a lover.'

'Haven't you?' Richard's mouth curved back in a sneer. 'Where did you go the night you were supposed to have stayed in Cambridge?'

'What do you mean?' The colour drained from Annabel's face. 'Laura told you – I went to visit Tom

Brocklehurst in hospital and then stayed at a hotel for the night.'

'You could have caught a late train home.'

'I preferred not to travel too late at night. Besides, you were at the House, Richard.'

'Actually, I wasn't,' he said. 'I gave it a miss and came home early – about nine. The telephone rang. It was your friend Selina. She said she'd rung the hotel and you weren't there so she thought you might have come home. When I told her you were staying in Cambridge over night she tried to cover for you and said she must have got the name of the hotel wrong, but I knew she was lying. I telephoned them myself and asked to speak to you. I was told that you had changed your mind – and that a gentleman had settled the bill.'

'You're making that up...' Annabel ran her tongue over lips that had suddenly become dry. 'It's because of Alice, isn't it? You want to pick a quarrel so that I shall forget about it, but I shan't. What did you do to her, Richard – or did you pay someone else to do it for you?'

'You're talking nonsense,' he muttered but she had seen something in his eyes, a momentary flicker of fear, and knew she was not mistaken. 'I don't even know your friend, Alice.'

'You could have had her followed. It would be easy enough for you, Richard.'

'I asked you about the night you stayed in Cambridge.' Richard had recovered himself and came towards her, his hand shooting out, gripping her wrist so tightly that it made her cry out in pain. 'This is nothing to what you're going to get. I know you went with him – Paul Keifer – that's his name, isn't it? I've been finding out about him, Annabel, and I know all I need to know. Some people I employ will shortly be paying him a visit; just a friendly little visit to warn him off. Nothing too terrible will happen to him this time – but if you go on seeing him he could end up in the river like your actress friend.'

'You wicked devil!' she cried. 'How dare you threaten Paul! I shan't let you get away with this. I'm going to the police. I'll tell them it was you; that you killed her.'

'They will laugh at you,' Richard said, a flicker of triumph in his eyes. 'I was miles away at a party when she was killed. You were with me, Annabel. You'll be able to testify on my behalf as a good wife should.'

'I know you had her killed,' she cried, losing all caution now as she lunged at him, striking out with her nails, wanting to hurt him as she was hurting inside. Alice was dead, her friend, the mother of Beth. Poor little Beth! How would she take it when she was told her mother was never coming back? 'I hate you, Richard. You're evil...'

'You would have a hard time proving it,' Richard mocked, catching her wrist as she lunged at him, gripping it so tightly that she cried out in pain. 'That slut deserved what she got. She tried to blackmail me. She had a letter she thought would incriminate me, and she wanted money or she was going to give it to the police.'

'I don't believe you! Alice wouldn't do that…' Annabel cried but there was something in Richard's manner that told her it was true. He was gloating over what he'd done. 'You are an animal. A monster!'

'She was just a greedy fool. I taught her the error of her ways. And now I am going to teach you a few lessons – things I should have attended to weeks ago. By the time I've finished with you, you won't be telling tales to anyone.'

Annabel fought him as he dragged her into the bedroom. She fought him as he ripped her dress away and then thrust her back on to the bed. She fought him as he hit her repeatedly across the face, and she went on fighting him as he raped her.

She had as much chance of stopping him as a fly. He was cold, almost clinical, showing little sign of anger as he humiliated her. Indeed, if anything he seemed to feel pleasure as she bit and kicked and struggled, even laughing as she threw every insult she could think of at him. But at last she was defeated and lay on the bed staring at the ceiling as he left her.

She was aware of him standing there, staring down at her.

'Well, you certainly won't be going anywhere this evening,' he said and held a handkerchief to his cheek where her nails had succeeded in scoring the skin. 'You've drawn blood you little she-cat. You fought better than your friend. I had her too before I let them get rid of her. All she could do was weep and beg me to forgive her and let her go.'

Annabel was silent, knowing that he was taunting her, trying to make her weep, but she wouldn't cry while he was there.

'The problem is what do I do with you, now? Maurice wouldn't take kindly to it if he knew that I'd had you disposed of the way Alice was. No, he likes you, can't see why but he does. Maurice isn't a man to be crossed so we'll have to keep him sweet, won't we, my pet?' Annabel didn't answer and he stared at her thoughtfully. 'You should have tried the cold treatment earlier. It might have saved you. You see, I respect you when you're a lady, Belle, but when you come down to my level, you're just another whore.'

Annabel refused to answer, and after a moment he turned away, locking the door behind him. She heard him making a telephone call. Presumably he was cancelling their dinner appointment. Her nails hadn't dug deep enough to scar him, but the mark was livid for the moment and he obviously didn't want to leave her behind and present himself with the evidence of their quarrel on his face.

She closed her eyes, refusing to let herself think about what had happened. It had been horrible and every time Richard touched her it made her want to vomit. She wouldn't think about it now. She made no attempt to move, certain that he hadn't finished with her yet, wondering what he would do next. He couldn't do much worse unless he was going to kill her after all.

'I told them you were ill,' he said, coming back into the room a few minutes later. 'I pretended to be concerned and begged them to forgive me because I couldn't leave you. I'll have to make some excuse for a couple of days until these scratch marks heal a bit. The thing is – what am I going to do with you? I can't have you running to Maurice or the police. I'd rather the police than Maurice actually, but that's neither here nor there. So I think we had better make another bargain, Annabel. I'll apologise for what I did earlier and promise it won't happen again – as long as you behave yourself.'

His rage seemed to have left him, and he was calm, controlled, seeming as if he hardly realised what he had done, or thought it unimportant.

'I would rather you killed me than have to go on living with you.'

'It would be a pleasure to oblige you,' Richard murmured silkily. His voice sent shivers down her spine. 'I might do it yet if you cause me too much trouble.'

Annabel sat up against the pillows, some of her earlier defiance returning. 'Why don't you do it now? Or haven't you got the guts? Do you always get someone to do your dirty work for you?'

'I killed Janie without meaning to,' Richard told her. His normality chilled her. It was as if he were discussing the weather. 'She was a whore just like you, Belle, only I paid her by the hour. She got a bit out of hand and I slapped her about that night. She died and Maurice got rid of her for me. He has held that over for me for a while now – that's why I found some people to do special things for me. I pay them and they keep their mouths shut or else. They know the score. I couldn't get rid of Maurice. He is too clever for that.'

'He knows too much about you and your business.'

'Your friend has been poking his nose into my business I suppose? Perhaps I should get rid of him.'

'Do that and I'll tell everything I know. The police won't laugh when I tell them about your dirty little business ventures…'

'No, perhaps not,' Richard said thoughtfully. 'So I'll make a little bargain with you. You keep your mouth shut and stay away from Paul Keifer and I'll let him live.'

'Paul can take care of himself,' Annabel said defiantly, though she was feeling sick inside. 'I'm going to leave you, Richard. I won't live with you.'

'No, perhaps it wouldn't work for the moment. Laura would see something was wrong and you might tell her. I can't risk that.'

'I'll go away somewhere.'

'To your friends at Kendlebury?' Richard smiled and shook his head. 'Oh no, my dear, that wouldn't do. Keifer has a workshop there – it's where you met him, isn't it? Don't worry. I'll think of something. For the moment I shall lock you in your room. I'll come back in the morning and we'll talk things over. If you've come to your senses I might send you abroad for a while. I could tell everyone you've been ill and need some sunshine.'

'Why don't you just leave me here to starve?'

'Don't tempt me,' he said, eyes glittering. 'Believe me, if it weren't for Maurice I might just do it. He would want to know where you were, Belle.'

She didn't answer him and after another minute or two he went out, taking the key and locking the door behind him. She heard him moving about in his own room for a while and then the front door of the apartment slammed and she knew he had gone.

For a moment Annabel sagged with relief. The tears of self-pity were very close, but she had no time to indulge in them now. She would cry when she was away from here, when Richard could not come back and find her.

Getting up, she went over to the wardrobe and took a spare key from the jacket pocket of her favourite suit. She had placed it there after her return from Cambridge, afraid that something like this might happen one day. Then she began to move about the room, throwing a few things into a small bag. She wouldn't take much with her. She had a little money saved and she could buy what she needed when she was ready.

She went into the bedroom and splashed her face with cold water, then applied a thick make up that she had bought for an emergency like this. It didn't completely cover the bruises but it made them less noticeable. Picking up her bag, she ran down the stairs. Fortunately, the porter was talking to someone and didn't notice her leaving.

Outside in the cool night air, Annabel began to walk fast. She wasn't sure where she was going. She couldn't go to Paul because Richard would come after them and he would have Paul killed. She loved Paul too much to risk his life. She would write to him explaining what had happened and why she had decided to disappear, but she wouldn't tell him where to find her. She couldn't tell anyone in case Richard found out.

Where was she going? Annabel had no ideas at the moment. She only knew that she had to get away, away from Richard and from London.

Nine

'Your key, sir. The room is exactly as you ordered with an adjoining bathroom. Ben will take your cases up. I hope you and Mrs Jackson have a wonderful stay with us.'

'Thank you, Mrs Tarleton,' the man said, giving her a broad smile. 'Me and the wife have been looking forward to this no end. It's our first time in the Lake District, you see.'

'It's our fortieth wedding anniversary,' Mrs Jackson put in, clearly excited. 'So Ted thought he'd spoil me.'

'She's worth spoiling,' he said and winked at Annabel as the youth came to pick up their cases. 'Nay, lad, you can't carry all them by yourself. Give me that big one and you take the others. By god, I reckon she's got the kitchen sink in here.'

Annabel smiled as the little party trooped off up the stairs. She had been working in the small, exclusive hotel for almost three months now and had discovered that she had a flair for looking after the guests. They seemed to like talking to her as much as she enjoyed talking to them, and she spent most of her day telling people where to look for the various attractions they had come to see.

Annabel had used her own name when she took this job more in defiance than anything. She'd left Richard but she wasn't going to deny her identity, nor was she going back to him if he found her, though she doubted his pride would let him search for her. Even so, for the first few weeks she had been nervous, half expecting Richard to walk through the front door and demand that she return to London with him. It hadn't happened and she had begun to feel more settled, enjoying her work more and more as each day passed. Oh, if only she'd had the courage to do something like this at the beginning! To just leave home and find herself a job rather than giving into Richard's blackmail. She might even now be Paul's wife.

For a moment she was swamped by dreams of what might have been, of a bright tomorrow, a future that would hold the kind of happiness she had never known. A happiness that was now denied her by the terrible secrets she carried inside her.

For a moment Annabel was overwhelmed by sadness. If only she could forget Paul, as she must, and that wonderful night she had spent in his arms. He was constantly in her mind, keeping her sleepless for hours. But she had made her decision to disappear and there was no going back on it – for Paul's sake.

She would rather endure her enforced loneliness than risk his life.

'You look very pensive, Annabel?'

'I was just thinking about the weekend, Mary.' She blushed slightly as she met the young woman's curious gaze, wondering what Mary would think if she knew what was on her mind.

Mary Foster was the wife of the hotel owner and it was she who had taken Annabel on when she turned up in answer to the advert she'd seen in a newspaper, even though she had no references and very little luggage. Somehow they had taken to each other from the start and their friendship had progressed as the weeks passed. Annabel sometimes wondered what Mary thought when one of her secrets became known, for she could not hide the fact that she was carrying a child for long.

'I'm going to take Beth out for tea on Sunday as you know, and I was wondering what to take her as a present.'

'You spoil that child,' Mary said, but without censure. 'Sending her letters, presents and cards almost every week.'

'Her mother was my friend,' Annabel said. 'Her fees at that school are paid until the end of the winter term but after that I'm not sure what will happen. I went to see Beth just after Alice died and she begged me not to desert her.'

Mary nodded. She hadn't been told all the details, she was sure, but she did know that Annabel had been through some kind of emotional trauma. She had been told of a friend's sudden death and that her new employee had left her husband because of a quarrel, more than that she had not asked, believing that Annabel would tell her anything she wanted her to know.

'Surely Beth has some relatives?' Mary asked now, wondering why Annabel seemed to believe the child was her responsibility.

'Yes. She has a grandmother,' Annabel said. 'I might go and see Mrs Rawlings this weekend, to ask her what she intends to do with Beth after Christmas.'

What Mary didn't understand was that the nature of Alice's death had made Annabel feel responsible. She hadn't been able to tell anyone that, could never tell of the terrible secret that weighed so heavily on her mind, even to Beth's grandmother, who was naturally stunned and grieving over her daughter's death.

'Why?' she'd asked Annabel when she'd visited her before going to see Beth the first time. 'Why would anyone do that to my little girl?'

Annabel had found it impossible to answer. How could she tell Mrs Rawlings the truth without going to the police – and how could she go to the police with her story? They would never believe her. She didn't have any proof, or anything against Richard that would stand up in court. It would only cause a huge scandal and endanger Annabel's own life, and perhaps Paul's. All she could do was to make amends in her own way as best she could.

Annabel had visited Beth after going to see Alice's mother, because Mrs Rawlings wasn't up to breaking the news to the child.

'You're not thinking of paying her school fees, are you?' Mary asked after a moment, because Annabel had seemed lost in thought.

'Unfortunately, I can't afford to at the moment,' Annabel said. 'But I want to help if I can. I could probably help towards the fees if that's what Beth wants.'

'She isn't your responsibility, Annabel.'

'No, perhaps not, but I promised her mother I would look after her and I shall as much as I can. Besides, she's a lovely child and I'm fond of her for her own sake, Mary. You would like her. Perhaps one day I'll bring her for a visit.'

'You're thinking of staying with us then?'

It had been agreed between them that Annabel would come for a few months to help out through the busy season. Mary had since hinted that she would like it to become a permanent arrangement, but Annabel hadn't taken her up on this because she hadn't been sure it was a good idea to get too settled in one place. If Richard was having her traced it could be dangerous. And there was the question of what to do once her child was born.

'I should like to stay for as long as I can, Mary.'

But would Mary want her once her condition became obvious? As time went by she might become more of a liability than a help to her employers. She wasn't sure what she would do then; there was no one she could turn to, because to do so might bring them into danger.

'You know we would love to have you.'

Mary was a warm, genuine person and something in Annabel's face when she arrived on that sunny morning in early July had warned her that the girl had suffered a terrible experience. She told her husband that she trusted and liked Annabel, even though there was clearly some mystery about her, and he trusted his wife's instincts sufficiently to take her on.

Mike Foster soon realised what a treasure he had in his new receptionist. Annabel was clearly from a good background, that much was evident from the way she carried herself and her speech, and her manners were excellent. She had just the right amount of authority mixed with a natural friendliness and it seemed that nothing was ever too much trouble for her. When she wasn't behind the counter, she was checking the sitting rooms to make sure they were tidy, finding guests' mislaid belongings and returning them, and had even turned her hand to bed making when necessary. Mary said she arranged flowers better than anyone they had ever employed.

'If I can, I shall stay,' Annabel promised impulsively. 'I'm happier here than I've ever been, Mary.'

'And that,' Mary said to her husband later in the day, is the saddest thing I've ever heard. 'It just shows she must have had a terrible life, doesn't it?'

'Well, it certainly sounds that way,' he said. 'But you mustn't get too fond of her, love. You never know how long she will stay…'

Annabel went for a walk when her duties were done for the day. She was usually off from six in the evenings. Mike Foster took over reception himself then for a few hours, and there was an elderly night porter who dozed in the hall from midnight until early morning.

They were just a short distance from the shores of the nearest lake, a large, beautiful, old rambling stone house built into the shelter of the hills, out of sight of the main roads and perhaps a little isolated for some. It was, however, very popular with those who knew it and guests returned every season to stay with the Fosters.

'The house belonged to my parents,' Mike told her when she first started to work for them. 'They started off taking a few guests to help with their income, and then, when it came to me, I decided to turn it into a hotel. We're closed in February, just for a month so that we can spruce the house up a bit, and then we have it to ourselves, but for the rest of the year we share it with our guests – most of whom have become friends over the years.'

It was a happy, friendly atmosphere, much like it had been at Kendlebury the Christmas Annabel stayed there, and she felt at home with her employers and their staff. She had been asked out by the chef, Keith Rivers, who was a man in his middle thirties, and a bit of a flirt, if Annabel was any judge, but in no way a threat. She had turned down his offer to take her to the cinema in the neighbouring town, but he was still just as pleasant to her when they met. As were all the others who worked in and around the hotel.

Annabel had no intention of going out with anyone, though Keith wasn't the only one to ask her. The young man who delivered their post in his van along with groceries from the village shop had hinted that he would be interested in taking her somewhere nice one evening, but she had thanked him and told him she was too busy for the moment.

She wasn't exactly afraid of going out with a man, though once when Mike had touched her arm inadvertently, she had felt cold shivers at the nape of her neck and recoiled from him. He'd given her an odd look but hadn't said anything. Annabel had asked Mary to apologise for her later.

'It's just that I don't like to be touched,' she'd said, not able to meet Mary's eyes. 'It isn't Mike, please don't think that. It's just something that happened before I came here...'

'Would you like to talk about it, Annabel?' Mary was sympathetic. 'Sometimes it helps to get things off your chest.'

'I couldn't at the moment,' Annabel replied. 'Perhaps one day – but for the moment I'm trying to forget.'

It wasn't easy to forget Richard's brutality to her that last night. The memory was there, lingering at the back of her mind, leaving a nasty taste in her mouth. It would be all right soon, she told herself. She just needed time to get over the humiliation of being used that way, to heal her spirit.

And now there was the child growing inside her. She hadn't been certain at first that her feelings of sickness in the morning meant anything in particular. Other women had talked about extreme nausea during the first months of pregnancy, but Annabel's symptoms were very mild. She was lucky, she supposed, for if they had been worse she might not have been able to do her work properly.

The worst of her problems, the one that haunted her thoughts night and day, was whose child was she carrying? Was it Paul's – or had Richard planted his seed inside her the night he raped her?

At first she had thought that if the child were Richard's she would want to tear it out of her body, but then, as the first horror began to subside, she realised that the child was hers. It did not truly matter who had fathered her baby, it was hers now. She must love it and protect it, for it would never know its father.

Annabel drew a deep breath, feeling her doubts slough off her as she walked, refreshed by the peace and solitude around her. The air up here in these hills and mountains was sweet enough to heal any ills, Annabel thought as she stood and gazed down on the lake, which was still some distance away. Too far for her to walk there and back before it got dark, but she liked to come here and watch the sun as it began to set over the lake, sinking towards the still waters in a blaze of fire.

A little sigh escaped her as she thought about Paul. If he could be here with her, by her side, then she might be able to put all the bad dreams out of her head. But she couldn't see Paul, mustn't contact him, even though she sometimes felt so alone.

She had written to Hetty, telling her that she had left Richard and would contact her when she could. She had sent the letter to Selina together with another to her friend, hoping that Tom was better and out of hospital, and asking that no details of her letters should be given to either her mother or Richard.

Jessie was the only one of her friends who had some idea of where Annabel was living, though even she had no address. Annabel had rung Jessie once or twice, just to tell her she was well, and to pass messages about Beth to Mrs Rawlings, but Jessie had promised that she would not give her away.

'Paul is very worried about you,' Jessie had told her the last time she rang. 'Won't you please see him, Annabel?'

'Paul understands why I can't see him,' Annabel told her. 'Please try to understand, Jessie. I'm not being selfish. I don't want to hurt him. It's for Paul's sake that I can't see him. It would be too dangerous. I can't tell you more than that, believe me, it's best that you don't know.'

Annabel had wondered if there might be something in the papers about her disappearance, but she saw most of the nationals daily because they were delivered for the guests, and so far she had not noticed anything. Richard must have told his friends she'd gone abroad for the sake of her health.

Annabel had considered sending a letter to Laura, because she knew that her friend might worry, and she hated letting her down – but Laura might tell her husband and then Richard would know. She was afraid of making him angrier than he must already be and preferred to let things stay as they were. The last thing she wanted was for Richard to come looking for her.

Annabel sighed again as she turned away and began to walk back towards the hotel. She would write some letters that evening and post them in Torquay when she was down there at the weekend to visit Beth at her school. The postmark was one she had used before and gave no clues as to where she was living.

Would she ever be free to see her friends and those she loved again? Sometimes she thought that this loneliness would go on forever – the loneliness of not being able to see Paul.

*

Beth had seemed disappointed when Annabel told her she might not be able to continue at the exclusive boarding school after Christmas, but not upset.

'I suppose I can live with Granny and go to school there,' Beth said. 'I don't mind if that happens,

Annabel – but you will still come and visit me, won't you?'

'Yes, of course I shall,' Annabel agreed, though it would make things more difficult for her because she might accidentally meet Paul while she was there, although Jessie said he didn't often visit these days.

'Annabel...' Beth said a little uncertainly as they were walking. They had been out to tea and were strolling in the park afterwards. 'You told me Mummy had an accident... can you tell me exactly what happened to her?'

Annabel had hoped this wasn't going to happen, but now she knew that she had to tell her the truth. Beth was nearly ten years old and you couldn't lie to her because she might discover the truth for herself one day.

'Someone hurt your mother,' Annabel said. 'I don't know how it happened, no one knows, not even the police, though they are still making enquiries.'

'Do you mean someone killed her? One of the girls told me she was murdered but I wasn't sure if she was just being a pig – some of the girls make up things like that. They say it even if it isn't true. They told one new girl that her father had been strangled and she had nightmares for weeks – and it wasn't true at all.'

Looking at her, seeing her anxiety but also the way she was being brave and facing up to her fears, Annabel knew it would be wrong to lie.

'I'm sorry, Beth, but it is true about your mother. I told you it was an accident because I didn't want to hurt you, but now you've asked I think it's best if you know. You mustn't worry too much. I think it must have happened very quickly. I don't think she would have known much about it.'

'That's what I wanted to know,' Beth said, her face very pale. There was a glimmer of tears in her eyes but she didn't let them fall. 'I didn't want her to be frightened or hurt.'

'Oh darling,' Annabel said. Beth was trying so hard to be brave and it was obvious she didn't understand why anyone would want to hurt her mother. How could she? Annabel found it hard to cope with herself. 'It isn't wrong to cry. I've cried lots. I loved your mummy too.'

She knelt down on the grass and put her arms around Beth, hugging her as they both shed tears. It was a while before Beth was comforted, but then she raised her head, still pale but proud and determined, her chin set.

'Thank you for telling me, Annabel. People think because you're a child you shouldn't be told, but it's worse not knowing – especially when some of the girls make things up.'

Annabel wondered at the cruelty of children. How could they taunt Beth with something so awful?

'Perhaps you might rather go to a school near your granny?'

'Yes,' Beth said, accepting Annabel's hanky to wipe her face. 'Yes, it might be better. That Shirley is horrible. She thinks I'm not good enough to be in her dormitory because my mother was an actress – and not married.'

'Your mother could sing beautifully,' Annabel told her. 'I saw her in a show in London and she was very good. You should be proud of her, Beth, and don't let anyone tell you any different. As for not being married, that's something that could happen to anyone. A lot of women give their babies away if they aren't married, but your mother kept you because she loved you. It wasn't easy for her and she had to struggle to send you to this school and look after you, but she did it because she wanted the best for you. She loved you very much. That is what is important and don't you forget it.'

Beth looked at her solemnly for a moment, then smiled. 'I'm glad Mummy brought you to see me that day, Annabel. You always make me see things better. It doesn't matter what Shirley says now, because you've made it all right.'

'Good.' Annabel smiled at her. 'Look, there's a man selling ice creams over there – shall we have one?'

*

Annabel took a taxi to Kendlebury after dropping Beth off at her school. It was very extravagant and she couldn't really afford it, but it was quicker than the bus which went round all the villages and she hadn't much time. She needed to see Mrs Rawlings and then catch the last train from Torquay. She would have to change trains in London and she didn't want to be there any longer than she had to.

Mrs Rawlings put her mind at rest immediately. 'I never did want Beth to go to that fancy school,' she confided. 'Alice insisted, but I'd rather have my granddaughter here. Especially now…' She broke off and dissolved into tears. 'I'm sorry, Annabel. You'd think I'd be over it now, but I still cry every time I think of what happened.'

'Yes, I know how you must feel. Beth asked me for the truth. I told her that her mother had been killed, because one of the girls had already been taunting her about the murder and she wanted to know the truth.'

'You never did!' Mrs Rawlings looked at her doubtfully. 'That's more than I could have done. Poor child. Will it give her nightmares?'

'I didn't tell her the details but I think she had to know the truth. Children are very cruel to each other sometimes, Mrs Rawlings, and Beth is old enough to be sensible. She seemed to take it well and of course, she already suspected something.'

'If that's what the girls are like at that school it's time she came away,' Mrs Rawlings said with a sniff. 'Poor little Beth. I don't know what things are coming to. Why did someone kill my girl, Annabel?'

'I don't know,' Annabel said, feeling guilt writhe inside her. Was it her fault? Had she caused Alice's death by seeing her that last time, or was Richard telling the truth when he said she tried to blackmail him? If that was the case then Alice's actions had caused an inevitable violent backlash. 'I wish I could explain. I wish I could make it as though it never happened,' Annabel said. 'I feel awful, but there's no way we can bring Alice back.'

'Lord, it isn't your fault. You've been kindness itself, coming down to see me and visiting Beth – and you with your own troubles.' Her eyes went over Annabel. 'And if I'm not mistaken you'll have plenty on your mind very soon now.'

Annabel blushed, realising that the older woman had guessed she was carrying a child, which meant that it wouldn't be long now before it was no longer a secret.

'My troubles are nothing compared to what happened to Alice,' Annabel said and again she was seared by guilt, as if somehow it was her fault that Alice was dead. 'You know I want to do anything I can to help with Beth's schooling. If there's a nice school she could go to here I shall be pleased to help with the fees.'

'Well, we'll see what happens after Christmas,' Mrs Rawlings said. 'I'm very grateful for all you've done.'

'I've done very little I'm afraid.'

'Money isn't everything. You've been kind to Beth and that's what matters to me.'

Annabel had tea with Beth's grandmother and then went to catch her bus to Torquay. She had decided against stopping off to visit Jessie at Kendlebury and thought she might just catch the last train to London, where she planned to stay the night, before continuing her journey the next day. It was as she was standing by the bus stop that a car drew up beside her and her heart quickened as she saw who was driving it. She had known she was running a risk by coming to Beth's school, which was so close to Torquay, but she'd hoped to get away with it.

'Get in, Annabel,' Paul said and leant across to open the door for her. 'I'll take you wherever you're going.'

She hesitated for a moment, then got into the passenger seat beside him. 'If you could take me to the station in Torquay I might just catch the last train for London.'

'I could drive you to London myself, if that's where you're going.'

'Paul... you know why I can't let you,' Annabel said, turning her head to look at him as he sat there. He hadn't made any attempt to start the car. 'If Richard or one of his friends saw us and he thought we were together...' she shivered with fear.

'Some of his friends may have been following me for a while,' Paul replied with a grimace. 'They don't frighten me and nor does Richard. He's just a rather nasty little man who thinks he can ride roughshod over everyone in his way, but this time he's met his match.'

'You don't know what he's capable of,' Annabel said and shuddered. 'He frightens me, Paul. He can be so violent at times.'

'Just what did he do that night?' Paul asked, looking at her intently. He reached out to touch her cheek but she drew back. She wasn't ready to be touched by anyone yet, not even Paul. 'You're not afraid of me? My God! What did that monster do to you?'

Annabel told him in a quiet, flat voice. She told him about the rape and that Richard had boasted about having Alice killed, her voice breaking at the last. But she didn't tell him that she was carrying a child, and that it might be his, because she knew that then he would never let her go.

'Why didn't you say anything about this in your letter?' Paul asked. 'You should have gone to the police, Annabel. He can't be allowed to get away with murder. He deserves to be punished for what he did to you, but murder...'

'I couldn't go to the police. They wouldn't believe me. Richard is a respectable man. He is an MP, Paul. I have no proof. He would deny everything, and he told me I was at a party with him the night Alice was killed. He's clever enough to get away with it. Besides, he threatened to kill you if I caused trouble for him. I couldn't bear that...' Tears trickled down her cheek but she brushed them away with the back of her hand. 'I love you too much...'

'Then let me take care of you, Annabel,' Paul said. 'We could go away together. Make a new life.'

'No! It wouldn't work,' she said, and more tears welled up inside her though she struggled to hold them back. 'You don't understand, Paul. I love you but I can't... I can't bear to be touched. Not by anyone. Not even by you.'

He stared at her in silence for a moment, a flicker in his cheek the only sign of the emotion working inside him.

'I wouldn't force you. Damn it, Annabel. I'm not like him. I wouldn't make you do anything you didn't want to do. I love you. I want to protect you.'

'Perhaps one day,' she said and blew her nose on the handkerchief he handed her. 'One day I'll get over it. I need time, Paul.'

'But you will let me see you sometimes, as a friend? Let me drive you back to wherever you're going, Annabel. Can't you see that it's tearing me apart not knowing where you are, wondering if something has happened to you.'

If she allowed him to visit her it wouldn't be long before he realised she was having a child, and she knew what would happen then. He would insist on taking care of her. It would be easy to let things drift, take advantage of Paul's generosity, but if she didn't stand on her own feet now she never would. She was determined that she would never again be dependent on any man. If she ever went to Paul it would be on her own terms.

'It's too dangerous. Supposing Richard found out?'

'We can be careful. Besides, I've been trying to find you and couldn't. What makes you think he would fare any better? I dare say he has given up on you. Why should he care what you do as long as you don't make trouble for him?'

'You don't know Richard. He hates to be thwarted.' Annabel sighed. 'Drive me to Torquay station, Paul. Let me catch my train this time. When I feel ready, I'll know where to find you.'

'I've been thinking of going to America for a few months. I've been offered work there,' Paul said, eyes narrowed as he looked at her intently. Annabel was pale but beautiful, yet there was something different about her. But then, he couldn't expect her to be the same after what had happened. It was shocking second-hand but she must have suffered terribly, must be suffering still. He loved her but perhaps it was selfish of him to push her; he ought to give her the time she needed.

'Why don't you do that?' she said and smiled at him. 'Please don't worry about me, Paul. I have good friends and I'm working. I have a job I like very much. I promise that I'll let Jessie know if I think I'm ready to see you again.'

'Are you all right for money?'

'I have a little,' Annabel reached out to touch him and then dropped her hand as a tiny shiver went down her spine. 'Would it be too much to ask for some help for Alice's grandmother? Beth is going to have to leave the boarding school after Christmas. She doesn't mind that and will live with Mrs Rawlings, but it's bound to be difficult for them. Mrs Rawlings has her cottage but only a little money her husband left her.'

'Yes, of course I'll do that,' Paul agreed. 'I was asking Jessie about it only this afternoon. She said that she will pass on any money I give her for Beth, and I'm going to make arrangements for an allowance for her. I liked Alice, too: we all did.'

'Yes, I know. I thought Jessie might help – and you.'

'I want to help you, Annabel. It can't be easy. You've never had to work for a living before.'

'Then it will be good for me,' she told him, a flash of pride in her face. 'I'm not helpless, Paul. I can manage.'

'I didn't mean it that way. I love you. I want to look after you.' He reached out to take her hand, but she pulled it back as soon as his fingers touched her. 'Sorry. I don't mean to upset you, but I love you. Seeing you makes me want to comfort you.'

'I know.' She felt the sting of tears. 'Don't you see, that's why I can't be with you yet, Paul. I would hurt you because I couldn't accept your love, not for a while yet. I feel… dirty. Used. And guilty. Can you understand that?'

'You weren't responsible for any of it,' he said. 'You mustn't let him ruin your life, Annabel. You have to fight it, forget Richard and the terrible things he's done.'

'Yes, I know, and I shall,' she said. 'I haven't stopped loving you, Paul. Believe me, I wish it could be as it was that night...'

'Annabel...' There was such longing in his voice, such need, that it almost tore the heart out of her. 'Please let me help you.'

'Ask your friends to find out what they can about Richard,' she said. 'I should like to see him punished for what he did to Alice. The rest of it is my problem, Paul. I have to fight my way through it. You can't help me, no one can.'

'I've already got people shadowing him day and night,' Paul told her, his face grim. 'I promise you that we'll find a way to make him pay – even if it isn't for what he did to Alice. It may never be possible to prove that, but he'll make a mistake one day and I shall know about it – and then he'll pay.'

'Yes, I can believe that,' she said and smiled. 'If Richard was in prison I think I could sleep easier. And now, I would be grateful if you would take me to catch my train.'

'If it's what you really want,' Paul said and started the engine.

It wasn't what she truly wanted, of course it wasn't. It was the way things had to be for the moment. She dare not let Paul visit her for his own sake. Not while Richard was still lurking in the shadows, waiting to strike. Paul wasn't afraid of him, but she was... very afraid of what he might do when he found her, especially if she was with the man she loved.

*

'I wanted to tell you, Mary,' Annabel said on the following evening. They were having a cup of coffee in Mary's private sitting room, the first chance they'd had to talk since Annabel got back that afternoon. 'When I came for the job I had no idea I was having the baby. I know it isn't fair to you, but I was hoping you would let me stay on for a while – until it gets too noticeable.'

'I'm hoping you'll stay on for good,' Mary told her. 'I did tell Mike a few days ago that I thought you might be expecting a baby and we discussed it then. You're staying in the hotel at the moment and you'll want a place of your own when the baby is born, but Mike has a little cottage that he sometimes lets out to visitors. It's empty most of the year. You could move in there. You'll want a few months off when the baby is born, but we hope you'll come back to us as soon as you can. We can make some arrangement about the baby for the hours you work. You could probably bring the child in with you.'

'Are you sure that's what you want? I never expected you would be prepared to have a child around.'

'I don't think our guests would object, they're a friendly bunch,' Mary said. 'Mike and I wanted babies, Annabel, but I can't have them. At least, it hasn't happened yet, though we still keep hoping. I think we would enjoy having yours as part of the family.'

'Oh, Mary…' Annabel couldn't stop the tears falling. She'd held them back all these weeks, even when she was with Paul she'd brushed them away, determined not to give way, but now she was crying helplessly. When Mary put her arms about her she stiffened for a moment, but then, almost at once, the fear was gone and she clung to her employer, accepting the comfort she had not been able to take from Paul. 'I'm such a fool…'

'Of course you're not a fool,' Mary said and hugged her tighter. 'You've been through a terrible time. I know that even though you haven't told me all of it.'

'Perhaps I ought to,' Annabel said, blinking and using her handkerchief to wipe away the tears. 'I'm all right now, Mary – but I think I should tell you a part of my story. If I'm going to stay it is only fair that you should know.'

*

It wasn't the first time he had been followed. Paul had sensed that he was being watched for days now; he was alert to danger but not unduly worried as he believed that he was being shadowed in the hope that he would lead them to Annabel.

He had waited for the right time and now he was ready, maintaining a steady pace just ahead of his shadow as he walked down the street, a place he had known since his days as a boy on the streets of the East End. Suddenly, he made an abrupt right turn into a narrow alley, seeking shelter in a side entrance difficult to see in this light unless you knew it was there.

He heard his pursuer's hurried step, then the hesitation as the man paused, unsure of his bearings and the whereabouts of his prey. Paul waited for his chance, then as the man turned his back, clearly waiting for an accomplice, he struck, grabbing him from behind, one arm about his throat and the other snatching his victim's arm up hard behind him.

'Bleedin' hell!' came the strangled gasp from the man he held. 'The bugger's got me, Mac...'

'I've not only got you, I'll break your neck if your mate tries to help you,' Paul muttered in his ear. 'Why are you following me? Is it on Hansen's orders?'

'You've got the wrong man,' his victim rasped. 'Never 'eard of the geezer.'

Paul jerked at his arm and he gave a scream of pain. A second man had appeared now and was standing well back, apparently considering the situation.

'I asked you a question,' Paul said. 'The next time it will be your neck that gets broken.'

'You've broke my bleedin' arm,' the man whined. 'Mac, he's broke my bleedin' arm.'

'Stop whining,' the other man muttered 'and listen to what he's sayin' else it will be your *neck*, fool'

'A sensible man, your friend,' Paul said. 'I know you've been following me for a couple of weeks, and I'm pretty certain I know who sent you – a man you've been working for, probably for a while now.'

'He's a bleedin' toff,' his victim muttered. 'I don't know 'is name, curse him. Let me go, me arm 'urts like hell.'

'I'll let you go when I'm ready,' Paul muttered. 'You're a fool if you work for a man like that. His days are numbered, as yours will be if you try any funny tricks with me.'

'I've 'ad enough,' the man muttered, sounding as though he was close to tears. 'Me bleedin' arm is killin' me.'

Paul let him go, giving him a little push towards the man he'd called Mac. The second man hesitated for a moment as if considering whether it was worth having a go now that his friend was free, but as Paul stepped forward Mac saw the flash of a steel blade in his hand.

'It's all right, mate,' he said, putting his hands up and backing away. 'We're out of 'ere. What he pays us isn't enough for this. He can do his own dirty work in future.'

'Just remember that I have friends in these streets,' Paul said. 'Any attempt to kill me will be repaid in full – and if I'm dead there are others who will hunt you down.'

'Call it quits,' Mac said. 'Come on, Bill, let's make ourselves scarce. Sorry, mate, we didn't realise you wus one of us or we wouldn't 'ave took it on.'

Paul smiled as the men slunk off into the darkness. His gamble had paid off and it had been worth the risk. He would remain alert, but somehow he didn't imagine he would be receiving any more attention from those two.

But that didn't ease Paul's mind as he emerged into the well lit street once more and paused to make sure the other men had made themselves scarce. He could take care of himself but Annabel was another matter. He cursed himself for a fool for letting her go back to wherever she was hiding, because if Richard couldn't get to him he might well turn his attention to her.

Paul was leaving on a trip to America in a few days, but he would tell his agents to redouble their efforts to find her, and to make sure she was safe once they did.

Ten

Annabel paused for a moment to rest, placing a hand to the middle of her aching back. She had just got off the bus from town, having been in to buy a few things for the baby now due in about two months' time, and she was feeling tired. She had put on an alarming amount of weight in the past month or so and was suffering from the effects.

'Are you going to Hightops?' a voice asked and she realised that it was Jack Roberts, who delivered the post to the surrounding villages and outlying homes, along with anything else that was ordered from his parents' shop. 'I'm going that way myself. I'll give you a lift, Mrs Tarleton.'

'Would you?' Annabel got in beside him gratefully, holding her various packages on her knees because the back of his little van was piled high with cardboard boxes and parcels. 'This is very kind of you, Mr Roberts.'

'Why don't you call me Jack?' he said and gave her a friendly grin. 'You've known me a few months now, no need to stand on ceremony with me, Mrs Tarleton – or may I call you Annabel?'

'I don't see why not,' she said. She liked the cheerful young man who came to the hotel with letters almost every day. 'I'm afraid I'm squeezing you a bit, there's a lot of me at the moment.'

'My sister was just like you in her last month,' Jack said. 'I expect you can't wait to get it over with now.'

'I shall certainly be relieved,' Annabel said. 'But I think I've got another two months to go yet.'

'I doubt it,' Jack said. 'I've got three sisters and two female cousins, all of them with several children apiece. I'll wager you won't go more than six weeks at the most.'

'Perhaps you're right,' she said, and her heart was gladdened. 'If the child was born in six weeks she could be certain that it was Paul's rather than Richard's.

'There's a letter for you in my bag,' Jack said, unable to hold back the curiosity in his voice. In all the time Annabel had been at Hightops, there had not been one letter for her, which was strange. The villagers gossiped about her because she was a bit of a mystery, but the tale was she'd left her husband, and some said Tarleton wasn't her real name, though so far no one had come up with an alternative.

Annabel smiled as she caught the note of curiosity. She had written to Hetty a week earlier, telling her about the baby and giving her an address, though with strict instructions not to tell anyone, including their mother. She had sent the letter to

Selina, because she wasn't sure where Hetty was at the moment, and Selina would pass it on for her.

'That will be from my sister,' she told Jack. 'I've asked her if she would like to come and stay when the baby is born – if she can. I'm not sure she will be able to because she is at college and she might not be able to get away.'

'Your sister, is it?' Jack said. His mother would be interested to learn that when he got back; a nice titbit of gossip for her. 'Well, that will be pleasant for you.'

'Yes, that's what I thought,' Annabel replied, knowing that the news would travel fast now that she had told Jack, because his mother was a terrible gossip and everyone visited her shop at some time or other; it was the lifeline of the village and saved a lot of tiring trips into town.

'You're settling down well here then?' Jack went on, anxious to find out what he could now that his passenger was at his mercy. 'Thinking of staying?'

'Yes, for the time being,' Annabel said. 'As you know, I shall move into the cottage after the baby comes. Mary and Mike Foster have been very good to me.'

'Well, you're an asset to the business,' Jack said. 'Mike thinks they were lucky to get you.'

'I'm not sure I'm an asset just at the moment.'

Jack chuckled. 'Mary won't mind that,' he said. 'She loves kids. It's a wicked shame she couldn't have her own. She'll be all over it when it arrives, you'll see.'

'Yes, you may be right,' Annabel agreed. Her friend, who had become more protective after learning why Annabel left her husband, was already constantly fussing her over her. 'Mary is a good friend.'

'Well, here we are then, lass,' Jack said and pulled to a halt outside the back door of the hotel. 'You sit there a moment and I'll open the door for you. We have to take care of you ladies when you're in this state.'

Annabel smiled at him as he helped her out of the car, taking her parcels from her and then handing them back. 'I can see your sisters have trained you well,' she said and he laughed again, then disappeared inside the back of the van and came back with an envelope, which he handed to her with a little flourish. 'Thank you.'

She went into the hotel kitchen without looking at the letter, being met by Mary who, because it was Keith's day off, was at the table whipping up one of her delicious puddings, which were famous with her regular guests. The radio was playing something by a blues singer and Mary was singing along, but as she saw Annabel she left what she was doing and rushed to take her parcels and beg her to take the weight off her feet.

'You must be exhausted,' she said. 'All the way up that hill. You should have telephoned from the village and let Mike come and fetch you.'

'Jack Roberts gave me a lift,' Annabel told her, but sat down in the chair Mary had pushed forward. 'I'm not sure I could have managed it if he hadn't. I think I weigh a ton and half.'

'Not quite that much,' Mary said and laughed. 'But you've certainly put on some weight. Are you sure you've got two months to go?'

'Jack tells me he'll be surprised if I go more than six weeks,' Annabel said and laughed as Mary raised her eyebrows. 'He's an expert on these things it seems.'

'It's all those sisters and cousins,' Mary said. 'They've got a couple of football teams between them, I reckon.'

'He gave me a letter…' Annabel looked at the writing and frowned. 'I thought it was from my sister but this isn't her writing – it's from Selina.' Mary looked curious and she explained. 'Selina Manners is a widow. She and her brother Tom were good friends of my family. I wrote to my sister care of her home, asking Hetty for a visit, but Selina has replied. I wonder why.'

'Open your letter,' Mary suggested. 'I'll put the kettle on…'

She was busy filling the kettle when she heard a little cry and turned to see Annabel staring at the letter, clearly in some distress.

'Is something wrong, love?'

'Yes. Yes, I'm rather afraid it is,' Annabel said, her face white. 'There's rather a lot of bad news. Selina's brother Tom died a few months back. Selina says she wants to talk to me about his will…'

'You were fond of him?'

'Yes, I was. I went to see him in hospital just before he died,' Annabel said. 'It isn't really a shock. I think he knew he was dying, but it's still upsetting. Selina must be devastated. If I'd known I would have gone to the funeral.'

'Selina didn't know where you were?'

'No. I didn't want anyone to know.'

'Because you thought Richard might follow you.' Mary nodded understandingly. 'It's a shame – but you couldn't have done anything.'

'No. He was pleased I went to see him in hospital that day. He said he wished that he'd asked me to marry him. He never liked Richard and he sensed that I was unhappy.'

'That was before it happened?' She avoided the word rape.

'Yes.' Annabel glanced at her letter again. 'Unfortunately, that isn't all the bad news. My sister has run away from her college. Apparently, she met someone when she was in France for a holiday – an artist. They have been writing to each other and she ran off to be with him. My brother went over to France to look for her but he wasn't able to find her. My mother has been very upset…'

'I imagine she might well be,' Mary said. 'It must be worrying for your family. Do you think you ought to go home and see them?'

'Not for the moment,' Annabel replied, frowning. 'I don't think I could cope like this, Mary. My mother is… well, she wouldn't understand why I left Richard. She would insist that I go back to him, and she would probably telephone him and tell him I was there.'

'Then I agree you should wait until the baby is born,' Mary said. 'But you could write to her if you liked. Mike would post it when he goes into Durham next week.'

Annabel considered. Durham was far enough away not to reveal her whereabouts. It should be safe enough, and she didn't want to involve Selina. Lady Tarleton could not be trusted to keep the source of her information to herself. If Richard suspected that Selina knew her address he might find some way of forcing her to tell him. Better to write to her mother and let Mike post it in town.

'Yes, that's a good idea,' Annabel agreed. 'I'll tell her that I'll visit in a few weeks' time but not when I'm going, that way I can surprise her.'

'Mike was saying…' Mary hesitated. 'One day you'll have to think about getting a divorce, Annabel. We know a good solicitor in Durham if you decide you want to be free of your husband once and for all.'

'Thank you, but I'm not ready yet,' Annabel said. 'Besides, I'm not sure Richard would agree to a divorce.'

She had told Mary about the rape, but there were certain things she could never tell. An icy chill went down her spine as she remembered Richard's boasts that night, when he'd told her that he had killed two women. What else had he done that he hadn't told her?

She had begun to forget these past months, her bad dreams becoming less and less frequent. She had even begun to think that she might telephone Jessie after the baby was born, ask if Paul was back in the country, but now a sudden fear rose up inside her and she thrust the wistful longings from her mind. Even if she was beginning to get over her fear of being touched, she still couldn't go to Paul for his own sake. Richard had left her alone thus far. She wasn't sure why. It might be that he hadn't been able to find her or perhaps he hadn't bothered because it no longer mattered to him.

She had looked for items of news about him in the papers, but had seen nothing for months. Clearly, he wasn't seeking publicity as much these days, perhaps because of Annabel's disappearance. Had it affected his career? If it had he must be very angry with her.

'Well, try not to worry about your sister too much,' Mary said. 'She will probably come home when she's ready.'

'She told me she was never going back home,' Annabel said. 'I think she was more unhappy than I'd realised. I was going through a bad time myself and I thought it was just a silly mood. Hetty got on better with my mother than I ever did – at least until my brother married. She didn't like his wife. She asked if she could stay with me sometimes. I suppose when I ran away she had nowhere to go, except Selina's.' Annabel wrinkled her brow as a thought occurred to her. 'It might be that what I did encouraged her to run off herself.'

'Now don't start blaming yourself, Annabel,' Mary said. 'You're not responsible for your sister's actions.'

'No – but if I'd been there it might have been different,' Annabel said and sighed. 'I suppose I should have told her where I was before this, but I was reluctant to involve anyone.'

'It isn't your fault,' Mary said again. 'Besides, it isn't the end of the world these days. We've moved on a bit from the Victorians. A lot of women have affairs these days, Annabel. Mike says they always did, of course, but it's more open now. Divorce isn't the shameful thing it used to be.'

'My mother wouldn't agree I'm afraid. She would condemn my sister for what she has done,' Annabel said and pulled a wry face. 'Hetty probably wouldn't be welcome in her house again – come to that, I dare say she won't be particularly pleased to see me. However, my brother will. He may be annoyed with me for not contacting him, but I couldn't because Mother or Helen would have been sure to see the letter. Ben could never hide something like that from them. He's far too easy going.'

'Well, he'll be pleased to see you then,' Mary said and handed her a cup of tea. 'It won't be long before the baby is born now, love. You can put all this out of your mind until then. After all, if your brother has looked for Hetty you couldn't do any more, especially in your condition.'

'No, of course not,' Annabel said and smiled, resting her hands tenderly on her swollen belly. 'I think Paula is getting as fed up with waiting as I am.'

'You've made up your mind what to call her if you have a girl then,' Mary said. 'What will it be if it's a boy?'

'She's going to be Paula Mary,' Annabel said. 'If it's a boy, and I don't think it will be, I'll call him Michael Paul.'

'That's lovely,' Mary said, and blinked because her eyes pricked with sudden tears. 'Mike will be pleased.'

Annabel put down her empty cup and picked up her parcels. 'I'm going upstairs for a little rest. I'll come down and write the menu cards for this evening in about an hour.'

'There's no need for you to do that if you're tired.'

'I shall be fine after half an hour on the bed,' Annabel said. 'I want to earn my keep, Mary, and don't say I don't need to – because I do.'

Mary smiled and shook her head but didn't argue. She blessed the day she had followed her instinct and taken Annabel in, because these days she was becoming more like a sister than an employee. She hoped that Annabel's news wouldn't take her away from them.

Annabel hadn't seemed interested in the news that Selina wanted to talk to her about her brother's will, but if he had thought a lot of her he might well have left her some money. Mary hoped it wasn't enough to make Annabel feel she didn't need to work for them, and then quashed the selfish thought. No, she didn't hope any such thing. It would be lovely if Tom Brocklehurst had left her a fortune. Heaven knows, Annabel could do with a bit of luck after all she'd been through – and Mary was sure she still didn't know the half of it.

*

It was six weeks to the day after Jack Roberts gave her a lift up the hill that Annabel gave birth. She had gone into labour during the night and Mike drove her to the small cottage hospital where she had made arrangements to have the child delivered.

He fussed over her as though he was the father, making Annabel laugh as he bullied the nurses into rushing to help her to her bed and telling them to take good care of her because she was very precious.

'Goodness, your husband is in a state,' one of them said as she helped Annabel into bed. 'It's a good thing men don't have to have the babies, that's all I can say.'

'Mike Foster isn't my husband,' Annabel said. 'I work for him and his wife, but they are good friends.'

'Well, I've seen husbands in a better state,' the nurse replied. 'I dread to think what your husband will be like when he gets here if your friend is in such a flutter.'

Annabel didn't tell her that her husband wouldn't be visiting.

Her pains were coming thick and fast now and she gave a little scream as her waters broke. The nurse looked startled and then nodded encouragement.

'Left it until the last moment did we? Well, it won't be long now, Mrs Tarleton, that's for sure.'

It seemed quite a while to Annabel, who was biting her lip to hold back the screams as the pains followed in quick succession, becoming so terrible that she thought she couldn't bear it any longer. But at last it was over and she looked at the tiny scrap they placed in her arms, touching the soft dark hair on her head with the tip of her finger. The child opened her eyes and looked up at her with Paul's eyes. A tremendous wave of love swept over Annabel and she cradled the baby to her protectively. She was Paul's daughter, there was no doubt left in Annabel's mind.

'She's beautiful,' the nurse who had admitted her said as she came to lift the child out of her arms. 'I just need to clean her up a bit, Mrs Tarleton, and then you can have her back for a while.'

'She is lovely, isn't she?' Annabel said, feeling a sense of loss as she watched the nurse washing the tiny baby. 'I'm going to call her Paula Mary.'

'Lovely name,' the nurse said. 'After your husband is it?'

'Yes,' Annabel said and smiled as she took the baby back into her arms, holding her tenderly. 'Yes, I'm naming her for her father.'

She slept for a while after that and woke again to be given her child to feed, then slept again when she'd had a cup of tea and some tinned fruit with jelly to eat herself. When she woke the next time it was to find Mary at her bedside with a huge bunch of flowers and a pink teddy bear for Paula.

'How are you, love?' Mary asked solicitously. 'The nurse told me Mike only just got you here in time.'

'Well, it wasn't quite like that,' Annabel said. 'But my waters broke almost at once, though she arrived a while afterwards.'

'These nurses have no idea what it's like,' Mary said with a snort. 'All they have to do is stand there and watch!'

Annabel laughed and agreed. 'It doesn't matter when it's all over,' she said. 'You forget the pain when they put that baby in your arms.'

'She is gorgeous,' Mary said. 'I went to see her before I came to you and she is such a little sweetheart. I'm so happy for you, Annabel. Mike said to tell you that the cottage is ready for you, but you can stay at the hotel in your old room for a while if you like.'

'I shall move into the cottage,' Annabel said. 'Thank you for the offer but your guests won't want a crying baby waking them. When she's settled and I feel up to it I'll bring her to work with me and we'll see how things go then.'

'She'll be as good as gold,' Mary said. 'They let me touch her and she grabbed my finger. She's really strong, Annabel. Perfect!'

'Yes, I know,' Annabel said and laughed at her friend's enthusiasm. 'I've been thinking, Mary. When I go to visit my mother I might leave her with you for a day, that's if we can get her to take the bottle. The nurse told me they are trying to give her some special milk from a bottle today; it seems my milk may not be enough for her on its own.'

'Yes, they told me she'd had half a bottle when I saw her earlier,' Mary said. 'Well, I suppose it's a good thing in one way. It doesn't tie you down so much if you don't have to breast feed all the time.'

'I want to try to as much as I can,' Annabel said. 'Besides, I can wait for a while before I visit my mother. As you said, it doesn't make much difference to Hetty. I can't persuade her to come home if I don't know where she is, can I?'

'All you have to worry about at the moment is getting strong,' Mary said. 'By the way, another letter came for you this morning. I'm sorry but I didn't bring it. I put it on my desk and then Mike called me and it's still sitting there. I think it was from your friend Selina again.'

'I wonder why she has written,' Annabel said and frowned. 'Oh, it doesn't matter. I shall soon be up and about again, Mary. Don't bother to bring it in, I'll read it when I get back to Hightops.'

*

Mike fetched Annabel when she was ready to leave the hospital a week or so later, driving her to the hotel first, because, as he told her, everyone wanted to see the new arrival. There were lots of cards, presents, admiring looks and good wishes before Annabel was finally driven to her cottage a couple of hours later.

A lovely fire was waiting for her in the sitting room, and the bedrooms were heated by cast iron radiators run from the kitchen range. Flowers had been arranged in pretty bowls on the sideboard and windowsill and a supply of food laid in for her, together with all the various bits and pieces Annabel had bought for her baby.

Annabel deposited her daughter in the cot lovingly prepared for her, which had been a gift from Mary, then made herself a cup of tea and took it to sit by the fire. She was reflecting on how lucky she was to have found such good friends when she remembered the letter she had slipped into her pocket and took it out.

Tearing the envelope she took out the three sheets of notepaper covered in Selina's handwriting and began to read, a frown creasing her smooth brow as its meaning became clearer. There was some mention of Ben having had a letter from Hetty, telling him not to worry, and of Lady Tarleton's anger at her daughter's behaviour.

As you may imagine, Annabel, your mother has been very displeased with you for some time,

Selina had written at the top of the second page.

However, in the light of recent events she has now begun to think that perhaps you had good reason to leave Richard. I have tried to tell her that you would not have done so without reason, and so has Benedict, but until now she was very much on Richard's side. Of course what has happened has completely changed all that...

Annabel wondered what Selina was talking about. What recent events? She turned the page, frowning again as she read on:

Of course nothing is proven as yet. No arrest has been made, but the old saying is that there is no smoke without fire and the papers would hardly print a story like that if it wasn't true, would they? It is quite shocking. As you know, I never liked Richard, never thought he was good enough for you, my dear, but I had no idea he was a violent man. You must have had a very unhappy time. I am so sorry, Annabel. All I can say is that I remain your friend and hope that you will find yourself able to visit me one day in the future, perhaps when this horrible business has been resolved.

What horrible business? Annabel scanned the letter from the beginning again but could find no clue as to what Selina was sympathising with her over. Clearly, she imagined that Annabel would know, as obviously it had been reported in the newspapers. Annabel hadn't seen many papers this past week, having been sleeping and resting in between learning how to look after her child.

A cold shiver ran down Annabel's spine. What had Richard done now? Had the police discovered the truth about Alice's murder? That hardly seemed possible, since Richard would have taken care to cover his tracks, but something had happened.

Who could she talk to? Who could she ask for the truth?

Getting up, Annabel went through into the bedroom to look at Paula, who was sleeping peacefully. For some months she had managed to put her fear of Richard out of her mind, but now it had returned with a vengeance. It seemed that he was in trouble of some kind and she was suddenly more afraid than she had been since the night she left him.

For a moment as she looked at her child sleeping so peacefully Annabel was tempted to scoop her up and run back up the hill to the safety of the hotel. There she would be surrounded by friends and protected from the wrath of a vengeful man, should he come looking for her.

What was that noise? Annabel started as she heard something, her heart racing with fear and then in another moment, realised it was only the wind sighing across the hills. She was being foolish, letting her imagination run away with her. Hardly anyone knew where she was, and certainly no one who would tell Richard. Besides, why should Richard bother to come looking for her now? If he hadn't troubled to find her in all these months, he wasn't likely to now, especially if he was in trouble.

One thing Mike's little cottage lacked was a telephone. Annabel had applied to have one connected but had been told it would be a few weeks before they could bring the line to her. She hadn't thought it would bother her that much, but now she wished that she had pushed a bit harder for the connection.

There was no point in wishing for something she could not have. In another moment her fear had faded and she could smile at herself.

She bent to kiss Paula on the cheek, then went through to the kitchen and started to prepare a light supper for herself. She switched on the radio to listen to the music, feeling better as the rich voice of Al Jolsen came over the air waves.

It was foolish of her to let Selina's letter worry her. If Richard had problems with the police he was hardly going to come looking for her now, was he? He would be worrying about keeping himself hidden and would not be concerned over the wife who had left him.

By the time she had eaten her meal and washed the dishes, Paula had woken and was demanding attention. Annabel went to feed her, change and bathe her, cradling her until she fell asleep again and was happy to be returned to her cot. She was an exceptionally good baby, and would be no trouble to take to the hotel with her, Annabel thought, smiling as she gazed down at her daughter.

There was no way that evening of finding out what Richard had done, and after reading for a while, Annabel decided on an early night. In the morning she would walk up to the hotel and make a couple of phone calls.

*

Annabel had thought she might not sleep after the worrying news from her friend, but she slept soundly with nothing to disturb her, not even the dreams that had troubled her for some months after she left Richard. She spent an hour or two tidying the cottage and arranging her things to her own liking, preparing Paula and herself for her visit to the hotel, but just as she was about to leave there was a knock at the door.

Opening it, she stared in shock and bewilderment at the man who stood there. He was the very last person she expected to see!

'Paul!' she exclaimed. 'How did you know I was here?'

'I asked Mary Foster. I discovered you were working at Hightops just recently and with this latest news, thought I ought to see if you were all right. Mrs Foster was reluctant to tell me anything at first, but when I explained that you might be in some danger she told me you were here.'

'You mean because of Richard?' Annabel stared at him. 'He's in trouble, isn't he? Selina wrote and told me some of it. I read her letter just last night, though she didn't say what he has done now – just that the papers printed a story about him.'

'Yes, he's in rather a lot of trouble,' Paul said. 'May I come in, Annabel? It's important that I talk to you.'

'Yes, of course.' She stood back, allowing him to follow her into the small but pretty sitting room. Paula was lying in her carrycot and there was no way she could prevent him seeing her. 'Did Mary tell you I had a daughter?'

'Yes. May I see her please?' At a nod from Annabel he walked over to look down at the sleeping child. 'She's lovely. Why on earth didn't you tell me you were having a child?'

'Because you would have insisted on taking care of me,' Annabel replied. 'I wasn't ready for that, Paul. I needed to stand on my own feet – and I wasn't sure if she was yours or Richard's.'

'And now?' He gave her a piercing look.

'I believe she's yours,' Annabel told him. 'She has your eyes. You can't see for the moment, but I knew as soon as they put her in my arms.'

'Why didn't you trust me? It wouldn't have mattered to me if she was his. I would still have loved you and her.'

'I know. Please don't be angry with me,' Annabel said. 'I can't explain, Paul, but I had to do this by myself. I couldn't let you take care of me. I had to live my own life, to be independent – as I ought to have done all along. If I'd had the courage then everything might have been different.'

'I told you it would be different for us. I'm not Richard. I had hoped you knew that, but it seems you didn't trust me enough to share your secret with me.'

'I was confused,' Annabel said, sensing his hurt. 'I do trust you, Paul, of course I do.'

'It doesn't seem that way,' he replied, and he looked angry although he was clearly trying to control his emotions. 'You gave Selina Manners your address. Not that she told me where to find you. I've had someone trying to trace you for months, and I finally got lucky.'

'I'm sorry. It was because of the baby…'

'Yes, I see that now,' he said, and there was a faint note of bitterness in his voice. 'I love you, Annabel. I thought you loved me once, but obviously I was mistaken.'

'Don't say that, Paul,' she cried, but he was looking at her so coldly that she held back all the things she wanted to tell him, how much she had missed him, how often she had wanted to break her silence.

'Well, it's not important for the moment. The thing is that you can't stay here alone, Annabel. The police are looking for Richard. He gave them the slip in London and has disappeared. If he came here looking for you, you would be vulnerable alone in this cottage. Don't imagine he doesn't know where you are. If my people found you, so could his.'

'What has he done?' Annabel asked, her mouth going dry with fear. 'Have they found out about Alice?'

'No, not as far as I know,' Paul said. 'There was another girl called Janie – the first girl he killed. Apparently some evidence has come to light and a witness has come forward, a girl who knew Janie. They worked and lived together for a while, sharing each other's secrets. She has been too frightened to make a statement but when the scandal broke about the other thing…'

'What other thing? Selina mentioned a scandal but I haven't read the papers and I don't know what happened.'

'Richard was in a brawl at a sleazy nightclub,' Paul said. 'He has apparently been drinking more of late and he'd had too much that night. He was slapping one of the hostesses about and Maurice Green tried to stop him. They had a terrific row and Richard attacked Maurice with a broken bottle. Maurice is in hospital at the moment recovering from wounds to the face and hands. He refused to press charges or Richard would have been arrested at once. However, it led to a thorough investigation, and the police have decided to press charges of a different nature. It seems that evidence of certain criminal activities has come into their possession…'

'That's because of your investigation, isn't it?' Annabel said, and he nodded. 'You said you would prove he was guilty of something and you have. I'm really glad, Paul. But this girl who came forward – do you suppose she's the one who telephoned me that time?'

'It's very possible. There's some talk of the first girl Richard killed having been her friend. She hasn't been named, of course, but is a waitress apparently; Janie shared a room with her and she says that she knows Janie met Richard the night she disappeared. Janie told her that she was frightened of him, because he had hurt her before. The witness is being held in protective custody at the moment so Richard can't get at her, but in his frustration he might try to punish you. I've heard that he became very bitter about you leaving him. It's the main reason for his split with his partner. Things have been going wrong between them ever since then, and that's what led to the fight at that club.'

'Richard must blame me,' Annabel agreed. She could imagine his anger at seeing his respectability crumble about him, helped by the scandal of her leaving him so abruptly. There must have been gossip, speculation and even some doubts about her safety, though she'd sent Laura a postcard in Torquay just to say she was well. She shivered, feeling cold and frightened as she pictured Richard's anger and what he might do if he found her here alone. 'You're right, Paul. It's best that I don't stay here at the cottage. I don't even have a telephone. It isn't safe until Richard is arrested.'

'I'll take you wherever you want to go,' he said. 'To the hotel or to Kendlebury. Jessie says you're welcome to stay there for a while.'

'It's very kind of her, and I know Mary would say the same,' Annabel said. 'But I don't think I ought to take advantage. If Richard does come looking for me it would make trouble for my friends. I think I should disappear again, change my name this time.'

He looked at her oddly. 'You would be safe at Kendlebury. I could stay there too.'

'No, I shan't risk their safety,' Annabel said. 'But I would be grateful if you could take me to see my family – and Selina. I want to see them before I vanish again, just to let them know I'm alright.'

'And afterwards? What do you plan to do then?' Paul frowned at her. 'Do you intend to hide from me again?'

'No, not this time,' Annabel said. 'Please don't be angry with me, Paul. I need your help. I need somewhere to stay until this is all over.'

'I know somewhere you can go – if you're willing to trust me?'

'Of course I trust you,' she said, but she could see that he still hadn't forgiven her. 'I'll need an hour or so to get ready – and I shall have to say goodbye to Mary before I leave.'

'Do you want me to help you?' Paul asked, and she shook her head. 'Then I'll go down to the village and make a couple of telephone calls. Lock the door after me and don't open it again, unless you're sure it's someone you know.'

'Yes, all right,' Annabel said. 'Thank you for coming today, Paul. I must admit that Selina's letter had made me a little uneasy.'

'I would have come any time you asked,' he said and went out.

Annabel stared after him for a moment. He was angry and hurt because he believed she hadn't trusted him enough to tell him about her child, but surely he knew she had been anxious about him? She'd been afraid that Richard might try to have him killed. Oh, please, don't let him stop loving her. She couldn't bear that, just when it looked as if they might have a chance of being together.

She didn't have time to worry about the future just yet. She began to move about the cottage, packing the items she would need for Paula in the immediate future. She thrust a few of her own clothes into a bag, but didn't bother with much more than a change of underwear and a few personal treasures. She could ask her mother for a few of the old things she had left at home when she married.

Annabel was conscious of a real fear that Richard would find her. Paul had managed it, which meant that Richard probably could if he wanted to. She would be glad to leave this cottage and half wished that Paul hadn't left her to make those phone calls. Now she was panicking and that was silly! Annabel took a deep breath to steady herself. Richard was probably too busy evading arrest to even think about her.

Nevertheless, she was relieved when she heard Paul's car return. She went to the window and looked out, ensuring it was him, before opening the door.

'Are you ready?' he asked and smiled as she nodded, pointing to the small pile of boxes and bags. 'Is that everything?'

'There's a lot more,' Annabel said. 'But I can manage with this and I shall come back when Richard is arrested. I like it here, Paul. Besides, the Fosters have been good to me and I've enjoyed working for them. I feel I'm letting them down as it is.'

'Mrs Foster seems a decent sort and so does her husband,' Paul said. 'They will understand you can't stay here in the circumstances.'

Mary agreed as soon as she heard Annabel's explanation.

'I always knew there was something you were keeping back, Annabel,' she said. 'It's not surprising you ran away from that dreadful man. But you will keep in touch, won't you? Come back to see us when you can?'

'Yes, of course,' Annabel said. 'Perhaps I can work for you again. I shall have to see what happens.'

'You know we will always be happy to have you,' Mary said, and hugged her, but she told Mike privately later that if she wasn't mistaken that nice Mr Keifer had very different ideas about Annabel's future.

Annabel was very conscious of Paul's reserved manner as he drove her away from Hightops. He had promised to help her and it was clear he meant to keep his word, but there was a distance between them that had never been there in the past, and Annabel wasn't sure she knew how to bridge it.

*

'Oh, Belle,' her brother said as he came to meet her outside the house. 'You deserve a good hiding for what you've put me through these past months. Why the hell didn't you let me know where you were?'

'I wrote to tell you I was safe.'

'Once! I know you wrote to Hetty and to Selina, and then recently to Mother – but you still didn't let me know where you were. I call that bad form, Belle. You knew damned well that I wouldn't have told Richard a thing.'

'Forgive me, Ben dearest,' Annabel said and hugged him, sensing the very real distress behind his expression of disgust. 'I know you wouldn't have told Richard, but Mother would – and you know how she has always been able to worm things out of you.'

'Well, I suppose – but she is very much against him now, Belle. Says she doesn't know what possessed you to marry such a wretched man.'

'Yes, I expect she does,' Annabel said. It would be too much to hope that her mother had changed. She would blame Annabel for marrying Richard now that his name had been disgraced. 'Oh, Ben – I want you to meet a good friend. This is Paul Keifer. He is a friend of Jessie Kendlebury.'

'Yes, we've met on a couple of occasions,' Ben said, and offered his hand. 'Paul was at Kendlebury when I went down to see if they knew where you were. We've all been trying to find you, Belle. It seems that Paul was more successful than I've been, but that doesn't mean I haven't been trying.'

'I know you were worried and I'm sorry. I truly am,' she said. 'Please forgive me. I need you on my side for when I speak to Mother.'

'Well, of course I'm on your side, always have been,' Ben said and arched his brows at her. 'You'd better come and face the dragon – she's been breathing fire all day, ever since Paul rang to tell us you were coming. Selina is here too. She invited herself to lunch when I told her you were expected. Wants to talk to you about something.'

'I wanted to see her before I disappear again.'

'Come off it, Belle,' her brother exclaimed. 'Now that is more than enough. There's no need for you to run off again. You're home now and you'll be safe enough here. I'll see to that.'

'I don't think it's a good idea, Ben.' Annabel reached inside the car to take out the carrycot. Paula was still sleeping. 'You haven't met my daughter yet – her name is Paula Mary…'

'Good grief!' Ben stared at the child in astonishment. 'You never said a word.' He gazed down at the child, then something clicked and he looked at his sister and then Paul. 'Is she… she isn't Richard's, is she?'

'No, she isn't,' Annabel said, giving Paul a shy smile. 'I was going to tell you about it privately, Ben. But I would rather you didn't tell anyone else for the moment – Mother or Helen.'

'Good Lord, no,' he said and grimaced. 'Tell one and you tell the other, they're like two peas in a pod.'

Annabel saw the shadows in his eyes and realised that her worst fears concerning him had come to pass. Her twin was not at all happy in his marriage, but knowing Ben as she did, she was sure that he would make the best of things.

'Poor Ben,' she murmured softly and heard him sigh. 'I suppose we had better go in.'

Annabel was glad that Selina was with her mother in the front parlour. She saw censure and hostility in the eyes of her brother's wife and coldness in her mother's. Discovering that Richard was not all she had thought him, hadn't improved Lady Tarleton's temper or her manner towards her elder daughter.

'Well, so you've had the decency to visit us at last,' she said. 'And to bring the child with you. If you're expecting me to take you in, Annabel, I have to tell you that I really don't think I can at the moment. My nerves are in a terrible state and I need my rest. It wouldn't suit me to have a baby in my house.'

'Belle can stay with me,' Ben said, risking a glare from both his mother and his wife. 'I don't mind babies. I'm hoping to have some of my own one day.'

'That is rather different,' Helen put in. 'Your mother is quite right, Benedict. Besides, under the circumstances, it might be better if Annabel went elsewhere for a while – just until this unfortunate business is cleared up.'

'Annabel is welcome to stay with me,' Selina said and smiled at her. 'Show me your baby, Annabel. Mr Keifer told me she was beautiful when he telephoned earlier, which was kind of him. It is quite important to me to have a little private talk with Annabel.'

'She is lovely,' Annabel said, setting the carrycot down on the floor next to Selina. 'I'm very lucky to have her.' She ignored the snort from her mother. 'Her name is Paula Mary.'

'A lovely name,' Selina said, her eyes knowing as she glanced at Paul standing uncertainly in the doorway. 'Do sit next to me, Mr Keifer. It was so kind of you to let us all know that you were bringing Annabel for a visit this morning.'

'The least I could do,' Paul said and came to sit beside her. 'Annabel told me that you and Tom were great friends of hers.'

'It's about Tom's will that I need to talk to you, Annabel,' Selina said. 'But perhaps we can have a few minutes alone before you leave?'

'Yes, of course,' Annabel agreed easily.

'I don't suppose you would consider staying with me for a while?'

'Not at the moment,' Annabel said. 'Richard will look for me at the homes of my friends. When… the police have him in custody, I should like to stay with you for a while, Selina.'

'Please don't mention that man in my house,' Lady Tarleton said in a pained tone. 'I cannot understand why you married him. You have managed to bring shame on this family. As for your sister…' She shuddered. 'I never want to see or hear of her again.'

'That's a bit harsh, Mother,' Ben said. 'I hope Hetty knows that if she ever needs help she can come to me. I shall always be glad to welcome her to my house – and in case you had forgotten, Mother, the Towers does belong to me.'

Lady Tarleton gave him an eloquent look but said nothing. It wasn't often that her easy going son dug his heels in, but in the matter of his sisters he refused to be budged.

'I know my opinions are of no consequence.'

'Now don't upset yourself, Mother dearest,' Helen said. 'Why don't you come up to my room and have a little rest? I dare say you have one of your dreadful headaches again.'

'At least I have you, Helen dear,' Lady Tarleton said with a sigh and allowed herself to be ushered from the room. At the door she glanced back. 'I expect you to be gone when I return, Annabel.'

'Take no notice of them, Belle,' Ben said when the door closed behind his mother and wife. 'It is my house, whatever the pair of them think, and you're welcome to stay.'

'No, I shan't do that,' Annabel said, but with a smile to soften the words. 'Mother and I never did agree and it would be worse now. Paul is going to take me somewhere. I'll try to keep in touch, but I shan't visit unless I'm asked. When things settle down we can meet somewhere.'

'I'd like a word in private,' Paul said, turning to Ben. 'Shall we leave Selina and Annabel to talk for a few minutes.'

'Yes, of course,' he replied. 'I want to know where you intend to take Belle, and how you're planning to keep her safe…'

Annabel sighed as the two men went out together and looked at Selina. 'I seem to have upset everyone, but there really wasn't much else I could do for a while. I was afraid to contact anyone.'

'Yes, I quite see that,' Selina agreed. 'Especially with the baby on the way. That must have made you feel more vulnerable.'

'Yes, it did in a way,' Annabel said. 'But I've made good friends. The hotel I worked at was a lovely old house, like Kendlebury in a way, but not quite as gracious or ancient – rather more sturdy, to suit the environment in which it is built. It's almost lost amongst the hills, hidden from the main roads and isolated, but the scenery is magnificent. I used to climb the hill and watch the sun setting into the lake in the evenings.'

'It sounds lovely,' Selina said. 'Shall you go back when Richard is safely under lock and key?'

'Perhaps. I don't know,' Annabel said. 'I shall certainly visit, because they have become good friends. It depends…'

'Well, you might like to know that Tom left you most of his money,' Selina told her with a smile. 'The house is mine because it was a family home and Tom thought I should have it, but he knew I had more than enough funds for my needs so he left the money to you.'

'He shouldn't have done that, Selina. It ought to be yours by rights. You are his sister.'

'And you are the woman he loved,' Selina said and took her hand. 'Tom loved you very much, my dear. He was worried about you because he disliked Richard, and he wanted to be sure you were safe. I'm afraid he tied a lot of the money up in a trust for you to protect it from Richard. You will have a rather splendid income for life – and there is a capital sum of twenty thousand pounds at your disposal.'

'Twenty thousand…' Annabel stared at her in dismay. 'But that's a fortune. Really, I can't accept all that.'

'But you must. You really must,' Selina told her. 'It is only a small part of the whole, though as I said, the rest is in a trust until you are forty, then you can break into it if you wish. My brother was a careful man. A little too careful perhaps, otherwise he would have followed his heart and asked you to marry him, Annabel. He was very fond of you, you know. Please accept what he has tried to do for you – for my sake if not your own. I should feel that I had let Tom down if you refused in my favour.'

'Put like that…' Annabel laughed and reached out to kiss her. 'I can only say thank you, to you and dear Tom. I feel unworthy of such generosity, but it will make a big difference to my life. It means I have real independence for the first time.'

'Precisely. That is exactly what my brother intended.' Selina beamed at her. 'Now that I've seen you we must keep in touch so that the solicitors can put everything in order. They have been asking me for months where they could contact you.'

'Yes, I do see that,' Annabel said. 'I'm not sure where Paul is taking me, but I shall phone you and write to you – and perhaps I can visit you soon.'

'We shall certainly remain friends,' Selina said firmly. 'Tom is not the only one who has always been fond of you. I should like to be one of Paula's godmothers when you have her christened, my dear.'

'Yes, of course,' Annabel said smiling at her. 'I shall look forward to that, though I don't know when it will be…'

‘No, things are a little difficult for you at the moment,’ Selina said. ‘We must just hope that the police do their duty very soon.’

Eleven

'I'm sorry if my mother wasn't exactly welcoming to you, Paul,' Annabel said as they drove away later that afternoon. At her twin's insistence his mother and wife had joined them for tea, but neither had been very talkative. 'I'm afraid she's the worst kind of snob.'

'I understand why you were unsure about inviting me to meet your family when I suggested it to you that first Christmas,' Paul said, glancing at her as he negotiated the car through a busy main junction. 'Has she always been like that with you?'

'Always,' Annabel said and sighed. 'It's Ben I feel sorry for. Both Hetty and I have escaped but he's stuck with Mother and Helen. It was his choice, but I suppose he didn't really have much of one. Most of his inheritance was lost in the Wall Street Crash.'

'He's too easy going for his own good,' Paul said. 'But I like him, Annabel, and he's very fond of you.'

'Yes, I know,' she said and smiled. 'Where are we going, Paul? You did tell Ben, didn't you?'

'I couldn't refuse. Besides, I doubt that even your mother would give that information to Richard now.'

'No,' Annabel agreed and laughed. 'Much as she disapproves of me, I think she is even more angry with Richard for letting her down. She was very proud of her son-in-law being an MP. Poor Mother. I'm afraid we've all been a disappointment to her.'

'You're very tolerant of her. I'm not sure I would be in your place,' Paul admitted. 'I'm taking you to the house of some friends of mine near Torquay. It's a large working farm and Matthew has three strapping sons who live and work on the farm. I think you will be quite safe there, Annabel. Rose is a lovely person and her daughter Sheila is about your age. They'll make sure Richard doesn't have a chance to get near you. That's if he ever discovered you were there, which isn't likely.'

'It sounds a good place to stay for the moment,' she said. 'I was frightened at first, but now I think it was all a storm in a teacup. Why should Richard bother to come looking for me? I'm sure he has enough to do keeping out of sight of the law.'

'You're probably right,' Paul agreed. 'But the cottage was too isolated for you, Annabel. I wouldn't have been able to sleep at night thinking of you there.'

'Yes, I know. I loved it but must admit I was nervous when I got Selina's letter.'

Annabel glanced at Paul's face as he drove. He didn't seem as angry as he had been on the way there.

Some of the reserve had gone but there was still a distance between them. She felt sad because she knew that she had hurt him. He believed she hadn't trusted him enough to tell him about the child, and she wasn't sure how to bridge the gap between them.

*

'Isn't she the little love?' Rose Harris said, looking at Paula as she lay sleeping in the large old-fashioned cradle in front of the kitchen fire. Paul had thought it unwise to send for the rest of Annabel's things until Richard had been taken into custody, just in case he discovered where she was hiding. But the carrycot wasn't suitable for Paula to sleep in at night, and Rose had remembered the old cradle in the loft. Matthew Harris fetched it down when his wife suggested it and because it was so beautiful Annabel hadn't bothered to buy a new one. 'She's such a good baby, hardly cries at all, except when she's hungry.'

'That's because she is thoroughly spoilt,' Annabel said and laughed. Rose was a plump, cheerful woman who kept her house spotless despite several men with large muddy boots tramping in and out all the time. 'You and Sheila make so much fuss of her she doesn't need to cry to get her own way.'

'Well, who could help it?' Rose said and turned to smile at Annabel, who was wearing an apron three sizes too big for her and had a smear of flour on her cheek. 'How is that bread coming on?'

'I think it is rising well,' Annabel said and lifted the damp cloth on the huge pudding bowl to have a peep at their latest batch of dough. 'It will soon be ready to bake. And I think those cakes I made are just about ready to come out of the oven if that delicious smell is anything to go by.'

'Fetch them out then, Annabel,' Rose said, 'and let's have a look. The last lot sank in the middle but I've hopes of greater things this time.'

Annabel took the tray of cakes out, shaking them on to a wire cooling rack and smiling as she saw that they were perfect.

'I'm learning,' she said. 'You will teach me to cook yet, Rose.'

'You're not a bad plain cook,' Rose agreed. 'But you still have a heavy hand with the pastry, lass. Some never manage to get the hang of that, though, so you're not alone. Two months isn't long. My Sheila has been at it for years and she still has her failures.'

'What's that, Ma?' Sheila asked, coming in from the yard with a bowl of eggs, which she took to the sink to wash. 'What have I done wrong now?'

'Nothing that I know of,' her mother said, 'but that means next to nothing, knowing you. I was telling Annabel you still have your failures with pastry.'

'We can't all be as good as you, Ma,' Sheila said, and grinned at Annabel. 'You're going to see Jessie this afternoon, aren't you? Would you ask her if they've got any honey to spare please? I bought some in Torquay last week but it isn't the same as that from Kendlebury.'

'Yes, of course I will,' Annabel said. 'I've got a list somewhere. Your brother Ken's wife wants some of Mrs Pottersby's shortbread.'

Annabel had a warm feeling inside as she moved about the large kitchen doing the routine chores she had taken on since her arrival just over two months earlier. At first Rose had tried to treat her like a special guest, but she'd been uncomfortable with that and once the family realised that she wanted to do her share it had all worked out very well.

There were always more than enough chores to go round in a working kitchen like this one. The men came in for a meal at about eleven thirty in the morning, and there was usually one of them popping in for tea when they happened to be in the yard. It was a busy time of year for the men with the fields beginning to show signs of the crops they would yield later, and since there were also cows and sheep on the farm there was never a dull moment.

For Annabel it was a completely new way of living, and one that she enjoyed very much. She was always so busy that she never had time to worry about Richard or what she was going to do with her life when she left the farm. Her time at Hightops had begun the healing inside her and these past two months had made her whole again. The bad dreams had stopped altogether and the memory of Richard's cruelty was fading and becoming almost dreamlike.

She was happy here with these people, much happier than she had been at home or during her time in London. It sometimes seemed to Annabel that she was a different person to the girl who had lived in dread of her mother's scolding, and she knew that she would never go back to that kind of life.

Having heard from Tom Brocklehurst's solicitors, Annabel knew that she was quite well off in her own right. She had enough money to live in London, take holidays in France, and perhaps have a cottage in the country as well. As yet she hadn't given much thought to what she wanted to do with her life.

She was, she supposed, waiting for a sign from Paul, but although he had visited the farm a few times, he hadn't said anything to her about the future. He was pleasant, friendly, and appeared at home in the kitchen with his friends, but when they were alone he seemed to keep his distance.

Matthew Harris had promised to drive Annabel to Kendlebury himself that afternoon. He had assured her that it was no trouble, because he had to make a small detour to a neighbouring farm on the way.

'If you don't mind waiting while I do a bit of business, lass, I'll take you there and gladly.'

'That's so kind of you,' Annabel said and smiled at the big bluff farmer. With his red face and callused hands, he was the kind of man her mother would have thought beneath her, but Annabel had found him good natured and generous.

He came in at eleven thirty to eat and then helped Annabel to carry all the things she needed for Paula out to his car, which was a rather battered old shooting brake, full of feathers, bits of sacking and other evidence of its working life. Matthew had laid a blanket on the back for Paula's carrycot to rest on, covering up the mess that had accumulated there.

'I've a bit of business as you know,' he said, 'but it won't take long. Ted Johnson is going to sell me a couple of his milking cows; he's got some Jerseys and I need them for the cream. Rose likes a lot of cream and them Jerseys are better than my Herefords for the cream.'

'Yes, I know Rose uses a lot of cream. That is what makes her cooking so delicious.'

Annabel was thoughtful as they drove through the beautiful countryside, winding their way through narrow lanes with high hedges. There were flowers growing in gardens behind some of the hedges and now and then it was possible to catch sight of a patch of colour and a pretty thatched cottage. Matthew's diversion looked as if it would take a bit longer than he had told her, because they seemed to be heading towards Torquay rather than Kendlebury. She suspected that she would actually be taking him out of his way, but it was like him to say it was no trouble even if it was.

They had been driving for several minutes when he turned off the road, going past a For Sale notice to the right and stopping at the end of the lane.

'Was that a house for sale back there?' Annabel asked, her interest piqued. 'I thought I glimpsed a big house in the trees?'

'Aye, that's Rowntree House,' he replied. 'Used to be a lovely place when I was young but it's been neglected for a while. Why don't you walk back and take a look while I do my business? I'll stop at the gate and honk my horn when I'm ready.'

'Would it be all right do you think?' Annabel said. 'The owners won't mind me looking?'

'Been empty for years now,' he replied. 'You take a quick peep at the outside, Annabel. If you want to look inside I'll get someone to arrange it with the agents for you.'

Annabel felt a surge of excitement as she walked back down the lane towards the For Sale notice. High, thick hedges protected the front of the house from prying eyes, but once she was through the gate she saw a long drive leading up to the house. It was larger than Tarleton Towers, but not quite as big as Kendlebury, and rather attractive. The front walls were heavy with ivy, which needed trimming back, because it was covering the long windows, but the style of the house was early Georgian and elegant. It was clear that it had been neglected for a long time and obviously needed a lot of repair work, and the paths were cracked and overgrown with moss. Shading her eyes with her free hand, Annabel gazed up at the roof. It looked as if some slates had come loose and it might need replacing. Even so, there was no denying that it was an attractive house.

She went closer to the house, mounting the steps to the front door and peering through the windows to either side. The rooms she could see were empty, dusty, and hung with cobwebs, but they looked to be a good size and she judged there must be at least ten or twelve bedrooms, perhaps more. She wandered towards the back, carrying Paula's carrycot by its handles; the path was slippery and actually broken in places. When she caught her heel and almost fell, she gave up and turned to go back. It would be better to leave Paula with someone and return to take a closer look by herself another day. She didn't want to risk a fall with Paula.

Just as she approached the gate she saw Matthew's shooting brake draw up and smiled as he leant across to open the door for her.

'You were quick, lass. Didn't appeal to you then?'

'Yes, it did, very much,' Annabel said. 'But the paths are a bit dangerous and I didn't want to risk a fall with the baby. I think I'll come back another day and have a look by myself.'

'Yes, why don't you do that?' he said and smiled at her. 'It would be nice if you were to settle in the area – when things are better.'

'Yes...' Annabel knew he was too tactful to mention Richard, but truthfully, she hardly thought about him at all now. He had managed to evade the police for two months and one report she'd read in the papers seemed to hint that he might have gone abroad. She really need not worry about Richard, and she was only staying on at the farm because she enjoyed being with her new friends, but perhaps it was time she began to think about the future. 'Yes, I might do that. I should certainly like to have a better look at the house.'

*

'She is growing,' Jessie said as she lifted Paula from her cot. The little girl opened her eyes wide and bubbled at her, making Jessie laugh as she settled her in the crook of her arm. 'Yes, you are very clever, darling. She's beautiful, Annabel. You must be so proud of her.'

'Yes, I am,' Annabel said. 'I think I've been very lucky, don't you?'

'In some ways,' Jessie said, and looked at her. 'You seem happier, Annabel. Are you feeling better now?'

'Yes, much better, thank you. I'm thinking about buying a house. At least, I'm going to look at one as soon as I can arrange it.'

'Really?' Jessie was interested. 'Where? In this area?'

'It's a bit nearer Torquay,' Annabel told her. 'I saw it this afternoon. Rowntree House. There was a For Sale notice and I went to look at it. I couldn't see much, but I'm going to go back and have another look soon.'

'Rowntree House?' Jessie gave her an odd look as she put the sleeping Paula back into her carrycot. 'Yes, I had heard it was for sale again. I believe it needs a lot of work to put it right.'

'So Mr Harris told me,' Annabel said. 'I don't suppose I shall buy it, but it looked rather lovely – or it would be if it was tidied up a bit.'

'Yes, so I understand...'

'Is something wrong? You and Harry didn't want to buy it yourselves?'

Jessie laughed and shook her head. 'For goodness sake no! We have more than enough to manage here. No...' then she hesitated, 'It's odd you happened to see it and think you might like it, because Paul told me he had arranged to go and see it with the agent this week.'

'Is Paul thinking of buying a house that size? It is very big...' Annabel wrinkled her forehead. 'I wouldn't want to live in it alone. I've been thinking... it might be nice to run a hotel. Not a huge place but something small and friendly.'

'A hotel?' Jessie laughed again. 'Well, if that doesn't just take the biscuit as my aunt would say. That is exactly what Paul was thinking of doing with Rowntree House if he bought it.'

Annabel frowned. 'Has Paul got time to run a hotel? I would have thought he was too busy.'

'He is busy, of course, but I suppose he would employ a manager.'

'I want to run it myself,' Annabel said and Jessie stared at her in surprise. 'I enjoyed working with Mary and Mike Foster, Jessie. They run their hotel like a big family house, with the guests becoming friends over the years. I thought it would be a nice way to live…' She blushed as Jessie continued to stare at her. 'Does that sound silly to you?'

'No, of course not,' Jessie assured her. 'I was just thinking how much you have changed from the girl who came here that first Christmas. You had very little confidence in your ability to do anything then, Annabel. Now you're thinking of taking on a huge responsibility. We only have a few guests at certain times of the year. I'm not sure I could cope with a hotel all year round.'

'But you have the workshops and the restaurant,' Annabel reminded her. 'It was because I was so happy here, and then at Hightops, that I thought… but perhaps I couldn't manage it alone. I suppose it was rather ambitious to think of it.'

'It might be a lot for you on your own,' Jessie said and looked thoughtful. 'Why don't you suggest to Paul that you buy the house together and then turn it into a hotel between you? Paul knows a lot about how to get things done, and you have a flair for getting on with people. If you pooled your resources you could be a good team.'

'Paul and I…' Annabel felt her cheeks growing warm. 'I'm not sure that he would want to go into business with me. I'm not sure he has forgiven me for disappearing the way I did.'

'Paul was worried and hurt that you didn't trust him,' Jessie said. 'But I don't think you need worry whether he likes you or not. He might not want to make the first move, but I'm sure he would appreciate it if it came from you, Annabel. Besides, you wouldn't want to bid against each other for the house, would you?'

'No – but we haven't seen it yet,' Annabel said. 'It might not be suitable for either of us.'

'Why don't you telephone Paul now?' Jessie suggested. 'I have to go and talk to my aunt about something. You can use the telephone here. Paul should be in London; the number is there on the pad on the desk.'

'Yes, perhaps that might be best,' Annabel said a little doubtfully. 'I wouldn't want to spoil Paul's plans...'

Jessie smiled and went out and Annabel sat down at the desk. She picked up the receiver and dialled Paul's number in London but there was no reply. Noticing another number further down the page, she tried that but with the same result. Clearly Paul was out for the moment, so she left the desk and went over to her daughter's cot as Paula began to whimper. Picking her up, she was trying to hush her when the door opened behind her.

'Paul wasn't at either of the numbers you have for him,' she said. 'I'll have to try again this evening.'

'Perhaps I can save you the trouble,' a voice said and she spun round to find Paul smiling at her from across the room. 'Matthew told me you were here so I came to save you the trouble of getting a taxi back to the farm.'

'Paul...' Annabel's heart beat faster as she saw his smile. 'Jessie told me you are interested in Rowntree House and I was going to ring you about it.'

'And I was going to talk to you about it after I'd had a proper look,' Paul said. 'I thought it might solve your problems for a while, Annabel. If I bought it with a view to turning it into a hotel...' He stopped as he saw the expression in her eyes. 'It's just an idea. You were happy at Hightops and you've made friends here. I thought...'

'So did I,' Annabel said, and laughed. 'I was telling Jessie that I'd had the same idea. It's been in my mind a long time, Paul. Since I first came here I suppose. I thought then that I might like to work in a hotel, and working with Mary and Mike Foster made me realise that I do have a flair for getting on with people. I enjoy meeting new people and looking after them and I... I don't want to be on my own. Nor do I want to live with my family. I don't think I could go back to London. At least, I would only want to stay there for a few days, just for a holiday or a shopping trip.'

'Then do you think...'

'Why don't we take a look at it together?' Annabel asked. 'Have you made arrangements to view?'

'Yes, that's why I came down today. I'm meeting the agent there in the morning. I could pick you up on my way if you like? Jessie has invited me to stay here for the night.'

'I should like that,' Annabel replied. 'Rose or Sheila would look after Paula for me for a few hours, and that would make it easier. I noticed that the paths at the side of the house are broken in places.'

'Yes, I noticed that too,' Paul said with a little frown. 'Did you go round the back at all?'

'No, I couldn't get there, because I had the cot to carry and I was afraid I might slip and drop her.'

'It might be just as well that you didn't,' Paul said. 'I went round to take a look myself and noticed there was a broken pane in the glass door of the kitchen. I thought someone might have been camping out there. As a matter of fact, I spoke to the agent about it and he said it often happens when houses are empty for a while. He was going to send one of his men to take a look, see if there was a tramp sleeping rough in the house or grounds.'

'I didn't see anything,' Annabel said. 'But, as you said, it is just as well I didn't explore further on my own. It will be much nicer doing it with you, Paul.'

'Will it, Annabel?'

His voice had gone soft, almost tender, and her heart quickened. He seemed to have forgotten the distance he'd kept between them as he smiled at her in the old way.

'You know it will. I'm sorry if I hurt you, Paul. I wasn't thinking clearly. In fact, I tried not to think for a long time, because if I had I might not have been able to cope.'

'Yes, I do realise that,' he said. 'Don't think I didn't understand, of course I did. Any woman would be upset after what happened that night. It was a shock when I found out about Paula, and I was angry with you for keeping it from me. She's my daughter too, Annabel, whoever fathered her. I want to love and protect both of you.'

'Oh, Paul...' Annabel moved closer to him, the child between them as he put his arms about her. 'I do love you and I'm so sorry...'

'I love you, darling,' he said. 'I've been keeping a distance between us because I couldn't trust myself not to want you, not to do this...' He touched his lips lightly to hers. 'Is it time, Annabel? You're not afraid of me now, are you?'

'It was never you,' Annabel said and looked into his eyes, her love plain to see. 'It was Richard – what he'd done...'

'I could kill him for that,' Paul said and there was a flash of anger in his eyes but not for her. 'If I ever found him I wouldn't be answerable for my actions after what he did to you.'

'Forget him,' she urged. 'It's over, done with, and I want to think about the future, about all the lovely things we're going to do together.'

'Yes, we'll think about the future,' Paul agreed and took his daughter from her, kissing her brow before restoring her to her cot. He then put his arms around Annabel, drawing her to him and kissing her with a hunger and sweetness that told her his love had never wavered in all these months and they were back at the beginning. 'I hope they find Richard soon so that you can start divorce proceedings against him.'

'Yes, I must speak to a solicitor about that,' Annabel said, though the prospect was horrendous because of the scandal. 'Do you think I have a chance of getting one?'

'We'll see what the lawyer has to say, but I should have thought you have a good chance with all the stuff that is coming out about Richard now. Once the police get him he's finished, Annabel. Maurice Green has been arrested now and apparently he's singing his heart out, telling the police all they want to know. My guess is that he'll put the blame squarely on Richard for as much as he can.' Paul frowned. 'I haven't wanted to trouble you, but the police have requested an interview with you. I've put them off for as long as I can, but it ought to be soon now.'

'Yes, I suppose they want to know what Richard told me about his activities,' Annabel said. 'They might bring charges for withholding evidence...'

'I doubt it,' Paul said, and looked fierce. 'You never had any evidence and you were in fear for your life. I don't think you need worry too much about that. Besides, my lawyers will be with you. They'll soon put paid to any nonsense of that sort.'

'Thank you,' she said, smiling at his fierceness, which was for her sake. 'Do you think Richard is abroad somewhere, Paul? The police can't seem to find any clues as to his whereabouts. I keep wondering if something... do you think he's still alive? Could he have taken his own life?'

'I don't know,' Paul said, looking thoughtful. 'If he was desperate he might but somehow I can't see Richard doing that. I'm sure he has money stashed away in other countries for emergencies. He probably got away before the police started looking for him. I doubt he's in this country now. But he won't be able to hide for long, not these days. People are so much more aware of what is going on, what with the Pathe News at the cinema, the telephone and the wireless. With any luck the international police will pick Richard up and he'll be sent back here to stand trial.'

'That's what I've been hoping,' Annabel said. 'I don't think I need to hide any more, Paul. Richard isn't a threat to me any longer.'

'No, I don't think he is,' Paul agreed and kissed her again. 'So we can start to make plans for our future together.'

*

Annabel felt excited the next morning when she got ready for her appointment with Paul, dressing in a pair of cream slacks and a yellow cotton blouse with a little stand-up collar and three quarter length sleeves. She chose a pair of flat shoes because it might be a bit dangerous at the back of the house and she didn't want to slip over and break something. Now that she had talked things over with Paul, she couldn't wait to start on their ideas for the future.

They might have to wait for some time before they could marry, but that need not prevent them being together or planning their hotel. It was going to be wonderful and Annabel felt as if the dark clouds had fallen away, as if Richard and all the unhappiness he had caused her had never been.

It was a lovely warm May morning and the sun was shining as Paul came to pick her up in his car. He smiled as he got out to open the door for her, catching her about the waist and kissing her softly on the mouth before letting her get in.

'You look beautiful,' he said. 'I was thinking we might go out for a meal this evening, Annabel. Jessie offered to have Paula for the night.'

'That would be lovely,' she replied, smiling up at him. 'Oh Paul, I'm so happy. It's all coming right for us at last.'

'Yes.' He reached across and squeezed her hand. 'Now you mustn't be too disappointed if the house isn't right, darling. It's just the first one we've asked to look at and I'm sure there are plenty of other nice houses for sale in the area. With the way things are at the moment there will probably be a lot more before long.'

'Are things very bad?' Annabel asked. 'I have seen reports in the papers, and of course there was that dreadful crash in Wall Street but Jessie says they are still doing very well at Kendlebury. And Mary wrote to tell me that they are booked right through the summer. She's very excited, Paul, because she thinks she may be having a baby at last, and she had thought it wasn't possible for her. They had been trying for so long and nothing happened so she'd given up. She says it was seeing Paula that gave them new hope, and this time they were lucky – she has her fingers crossed.'

'Well, that is good news. Let's hope it works out for them,' Paul said and smiled because the news had pleased her. 'As far as Kendlebury goes, Jessie works at that place to make it as popular as it is. There's still money about in certain areas, but in others it's getting very tight. I believe there's a huge slump coming – in America as well as here. I know some investors lost an awful lot of money in the crash, and it will take time for their economy to recover. I believe we are going to have what the economists call a depression. I'm afraid the gaiety of the "Twenties" has finally fizzled out, and we're all going to have to be more serious about life from now on.'

'How dreadful,' Annabel said and looked at him anxiously. 'I didn't realise things were that bad. Will it affect your business, Paul?'

'It's bound to affect orders,' he said. 'I've diversified as much as I can without stretching myself too far, but I can weather the storm. Don't worry about me.'

Annabel nodded. 'I don't know how much the house is but I have capital of twenty thousand pounds that Tom left me – as well as the income from the trust.'

'I think we might get the house for five thousand or less considering the state it is in,' Paul said thoughtfully. 'But we shall have to spend another five at least to get it into shape.'

'That will still leave quite a bit for expenses until it begins to pay for itself,' Annabel said. 'I could buy the house if you need your money for the business, Paul.'

'We'll buy it together,' he said. 'I want this to be something of ours, Annabel, to start our life together in the right way.'

'Yes, perhaps that's best,' she agreed and smiled at him. 'It will be our house, Paul, our hotel.'

They had reached the house now and as Paul drew his car into the drive they saw another one was already there. The agent got out as they did and came to greet them.

'Timothy Bromley,' he said and shook their hands. 'I hope you won't be too disappointed when you see inside, Mr Keifer. I know the house has been neglected for a while. An elderly lady lived there for years. She left it to her nephew but he never bothered to visit. We sold it once, or thought we had, but that fell through about two years ago, and since then it has been as you see it now. No one has asked to look at it for months.'

'Did you send someone to find out if you'd had intruders?' Paul asked.

'Yes, as soon as you told me. My lad said he thought someone might have been there for a while but there was no one about when he got here. I've arranged for the glass to be replaced and it should be done later today or tomorrow at the latest. Shall we go in?'

Annabel looked at Paul as he followed the agent, her heart racing with excitement. The house looked even nicer on a day like this with the sun shining on the windows. They were dirty, of course, but she could imagine what it might look like when it was cleaned up and ready for occupation.

They entered by the front door, stepping into a large hall. The door had stained glass panelling and the sun shone through it, casting a myriad of colours onto the black and white marble flooring. The floor was dusty and there was debris where leaves had blown in at some time, but the marble looked in good condition, as did the impressive mahogany staircase.

'There's some damp on the walls and wallpaper is hanging off in places,' Paul observed. 'Is that a problem or just a consequence of the house being empty for a while?'

'Mrs Oakes would never have central heating installed,' the agent explained. 'She thought it a new-fangled idea and refused to consider it even though her nephew advised it years ago. I am sure that any problem would be solved by putting a heating system in, but it may be necessary to strip away some of the old plaster and have new. I would also advise a complete rewiring. I think there may be some electrical points here but they would not be up to today's standards.'

'Yes, it certainly needs a great deal of work,' Paul agreed with a frown. 'On the other hand, the proportions are good. I think it is worth exploring further – don't you, Annabel?'

'Yes. Yes, I love it,' she said. She had gone through to the back of the house into a large sunny sitting room. It was warm because of being south facing and there was no sign of damp or peeling wallpaper here. 'Oh, look, Paul, what a beautiful garden.'

There was a summerhouse shaped a little like a Grecian temple about halfway down the garden with lawns leading up to it and a pond with what might be water lilies crowding the surface. Robins and blackbirds were feeding on the grass and the whole scene had an idyllic, peaceful atmosphere.

Paul came to stand by her side and look out. She turned to him eagerly and he smiled as he saw that she was already convinced.

'There are another five reception rooms, what used to be the library, and the kitchens in the basement to see,' he said. 'I believe there are twelve bedrooms upstairs and some further attic rooms, which could be converted. There's also a possibility of converting the old stable block into more guest accommodation, but that's for the future.'

'I love it, Paul,' she said. 'It feels right for us.'

'Well, don't tell Mr Bromley that just yet,' he said with another smile. 'I'm hoping to get a few hundred off the price.'

Annabel arched her brows at him. She would have said yes straightaway, but she knew that Paul was far too good a businessman to do any such thing. He would assess the work necessary and the likely cost and then put in his offer – but she knew this was the house she wanted.

They spent some time looking round the upstairs, which was in even worse condition than downstairs and made Annabel's heart sink. The bathroom was Victorian and badly stained where water had dripped, which meant it would all have to be renewed. She didn't think that was a serious problem. Yet Mr Bromley was shaking his head over it and Paul was agreeing.

Was it really as bad as the two men thought? Surely it could be put right? She loved the house and the beautiful wild garden. She wandered off to look at the garden as the men examined some of the antiquated plumbing.

'I'm going to explore,' she called and Paul turned his head to smile at her as she went out, telling her he wouldn't be much longer before he joined her. 'I want to look at the summerhouse…'

It was so warm in the sheltered garden! Annabel could hear the drone of bees and birdsong. There was such a peaceful, tranquil feeling about the garden with its beds of old-fashioned flowers, roses and lavender, that she felt as if she had stumbled upon some secret place in a fairytale.

It was a very long garden, Annabel discovered, and went on for ages behind the summerhouse. She went inside the little pseudo Grecian temple and sat on the stone bench for a moment, dreaming in the sunshine. She could see her children growing up here, running around in the garden, playing and laughing in the shrubbery. Yes, she really must have this house, she decided, even if it cost more than they had originally thought to put it right.

She got up and began to wander down to the far end of the garden. It looked as if there was a small barn or outhouse hidden behind a bank of trees – possibly the old stables Paul had mentioned – and what might once have been an orchard. Paul was calling to her and she turned to wave but didn't wait for him because she wanted to see what was there; it looked as though there might also be a Victorian glasshouse of rather splendid proportions.

'Wait for me, Annabel!'

Something in Paul's voice made her stop just before she reached the stable block. She shaded her eyes to look back at him as he came striding towards her. What was worrying him? He seemed anxious about something.

He had almost reached her when she heard a grunting sound behind her and swung round to see a shape looming towards her from the direction of the outhouses. It must be the tramp the agent had spoken of, was Annabel's first thought, and then, as she began to focus more clearly, she suddenly realised that although the man had clearly been sleeping rough he was not a tramp. For a moment she could not believe the evidence of her own eyes. It could not be. It was not possible – he couldn't be here. Not here in this lovely place!

'Richard…' Annabel wasn't sure whether she had spoken or just thought his name. She was too stunned to move as the dishevelled figure lunged at her, taking her down to the ground with him, her scream belated as she came to life, struggling beneath him as the fear became only too real. 'Paul, help me!'

Richard's hands were at her throat. He seemed intent on strangling her. She could hear him cursing, feel the heat of his breath against her face, but it was all happening as from a distance. She was in a haze of disbelief, unable to take in what was going on around her, though she could hear shouting. And then, before she had time to resist, Richard's weight was hauled off her and she could breathe again.

She lay still for a moment, winded and stunned. She was hurting, her body bruised, throat painful where Richard's hands had pressed so cruelly for that brief moment. Any longer and he might have killed her. Confusion held her mind as she struggled to make sense of what had happened, but then the sounds of a fight broke into the haze and she pushed herself up to a sitting position, trying to focus on the struggle between Paul and Richard.

'Are you all right?' Annabel became aware that the agent was bending over her now, clearly anxious and bewildered by what was happening. 'Forgive me. I was told the tramp had gone. I had no idea he was here. I can't apologise enough. I can't think what to do – this is terrible. Terrible…'

Annabel saw from eyes that still refused to focus properly that he was actually wringing his hands. It struck her as funny but her throat hurt and she hadn't the strength to do anything. She could only stay where she was and watch the struggle going on between Paul and Richard, her fear very real as she saw how desperate it was.

'He will kill him,' she croaked, her voice husky, throat aching from the imprint of Richard's hands. 'He hates him… blames him for everything… almost as much as he hates me…'

'Oh dear, oh dear,' Timothy Bromley muttered and wrung his hands again. 'What ought I to do, Mrs Keifer?'

Annabel's head was clearing. With the agent's help she struggled to her feet just as she saw Paul land a blow to Richard's chin, which sent him staggering backwards. He seemed to hang off balance for a moment, swayed and then fell to the ground, where he lay still.

'Paul...' Annabel ran to him, as he stood motionless, seemingly stunned, exhausted after the fight. 'Are you all right? Are you hurt?'

'I'm just winded,' Paul said and looked at her. 'He was trying to kill you. Thank goodness I came out when I did. God knows what would have happened if Bromley hadn't happened to mention that this place belonged to Richard – Mrs Oakes was his aunt, it seems.'

'Belongs to Richard...' Annabel stared at him as the horror dawned on her. Suddenly what had seemed impossible became understandable and made sense in her mind. If Richard owned the property he would probably feel safe here, hiding out in the old stables or even the house itself. 'I couldn't believe it but that's why he was here... he's been hiding here all the time the police have been looking for him.'

'Well, perhaps not all the time,' Paul said. 'The police may have made a search here at some time or again, knowing them, they may not. Bromley hadn't made the connection himself. Certainly I had no idea nor was it in the reports I gave to the police. Bromley only mentioned it because I asked how soon we could complete the sale. He said it might be difficult because Mr Hansen had gone missing and it all fitted into place. I was afraid the tramp his boy suspected might be Richard and I was right.'

'Mr Keifer!' Timothy Bromley was bending over Richard as he lay on the ground. 'Would you take a look please? I think he may be dead. He seems to have hit his head on something when he fell.'

Paul swore and went to kneel on the ground beside Richard, feeling for a pulse. He was a moment before he looked up and Annabel's heart stood still as she caught her breath. She didn't want Richard to be dead, not at Paul's hand, not this way.

'It's all right, Annabel,' Paul said, understanding the expression in her eyes. 'He must have hit his head as he fell. He is unconscious but he's still alive. I think we need an ambulance and the police, Mr Bromley. I noticed a phone box just down the road. If you will wait here with Annabel, I'll make the call.'

'Paul...' Annabel said but he shook his head at her and set off at a run. She heard his car start up a few seconds later and turned to look at the estate agent who was on his feet again, though obviously shaken. 'There's a bench just here,' she said. 'Perhaps we should sit down until Paul gets back?'

'I suppose he will come back?' Timothy Bromley shook his head, clearly much troubled. 'I don't know about all this, Mrs Keifer. It's very strange. I don't know what to make of it all.'

'I'm not Mrs Keifer,' Annabel said. 'Paul is my friend – Richard is my husband. Richard Hansen…'

The agent looked stunned and then horrified. Annabel was sure he half suspected them of somehow arranging this incident, as if he thought Paul had deliberately tried to kill Richard.

'You saw him attack me,' Annabel said. 'Paul had to do something or he would have killed me.'

'Oh dear, oh dear, this is most regrettable,' the agent muttered uncomfortably. 'I was locking up and really didn't see anything until I heard the screams and shouting. You were lying on the ground and Mr Keifer was fighting with…' He glanced down at Richard, who was still lying there with his eyes closed. 'Is that really Mr Hansen… *the* Mr Hansen? The Conservative Member of Parliament who…'

'Haven't you met him? You knew he owned the house.'

'No, I've never met him. I've only been with the agency for a few months. I was told that there might be a difficulty only yesterday when Mr Keifer made the appointment to view… because of Mr Hansen being in some trouble… Oh, dear, oh dear, this is terrible.'

'What is terrible is that my husband tried to kill me,' Annabel said. 'We had no idea this house belonged to Richard. If we had we would never have dreamt of coming here.'

'Of course you won't want to buy it now.' Mr Bromley looked mournful. 'This really is most unfortunate, Mrs… Hansen.'

'Yes, for more reasons than one,' Annabel replied, feeling annoyed with the man. If he didn't stop making inane remarks she would scream! As if they could somehow have planned the incident!

She heard the sound of a car returning and a few moments later, Paul was striding towards her. She ran to greet him, looking at him anxiously.

'The ambulance is on its way,' he told her, 'and the police said they would get someone out to us immediately. You're sure you're all right? He touched the marks on her throat with the tip of his finger. 'He hurt you, Annabel. I hope the bastard dies!'

'Really, Mr Keifer,' remonstrated Timothy Bromley. 'That is not the thing to say at all when Mr Hansen is lying there… not the thing, sir.'

'You have no idea what you're talking about,' Paul snapped. 'Kindly keep your opinions to yourself. That man is a murderer and deserves whatever is coming to him.'

The other man's face turned pale and he backed off, muttering something beneath his breath. He looked like a frightened rabbit and Annabel thought he might have turned tail and run like one if the sound of a police siren had not stopped him in his tracks.

'Ah, the police are here,' he said and an expression of relief came to his eyes. 'Now we shall be all right, Mrs Hansen.'

Annabel didn't answer. She held tight to Paul's hand until he went to greet the police and tell them what had happened. She sat down heavily on the bench, feeling sick and faint as she suddenly realised how close she'd come to death. Another few minutes and Paul would have been too late to help her. She put a hand to her throat, feeling the pain of Richard's brutal assault on her.

Paul seemed to be talking to the police officer a long time. They bent over Richard's body again, the police constable feeling for a pulse and shaking his head at Richard; then there was the sound of another siren and a few minutes later two ambulance men came round the corner. They consulted with the police and then Richard was lifted onto a stretcher and carried away.

The younger of the police officers came over to Annabel.

'I understand Mr Hansen attacked you without warning, Mrs Hansen?'

'Yes. I wanted to explore the garden. Paul was talking to the agent and I left them in the house and came out. I think Richard was hiding in the barn and… and he must have seen it was me. He hated me, you see, for leaving him.'

'Yes, Mr Keifer has told me something of your history, Mrs Hansen. I won't trouble you for the moment, but I shall have to ask you to give us a statement when you are feeling better. We shall want to know exactly what happened between the three of you. You didn't know that Mr Hansen was hiding here?'

'No, of course not. I have been avoiding such contact for months. I would never have come here today if I had thought it possible. It was a complete surprise and not a pleasant one. I thought I was going to die. I would have done if Paul hadn't dragged Richard off me.'

'It was a terrible shock for you.' Annabel held her throat, which felt sore, but said nothing; the officer continued his questioning. 'So you didn't know your husband owned this house?'

'I had no idea,' Annabel croaked. 'I saw it was for sale only yesterday. I wanted to look inside. We were thinking of turning it into a hotel…' she broke off and shivered as she thought what might have happened if she had walked round to the back of the house the previous day. 'You do realise that Richard tried to kill me? It isn't the first time he's hurt me either.'

'You can give us your statement another day,' the police officer said. 'Mr Keifer will take you home when you are ready. You are both free to go now. We shall want statements from everyone, but for the moment that's all I need to know.'

'Thank you,' Annabel said and stood up. The young officer had been pleasant enough to her for the moment but she had an uncomfortable feeling that he didn't quite believe her.

Twelve

'But that's ridiculous,' Ben's voice sounded indignant and Annabel smiled to herself. 'As if you would have gone to the wretched house if you'd had any idea Richard would be there.'

'I tried to tell the police officer that but he seemed a bit sceptical,' she said. 'Anyway, I thought I should telephone and let you know what had happened. The police have asked me to go in and give my statement this morning and Paul has arranged for his lawyers to meet us there. I hope it will all be straightforward but I can't be sure they won't bring some silly charge against us.'

'I'm glad you telephoned me, because Mother will go mad if all this gets into the papers, but I shall be prepared for it. If there's anything I can do to help, Belle, you know I will.'

'Yes, of course I know,' she said. 'But I'm sure you have enough problems of your own.'

'I've had a letter from Hetty,' Ben said. 'She says she's well and happy, but she would like to know if I have any news of you. She has given me an address where I can contact her in Paris. I think I may take a trip over to see her when I can get away.'

'I should like to come with you,' Annabel said. 'If I can that is...'

'You don't seriously think the police might suspect you and Paul of trying to murder Richard? How is he by the way? Have you heard?'

'He was still unconscious last night. Paul rang a friend of his with contacts at Scotland Yard, and he said Richard is in hospital and has a fifty-fifty chance of coming out of this.' Her voice was breathy with anxiety as she said, 'I pray he does recover, Ben. I don't want Richard's death on Paul's hands. I know what he did was for my sake, but it would hang over us for the rest of our lives.'

'In my opinion they should give Paul a medal for services to the community,' her brother said. 'Richard doesn't deserve your pity, Belle, not after the things he's done.'

'I know. It's Paul I'm thinking of, not Richard.'

'Well, these things happen. He couldn't stand by and let Richard strangle you in front of him, could he?'

'No, of course he couldn't,' Annabel said. 'I was thankful he was there – but you know what I mean.'

'Yes, though I think you're worrying for nothing. Anyway, I'm glad you telephoned because I wanted to let you know about Jonah. His grandson told me that he passed away in his sleep last night. It was very peaceful and he hadn't said anything about feeling ill, so at least he didn't suffer. I thought you might want to send flowers or something?'

'If things were normal I should have gone to his funeral,' she said feeling upset by the news. 'I don't feel I can face Mother at the moment – but I shall certainly send flowers. I was very fond of Jonah.' Why did everything happen at once? As if she hadn't got enough on her mind without this news.

'Yes, I thought you were – so was Hetty. I shall attend myself, so at least one of the family will be there. Ring me again and tell me how you get on with the police, won't you?'

Annabel agreed she would and replaced the receiver. As she turned away the phone rang and she picked it up, thinking it might be her brother ringing back to tell her something he'd forgotten.

'Green Farm,' she said. 'How may I help you?'

'Annabel,' Paul's voice had an urgent note. 'I'm sorry but I shall be late. Take a taxi and ask for Mr Tetley when you arrive. Don't let yourself be interviewed alone.'

'I'll do as you say but what's happened? You sound odd.'

'Harry went out earlier to an appointment and Catherine has collapsed. Jessie is naturally upset. I would like to stay with her until the doctor has been.'

'Yes, you must,' Annabel said at once wondering what else was going to happen. First she'd had bad news about Jonah and now it was Catherine. 'Don't think about me, I shall be fine. Jessie must be very worried.'

'I think the doctor has just arrived. I'll talk to you later.'

'Goodbye.'

Annabel replaced the receiver and turned to find Rose wiping her hands on a towel and looking anxious. 'I heard you talking. Has something happened at Kendlebury?'

'Catherine has been taken ill. Harry went out earlier so Paul is staying with Jessie for the time being. I think it must be serious.'

'The poor little lass,' Rose said and shook her head. 'They've always known something could happen, but Jessie is that fond of the girl. She's been better than a mother to her.'

'Yes, I know. It must be terribly worrying for her. Paul was anxious about me, but I can quite easily ring for a taxi to take me into Torquay.'

'You won't do that,' Rose said. 'There's bound to be one of the lads in the yard. Someone can take you in. Get yourself ready and come down. We'll have you there on time, don't you fret.'

It was easier to agree than argue, besides, she was feeling distressed, both by what her brother had told her and her concern for Catherine. By the time she had put on a light coat and tidied her hair, Rose's eldest son had the shooting brake waiting for her in the yard.

'This is very kind of you,' she said as she got in. 'I do hope I'm not taking you away from something important.'

'Nothing that can't wait,' he said and grinned. 'Besides, when Ma tells you to fetch the car you fetch the car.'

Annabel laughed. It was quite true that the cheerful Rose kept her menfolk in order and she could only be glad of their help and kindness. They had certainly made her welcome, looking after her as if she were one of their own these past weeks. She had wondered if she might have bad dreams after Richard's attempt to strangle her, but Rose had fussed over her like a mother hen, sending her to bed early with a mug of warm milk laced with brandy, and she had slept soundly.

The shadows that had hung over her for months seemed to have lifted, as if the incident with Richard had taken away her fear, though she was a little anxious over her coming interview with the police.

Arriving at the police station some twenty minutes or so later, which was five minutes sooner than she need have been, Annabel was asked to wait. A quarter of an hour later a young constable came out of the office to speak to her.

'Inspector Morrison is sorry to keep you waiting, Mrs Hansen, but your lawyer hasn't arrived. We've just had a telephone call to say he will be an hour late.'

'Oh dear,' Annabel said. 'That is rather a nuisance, isn't it? Shall I go away and come back later?'

'Inspector Morrison has appointments later this morning. He wondered if you would mind having a talk to him now, madam. He thinks it's a waste of your time and his making another appointment.'

'Well…' Annabel recalled Paul's warning not to allow the police to interview her alone, but what harm could it do? 'I suppose it will be all right.'

She followed the young man into a small, rather austere room and was left alone once more, but in seconds, rather than minutes, an older man joined her. He was of medium build with a grey moustache and a fatherly air. His manner immediately put her at her ease.

'Thank you for agreeing to see me without your lawyer,' he said. 'It is tiresome of the man to be late, but apparently his train has been delayed somewhere.'

'I don't suppose it matters,' Annabel said. 'We told the police constable yesterday all there is to say really.'

'I would like to go back a little if that is all right with you, Mrs Hansen. I understand that you left your husband some months ago – would you mind telling me why?'

Annabel raised her head and looked at him. 'Richard Hansen was a violent man, Inspector. I left him because he inflicted pain on me several times and when I resisted, he raped me. He had threatened more violence if I did not do as he wanted and I was afraid he might kill me. He tried to strangle me yesterday.' She touched her throat, which had black marks where Richard's fingers had been, bruising the tender flesh.

'That fits with what I have been told about him,' Inspector Morrison agreed and frowned. 'Did you quarrel with Mr Hansen the night he raped you – prior to the rape?'

'Yes. It was over a friend of mine that he did not wish me to see.'

'Male or female?' The Inspector's eyes narrowed.

'There was more than one quarrel over my friendships, with female and male friends,' Annabel replied. 'Richard suspected me having an affair with someone.'

'And were you?'

'Yes, as a matter of fact there was someone. I should never have married Richard. It was a mistake from the beginning.'

'And would the man in question be Mr Paul Keifer?'

Annabel looked at him warily, remembering that Paul had warned her to be careful. 'Does all this really have any bearing on what happened yesterday, Inspector? Neither Paul nor I expected my husband to be at the house. If we had known we should never have gone to look at it.'

'Are you certain that Mr Keifer did not know it was your husband's property?'

'I really do not understand your line of questioning,' Annabel replied. 'Richard attacked me without provocation. Had Paul not come when he did he would have killed me. You already know that my husband has been involved in criminal activities – in fact I believe he has killed more than one person…'

'What makes you say that?' Inspector Morrison's gaze narrowed suspiciously. 'Have you spoken of your belief to anyone before this – to the police or a lawyer?'

'No, of course not. I have no proof. Richard told me the night he raped me. He was gloating over it, taunting me with his power – but that doesn't amount to proof. I knew that the police wouldn't believe me if I had gone to them with my story. Besides, I've been hiding from my husband. I was afraid of what he might do if he found me.'

'Were you with your lover?' The inspector's brows rose. 'Was your husband a jealous man, Mrs Hansen? Did you want to be rid of him once and for all? Is that why you and Mr Keifer went to Rowntree House, hoping to provoke Mr Hansen into making an attack on you – thus giving Mr Keifer a chance to retaliate?'

'That is ridiculous,' Annabel said, angry that she had allowed herself to be led into this trap. 'I keep telling you that I was afraid of my husband because he was violent. I believed he was capable of killing – why would I go near him and risk being attacked?'

'Mr Hansen is a very rich man…'

'I consider that an insult! I have no interest in Richard's money.'

'And yet that was the reason you married him was it not – for the money?'

Annabel shivered as she met his hard gaze. Did he really think that she had wanted Richard dead, that she and Paul had conspired to arrange the incident at Rowntree House? Knowing the truth it was inconceivable that anyone could be so mistaken about her motives.

'My reasons for marrying are my own,' she said. 'I do not believe that is your business, Inspector. And I think I would prefer to terminate this interview now. If you wish to speak to me again, I shall ask my lawyer to be present.'

'Oh, I imagine we have more to say regarding this unhappy affair, Mrs Hansen,' he said. 'But I don't think I need trouble you further today. I must just ask you not to think of leaving the country for the time being. That is, you and Mr Keifer. I had expected Mr Keifer to accompany you today, but perhaps he was also delayed?'

'Yes, it was unavoidable. He stayed away to help a friend whose child has suddenly fallen sick,' Annabel said, but could see from his expression that he was sceptical. 'I am sure he will be pleased to make an appointment with you another day.'

'We must hope so. In the meantime, thank you for your own time, Mrs Hansen.'

Annabel lifted her head, giving him a look that would have had lesser men quailing in their shoes, but did not deign to say any more. It was so ridiculous and humiliating – and she was very much afraid that she had been foolish to agree to the interview.

She was angry as she left and a little uneasy as she realised what an invidious position they were in. How could they prove they had no prior knowledge of Richard's connection with the house?

*

Annabel did a little shopping in Torquay and then caught a bus back to the farm, walking the last few hundred yards down the lane. It was such a lovely day now, warm, the scent of blossom in the air filling her with a sense of peace. She was foolish to let Inspector Morrison worry her. Besides, as far as she knew Richard was still alive and there was surely no charge for anyone to answer. Richard had tried to strangle her and Paul had acted in her defence.

Rose was in the kitchen baking when Annabel went in with her parcels. She looked up but didn't smile and Annabel sensed that something was wrong.

'Is it Catherine?'

'Yes, I'm afraid so. Paul rang a few minutes ago. He'll be here this afternoon, but Harry hasn't been able to get back yet – and Catherine died about half an hour ago. Paul said it was quite peaceful in the end, she just went to sleep the way she so often does... poor little lass. She hasn't had much of a life, has she?'

'She certainly hasn't had a long one,' Annabel said. 'But I think she was happy. She always seemed to be busy, helping Jessie and Mrs Pottersby in the house.'

'I know Jessie tried to make life as normal as possible for her, and I know she loved her. I suppose no one can ask for more than that – but it's such a shame. They lost Harry's first son from a riding accident when he was just a small boy, you know – and then Harry had his accident. I don't know what the family would have done if it hadn't been for Jessie. I suppose that's why I feel for her now.'

'Yes, I know she will be very upset,' Annabel said. 'I don't think I'll telephone or go over today. Jessie won't want visitors at the moment, and she has her aunt with her.'

'It's always awkward at times like these,' Rose agreed. 'Saying you're sorry never helps and it brings on the tears.' She looked at Annabel with raised brows. 'How did you get on, my dear? All over, is it?'

'I'm not sure,' Annabel said. 'The police seem to have got some foolish idea that we went to the house in order to provoke a fight with Richard. They questioned me about things that had nothing to do with the incident at Rowntree House and in the end I refused to continue the interview without my lawyer. Well, he's Paul's lawyer really, but he didn't turn up and I agreed to be interviewed alone, which may have been a mistake.'

'Oh, it's just some over officious officer doing his duty a little too enthusiastically,' Rose said. 'I shouldn't worry about it if I were you, Annabel.'

'No, I shan't. Besides, it seems so trivial compared to Jessie's trouble, doesn't it?'

'Death always makes you feel like that,' Rose agreed solemnly. 'But the death of a child is worse than anything else. And Catherine was such a lovely girl.' She dabbed at her eyes with her apron. 'But crying won't help and I've got a family to feed.'

Annabel asked if she could do anything but was told everything was under control so she took her shopping upstairs and then went for a walk over the fields. She had avoided taking long walks on her own these past months, but now she felt in need of the exercise to blow away the cobwebs in her mind. She was much refreshed when she returned to the farm nearly two hours later to find that Paul had just arrived.

He had been looking at his daughter in her cot in the kitchen but came to meet her and they embraced, talking for a minute of their mutual sadness over Catherine's sudden death.

'Jessie knew it could happen,' he told her. 'But she was distraught. She's always so calm and competent that I felt I had to stay with her until Harry got home. She will be all right now he's with her.'

'Yes, of course. It isn't like Jessie to fall apart, is it?' Annabel felt the prick of tears but held them back. 'She's such a strong person.'

'She always has been, but I suppose even the strongest of us have our breaking point and with Jessie it was Catherine. She has always been so protective of her.' He put his arm around Annabel's shoulders. 'But what about you? No nightmares?'

'No, I slept well,' she said. 'But I think I've been foolish this morning, Paul.' She recounted her interview and he frowned. 'I should have done what you asked, shouldn't I?'

'You would have saved yourself some unpleasantness,' Paul said, 'but I don't think much harm was done. Morrison's line of questioning was unnecessary and Tetley would have stopped him as soon as it started, but as I say, there is no need to worry. We neither of us had any idea Richard was there – and they have to prove otherwise.'

'Yes, I know you're right, Paul, but I couldn't help feeling stupid for agreeing to the interview in the first place. He seemed such a fatherly man. I never dreamt he would ask questions about our personal life. He can't do anything to us, can he, Paul – if Richard dies?'

'Richard banged his head as he fell. It was an accident. I was merely protecting you from his attack. No jury would ever bring in a verdict of murder or even manslaughter.'

'I should hope it wouldn't come to a trial!' Annabel was shocked.

'It depends on whether Richard recovers consciousness or not, I suppose. The police might try something if he doesn't – though I have friends in the force and in the circumstances I think it's a nonstarter. As I said, I don't think we have a thing to worry about.'

'Then I shan't,' Annabel said and smiled at him. 'We had such a happy day planned yesterday and it all went wrong, and now Catherine – it seems as if we're destined to be parted, Paul.'

'That's just unfortunate,' Paul told her and touched her cheek with his fingertips. 'We are going to spend our lives together, Annabel, don't let the doubts creep in. What happened was just a temporary setback. We'll find another house for our hotel – perhaps something a little larger.'

Annabel nodded, feeling disappointed though she wouldn't say so. She had loved the house, felt it was right for them, but she supposed it would be overshadowed by Richard's attack on her now. It would be best to look for somewhere else, though the memory of that sun-dappled garden would live with her for a while. What had happened later was something apart, and already it was fading into insignificance in her mind – at least it would if she could be sure that Richard would recover and Paul would not be charged with assault or something more serious.

'Yes, we'll find something else,' she agreed, and then, to change the subject. 'I spoke to my brother on the telephone earlier. Our old gardener has died in his sleep and Ben says he's heard from Hetty. He may go to Paris to see her.'

'Shall you go with him?'

'I was asked not to leave the country.' Annabel laughed as he swore. 'Ridiculous, isn't it? But when this is over I should like us both to visit her – unless Ben can persuade her to come home.'

'Do you think that likely?'

'No, if I'm truthful I don't think it would be possible. Mother would either demand that she return home and then treat her like a criminal, or refuse to have her in the house. Either way, I can't see Hetty agreeing – unless she is in trouble. If this artist deserted her…'

'She could live with us if she wanted,' Paul said. 'Ask your brother to tell her that when he goes to see her. If she is ever in trouble she only has to come to us and there will be a home for her.'

'Oh, Paul,' Annabel said, her heart brimming with love for him. 'It's just like you to say that. Thank you for the offer, though I have a feeling that my sister will go her own way whatever we say.'

'I'm definitely taking you out for a meal this evening,' Paul said, his arm around her waist. 'I have to make a business trip tomorrow and I shall probably be gone for several days, but I'll telephone and I'll be back as soon as I can.'

'I shall miss you,' she said and lifted her face for his kiss. 'Do you think we could stay somewhere tonight, Paul? I want to be with you... truly with you. We've wasted too much time already, and that is my fault.'

'Is that what you really want, my darling?' Paul asked and lifted her chin with the tip of his finger so that she gazed up into his eyes. 'You know it's what I want, but if you're not ready...'

'I am ready,' she said a little shiver running through her. 'I could have died yesterday, Paul. I keep thinking what might have happened if I'd gone round to the back of the house the day before and Richard had seen me...You saved my life. I'm not going to let Richard or what he did to me stand between us again. I love you and I want to be yours – your wife as soon as I'm free. I'm going to take a trip to London while you are away to see my own lawyers, and I'm going to start divorce proceedings. I should have done it months ago.'

'You were hurt,' Paul said. 'I was hurt too, and angry because you didn't trust me, but that's behind us now. All we have to do is look forward to the future.'

*

Annabel was smiling as she waved goodbye to Paul the next day. He had insisted on taking her and Paula to London, because, as he'd told her, it was on his way and he would enjoy having her company for a little longer.

'I don't want to part from you at all, my darling,' he'd said as he kissed her goodbye. 'But it will only be for a few days. I shall see you at Catherine's funeral if not before.'

'Yes, of course. I'm only staying in London for a couple of days,' Annabel said. 'I want to buy some new clothes, because a lot of mine are too smart for country living – and I'd like to see a few friends – if they are prepared to forgive me for ignoring them all these months.'

'I'm sure they will,' Paul said. 'Whatever happens you will always have me.'

Annabel had made a reservation at a small hotel. She had no wish to return to Richard's flat or to avail herself of the clothes she had left behind. She was determined to make a new life for herself and she had a very generous income with which to buy as many clothes as she needed.

After registering at her hotel and leaving her small overnight bag, she called for a taxi and went to visit some of her favourite shops: Swan and Edgar, Selfridges and others. She saw that the "battle of the hemlines" was raging in the shop windows as it was in the newspapers. For the past two seasons the fashion designers had been trying to popularise the longer length, but many women felt it was an infringement of their freedom. Annabel thought the longer length rather attractive and feminine, a view she shared with the Queen, but the shorter dresses were more practical for everyday and working. However, she indulged in one very elegant afternoon dress for herself and some practical skirts and blouses for mornings, before having a light lunch in a little restaurant in Knightsbridge. She used the ladies room to give Paula her bottle and change her wet nappy, thinking herself lucky that her daughter was such a contented baby.

The sun was shining as she left the restaurant, an obliging waiter helping her to get the pushchair through the door. It was as she was about to cross the road to Harrods' impressive store that she heard a woman calling her name and spun round to find herself face to face with Laura Bristow.

'It is you, Annabel,' Laura said. 'Thank God! After all the stuff I've been hearing about Richard I was beginning to think he had murdered you.'

'Laura…' Annabel was swamped by guilt as she saw the real anxiety in her friend's face. 'I'm so sorry if you were worried…'

'If I was worried!' Laura exclaimed indignantly. She glanced at the pushchair but didn't mention the baby. 'Of course I was worried. Richard told us all that you weren't well and didn't want any visitors, then he said you'd gone home, but when I rang there your brother said he hadn't seen you – and then Richard told us you'd gone abroad for your health.'

'He didn't know where I was,' Annabel admitted. 'We… quarrelled and I left him while he was out. I didn't tell anyone where I was for months.'

'Because you were frightened of Richard's violence?' Laura pulled a face as Annabel was silent. 'I've heard such shocking things since all this broke, my dear. I feel so foolish, letting him charm me so easily, believing all his lies – but I suppose it was the same for you. You must have believed in him at the beginning or you wouldn't have married him.'

'I didn't know he could be violent when I married him,' Annabel agreed. 'But my marriage was a mistake from the start. I should never have let myself be persuaded into it.'

Laura looked distressed. 'Oh, my dear, I'm so sorry. You've had an unhappy time I think – but you won't disappear again, will you? So many people were asking after you. Your card reassured me as to your… health, but we were all upset when this latest thing happened.'

It was obvious that Laura hadn't heard the very latest in the sorry saga and Annabel suggested having coffee together so that they could talk. Laura listened sympathetically as Annabel told her the bare bones of her story, shaking her head when she told her about the attitude of the police in Devon.

'But that's so stupid,' Laura said. 'I am sure it will all get sorted once Scotland Yard get involved. I had a very nice Inspector Smith visit me and what he told me about Richard was horrifying. I don't know how much you are aware of, my dear, but it doesn't make very pleasant listening I can tell you. My husband and I were quite taken in by Richard, as your family must have been. It is all very shocking.'

'Yes, it is. But how were any of you to know?'

Annabel did not enlighten her concerning her own suspicions about Richard. She had no more proof now than she'd ever had and there was no point in making accusations without it.

'Well, I must get on,' Laura said and glanced awkwardly at the pushchair once more but made no comment.

'She's mine,' Annabel told her as she saw the glance. Laura was curious but too embarrassed to ask questions. 'But not Richard's. I was in love with her father before I married but he doesn't have the right background and wouldn't have suited my mother; there would have been terrible quarrels. I was in love with Paul but too young and innocent at the time to realise that sometimes you have to go after what you want no matter what. I grew up very quickly once it was too late. After Richard's behaviour became too violent to bear I knew I would have to leave him one day. I had planned to leave him, even if he hadn't... well, I've told you that bit already, haven't I?'

Oh...' Laura seemed faintly embarrassed by this last revelation; she probably didn't approve, though she sympathised with Annabel's reasons for leaving her husband. 'I have to rush now. You will keep in touch, won't you? We should like you to come for a meal – perhaps lunch on Sunday?'

'I shall be back in Devon by then,' Annabel said. 'I'm staying in a hotel for a couple of nights. I have to go back for a funeral. Jessie Kendle's daughter has died and I want to be there.'

'Yes, of course, you must,' Laura agreed at once, relieved to be back on firmer ground. 'These things are always so sad. But do keep in touch and come and stay with me one day.'

'Perhaps,' Annabel said. 'I'm not sure what I shall be doing – but I should like to meet in town for lunch sometimes and perhaps help with your charity work if I can.'

They parted on good terms and Annabel finished her shopping, returning to her hotel with several parcels. She reflected that she would have some difficulty carrying them all back to the farm if she went on like this, but it had been fun buying new clothes for herself and Paula and she was feeling as if the clouds had lifted a little.

She spent the next half an hour phoning friends, some of whom seemed a little reserved, but others genuinely pleased to hear from her. She was lucky enough to find Georgie Barrington at home on her second attempt.

'Is it really you, Annabel?' Georgie said, sounding odd. 'I'd heard you were all right, though still a bit anxious one way or another – but I do think you might have rung me before.'

Annabel felt guilty as she heard the reproach in her friend's voice. 'Yes, I know. Perhaps I was a little foolish to disappear as completely as I did, Georgie – but a part of it was because I didn't want to cause trouble for the people I care about.'

There was silence for a moment as Georgie absorbed this, then, 'that's what your brother said when I spoke to him. He told me not to worry because he was sure you were all right so I suppose I shall have to forgive you. Look, I'm going down to Catherine's funeral in a couple of days and may stay there for a while. Perhaps we could meet, have lunch together one day?'

'Yes, of course we can,' Annabel said. 'Have you heard that Richard is in hospital?'

'Yes, Ben mentioned it,' Georgie said and again there was something odd in her voice. 'You're worried his death might hang over you and Paul, aren't you? I shouldn't let it bother you. It was clearly an accident.'

'I'm trying to put it out of my mind. Anyway, I'm going back to Devon tomorrow afternoon so I'll see you at the funeral if not before. And I am sorry if you were worried, Georgie.'

'Well, I know Ben was upset for a while, but it's all sorted now so let's forget it, shall we? Just don't do it again!'

'I promise I shan't,' Annabel laughed and replaced the receiver.

Georgie had sounded a little odd when she mentioned Ben – and she had mentioned him several times. Annabel recalled having thought they were ideally suited to one another the morning Georgie took him for a spin in her sports car. Ben had already been committed to Helen at the time, but his marriage was not happy.

Was there something going on between her brother and Georgie?

Annabel dismissed the idea as unlikely. Ben wasn't the sort to stray, and she couldn't imagine Georgie's family being keen on a messy divorce – as it would be. Helen would not give Ben his freedom without a fight, of that Annabel was certain.

Paul telephoned the farm the evening she got back, telling her he would be down the next day so that they could attend Catherine's funeral together the following morning.

'I've missed you,' he said. 'I hope we can get everything settled in the next few days, and then we'll sort something out for the future.'

'Have you heard anything of Richard?

'As far as I know he's holding his own. I was told he had recovered consciousness, but I'm not sure if that's true. I see no reason why he shouldn't.'

'I would rather he didn't die because of what happened that's all.'

'I would prefer that myself – but have you thought of the alternative? It will mean a sensational trial and you will have to divorce him. Your mother will not be happy about any of that?'

'I still hope it happens that way. I know it will take ages to get a divorce,' Annabel said. 'But I don't think that should stop us being together, Paul. I'm going to start looking in earnest for our hotel.'

'I'll help you when I get back,' he said. 'I've been too busy to check on the estate agents in the area, but now my business is settled up here I should be free for a while.'

'Take care of yourself. I love you.'

'I love you, too. Expect me about six thirty and we'll go out somewhere for a meal.'

'I shall look forward to it.'

Annabel went over to Kendlebury to see Jessie the next day. She could sense the underlying sadness in her, but she was back to her usual calm self and told Annabel that in her heart she had been expecting it to happen.

'Catherine hadn't been herself for a few weeks,' Jessie said. 'She didn't want to do much and she was quiet, which was unlike her. As a small child she was often quiet but when I married Harry and everyone started to make a fuss of her she became much more talkative, and she always wanted to be doing something. The doctors had already told me it was unlikely she would live more than a few more months, but it was still a shock when it happened. The boys are so upset; both Jonathan and Walter were proud of their big sister. We shall all miss her about the place, some of the customers loved her too.'

'Yes, of course you will miss her,' Annabel said. She was close to tears herself but didn't want to start crying in case she made things worse for Jessie. 'I didn't see much of her when I was here, but she was a lovely girl. Everyone says the same thing.'

'Cook hasn't stopped crying and nor has Maggie,' Jessie said. 'By the way, Maggie was asking if you were still going to set up that hotel at Rowntree House. She has a friend who is looking for a job as a cook's helper, and Rowntree is nearer for Josie than Kendlebury.'

'I'll have a word with her before I leave,' Annabel said. 'I shall be needing staff, though not for a while. I'm not sure what we're going to do about that particular house, though. It was exactly what I wanted but it belongs to Richard and it might be awkward now. I suppose we shall have to look for something else.'

'That was so strange, wasn't it?' Jessie said. 'Both you and Paul fell in love with the house and then it turns out that Richard had been hiding out there for weeks.'

'The police think we must have known about it. I think they half suspect that we planned the whole thing in order to murder Richard.'

'Oh, they couldn't!' Jessie looked at her in disbelief. 'How could they? That is so foolish. Neither you nor Paul would dream of such a thing. I know Paul has spoken of his wish to give Richard a good hiding for what he did to you – but he wouldn't have wanted this.'

'No, of course not. It's foolish as you said – but I confess it worries me a little,' Annabel said. 'Paul thinks it is nothing to worry about but I can't help it. Especially if Richard should... well, you know.'

'Yes, I see.' Jessie was thoughtful. 'I'm sure you're worrying for nothing, Annabel. You'll see. It's just a storm in a teacup. It will all be sorted soon enough.'

'I expect so,' Annabel agreed and smiled wryly. 'Paul will be here this evening and then I can stop worrying. Things always seem better when he's around.'

'I know what you mean,' Jessie agreed. 'I can cope with anything as long as I have Harry. Which reminds me, I need to talk to him about something if I can find him. I dare say he will be in the barn. You could walk down with me if you like, Annabel?'

'Another time,' she said. 'I'll go and have a word with Maggie and Cook if that's all right with you, and then I'll phone for a taxi to take me back to the farm…'

Thirteen

Annabel didn't start to worry until it was past seven o'clock. She had assumed that Paul had been delayed for some reason, but as the time crept towards eight she began to feel anxious. It was almost nine when the telephone rang. Matthew Harris went to answer it and came back to tell her the call was for her.

'Is it Paul?' she asked, her heart jerking with fright as she saw his expression. He looked so serious that it made her knees tremble. What had happened now? 'Is he all right?'

'It's a Mr Stephen Tetley,' Matthew said. 'I think you'd better talk to him, Annabel.' He exchanged an ominous look with his wife as Annabel went into the hall and began to speak in whispers.

'Mr Tetley?'

'Mrs Hansen? I'm afraid I have some unpleasant news. Your husband died this morning and Mr Keifer has been arrested. The police have some idea of charging him with manslaughter.'

'Oh no!' Annabel was alarmed, the shock making her feel shaky. 'Surely they can't do that? Richard was trying to kill me. Paul stopped him and the fight was a matter of self defence after that.'

'You may have to testify in court to that end. Would you be prepared to do that?'

'Yes, of course. Anything. Paul saved my life. Richard would have killed me if he hadn't stopped him.' Annabel's nails turned into her palm as she clenched her free hand, finding this news almost unbearable. 'It was Richard's fault. Paul had no choice but to defend me – and himself.'

'So I understand.' The lawyer hesitated, then, 'I have an interview with Inspector Morrison at ten in the morning. I shall travel overnight to be sure of arriving on time. I hope to arrange bail for Mr Keifer and I think it advisable if I hear your story more fully, Mrs Hansen. Would twelve suit you?'

'Could you make it later in the day please? I have a funeral to attend. Two in the afternoon would be much better.'

'Ah yes, I remember Mr Keifer mentioning it. Shall I come out to the farm?'

'That would be very kind. Shall we say at two then?'

Annabel returned to the comfortable kitchen to tell Rose and Matthew the news. They were both concerned and shocked by Paul's arrest.

'That Inspector Morrison is a damned fool,' Rose exclaimed in disgust. 'I should like to give him a piece of my mind.'

'Come and sit down, lass, 'Matthew Harris said. 'It must be a shock for you – with your husband and all…'

'In a way Richard's death is a relief,' Annabel admitted as she sat down in the chair he'd vacated for her comfort. 'But I wish it hadn't happened as a result of the fight. I'm afraid Paul may be sent to trial because of it – and that's so unfair.'

She caught back a sob at the thought of Paul spending the night in a prison cell. It was wrong that he should suffer for something that was Richard's own fault. If he hadn't attacked Annabel it wouldn't have happened. But he had always been prone to unpredictable rages and seeing her there suddenly in the garden of his refuge must have been as provocative as a red rag to a bull.

'Don't you fret, lass,' Rose said as she saw how near Annabel's emotions were to the surface. 'You sit there quietly and I'll make you a nice cup of tea and a sandwich. You've had nothing to eat all evening.'

'Paul was taking me out to dinner…' Annabel felt the tears building inside. She tried to hold them back but suddenly she was weeping. Making a mumbled excuse, she fled the room and lay on her bed until the storm had passed.

It was more than half an hour before she was sufficiently in control of her feelings to go back down and apologise for her lapse. She'd taken time to wash her face and tidy herself, but she was still visibly shaken and Rose substituted hot milk and brandy for the tea.

'It's foolish of me to give way, 'Annabel said and blew her nose. 'I know others have far more to bear but I was looking forward to seeing Paul this evening. It just seems as if we're fated to be kept apart.'

'Things will sort themselves out,' Rose said kindly. 'You take that drink to bed. It will all seem different in the morning.'

Annabel smiled at Rose's mothering and went meekly to bed as she was told but despite the stiff lacing of brandy in her drink, she found it difficult to sleep. She had hoped that the future held new promise but if Paul was sent to prison – No, it could not happen! It was wrong that he had been arrested. Yet she knew that sometimes things like this did happen; people were wrongfully arrested and imprisoned for crimes they had not committed and it was sometimes impossible to prove a miscarriage of justice.

The thoughts went round and round in her head, keeping her wakeful and making her realise how empty her life would be without Paul. At last she fell asleep and her dreams were pleasant for she saw herself in a beautiful house with Paul and her children.

*

It felt wrong to be going to Catherine's funeral without Paul, because she knew he would have wanted to be there. Annabel shed a few tears during the service and she wasn't the only one. The church was filled to capacity and some of the local people had gathered outside, standing in the warm sunshine to join in the service. Annabel felt the overwhelming flow of feeling towards Jessie. People loved her and the child she had taken to her heart.

A large gathering had been invited back to the house for a celebration of Catherine's life, because as Jessie had said when she stood up in church to talk about her beloved daughter, they had all been privileged to know Catherine.

Annabel apologised for Paul's absence as soon as she had the chance. 'He wanted to be here,' she said. 'But I'm sure you knew that.'

'Yes, of course. He sent the most wonderful flowers. Did you see that huge teddy bear made out of carnations? That was from Paul as well as the flowers you both sent. He was always giving her soft toys. She must have hundreds of them upstairs.'

'Yes, I know how generous he is,' Annabel said, thinking of his offer to provide a home for her sister if Hetty should ever need it.

She was mindful of her appointment with Stephen Tetley and prepared to leave at just after twelve. As she was about to go, Georgie came up to her.

'You're not leaving already?'

'I have to, Georgie,' Annabel explained and her friend nodded. 'But I was going to say goodbye. You've been busy ever since we got back from church and I haven't been able to find you alone.'

'I had to help out with all these people here,' Georgie said. 'We can't talk properly now. Perhaps I could come out to the farm this evening? Jessie said you're stopping with Rose Harris.'

'Yes, that's right. Paul arranged it and they've been very kind to me in sharing their home. Rose will let us have the parlour so that we can talk in private. We have a lot of catching up to do.'

'I've got something to tell you. I'll come after tea. It should have calmed down here by then.'

Annabel agreed, kissed her cheek and went out to her taxi. She thought that if she were going to be living in the country she would have to learn to drive a car. Perhaps Paul would teach her… if he were able. She might know more about that after the lawyer had been.

*

Mr Tetley arrived at five minutes to two. He was a small, thin man who wore gold-rimmed spectacles perched precariously on the end of his nose. At first sight Annabel wasn't inspired with much confidence in his ability, but as they talked her respect for him grew. He obviously knew what he was talking about and she understood why Paul trusted him when he told her he had known Mr Keifer for years.

'It's this Inspector Morrison,' he said. 'He has taken some foolish notion in his head and doesn't want to let go of it. He was resisting bail this morning and then for some reason changed his mind. I've applied but it may take some time. I doubt Mr Keifer will be free before tomorrow.'

'Paul has to spend another night in prison?' Annabel's eyes widened in distress. 'That's awful. How can they do that to him?'

'I'm afraid it's the way things work. I'm sorry but it takes time to get the legal stuff sorted out. I'm going to see someone in Torquay this afternoon to try and hurry it along, but I don't hold out much hope of a release before morning.'

'I'm sure you will do everything in your power to help him.'

'You can rely on that, Mrs Hansen. And now I'd like to take a full statement from you – about what happened that day and other things. I may have to ask personal questions that make you uncomfortable, and I shall apologise in advance, but it is all to assist me in my efforts to help Mr Keifer.'

'Yes, I understand. I'll tell you all I can.'

*

Annabel went for a walk after the lawyer had gone. He'd done his best to reassure her that Paul would soon be free, but a cloud of anxiety hung over her and she was restless.

She was glad when Georgie arrived at about four. Rose told them to make use of her best parlour.

'You'll be private in there, my dears, and there's always someone running in and out of my kitchen.'

'She's nice,' Georgie said, when they were alone in Rose's shining parlour, the rosewood furniture polished to perfection even though the room was rarely used apart from special high teas on a Sunday. 'This is a rotten business for you, Annabel. You'll be glad when it's all over.'

'Just as long as Paul doesn't have to stand trial for manslaughter.' Annabel shivered as a chill crept down her spine at the dreadful thought. 'I can't stop worrying about it. If he should go to prison...'

'He won't,' Georgie said. 'Stop worrying, Belle. It's unpleasant but the lawyer will sort it out eventually.'

'I do hope so – but you had something to tell me?' She raised her brows. 'It sounded important.'

'Yes,' Georgie hesitated, 'I'm getting married next month. I haven't got an engagement ring, but I shall have on Sunday when I see Arthur next.'

'Oh!' Annabel was surprised. She'd half expected something rather different. 'That is good news, Georgie. I'm so pleased for you. Do I know the lucky man?'

'No, I don't think so. Arthur Bridges is a friend of my father's. He's some years older than I am, well off, but not terribly rich, and nice. Yes, Arthur is a nice man. I like him.'

'You like him? Does that mean you don't love him?'

'No, I'm not in love,' Georgie admitted. 'Arthur says he loves me. He wants to marry me even though he knows... he knows I don't love him in that way.'

'Is there someone else?'

'Yes. I can't lie to you. I'm in love with someone but it's impossible. He's married. He couldn't leave his wife for various reasons.' Georgie fiddled in her pocket and brought out a packet of crumpled cigarettes and a box of matches. She lit a cigarette, offering them to Annabel, who shook her head. 'I shouldn't really, but I find they help sometimes. One of the reasons he can't leave her is that she's having a child. He told me in confidence though no one else knows as yet – she wanted it that way until she is sure everything is all right.'

'I'm so sorry, Georgie. Are you sure you should marry Arthur, feeling as you do? It isn't always a good idea to marry for convenience's sake. I should know.'

'Your case was very different,' Georgie said, drawing deeply on her cigarette. 'I never liked Richard. I've thought about it for ages and I believe it's the right thing for me. Arthur knows the situation and still wants to marry me. It will be a proper marriage; I want children if we can have them, and I'm fond enough of him to make that side of things all right. Besides, I don't want to stay single forever.'

'And there's no chance of the man you love getting a divorce?'

'None. He's too honourable for his own good.' Georgie's laugh was slightly bitter. 'Nothing has happened between us, except for a kiss. We had both tried to hide our feelings but it all came out – over you actually. We had an argument and then we were suddenly kissing. Ben broke it off before it went too far, of course. I was ready to do anything he wanted – run off, have an affair, but he said it wasn't right or fair to any of us.'

'Yes, that's like Ben,' Annabel agreed. 'I had wondered if there was something between you but I didn't think he would have an affair. I'm sorry,

Georgie. You are perfect for each other. I wish he hadn't married Helen. It was for the money, as you know of course. I'm afraid we've both made a mess of things. We should have had the courage to make independent lives for ourselves. Mother was responsible for much of it but the ultimate responsibility lies with us.'

'But you have something to look forward to,' Georgie said. 'You left Richard and you're in love with Paul. At least you had the courage to put your mistakes right.'

'I left Richard because he raped me and because I believed he was a murderer,' Annabel said. 'Without that final push I might never have done it.' She smiled wryly as her friend blanched with shock. 'The truth isn't very pretty is it? Ben didn't tell you that bit then? I suppose he didn't want to mention it. I'm fairly sure that Richard has killed two women. He would have killed me the other day if Paul hadn't stopped him. That's why it's so unfair…' she broke off as the emotion welled up inside her, choking her. 'It's no use going over that. I have to wait and see what happens.'

'What will you do if Paul goes to prison for some years?'

'I'll visit him and wait for him to come out,' Annabel said. 'I'm going to run a hotel, with or without Paul's help. It's what I want to do with my life. I have Paul's child and I'll get through somehow. I shan't stop loving him and one day we'll be together. I shan't give up on that hope, Georgie. I can't.'

'You're so brave,' Georgie said, giving her an admiring glance. 'You've changed so much. I never thought you had it in you. You always let your mother have her own way.'

'It was easier,' Annabel said, a wry smile curving her soft mouth. 'I let Mother bully me for years, but there's only so much you can take, Georgie. You either give in and go under or you fight. I decided to fight.'

'What is that old saying? It's always darkest before the dawn? I think your new dawn is breaking, Belle. Whatever happens now you will cope with it and life has to get better. You're not overshadowed by fear of anyone any longer. You're free.'

'Yes, I'm free,' Annabel agreed. 'I just wish Paul was here with me.' She sighed and lifted her chin. 'Perhaps you're right. It may be that's there's a new beginning waiting just round the corner.'

'When Harry was injured so badly Jessie asked him to give her tomorrow. They've built their lives that way, taking one day at a time. There will be a bright tomorrow for you too, Belle. It might not be yet but it will happen.'

'Yes, I think you're right. But what about you and Ben? Why don't you wait for a while? Ben might realise what he is losing if you gave him a little time. He must care for you a great deal, Georgie. He hasn't even told me about the baby yet.'

'That's because she didn't want him to, Belle. She's jealous of you – don't you know that?'

'I thought she might have got over that by now. But won't you think about what I said – wait for a while before you marry?'

'No, I don't think so,' Georgie said. 'Ben is fond of Helen in his own way and when he discovered she was pregnant there was just no chance he would leave her. He would feel awful about hurting her. And there's your mother – she has been terrible to live with, just imagine what she would be like if Ben walked out on his marriage too? It's hopeless. I've got to get on with my life and marry Arthur Bridges.' Georgie absentmindedly picked up a pretty dish decorated in the Art Deco style and turned it over to look at the bottom. 'Oh, this is one of those new ones decorated by Clarice Cliff. I do like her work, don't you?'

'Yes, very much. I bought it for Rose as a thank you for her kindness,' Annabel told her. 'But you were telling me about Arthur?'

Georgie nodded and put the dish down. 'He was a major in the war and won medals for bravery. I know he's a lot older than me but he's a dear and I think I shall be content. We're going to live in the country. It's a pretty house. They call it Mulberry Cottage but it's too big for a cottage. About the size of Tarleton Towers but much nicer, cosier. I like it a lot and I shall enjoy living in the country. Arthur has land and a small timber business. As I said, he's comfortably off rather than wealthy, but I have money of my own. We shall manage very well together.'

It was a long speech and Annabel felt that it was as much to do with convincing Georgie herself as anything else, but there was no more she could say in the circumstances. Georgie was convinced it was hopeless and perhaps it was.

'I suppose you are right. I just wish Ben had married you instead of her, Georgie.'

'It's no good wishing for the moon,' Georgie said with a grimace. 'I always thought I would make a sensible marriage and I shall be doing just that so there's nothing to repine over.'

'Not if you look at it like that.'

'Well, I shall. I must,' Georgie said and stood up. 'I'd better be getting back. Jessie has people staying over and I want to help where I can. You will come to my wedding, won't you?'

'Of course I shall.' Annabel hugged her impulsively. 'Be happy, Georgie.'

'I'll do my best,' Georgie said and gave her a wobbly smile. 'Let me know how things turn out for you and Paul, won't you?'

Annabel assured her that she would and went to wave her off in her car. Why did everything have to be so miserable? There was Ben, desperately unhappy and yet unwilling to end his marriage; Georgie was marrying a man she did not love because she couldn't have the man she wanted, and Annabel herself was facing an uncertain future.

She put on a brave face as she joined Rose and Matthew in the kitchen. They talked about various houses that were for sale in the district and Annabel decided to telephone round the agents in the morning. Even if she had to make the inspection visits alone she would do it. She wouldn't give in to despair, because then Richard would have won after all.

*

After a sleepless night Annabel contacted several estate agents. She was told about three houses that seemed suitable for her purpose and made arrangements to view them the next day. She spent the rest of the morning helping Rose with the baking and looking after Paula, one ear listening for the telephone. It remained stubbornly silent and after helping to wash the dishes after their meal, she left Paula sleeping with Rose to keep an eye on her and went out for a walk.

Her nerves were on edge and she felt as if she might have had hysterics or started screaming if she stayed at the farm any longer. Everyone was so concerned for her and she couldn't bear their anxious silence another minute.

What was taking so much time? Surely all the formalities must be over by now? But supposing bail was refused? Paul might be forced to stay in prison until the trial – and what would happen then? He had been confident that no jury would convict on such slim evidence, but Annabel found it unbearable to contemplate.

She returned to the farm at about three. She walked slowly, her head down, lost in thought, not seeing the man coming eagerly towards her until he was almost upon her.

'Annabel...'

Her head came up sharply as she heard the sound of Paul's voice. She stared at him in disbelief, hardly daring to believe it. Then she gave a cry of surprise and delight and ran towards him, to be caught in his arms.

'Paul! Oh, Paul, I had begun to think you weren't coming – that they would keep you there forever. What did they say? Why did it take them so long?'

'It took a long time because we were asked to wait by an Inspector from Scotland Yard. I'm glad we did, because it was worth it to see Morrison grovel in the end.'

'What do you mean? Are you on bail – what?'

Paul laughed as she clutched at his lapels in her urgency. 'No case to answer. Richard's death was due to a condition in his brain apparently. He would have died soon anyway. It seems there was pressure and the tumour was growing so large that it would have killed him even if he had not fallen and hit his head. The concussion was due to blood leaking from the tumour it seems and not the fall, though that may have contributed in a small way. It may account for his violence towards you and others, which had escalated these past months. Everyone who knew him says he became impossible after you left. He drank too much and was moody and argumentative, which according to the doctors was a symptom of his illness, though no one knew it at the time. I doubt if he knew himself.'

'Richard was ill…' Annabel stared at him, hardly daring to believe the nightmare was over. 'So they aren't going to prosecute?' She didn't want to think about Richard's illness for the moment, or what bearing it might have had on his behaviour towards her. She could not forgive him so easily whatever the circumstances, she wanted only to forget. 'It's really over?'

'Morrison was out of order in the first place and he knows it. He was told to wait for instructions from London but he's retiring soon and I suppose he wanted to go out in a blaze of glory. As it is he has a large amount of egg on his face. At least he had the decency to apologise.'

'It's really finished?' Annabel laughed as he put his arms around her, drawing her closer. 'That's such a relief. I've been so worried about you, Paul, thinking the worst.'

'I tried to telephone earlier but the line was engaged and I couldn't get through, and afterwards there wasn't time. I just drove straight here as soon as they said I wasn't needed any longer.'

'I'm so glad you're here,' she said and clung to him. 'I don't think I can bear to be parted from you ever again.'

'That's just what I wanted to hear.' He kissed her softly on the mouth. 'How soon will you marry me, darling? I suppose we have to wait for a while for the sake of appearances...'

'Be damned to that!' Annabel said in such a fierce voice that he shouted with laughter. 'I'll marry you as soon as you can buy the special licence, Paul.'

'Then I suggest early next week. Unless you want a big wedding?'

'We'll invite our closest friends,' Annabel said. 'And I'll wear a pretty dress, but I think Jessie might arrange a small reception for us at Kendlebury if we asked.'

'Yes, I'm sure she would,' Paul agreed. 'All we have to do then is find somewhere to live.'

'I've arranged to see three houses tomorrow. But if we don't find what we want immediately we can rent somewhere for the time being.'

'My own apartment isn't suitable for a permanent home, though it would do for a few months I dare say – until we find our dream house.'

'And we'll start looking tomorrow.' Annabel smiled as she lifted her face for his kiss. 'It's going to be a bright new day after all.'

*

Paris had never seemed this exciting before, Annabel thought as they dodged the honking taxis, holding hands to run across the crowded square. The buzz of traffic and the sound of lively music coming from inside one of the cafés added to the atmosphere, which was made even more tantalising by the delicious smell of roast coffee beans and fresh croissants mingling with the scent of flowers in tubs all around them.

'Buy your lady flowers, monsieur?' an old woman asked, giving them a toothless grin. Paul took a note from his pocket and held it out to her, presenting Annabel with a posy of sweet smelling roses.

'Thank you.' She smiled at him, love flowing between them. She was conscious of being truly happy, content in a way that she had never expected. Her second wedding day – and night – had been so different from the first and she knew that whatever happened in the future she would always know that she was loved. 'Oh, look! There's Hetty. She's waving to us – and that must be Henri with her.'

Paul had brought her to Paris for their brief honeymoon, brief because they wanted to begin getting their future home ready as soon as possible. Annabel had taken the opportunity to arrange this meeting with her sister and her artist lover.

She hurried towards the open air café and Hetty came rushing to meet her. They embraced, hugging and kissing, the questions flying fast and furious until Annabel laughed.

'Slow down, dearest. You haven't met Paul yet – and I haven't met Henri.'

There was a faint colour in Hetty's cheek but her eyes were fearless, her manner proud as she looked at her sister.

'We aren't married. Henri doesn't believe in marriage. He says love is enough – and I agree with him.'

'Yes, I think I do too,' Annabel said. 'If you are happy with him that's all that matters to me, love.'

Hetty looked surprised, as if she had expected something different, then she laughed. 'You wouldn't have said that once, Belle.'

'No, perhaps not,' Annabel said. 'I've changed, grown up – and so have you, Hetty. Now, introduce me to your Henri. I see he and Paul are already talking. They've got tired of waiting for us.'

'Henri never waits for anything or anyone,' Hetty said. 'He's like a greedy child, Belle. He wants it all now, at once.'

'But you don't mind that?'

'I'm very much the same,' her sister admitted with a laugh. 'We argue all the time but then we make it up in bed and it's wonderful.'

Annabel felt a flicker of fear for her sister's future but then, as she saw the way Henri looked at her, it faded. There was no doubting the love between them. It might be demonstrated in an unconventional way but it was there. No one knew what tomorrow might bring. You just had to take what happiness you could along the road.

Annabel was smiling as she went forward to greet Henri… He was an artist of some repute, she knew, and she wondered what had happened to Hetty's desire to paint. Did Henri help her or was she content to be his model and lover? It wasn't for Annabel to question. Hetty must find the right path for herself.

*

Later, when she lay in Paul's arms, basking in the feeling of wellbeing that comes after mutual pleasure in loving, Annabel nuzzled his bare shoulder and asked what he thought of Henri Claremont.

'He has charm and talent,' Paul said thoughtfully. 'I think he is probably very selfish, but in someone as talented as Henri that is quite expected. I am sure he loves Hetty, but I think she may grow out of him in time.'

'What do you mean?' Annabel raised herself to gaze down at him, her hair falling forward over her breasts like a curtain.

'Hetty is very young yet. She doesn't know her own potential, my darling. One day she may wake up and decide she wants more out of life. She's an intelligent girl but she is just a girl at the moment. When she becomes a woman – who knows?'

'I felt something like that,' Annabel said and snuggled up to him again. 'But I couldn't tell her.

She's happy now and it's her life to live as she chooses.'

'She wouldn't listen whatever you said,' Paul told her and kissed her neck, his hand moving lazily over her thigh. 'Hetty is very much in love. No one listens to another person's opinion when they're in love, and perhaps it's just as well. We can observe but we can't know what she truly wants, my darling – we can only try to please each other and be happy ourselves.'

'I am happy.' Annabel pressed herself against him. 'Once I thought my life was over, now I know it is just beginning.'

'Being here with you like this is a dream come true for me,' Paul said and kissed her mouth softly, his tongue teasing her as he pushed inside her mouth briefly, tasting her sweetness. He kissed her eyelids, the tip of her nose, her throat, and lastly her mouth. Withdrawing, he smiled down at her as she opened her eyes and looked up at him. 'And, my darling, the best thing of all is that I know it is going to get even better…'

Afterword

They had all come for the opening of the hotel, all her dearest friends. Jessie, Harry and Aunt Elizabeth. Maggie and Cook and Pam Bates, Rose and Matthew Harris, Mary and Mike Foster, Mary with a new baby in her arms. Then there was Ben standing with Hetty and Selina; neither Helen nor Henri had come but Georgie was there with her husband.

Arthur was a dear just as Georgie had said, and very proud of his wife, who, he confided to Annabel, was already carrying their first child. And then there was Beth, looking very grown up and smart wearing her first grown up costume, together with her grandmother, both of whom were going to live in the newly converted accommodation at the bottom of the garden.

Annabel noticed that Selina had a handsome escort. Lady Tarleton had declined the invitation, as had Laura, who had sent a card and flowers, but apologised for her absence on the grounds of a prior engagement; but in the main everyone was there to support Annabel on this special day. Even Charlie Fortescue, who had rung her up after reading about the opening in a newspaper and demanded an invitation on the grounds of friendship, and had sworn that he would recommend her hotel to all his friends.

Paul was lifting his champagne glass, the buzz dying down as he made his toast.

'To my darling wife who has worked so hard to make this day possible,' he said, looking at her lovingly. 'We had almost given up on our dream, because it seemed impossible to find the right place, but Annabel knew what she wanted and she had the courage to go for it. My friends and loved ones, I give you Annabel and Rowntree House Hotel. Long may they continue to flourish.'

There was a chorus of laughter and cheers. Annabel smiled through her tears. It had taken patience and determination to cut through a mountain of red tape, because it would be years before the wrangling over Richard's estate was finally finished. Annabel didn't care what happened to his fortune, much of it illegal and subject to Government investigation and restrictions. The lawyers said that she would probably be entitled to whatever was legal when it was all settled, but she'd told them that she didn't want a penny. Anything that was finally allowed to come to her could be donated to one of the good causes she still helped Laura with when she had time.

Annabel had all she needed or wanted. She had, by means of persuasion and her lawyer's hard work, managed to buy the house she wanted for a nominal sum. Although the times were hard and it wouldn't be easy to make the hotel a paying concern, Annabel had been determined to carry out her plans for the future.

Paul had asked her a hundred times if she was certain she wanted the house. Everyone had voiced their doubts about the wisdom of buying it because of what had happened the day Richard attacked her, but Annabel had held true to her vision. And today, surrounded by all those she cared for, she knew without the shadow of a doubt that it had been worth it. She raised her glass to Paul, blessing the day she had met him, her whole body suffused in the warmth of his love.

'Thank you all for coming,' she said. 'I've never been happier than I am at this moment, and as Paul so often tells me, this is only the beginning.'

We hope you enjoyed this book!

Rosie Clarke's next book is coming in summer 2018

More addictive fiction from Aria:

Find out more
http://headofzeus.com/books/isbn/9781786694966

Find out more
http://headofzeus.com/books/isbn/9781786690814

Find out more
http://headofzeus.com/books/isbn/9781786692535

About Rosie Clarke

ROSIE CLARKE is happily married and lives in a quiet village in East Anglia. Writing books is a passion for Rosie, she also likes to read, watch good films and enjoys holidays in the sunshine. She loves shoes and adores animals, especially squirrels and dogs.

Find me on Twitter
https://twitter.com/AnneHerries

Visit my website
http://lindasole.co.uk

A Letter from the Author

Dear Reader,

I just want to say thank you to all those lovely people who buy and read my books. Writing them is a great pleasure and I always feel it a privilege that they are actually published. I like to know what my readers think of the books, which ones they like best and why. A review is always welcome, as is a tweet because it makes other readers aware that the books gave you pleasure. If you can either leave a review or tweet about the books that would be wonderful.

I reply whenever I can, both from the website and on Twitter, so please do feel free to follow and message me on there following the buttons below.

I do hope you enjoyed the book you have just read and that there were no silly typos to annoy you. My editors and I do all we can to eliminate them but somehow they occasionally get through; if they did, my apologies. Please forgive me and enjoy the stories which are meant to please and entertain you.

My heartfelt thanks for being a reader!

Rosie Clarke

Find me on Twitter
https://twitter.com/AnneHerries

Visit my website
http://lindasole.co.uk

About The Workshop Girls Series

Find out more
http://headofzeus.com/books/isbn/9781784977146

Find out more
http://headofzeus.com/books/isbn/9781784977160

Find out more
http://headofzeus.com/books/isbn/9781786692979

About the Mulberry Lane Series

Find out more
http://headofzeus.com/books/isbn/9781786692573

Find out more
http://headofzeus.com/books/isbn/9781786692474

Visit Aria now
http://www.ariafiction.com

Also by Rosie Clarke

Find out more
http://headofzeus.com/books/isbn/9781784977177

Find out more
http://headofzeus.com/books/isbn/9781786692986

Visit Aria now
http://www.ariafiction.com

Become an Aria Addict

Aria is the new digital-first fiction imprint from Head of Zeus.

It's Aria's ambition to discover and publish tomorrow's superstars, targeting fiction addicts and readers keen to discover new and exciting authors.

Aria will publish a variety of genres under the commercial fiction umbrella such as women's fiction, crime, thrillers, historical fiction, saga and erotica.

So, whether you're a budding writer looking for a publisher or an avid reader looking for something to escape with – Aria will have something for you.

Get in touch: aria@headofzeus.com

Become an Aria Addict
http://ariafiction.com/newsletter/subscribe

Find us on Twitter
https://twitter.com/Aria_Fiction

Find us on Facebook
http://www.facebook.com/ariafiction

Find us on BookGrail
http://www.bookgrail.com/store/aria

Addictive Fiction

First published in the UK in 2018 by Aria, an imprint
of Head of Zeus Ltd

9 7 5 3 1 2 4 6 8

A CIP catalogue record for this book is available
from the British Library.

ISBN (E) 9781786692986

Aria
c/o Head of Zeus
First Floor East

5–8 Hardwick Street
London EC1R 4RG

www.ariafiction.com